Laila Manning

A.M. McCoy

COPYRIGHT

Copyright © 2025 by A.M. McCoy

All rights reserved.

contents

CHAPTER 1 – LAILA

His large hands gripped the backside of my thighs tightly, pushing them against my chest to open my pussy up for his hungry mouth.

"Yes." I whimpered, thrashing my head back and forth on the bed. "Don't stop," I begged.

I hated begging. I hated asking for anything in life, but this man—did things to me. He reduced me to carnal needs and incomplete thoughts, leaving me begging him for more of the pleasure he promised me.

"You taste so good, Laila." His deep baritone rough voice hummed against my clit and my back bowed involuntarily. His eyes snapped up to look into mine, and the cool blue depths of them made me feel like I was crashing into the ocean headfirst. "I can't get enough of you."

"I don't want you to." I panted. I needed him more than anything else I'd ever experienced before. I needed the calm he brought to my soul.

He took his tattooed hands off my thighs and pushed two fingers deep inside of me and curled them forward, rubbing them against my G-spot while stroking his pinky against my ass. He pushed his finger into my ass slowly, letting the saliva and wetness from my two previous orgasms coat his skin and help with the intrusion. "Damn, your ass is so tight, baby." He cursed, sucking powerfully on my clit.

"I'm going to come!" I gasped, curling forward, and watching his mouth and fingers attack my body. It was the sexiest thing I'd ever seen before, and it was my undoing. "Yes!" I screamed and fell back onto the pillow as my brain misfired, and pleasure rocked my entire system. "Please, Zeke!" I chanted. "Please fuck me, I need more."

He pushed another finger into my ass and kept the suction on my clit as my orgasm wrecked me, crashing through my body, and destroying me in its wake. My chest heaved as I struggled to catch my breath as his talented mouth and fingers never let up their delicious torture.

"Laila!" He panted, "Laila!" Something in his tone made me open my eyes and look down my body at him, but he was no longer lying between my legs.

Zeke was kneeling on the bed next to me, staring down with a scary and intense glare. His large hands gripped my shoulders tightly and shook me gently as I gasped.

Gone was the erotic high buzzing through my body, and in its place was fear.

"Zeke?" I whispered, suddenly unsure of what was going on.

"You were dreaming." He said deeply, letting his eyes travel down my body where I lay twisted up in my sheets. I followed his gaze down my body and saw that my thin nightshirt hung awkwardly off my shoulder and the top of my breasts were bare to his eyes.

It was all a dream.

It was all a sex dream.

With Zeke!

I lay frozen in place as he finally slid his hands from my shoulders, and I took in his appearance. He wore nothing but a pair of tight black boxer briefs with a gun tucked into the waistband.

And tattoos.

Nearly every inch of his arms, legs, chest, and abdomen were covered in a mix of black and brightly colored ink.

"I'm sorry," I whispered, snapping my eyes back to his as the ghost of a smile kissed his manly lips while I got caught staring at his twelve-pack of abs and the deep v that disappeared beneath the thin black fabric of his briefs that hid—almost nothing.

His scowl returned as he stood up to his full height and stared down at me, I didn't right my shirt, don't ask me why, but I liked the way his eyes looked troubled as they flickered back and forth from my chest to my pupils. "You were screaming." He finally said as he rubbed a hand over the back of his neck, squeezing the muscles that flexed under the colored skin. "I was worried about you."

I pushed myself back against the headboard and awkwardly lifted my shirt onto my shoulder, covering my cleavage, cursing myself for wanting his attention at all now that he was mentioning my night terrors. "I'm sorry I woke you." Shame filled me before curiosity took its place. "How did you–how did you get in here?"

I looked past him to the brightly lit hallway between our apartments and into his space through both open doors. It was my first glimpse of his personal living space.

"I have a key." His deep voice rumbled, and my lips parted in surprise.

"Have you always had a key to this apartment? Or just since I started staying here?" I asked. When his eyes dropped to the bed and he didn't answer right away, I had my answer. "You have a key because of me, specifically." I couldn't help the humiliation that filled my nerves as I processed that. "Because I need to be babysat."

"I have a key in case you need me." he said firmly, staring back into my eyes as his brows dropped into an almost menacing scowl. "Not because you need to be babysat."

"Right," I whispered, and took a deep breath, pulling my blanket up to my chest to hide where my nipples poked through the forest green shirt, searching out for the man who had been doing delicious things to them in my dreams.

But it was all just a fantasy.

Not real.

Nothing seemed real anymore.

"Thanks for waking me, I'm sorry I disturbed you. You can go back to bed now." I said firmly, but I wouldn't meet his gaze.

"Want to talk about it?" he said, leaning back against the wall and crossing his arms. I looked up at him as he did it and fought to keep my eyes above his incredible chest and on his face.

Did this man have any idea how sexy he was? His shaved head and perfect beard paired flawlessly with the ink and chiseled muscles that he always hid under his tailored suits.

In fact, in the three months since moving onto Ryker's estate, in the barracks, I'd only ever seen Zeke in anything other than a suit a dozen times or less. It was usually when he wore workout clothes, and while that was a sight to behold, nothing compared to him nearly naked in briefs.

"No," I blurted, feeling a blush creep across my face as I brought my knees up to my chest and wrapped my arms around them. "Not in the least."

"You know," he said, pausing like he was trying to choose his next words carefully, "I hear you most nights. But tonight was different." I blushed even deeper as he kept talking, praying the world would open up and swallow me whole. "Your screams were more—intense. But they didn't sound as pained."

"Jesus." I groaned and ran my hand through my hair. "I don't ever remember what I dream about, other nights or tonight. They fade as soon as I wake up." I lied quickly trying to end this embarrassing conversation.

He didn't say anything right away, but his crystal-blue eyes stared deep into mine. Did he have any idea how painful it was for me to maintain eye contact with anyone, let alone him? Finally, he stood up off the wall and uncrossed his arms, "If that's how you want to play it." He said pensively and frowned.

"What the fuck is going on in here?"

We both snapped our heads toward the open door to my apartment and saw the giant outline of my brother standing in the doorway. Even with the light behind him, I could see the dark glare on his face as he stared at us.

"Jed." I gasped, looking from him to Zeke and back. My mouth hung open at the assumptions I knew he was making about the two of us right now, but I couldn't get words to come out of my mouth.

"Laila was having a nightmare. Her screaming woke me up, so I came over here to wake her up." Zeke said plainly, not shrinking down at all as Jed walked into the room. Their dynamic had intrigued me since coming to live with them.

They were friends who respected each other, but I'd seen Jed fall into an alpha role around Zeke recently when I was around, and I didn't necessarily like it.

"Are you okay?" Jed asked, deflating a bit as he walked over to me and sat down on the edge of my bed. He was a total stranger to me as an adult, but there were times like this when I'd see small bits and pieces of the boy he was when we were younger, trying to protect me from the evils of the world.

And I knew what that choice had cost him all those years ago.

"I'm fine," I said, putting my hand on Jed's between us on the bed and squeezing it briefly before putting mine back in my lap, twisting the blanket between my nervous fingers.

He watched me closely, letting his eyes bore into me as he remained quiet before finally blinking and nodding his head. "Okay."

"What are you doing here?" I asked, looking at my phone next to me. It was only three a.m.

Zeke still stood against the wall in his tight boxers, and I tried *really hard* to keep my eyes from looking in his direction at all. I didn't want Jed to see something there in them that I wasn't ready to process myself yet.

"I just got home from a job, and I saw Zeke's light on, so I came over to walk through and check on you both," Jed said, looking over at his scantily clad friend, raising an eyebrow at him. "Care to take your naked ass out of my sister's apartment?" He bit.

I snapped my eyes over to Zeke, appalled by my brother's rudeness, but Zeke just smirked at him, highlighting a dimple on his cheek under his short dark beard. He nodded his head and looked over to me, drawing my eyes into the deep blue of his. "You know where to find me if you need me, Laila." he said, and his voice caressed my skin like a physical touch.

I nodded back to him quickly and gave him a small smile before dipping my head and staring at my hands, avoiding Jed's watchful stare as he observed our interaction with interest. Zeke walked out, softly closing my door behind him, and I listened as his own door shut across the hall before I took a deep breath, laying my head back against the headboard as my shoulders deflated.

Jed reached over and flicked on the lamp next to my bed, "Talk to me," he said firmly as I stared up at the dark ceiling.

"I—" Stammering, I swallowed away the anxiety, "I don't know how to," I finished, hating the uncertainty I felt in my heart being in a small space with him. The vicious things my grandparents had told me about Jed over the years, beating them into my brain, were hard to un-believe. Even after spending three months living in his world and seeing who he really was now.

I looked down my nose to watch Jed as he processed that, and I saw the hurt in his eyes before he dropped them to the bed between us.

"I never should have let them take you from me." He said quietly. It was the first time he had spoken of our grandparents or our past at all. Neither of us had wanted to rehash those painful days when I got out of the hospital and somehow, we both silently agreed to just move forward, forgetting the past altogether.

But I knew from Carly that it killed him not knowing what happened in the nearly two decades that we were separated.

I was an adult now, but with just a few words, I was transported back to being a kid cowering in my big brother's arms begging him to make the monsters of the world stay away.

"You didn't have a choice. And you didn't know any better, Jed." I said, lifting my head off the headboard to look him square in the eye, something I struggled to do with anyone, especially men.

"Are your nightmares–" He started and stopped, rubbing his hand over his face, and taking a deep breath. "Are they about what happened when we were kids, or about after that?"

I didn't want to have this conversation, especially at three a.m., fresh out of a sex dream with my biggest fantasy brought to life from across the hall. But I wanted to try to give him *something*. Jed deserved every bit of loyalty and selflessness I could give to him for saving my life, not once but twice. So, I ripped the Band-Aid off, ignoring the way my heart raced in my chest as I tried to articulate my feelings into words.

"I don't remember much about that night when we were kids," I said, taking a deep breath and forcing myself to hold his gaze as I swallowed down my fear and discomfort. "I remember what happened before he attacked me, and I remember you carrying me." His pupils dilated and he swallowed quickly as I watched the muscles in his neck work beneath his skin. "I remember the way you smelled as you carried me to the Thompson's." I chewed on my lip and dropped his gaze, feeling my brow sweating from even trying to look into his eyes for that long. "I remember it calmed me down because I knew I was safe with you, even when I couldn't see through my swollen eyes."

"I had no idea then that it would be the last time I got to hold you." He said, and I could feel the grief in his words without even looking at him. "They took you from me before I even realized they could do that."

"I know," I whispered as pain burrowed its way into my chest at the painful memory. "They lied to me for months, telling me they had to wait for the court to release you, and then they had to wait for paperwork." I shook my head. "I think they were just hoping I'd forget about you or something if enough time passed." I shuddered at the intensity of his brown eyes locked on mine. "But I never did, Jed. I never forgot you or stopped wanting to be near you again. Please know I didn't just move on while they abandoned you." I hiccupped as emotions bubbled up and tears blurred my vision.

I swiped at my face as the salty moisture rolled down my cheeks and Jed moved swiftly, sliding up the bed to sit at my feet, before pulling me against his chest, wrapping his strong arms around my shoulders, and holding me as years of pain broke free. I sobbed, clinging to him as he rocked us back and forth, soothing me as I struggled to get myself under control.

Human touch hurt. Physically, it felt like I was being burned alive as he hugged me, but I let him anyway.

He needed it. So, I endured. For Jed, I would endure.

"I never stopped thinking about you, Laila. I tried looking for you when I got with the crew, but they changed your name, and I couldn't find you. And I struggled with so much self-doubt that you were better off without me. I was a thug, with an anger problem and a habit of using my size and power to make others bend to my will. I was in no shape to be a good influence in your life." I felt his own tears hit the top of my head as he held me in a vice grip, working through his own emotions. "But then—Carly whispered to me as she walked by me in that brothel that you were there, and every lie I'd ever made myself believe about you being better off without me burned to ash. I'm so sorry." He cried.

"I'm sorry you had to see me there," I said firmly. "I know you blame yourself, but you can't. My own decisions led me into that life, I trusted the wrong people, and before I knew it, I was imprisoned." I pulled back and looked up at him and took a deep breath. "But you saved me. Again. And I'm going to spend the rest of my life healing. But I'll find my purpose and happiness again, and when I do, I hope you can let go of that guilt and grief alongside me."

I puffed a giant breath of air out, blowing my loose bangs out of my face for the hundredth time in the last six hours. My feet ached from the unsupportive sneakers I was wearing that went with the dress code as I made a mental note to go buy some new ones the next time I got paid.

"Are you even listening to me?" The woman on the other side of the counter snapped at me. She was about my age but wore a fancy business pantsuit and had a giant diamond weighing down her ring finger as she snapped her hand in front of my face.

"Yes, I'm sorry." I stuttered and looked back down at the computer screen in front of me. "Large nonfat latte with extra whipped cream and extra chocolate sauce? Anything else?" I asked, looking back up at her with a smile on my face that I hoped was genuine-looking.

Nonfat with extra whip and chocolate syrup?

Because that made sense.

"That's it." She bit at me again, snapping her gum obnoxiously.

"Name?"

"Victoria!" She all but screamed at me. "I'm here every day! Don't you pay attention?"

"I apologize," I replied on autopilot as she slid her platinum card through the reader, I wrote her name on the side of her cup and passed it to my runner.

It was a Tuesday, right after the lunch rush, but we were still swamped, and I wanted to be anywhere else in the world than here at this quirky coffee shop that catered to the needs of Shadeport's most snobby coffee drinkers.

Well, almost anywhere else.

I'd been in worse places than this.

And that mental reminder was the only reason I came back every day. I'd gotten the job as a barista a month ago because I needed to have a task every day. Sitting at Ryker and Ellie's house, while lovely and relaxing as it was, left me way too much idle time to think about everything that had happened over the last few months.

Or the last few years, really.

And idle time was the opposite of helpful, even though my new therapist had insisted that talking about my past would help heal my emotional wounds.

But I just *couldn't*.

I didn't want to.

So, I worked myself weary in this upscale coffee shop until I was so tired that I was left with no choice but to return to my quiet piece of serenity and fall into an exhausted sleep for an hour or two. Then I'd get up and try to pretend I hadn't been held captive in a sex trafficking brothel for years as I got to know my brother and his beautiful fiancée and their friends. Only to pass out and dream all night long and wake up at four a.m. to do it all over again.

I was living the dream.

But at least it was my dream, and I got to decide what to do with it now.

"Are you daft?" The woman asked with a sneer as she took the large coffee from my hands, spilling it over the edge and burning my fingers. I didn't remember my runner even handing it to me, yet there I stood, holding onto it, and gazing off into space.

"Shit." I cursed, wrapping my hand in my apron as tears burned my eyes from the pain.

"That was your fault." She accused. "You're so stupid you can't even hand someone a coffee the right way."

My boss, Nate, walked forward to the counter and handed her a pile of napkins.

"I'm so sorry, Victoria. Your next one is on the house. I'm sorry for all this, she's—difficult." He said in a nasal, heavy voice that drove me absolutely insane.

He was eighteen and had been promoted to manager by his dad, the owner of the store, but he was the worst kind of boss out there.

I held my burned hand to my stomach still, even though he didn't spare me a second glance.

Victoria started to say something to me, no doubt another insult, when a shadow descended on her, and a large, imposing man walked right up against her back. I looked up into the eyes of the scariest man I'd ever met .

"I think you need to think twice about whatever that cunt mouth of yours was about to say to her." He warned in his dark tone.

"Diesel." I hissed, my eyes jumping from the woman who went as white as a ghost as she looked up into the face of the notorious president of the Reaper MC. My boss stood next to me with his mouth agape and was also silent for once in his pathetic life.

Diesel Ames turned to me and raised an eyebrow as he let his eyes drop over my body from hair to toes and back. I should be revolted by his gaze, or at least wane under it, but for some reason, I never shrunk around him.

And he had been coming around more and more lately.

"Laila. Is there a problem here?" He turned, looking down his nose at the woman who probably had never been looked at like that before a day in her life.

"What?" She stammered and stepped back away from him as he came to stand at her side, cocking his hip against the counter. "No! No problem." She finished in a whisper.

"Good, because I know of about ten different ways off the top of my head to make a cunt like you beg for forgiveness, and not a single one of them leaves you alive in the end." Diesel snapped back at her. He turned his attention to my teenage boss, "Your employee is hurt, and you ignore her pain to take the side of your bitch-ass customer? Do you have any idea who the fuck she is?" He challenged the kid and, as expected, my boss shrunk under his intense stare and menacing words.

"Uh, my apologies–" Nate the snake said, looking away from Diesel to me, but I just rolled my eyes.

"I'm done," I said, realizing that even without Diesel stepping in and scaring my boss, there was no way I could do this stupid job anymore. "I quit." I took off my apron and threw it on the counter before going to the back to get my bag and walking back out around the front counter. The entire coffee shop was silent as patrons and employees watched on in morbid fascination while Diesel stood rooted in place with his arms crossed over his chest and his leather vest hanging open over his clean white tee.

I didn't stop to talk to him or anyone else as I walked to the door, but on my way, I heard his warning loud and clear. "Laila Manning is protected by the King of the Shadeport Crew himself, as well as the Reapers MC. Fuck with her again and I'll skin you alive."

I pushed my way out onto the sidewalk and gasped a deep breath of fresh air to calm my spiraling nerves. The tingling in my hand was fading, so I knew it wasn't severe, but my chest was tightening more and more, and I knew if I didn't get out of my head, I'd be falling face-first into a panic attack in minutes.

"Hey, wait up." Diesel said as I ran my hand through my hair and looked around for a way out of this mess.

"I have to go," I said quietly, looking anywhere but at him. I grabbed my phone from my back pocket and pulled up a ride-share app, but my hands were shaking so badly that I dropped it and the screen shattered on the rough concrete. "Shit!" I hissed and clawed at the collar of my shirt. It was suffocating me.

"Laila, hey!" Diesel tried again, putting both hands on my arms, and turning me towards him. He leaned down to look at me, and I focused on the top of his man bun for mere seconds before turning away and looking for an out. "You're having a panic attack, aren't you?" He asked. His voice lost the edge that I usually heard in it and softened.

I nodded quickly and closed my eyes as tears soaked my lashes. "I have to get out of here," I whispered, keeping my eyes closed.

"Let's go." He said, pulling me towards his bike parked a few spots away. Red flags flew into my vision like a downhill skier as I followed after him, but I didn't know what else to do. My phone was useless, and I couldn't wait for the bus to take me home. I just needed to get home and into *my* space, and I'd be able to calm down.

Diesel swung his leg over the large hunk of matte black metal, and I froze. The seat on the back was tiny, and I fought the memories trying to assault my brain that associated motorcycles with pain from my experiences with the Youngblood MC.

But they were all dead.

Because of Jed and Diesel's men.

I could trust him. He killed for me.

"Get on, Laila." He commanded, and my feet moved again without thinking as I threw my leg over the back and pressed my chest against his body. He smelled of leather and cigarette smoke, and I closed my eyes and tried to ground myself to that one single sense instead of paying attention to all five. Wrapping his hands around my ankles, he lifted my feet onto the pegs behind his legs before taking my hands and wrapping them around his stomach. "Hold on to me, and don't let go. Got it?"

"Got it," I nodded and kept my eyes closed. My crossbody bag rested against my back as he turned on the bike and it roared to life. I felt him move his legs, and in seconds we were pulling away from the curb and thundering down the busy city street. He weaved in between cars, and my arms wrapped tighter around his stomach as the bike leaned from side to side.

With my eyes closed, the sights passed by unseen. I couldn't hear over the rumbling pipes; all I could do was smell and feel—it was perfect.

I rested my forehead against his back as we ate up the pavement, and I felt my anxiety melting away with each wisp of air blowing through my hair. Diesel rested his warm hand on my jean-clad knee, and he patted it reassuringly.

I finally felt relaxed enough to open my eyes and saw that we were nearing the East Valley, where Ryker's property lay, and I felt my quiet apartment beckoning to me from here.

When we got to the gate at the Valley entrance, the guard eyed Diesel crudely before looking back at me and raising the gate, but before we were even under the arm, he was on the phone from the booth.

And I knew exactly who he was calling.

I was in trouble. As we got to Ryker's driveway, the gate opened without us even nearing it and Diesel chuckled, gently shaking his head.

"Think they're all going to be waiting for us?" he asked before opening the throttle and roaring loudly down the driveway. I cringed inwardly, hating the idea of Jed or Ryker seeing me on Diesel's bike, while also worrying about the noise for little Gavin. If Ellie had him sleeping and Diesel woke him up with his pipes, she'd have both of our heads.

Babies were fucking tough.

As we neared the mansion, I groaned as I watched my brother and Ryker both rush out of the garage to stand with their hands on their hips watching our approach, and Zeke and Carly stood with them.

Carly had a smirk on her lips, and I wanted to flip her off.

Lovingly, of course.

Because that girl had a meddling bone that she loved to use every chance she got.

But the thing that surprised me the most was the downright enraged look on Zeke's face as he stood between Jed and Ryker. I shrunk back behind Diesel further when he pulled to a stop in front of them and killed the engine.

"What the fuck do you think you're doing?" Jed snapped, scowling at me.

I guess he forgot our heart-to-heart in my bedroom last night when he was angry. I put my feet down, and Diesel held my hand as I slid off the bike on unsteady legs, never letting go of me until I was stable.

"Thanks for the ride," I told him quietly, hoping he'd catch my drift and leave quickly. But I should have known he would have something to say before he did any of that.

He turned to my brother, stepping off the bike and standing to his full height, toe to toe with Jed as he bit out, "Do you have any idea what conditions she works in at that fucking place? Are you too fucking busy with your little family here to support your blood financially while she figures shit out?"

Jed's scowl darkened, and Carly put her hand on his arm, pulling him back a step before putting herself between them. "Diesel, stop." She ordered, pointing her finger at him sternly while keeping a hand pressed against Jed's chest before looking over at me where I stood on the other side of the bike wringing my hands together. "What happened, Laila?" She asked in the gentle voice that she used with me. The one that screamed 'pathetic' and 'wounded animal' every time she did. Because she had seen my abuse firsthand, the sounds of my screams and the sight of my injuries haunted her.

I just wanted to be normal.

"Nothing," I said, looking at her shoes instead of her face.

She sighed, and I felt even worse about myself for disappointing her.

"Some cunt burned her hand, and her bitch ass boss did nothing about it. Then she had a panic attack and broke the screen on her phone, so I got her the fuck out of there." Diesel said, and I watched as he leveled Jed with a pointed look. "A thank you would have been a more respectful greeting, boy." He spoke.

Jed clenched his jaw so tight I was afraid I was going to hear his teeth crack from ten feet away.

"Thank you." He bit out, keeping his stare locked with Diesel's.

Ryker stepped forward and held his hand out to the MC president, and Diesel finally looked away from Jed and turned his attention to the King. They shook hands, and Ryker spoke, "I didn't realize you drank coffee." he said with a curious look on his dark face.

Diesel finally dropped his offensive stance, lowering his shoulders and relaxing with a smug smirk on his face. "I don't go there for the hippie coffee." He said plainly, and Ryker's eyebrows rose as Jed cursed before being shoved backward again by Carly, who was surprisingly strong for her tiny frame.

I didn't want to know what Diesel meant by that, so I just turned and walked away towards the barracks, aching to be in the dark quiet of my space.

I walked in the main doorway and was halfway down the hallway when I heard the door open behind me, and I fought down the panic inside of me that rose with the sensation of being followed.

"Laila." A deep voice echoed down the hall, and goosebumps erupted over my skin as if I'd touched an electric fence, feeling the voltage burn in every cell.

CHAPTER 2 – ZEKE

"Laila," I repeated when she froze with her hand on her door-knob, refusing to turn around and look at me.

God, she was infuriating.

And perfect.

And scarred.

And flawless.

I stood in front of her, waiting for her to acknowledge me. I was always waiting for those bottomless brown eyes to meet mine, and it usually took her a while, but she eventually always looked at me.

But not for long. Laila never held a person's stare for more than a few seconds at a time.

She sighed and dropped her hand off her doorknob before squaring her shoulders like she was mustering up the physical strength to look at me.

And then she did.

And it was like every other time that she made eye contact with me.

Everything else faded away, and I was lost to the pain and darkness inside of her soul, shining through her brown and golden eyes.

"That's better," I said, acknowledging her effort to look at me. "Let me see your hand."

She flicked her glance past my head to the ceiling, and her nostrils flared a few times like she was on the edge of losing her composure completely, but eventually, she raised her hand to the space between us and swallowed. "It's fine."

I glanced down at her hand and saw the angry red welt on the webbed flesh between her thumb and first finger and grimaced. "That's not fine." She looked down at her hand and then dropped her shoulders, accepting the truth. "Come with me," I took her good hand, touching her for the first time while she was awake, and fought the full-body tremor that tried to lead my body into convulsions. I pulled her behind me to my door and felt her fight my hold as I opened it and led her inside. "I have burn cream."

"It's fine." She tried again, but I ignored her. It was surreal having her inside my space, but it didn't feel wrong either. "Zeke." She dug her heels in when we were in the center of the studio apartment, making me stop. "I can't."

I turned around and faced her again, noting the way her eyes flicked back and forth over the furniture inside of the space, and then to the windows on the wall on each side of my bed, and the closed door to my bathroom.

"Why?" I asked, keeping her hand in mine as she took a step back, and then another. I followed her move, keeping the same amount of space between us as she tried to retreat. "What's wrong?"

"I can't." She repeated before closing her eyes and shaking her head. "It's too small." Her chest rose and fell, straining against the white fabric of her uniform top. "I can't be in here."

"Shh." I tried to soothe her, but as I tried to rub her arm, she flinched and pulled back, breaking all physical contact. I tried to ignore how her reaction to my touch felt, but that was impossible.

"I'm sorry." She shook her head, backing up again until she was in the doorway to my apartment. "I can't come inside." Her eyes were wide, and I recognized the panic building inside of her, so I didn't chase or confront her about it.

"I'm sorry." I held my hands up, showing I was giving up. "I'm just trying to help."

Her lips quivered as she cradled her burned hand against her stomach, fluttering with each breath, like she was on the verge of losing all control. "I'm past the point of help, Zeke." She shook her head again as a tear slid over the edge of her eyelashes, "I'm too far gone."

"You're not," I said firmly but didn't close the distance like I wanted to. I never closed the distance like I wanted to with her, and it sucked. "You just have to let us in. All we want to do is help."

"I'm sorry." She said before bolting out the door and straight through hers, turning the locks ominously in her silent wake as she once again hid from the world.

I stood in the center of my apartment, kicking myself for how I had handled her while simultaneously listening for any signs of distress from behind her door. But there were none.

There was always just silence.

From her apartment.

From her.

But I knew without a doubt that there was no silence within her soul. I knew from the times her screams cut through the night that she had no peace.

And I had no fucking place amongst her pain.

I was the devil himself.

I offered her nothing but more terror and darkness, so I needed to stay away.

I threw myself into the driver's seat and turned the engine on as Ryker got in the passenger seat and Jed climbed in the back. Normally, riding anywhere with the only two men I trusted in the world would bring peace to my chaotic mind.

But not today.

Today, I wanted to kill something.

Someone.

"You good?" Ry asked as I tore down the street away from Lux, his strip club.

"Perfect," I responded, ignoring the glare from Jed in my rearview mirror. "Let's just find these assholes."

"Proof you aren't good." Ry sighed, adjusting himself in the seat to my right. "You're supposed to be my calm and levelheaded one. I can't have two hotheaded fuck offs riding alongside each other."

"Hey," Jed grunted from the back seat. "I'm not a hothead."

"Are too," I argued, tightening my hand on the steering wheel. "I'm straight."

"Want to talk about it?" Ryker challenged, ignoring my previous statements. "Or about whom."

"Say her name and I'll break all the bones in your face," Jed warned ominously from behind me.

"I was talking about Diesel." Ryker butted in, stopping me from slamming the brakes hard enough to send the giant asshole in the back through the windshield for even bringing her into this.

Laila.

He didn't have to say her name, but I knew who he meant.

"I'm straight," I repeated. "I'm allowed to want to break some skulls occasionally."

"Hmm." Ryker hummed, disbelieving. "Whatever you say. But the reapers are off limits, and that includes Diesel."

I grunted.

"Is that an order, Dad?" Jed asked, "Because if he puts Laila on the back of that motorcycle again and I'm declaring war, your order be damned."

"That we can agree on," I murmured as we rounded the building outside of Shadeport city limits that we were planning to burn to the ground.

Much like the Reaper clubhouse, if that piece of shit ever touched an inch of Laila's body again.

"You two are insufferable." Ryker took his seat belt off, leaning back to get comfortable as I parked down the street. "If you two would get on the same team instead of fighting against each other all the time, you might actually do that girl some good."

"We're not fighting. And there is no same team." Snapping, the entire situation annoyed me. "I have no claim there," I held my hand up when Jed opened his mouth, sensing the movement without even seeing it. "I'm not interested in one either. She sleeps across the hall from me, and I care about helping her get over the absolutely atrocious things that were done to her because she's your sister." I locked eyes with Jed in the mirror. "That's it."

"Good." He declared. "Because you're the last person she needs to get mixed up with."

Ryker snorted and looked over his shoulder, "You say that like Zeke's the boogeyman, Jed." Even though he showed no other signs, Ryker ran his thumb across his lip, just as he did when stressed. "She could do worse, man."

"She could do a lot better too," Jed argued, annoying me even further. "Zeke's worse than the boogeyman." He stared at me in the mirror again as he finished. "The things he's done would scare the boogeyman to death. And that's exactly what Laila doesn't need in her life. Romantically or friendly-wise."

"Message received, Jed." I clenched my teeth and looked back out the front window.

"Are you two done?" Ryker interrupted. "Because there's the scum bag now." He nodded toward the man who went by the name of Wickham. The piece of shit was walking in broad daylight toward the nightclub he trafficked girls straight out of. He forced them into places like the brothel where Carly ended up. The same one Laila was a prisoner in for years too.

Right under our fucking noses. And he was going to pay for it with his life.

After we made him beg for death.

Chapter 3 – Laila

I watched the blades of fern grass billow in the breeze as I walked up the long path to Carly's house. The path was familiar, and it had never caused me any pain, yet each time I walked it, it felt like I was nearing my death.

It felt like that every time I walked down any type of path.

A hallway.

A paved sidewalk.

The annoyingly long roped-off queue line at the DMV.

Every path created the same panic inside of me.

The same phantom pain.

As if something at the end of that path would tear another piece from my soul away.

Again, none of those things happened to me after Jed rescued me from the brothel. Regardless, any route felt like a walk to the gallows for me.

Most days, I walked through the grass instead of the paver-lined walkway to the front steps. But today I wanted to be brave. I wanted to force myself to be strong.

Even if I felt anything but.

"Hey," Carly called, walking out of her front door with a coffee cup in her hand, wrapping a cardigan sweater around her waist tighter. "Brrr, it's chilly out here."

"Hi," I responded on autopilot. "Yeah, I guess winter came early."

"Hmm." She hummed and tilted her head. "Porch or inside?"

Every day I walked to Carly's front porch, and we *visited*. Most days we sat next to each other on the front porch, and she chatted aimlessly about her life, and all the great people she surrounded herself with. And I just listened.

Because I couldn't return her stories or inquiries into my day; I simply had nothing to offer her.

Some days, we went inside her cute little cottage for our visits.

Those were brutal days, but I forced myself to do them anyway. If I didn't move forward, even on brutal days, I would not get better.

At least that's what my therapist said.

"Inside." I took a deep breath and squared my shoulders.

Carly's affectionate smile lit up her face before she forced it back and nodded her head like I'd just said something menial and unim-pressive. "Inside, then." With a soft click, she opened the front door, stepping inside and leaving it slightly open, inviting me to follow at my own pace. The scent of wood-smoke hung in the air.

Even without telling her anything, she *knew*.

Carly picked up on things and made observations without asking questions. It was unnerving how much she could piece together from body language and one-word answers. But I guess that was a skill she picked up as a dancer at Ryker's club.

And probably the fact that she witnessed my torture from inside that hellhole. She simply understood me better.

"So," Carly called from the kitchen island, where she poured creamer into a cup of tea for me when I finally entered her home. "I was thinking about that stupid barista incident."

My blood ran cold as my foot landed on the hardwood floor of her foyer, but I forced myself to keep my chest open and unrestricted, forcing full deep breaths of fresh oxygen into my lungs so I didn't pass out.

Again.

It was mortifying enough the first time I'd done it on her floor.

"I can't go back." I shook my head as I passed the couch between the two spaces, running my fingertips over the lush soft blanket draped over the back as I went. Grounding me in the comforts provided inside the warm home. "I blew it."

"That's not true," She shook her head, sending her perfectly blown-out blonde locks swaying. "But it's irrelevant because I don't think you should go back to that place anyway. It was a shitty job, and I understand why you took it, but you're better off without it." She slid the mug of warm tea across the countertop to me and then walked around the other side to the couch, giving me a wide berth.

She knew I didn't enjoy being too close to people when I was inside.

Even though I'd never spoken those words to her.

"I'll find something." I dipped my head over my mug and followed her to my favorite chair by the window. The window overlooked the front porch, so I could see who was coming and going before they arrived. It also gave me an exit point if I needed one.

Escape was paramount; the threat of slashing my arteries wide open wouldn't stop me from leaping out the window if I had to.

"I have something in mind." She cut off my train of thought as I settled into a comfortable chair the same color as her eyes.

Turquoise blue.

Everything about Carly was angelic and unthreatening.

"How do you feel about kids?"

"Kids?" I mumbled, confused and surprised. "Huh?"

"Gavin in particular."

"What about him?" I wondered where she was going with the conversation about Ryker and Ellie's baby. He was the cutest, sweetest baby in the entire world, with his chubby little teddy bear cheeks and Ryker's signature scowl.

"How do you feel about babysitting him?" She watched me closely as she asked, waiting to read my cues before I even realized I had given them.

"When?" I asked, "Where would Ellie or you be?" Ellie hardly ever left Gavin at home when she left, and if she did, Carly watched him.

"Out," She shrugged her shoulders, "Date night, or girl's days. Whatever the occasion, you could watch him instead of Ellie leaving him with Ryker or the nanny." She rolled her eyes, "Gavin loves you."

"I don't know—," I shook my head, "I don't know much about kids."

"You absolutely know enough to take care of him for a few hours at a time." Carly countered, "And you know that. You're great with him."

"I'm—," I fought for the right words but came up short. "It's not a good idea."

"Why?" She sipped her coffee, watching me.

"Because I'm unreliable." I quoted my old boss, the teenager. "And flighty."

"You're healing." She countered, squinting her eyes, "And human."

"Both are terrible qualities with children." I shrugged as if that would keep the words from hurting. Because once upon a time, I wanted nothing more than to be a mom someday.

Now, it wasn't even a possibility anymore.

"You're wrong." She tsked her tongue and leaned back in her chair across from me. "You'd do nothing to harm Gavin. Tell me I'm wrong."

"Not intentionally," I replied.

"Not at all, Laila," She tried. "You know that."

"It's not worth the risk." I shut her down, looking into my mug to signal that the conversation was over.

She sighed, and took a deep breath, before moving on in a way that only Carly could.

"So, Diesel, huh?"

I groaned and rolled my eyes, cringing at the whole endeavor.

"Carly."

"What?" she asked innocently. "I mean, he's not my first pick of a friend for you. But you could do worse."

"Worse?" I shook my head. "The man no doubt has a little black book filled with names of hookups right next to the names of people he's killed."

Her brows rose, and a smirk covered her lips, "You're thinking about women he's slept with?"

"Ugh," I groaned. "You're exhausting."

"Okay, let me ask you a better question." She hurried on, ignoring my discomfort. Because to be honest, it was a different discomfort than we were used to dealing with between us. This was the embarrassing uneasiness that people tried to avoid, not the physical pain kind of discomfort I was usually in when I was outside of my apartment.

"I'd prefer if you didn't."

"Zeke." She said effortlessly, like that was the entire sentence.

The flush of even more embarrassment crawled up my chest, and I fought the urge to run from the room completely.

"That's not a question," I said, and she opened her mouth to butt in, "Or a topic I'm willing to discuss."

She smiled knowingly, "Yet that answers so much, all on its own."

"You're insufferable," I murmured and took a sip of my tea, letting the gentle taste soothe the wounds inside of my throat that were no longer there, yet permanently marked in my mind.

"You love me anyway." She winked and crossed her legs under her like a kid at school on the story rug.

Before I could reply, movement outside caught my eye, and I turned and watched Ellie walking up the path with baby Gavin in her arms. A soft black blanket, fit for the world's most prized possessions, cradled him.

"Ah," Carly smirked as she waved to Ellie through the window, "Seems Ryker misinterpreted the message this morning."

"What does that mean, exactly?" I questioned her as the front door opened, but Elora's frustrated voice rang out, interrupting Carly's chance to clarify.

"That man is the most unbearable man in the entire world!" Elora complained, slamming the door behind her and kicking off her shoes as she rounded the corner. "Work." She huffed, "Can you believe he turned me down? For work!" She yelled.

Gavin babbled in her arms excitedly, picking up on the heightened energy surrounding him as he twisted around to see who was on the other side of his warm blanket still snuggling him.

Carly giggled and raised an eyebrow at her best friend with a know-ing look. "I told you they were doing something important. I haven't seen Jed for over five minutes in days." She looked across at me. "Has Zeke been as MIA as our men have been ?"

"How would I know?" I questioned, even as a blush warmed my cheeks. Elora's shoulders relaxed as she chuckled and came into the warm living room.

"I thought you'd hear him come and go, is all." Carly shrugged, holding her hands out for Gavin as Ellie handed him off to his favorite aunt. "Considering Jed said he found him half naked in your room at three am the other night."

"What?" Ellie gasped, pulling off her sweater and throwing herself down on the couch with excitement in her eyes. "Why am I just hearing about this?"

Carly shrugged, ignoring her overly eager friend to keep her eyes on me. "Care to share with the class?"

"There's nothing to share." I bit out a bit more forcefully than I planned and cringed. I never raised my voice or yelled, especially not at Carly.

Never at Carly.

"Why was he in your room, then?" She challenged me, pushing me further out of my comfort zone. She always knew what boundaries to push and which ones to avoid.

"I was having a dream." I stammered, "He said he could hear me screaming." Overwhelmed by the urge to sidetrack myself with my favorite chubby-cheeked distraction, I shrugged and stared down at my tea. My resolve lasted an entire five seconds before I put my mug on the table and slid down to the floor, instantly getting what I wanted.

Gavin squirmed in Carly's arms when he saw me on the floor, and she smirked as she set him on the floor at her feet. He quickly crawled across the space and threw himself into my lap like he had been wanting it as badly as I did.

"What kind of dream?" Elora asked, pushing the conversation on. And with her sweet little baby in my arms, I could almost ignore the normal anxiety that talking gave me, leaving me able to do it without a second thought.

"A naughty one," I answered truthfully, as I helped Gavin stand up in front of me. His sweet blue eyes were bright and round as he tried to balance with my support. "The kind a girl like me shouldn't be having about anyone." I sighed, "Let alone Zeke."

"A sex dream?" Ellie licked her lips and leaned forward on the couch. "You could definitely do worse for sex dream partners than Zeke Evans!" She winked. "The man is sexy."

"I shouldn't be having those kinds of dreams about anyone." I grounded myself, keeping my eyes on Gavin's innocent blue ones. "Besides, he thinks it was a nightmare, and that just adds to the embarrassment of it all. So, let's not talk about it. Please."

"You are allowed to be normal, Laila." Carly cut in, waiting for me to look at her before she finished. "Women dream of men sexually every single night. It's normal. You are normal. And you are allowed to enjoy sex. Both physically and mentally."

"You sound like—"

"Your therapist." She cut me off. "Because I'm right. And so is she."

"Are you attracted to Zeke?" Ellie asked, sliding down onto the floor so Gavin could take a few practice steps with our help between us.

"I don't know," I replied.

"Try again," Carly instructed, detecting my lie.

"I don't know how to be attracted to a man," I admitted, answering truthfully, without giving anything else away.

"Sex is empowering when we let it be," Carly said firmly. "What they did to you—," She paused and shook her head, skipping the words no one in the room needed to hear ever again. "Does not take away your power for the rest of your life. You are powerful. You are strong."

"I'm weak." My gaze fell on Gavin as he retreated. "I can't even—" I shook my head. "Never mind."

"Say it," Carly encouraged. "Get it off your chest."

I sighed and forced myself to meet her crystal blue eyes, fighting my discomfort to give her something of myself she deserved. "I can't even stand to be inside a room with anyone," I looked at Ellie, "Besides the three of you, that is. And even now, I'm on edge and I'm fighting the urge to escape this house completely before someone can imprison me inside of it." Fighting the urge to claw at my skin until I bled, I took Gavin's hands in mine and gave him my full attention, desperate to feel something besides the phantom pain of my past. "Every hallway, sidewalk, and path remind me of the torturous nightly walks to face another abuser." I blinked back stupid tears that I had fought every day for years because they didn't do me any good either way. "I can't even walk into Zeke's apartment without remembering the way it felt to lose my virginity in a horrific way."

"You've never had consensual sex before?" Carly asked gently. "Were you a virgin when they abducted you?"

I swallowed and kept my eyes firmly on Gavin's perfection. "They stole everything from me."

"Laila." Ellie sighed quietly, but I shook my head, and Carly put her hand on her shoulder, silencing whatever pity she was going to throw my way next.

Pity was something I couldn't stand. I hated it. I'd rather feel the physical pain of torture again than feel someone's pity, somehow, it felt worse than anything else.

"You are in control of your life now, Laila." Carly affirmed, like she had been in the room with my therapist every week. "I understand why you feel the way you do right now, but it won't be like this forever." She tilted her head and gave me a soft smile. "Look at how far you've come already."

I scoffed, dropping my gaze as self-doubt filled my head. "I'm going backward, not forward."

"Wrong." Ellie countered. "You couldn't even come inside when you first moved here." She raised her eyebrows at me as she took Gavin back in another handoff. "You locked yourself away in your apartment and didn't come out for weeks." She raised her hand, showcasing the interior of Carly's home. "And now we're hanging out inside and having girl time."

"And it physically hurts to do it." I challenged, hating the way her face pinched at the accusation in my voice. "I'm sorry." Sighing, I rubbed my forehead.

"What about Jed?" Carly questioned, staring me down. "Besides that first night at the brothel, you didn't let anyone touch you. Ever." She raised her eyebrows. "He said you clung to him and cried for a long time the other night." I groaned at the mental embarrassment that moment of weakness brought upon me. "You don't realize what that moment," She shook her head excitedly, "That *trust* you put in him, did for him right then and there. He came home and clung to *me* for hours, sobbing for all the pain he could finally let go of. All from having a piece of you and your relationship back, Laila." She fell to her knees in front of me, but didn't touch me, "You are healing decades' worth of pain and trauma, for both of you, with every single victory you make. Every piece of you that you allow us to help you heal, you're giving him peace, too. All of us. We ache to help you heal as much as you do," Reaching forward, Carly took my hand, and the contact burned like a jolt of electricity, but I forced myself to stay still and eventually the pain subsided and something else took its place. Something like comfort. "We want you to get every bit of peace and happiness you deserve, because you deserve the fucking world, Laila. And we're all going to make sure you get it."

"You make it sound so easy," I whispered, tightening my hand in hers and reveling in her unwavering support.

"It won't be easy." She shook her head. "What I'm asking you to do is painful and traumatic, and I'm not unaware of that. I promise you. But it's going to be so fucking worth it." She shook her head as her blue eyes misted over. "And it's possible. It's within reach. Your joy and happiness, both in yourself and in a relationship with someone someday, are within reach."

CHAPTER 4 – ZEKE

Something about Ryker's gated community in the East Valley always felt unsettling as I drove through it. No matter how many years I'd done it. Technically, I lived in the East Valley too, being that I lived inside Ryker's estate. But it wasn't where I belonged.

At least not until lately.

Before the repetitive sameness of the HOA village's tree-lined streets, with their quiet, almost oppressive order, fueled a powerful longing to escape each time I drove through.

Lately, though, I almost looked forward to returning after a long day of skull busting and deal-making.

Lately, I ached to feel the draw of electricity that burned in my gut every time I neared her door.

Lately, it was almost enough to be in the presence of her innocence, to feel like the weight of my darkness no longer threatened to shove me into the ground, inch by inch, until I was six feet under.

At least, that was until someone reminded me of all the reasons I shouldn't even share her air.

Laila.

The name of the angel with the spirit of a wounded animal.

As if the mere thought of her could conjure her perfection, I caught sight of her on the sidewalk standing still, unmoving outside the mansion that belonged to a sleazy politician on Ryker's payroll.

I pulled my blacked-out SUV over on the side of the street and put it in park, watching the mysterious woman as she stared up at the brick façade, still motionless. Her usually sharp senses were dulled, and she didn't notice me approaching; her alertness was gone.

Lost in thought, she didn't notice me silently stalking her from twenty yards away; the only sounds were the gentle breeze and the rustle of leaves under my feet.

Which meant that the house meant something to her, or something happened again.

Before I could think twice, my hand pulled the door handle, and I slid from the car, quietly closing it behind me as I walked up the sidewalk toward her.

Still, she didn't move.

"Laila," I called quietly so as not to spook her. If jumpy had a picture in the dictionary, it would be Laila with those big brown eyes rounded in surprise at every little noise or movement. Those eyes with flakes of gold in them made the monster in me wonder what they would look like swimming in tears, staring up at me as she kneeled at my feet.

Fuck.

"Laila," I growled out with more force, trying to straighten out my thoughts, and as if on cue, her body jolted as she swung around to face me with that startled expression on her face.

And those deep, bottomless chocolate eyes staring up at me.

"Jesus." She gasped, covering her heart with her hand as she twirled around, finally taking in her surroundings.

"What are you doing?" I questioned, keeping a couple of feet between us.

"What are *you* doing?" She avoided my gaze, staring just off to the side of my head like she normally did before glancing back at the house beside us.

"Trying to understand why you're frozen stiff on the sidewalk, staring up at Senator Lupold's house." I nodded to the house again, and her jaw clenched slightly.

"Senator." She repeated quietly before looking away from the house completely and facing me, straightening her spine, and taking a deep breath. "I got distracted. That's all."

"Distracted," I repeated, not buying it. "Where are you going?"

"Nowhere." She countered, chewing her bottom lip the tiniest bit. And that was her tell.

She always chewed on her lips when she lied or avoided the truth.

"Laila." I urged, deepening my voice and drawing her attention back to me. "Don't ever lie to me."

"I'm not—," She stopped and swallowed. "I'm just walking."

"Where to?" I questioned. "Jed said you quit your job."

Annoyance flared in her normally sweet eyes for a second before she turned and simply walked away from me, like I hadn't interrupted her in the first place.

I stood rooted in place as she walked down the sidewalk away from me, stunned at her bravery. A sinister grin pulled my lips to the side while something akin to excitement burned down my spine as she got further away from me.

With a flick of my wrist, I locked the SUV with my fob and followed her. A fire ignited within me, growing stronger with each footfall on the concrete behind her.

She was defying me.

She'd never defied me before, or anyone for that matter.

The sound of my approaching footsteps caused Laila to glance back, her dark brown hair streaming behind her, fear widening her eyes.

But she turned around and faced forward, quickening her step. As we walked along, my smile grew wider and more intense with every nervous peek she took over her shoulder. The quick pace she kept made her jeans hug her ass in a way that called to the animal in me, but I pushed it down, silencing the desire.

Finally, she paused and turned on me. "What are you doing?"

"Following you," I replied honestly.

Her eyes squinted a fraction, "Why?"

"Because you lied to me. Then you rebelled against me." I tilted my head to the side, and the pulse in her neck beat rapidly as she watched me. "And you've never done that before."

"I didn't realize you were my babysitter." She snapped, "Or my boss."

Fire brewed in her eyes for the first time in months, and pride grew in mine.

"Do you need a babysitter?" I challenged. "Or a boss?"

The innuendo in that statement burned in my gut, but it missed her innocence by a mile, and she never caught on.

Which was good. Because she was the last woman on earth I needed to dominate.

Even if I'd never wanted to see a woman beg more than her before.

"I need to be left alone." She huffed.

"Why?"

"Because." She fired back.

"You're cheeky today."

"And you're bossy."

"Always." I raised an eyebrow at her, and she sucked her teeth. "So, I'll ask you again. Where are you going?"

"To therapy." She snapped.

"You go to therapy across the city." I scowled. "Do you plan to get there on foot?"

"How do you—?" She closed her mouth. "Never mind, I'm not even surprised you know that."

"Good," I replied. "One less thing to cover. So, where are you really going?"

"I just told you. I'm doing therapy."

The way she said doing therapy instead of going to therapy alerted me to what she meant, even if she didn't intend it to.

"Walking around East Valley is part of your therapy?"

She clenched her jaw, looked around at the deserted streets around us, and sighed. "Walking on a sidewalk is."

I raised my eyebrows at her but kept the quick-cutting retort I had ready to myself. "Why?"

She rolled her eyes. "How is this any of your business?"

"Isn't this something a friend would know?"

"Friend?" She raised her brows at me in surprise and then rolled her eyes again, making the alpha in me ache to correct the bratty attitude. "We're not friends, Zeke."

"Ouch." I feigned insult, and she smirked the tiniest smile before dropping her gaze to her feet and hiding it. "So let me be your friend. For five minutes."

"Why?" She shook her head, sneaking a glance up at me. "What do you care?"

"Humor me. Let me know something about you."

She scoffed and kicked a stone with her sneaker. "You already know the worst parts of me, Zeke." She replied quietly, "Everyone does." A redness crept up her neck, but it wasn't from embarrassment. It looked like anger. "Everyone knows the darkest and most terrible parts. Don't I deserve to have anything that's just for me?"

"You're wrong, because I don't know you at all." I argued, waiting for her to look up at me before continuing. "I know the darkest and most terrible thing that happened to you, but I don't know anything *about* you. Things that happen *to* us do not define us." I took a step forward, closing the distance between us, and swelled with undeserving pride when she didn't take a step backward like she usually did. "So, for five minutes, let me be your friend."

She mulled it over, but I thought she was going to just remain mute indefinitely until she sighed and turned back away from me. Instead of walking away from me, she looked over her shoulder and nodded for me to walk beside her.

"What about your car?" she asked as we started down the sidewalk away from my car.

"Do you think someone in East Valley is going to steal it?"

She shrugged her shoulders, "I grew up in a neighborhood not much different from this one." She kept her gaze forward, "And terrible things happened there, so who knows."

I smirked at her attempt at sarcasm, but kept my mouth shut, giving her control of the conversation. It was one of the first conversations we had if you didn't count the one in her bedroom the other night.

I didn't count it, because I couldn't focus on a single thing besides how good she looked in her cute little pajama set, rumpled and sleepy as she stared up at me.

Or the noises she made as she dreamed. God, those noises.

"I'm practicing walking down sidewalks." She finally admitted. "For therapy."

All sexual thoughts I'd been having about her faded away as the gravity of that statement hit me square in the chest. I pressed carefully, not oblivious to the fact that she was finally giving me a glimpse into her life, and I didn't want her slamming the door in my face just yet.

"What is it about walking down sidewalks that bothers you?"

"It's not sidewalks in particular." She hummed and took another deep breath. "There was a long hallway," She paused again, like the words were evading her. "Every time they ushered me down that hallway, I was hurt."

"And now walking down certain hallways," I motioned to the long strip of concrete ahead of us, "leaves you triggered."

She peeked up at me from under the curtain of hair blowing around her face and nodded.

"I see." I acknowledged, focusing on maintaining my strong composure when the small tidbit of information rattled me. "How are you feeling right now?"

She scoffed a bit with a smirk. "Like I've fallen into some alternate universe and wound up with you walking down a sidewalk with me while I try not to have a panic attack."

I snorted from her attempt at deflection and humor but kept walking with her. "Anxious." I looked at her, and she rolled her eyes before nodding in agreement. "How do you combat your anxiety?"

She sighed, sliding her hands into the pockets of her tight jeans, and kicked a stone with the toe of her sneaker. "Besides a near-lethal dose of medication?" She shrugged, "Meditation and journaling have helped, I guess."

"What do you journal about?" I asked as I pinpointed a black sedan rolling down the road toward us, slower than usual, even for the residential street.

"Uh," She shrugged again, peeking up at me, drawing my eyes back to hers. "The past. The present." She licked her lips. "My dreams and my hopes for the future."

"Manifesting what you want out of life is a great way to put into action." I tried to sound sure and supportive. But I didn't have a fucking clue how to be a self-help guru. Damn if I wasn't trying, though.

"That's what Carly says." She chuckled, shaking her head.

"Carly's one of the smartest people I know, so that makes sense," I responded, looking back at the car as it slowed to a stop next to us. I turned toward it, sliding my hand down Laila's arm, tucking her behind me as the tinted window on the vehicle's back door rolled down. One hand was on her, and the other was next to the gun in my waistband.

"Zeke." A sickly-sweet voice called from the darkness inside as its occupant leaned forward, revealing herself.

"Mrs. Lupold." I nodded, relaxing my hand near my gun, but not on Laila's arm. I felt her tense when I responded, and she slid her hand into mine and squeezed like she was on edge. "What can I do for you?"

"Always so formal." Clarissa Lupold sucked her perfectly white teeth as she eyed me up openly. Her flawlessly curled blonde hair framed every inch of her face, perfectly made up, a picture of polished beauty.

She looked porcelain and perfect for her role as a Senator's wife because of it all.

But I knew there was a slimy, repulsive creature that lived beneath her perfect appearance.

Clarissa smiled brightly and flicked her bright blue eyes to the figure standing behind me, still clinging to my hand.

"Out for a stroll today, Zeke? Or were you coming over for a visit?" Clarissa tried again, "I hardly ever see you outside of those massive gates. Well," She paused with a smirk, "besides at special functions, that is."

I tensed at her thinly veiled statement and scowled at her, which only made her sickly smile deepen.

"Have a nice day, Mrs. Lupold." I nodded, turning back to the sidewalk, keeping my body in front of Laila's.

"Oh, I will," Clarissa called from the window as we walked away. "Until next time."

Laila's hand shook in mine as she peeked over her shoulder to where Clarissa's car started back down the street, pulling into the driveway of the estate Laila had been staring at when I found her.

"Who was that?" Laila whispered as I finally looked down at her, finding those eyes rounded as she stared up at me, fulfilling that sexually deviant side of my soul again.

"No one," I replied, as my eyes flicked down to her plump lips that were parted in surprise from the entire encounter. "She's a nobody."

"She called you Zeke," Laila whispered, staring up at me while still clutching my hand like she wasn't even aware that she had touched me. "I've only heard Carly and Ellie get to call you Zeke. Every other woman calls you Mr. Evans."

"Everyone but you." I reminded her. "You call me Zeke."

She licked her lips and swallowed, suddenly aware of our closeness and the intensity burning between our bodies. "Why did you block me when you talked to her?"

"I didn't know who she was at first," I admitted. "If she were a threat, I needed you behind me to protect you."

Laila dropped her eyes, staring at my arm before shaking herself free completely, abandoning my hand and creating space between our bodies again. "She's related to that Senator." She glanced back down the sidewalk toward the estate again. "The one who lives in that house."

"She's his wife."

"Yet you sleep with her." She replied instantly and then tensed.

My brows rose in surprise, and my first inclination was to deny it. But something made me want to be honest with her. Perhaps giving honesty would get me honesty.

"I have in the past." I acknowledged. "How did you know?"

She rolled her eyes and scoffed. "Curse of the trade." She said, not elaborating, but I knew what she meant.

She could read sexual situations because of her extensive time in the sex work world. Just like Carly could.

But Laila's experience was never her choice, yet she still gained the same sixth sense from it.

My phone rang in my pocket as I started to respond, interrupting me and destroying the honest moment between us. Looking at the screen, I sighed.

Jed.

Exactly the man I didn't want to talk to at the moment.

"Thanks for the five minutes," Laila said, drawing an end to our impromptu friendship as she backed away down the sidewalk. "See ya around." She smirked a tiny smile. "Zeke."

I couldn't resist the smile that burned my cheeks as I shook my head at her brazenness. "Have a good therapy session." I nodded to the sidewalk, and she tipped her head back and chuckled.

"Mmh. Will do." She saluted and then turned around and walked away from me. I stood rooted in place, unable to move as she got further down the street before she turned the corner and walked around the block, disappearing completely.

CHAPTER 5 – LAILA

"I need a favor." Carly clasped her hands together in front of her as she rocked back and forth on the balls of her feet at my door.

I'd never admit it, but I was slightly disappointed when I opened it to her instead of my mysterious neighbor from across the hall.

Four days ago, Zeke walked with me down the sidewalk while I did a therapy exercise, and it felt like something passed between us, yet I hadn't seen or heard from him since.

Nothing. Not a casual smile, in passing down the hallway, or even the noise of him coming or going to his place late at night like usual.

Just silence.

So, when someone knocked on my door, my stupid heart sped up with excitement that it could be him coming to say hello.

"No." I shook my head, forcing myself back to the present. "I mean, I can't. I'm busy."

She rolled her eyes and glared at me. "You don't even know what I'm asking of you yet."

"Doesn't matter. I can't." I shook my head again.

"Elora and Ryker need a babysitter tonight. Their nanny has the flu, and they have plans."

"No." I shook my head, trying to shut my door as panic flushed through my body at the mere mention of watching Gavin alone. "You do it."

"I can't!" Carly cried, blocking my door with her foot and pushing it open, ignoring my attempts to run. "I must go, too. We have tickets to a concert, and I'm not missing it. They're my favorite band."

"There are no less than twenty staff and crew members on this estate at any given time. Make one of them do it." I scoffed.

"Ellie doesn't trust anyone else with Gavin, and you know that!"

"Not my problem!"

"Laila!" She sighed.

"Carly." I mocked. "We talked about this. I can't."

"You can." She challenged. "You just won't try."

"Rude." I pursed my lips at her, and she smirked, tilting her head to the side.

"He goes to bed in two hours; we're leaving in one. That's just one hour of babysitting duties and then bedtime, and you can just hang out for a few more hours until we get back."

"Carly." I groaned. "I'm not comfortable—"

"You have to try new things, Laila." Carly prodded, reminding me of my therapist's orders at my last session. She called me sedentary and complacent about letting life pass me by.

While I first balked at her lack of tact, she wasn't wrong.

"A baby is not an appropriate test subject."

"He'll be fine." She reasoned. "We trust you, Laila. You have to trust yourself."

I groaned, knowing she had me by the throat because I couldn't *actually* tell her no. Or Elora and Ryker, for that matter, after how much they'd done for me.

She smiled brightly before squealing and taking my hand in hers. "Yay!" She bounced around on her toes. "Come to the mansion in forty minutes and we'll give you a quick recap of his routines and where to find stuff." She excitedly turned down the hall and headed toward the exit but stopped and looked back at me. "I'm proud of you, Laila." She smiled. "Thank you."

In the deserted hallway after the exterior door swung shut, I stood silently, focusing on my breathing and heart rate to prevent a panic attack.

"I can do this," I whispered to myself, tightening my hold on the doorknob of my apartment to ground me. "I can do this."

"If you have questions, just text me." Carly rubbed her hand up my arm reassuringly. "You're going to be just fine."

"I know," I replied, smiling back at her, believing in myself. It took a massive pep talk in my apartment before coming over to the mansion, but I felt fine about being left with Gavin.

"The guards will go in and out through the security room entrance," Ryker informed me as Ellie slid her leather jacket on next to him. "I've given them strict instructions to stay out of the main living areas unless summoned."

"Got it." I nodded, switching Gavin to my hip as he cooed and played peek-a-boo with Jed over my shoulder. "I'm good. Really. We'll be fine." I repeated Carly's affirmation. "Have fun."

"It's going to be a blast." Ryker rolled his eyes, and Ellie elbowed him in the ribs. "What?" He scoffed. "I'm too old for a mosh pit."

"And I'm too young to stay home every night," Ellie argued, winking at me before kissing Gavin's cheek. "Be good for Auntie Laila, Gav. I'll see you in the morning." She pulled back. "Thank you so much for filling in."

"No problem. Get out of here before you hit traffic." I waited at the bottom of the stairs as they started leaving, pausing when Jed came up to me.

"Say the word, and I'll stay here." He said firmly, not elaborating.

"And leave your girl, looking that good, all alone at a rock concert?" I deadpanned, looking around his shoulder to where Carly zipped up a pair of black leather thigh-high boots to match the mini leather skirt that barely covered her bits. "Yeah, right."

She winked at me and backed toward the door. "I had to beg, borrow, and plead to get him to agree to this, Laila. I wasn't leaving anything to chance for getting him out the door." She blew Jed a sultry kiss. "Come on, big boy. Let's go rock and roll."

He groaned but followed her with a grimace my way. "Text me if you need anything, and we'll come right back." He stared me down. "I promise."

"We're good." I waved Gavin's little hand at his parents as they left, while he happily giggled and chewed on his other hand. When the door shut behind them and I was alone in a house filled with other people just out of sight, I quietly asked myself. "We're good, aren't we, little man?

Men.

The house was filled with men.

Men who were big and scary and trained to fight and kill at a moment's notice. But who were also supposedly friends.

Allies.

Memories assaulted me from a time in my past when other men were supposed to be my friends, my allies.

Yet they were the ones who hurt me first.

"Let's go play with all your cool toys." I fussed at Gavin, distracting myself from the panic again.

Carrying Gavin through the house, I avoided the kitchen like the plague on my way to the den and sat in the middle of the floor with him, surrounded by his happy, colorful toys. He crawled away to his favorite set of blocks, intent on destroying any remnants of towers left standing from the last time he was here to play as I sat back against the couch and watched him.

He was so perfect and innocent. Sometimes, when he was near, I felt like his innocence could almost silence the damage done inside my head. Like somehow his pure goodness could heal something inside of me.

Then there were other times that I worried my darkness and trauma would taint his cleanness, leaving him contaminated and broken like me.

I wouldn't survive that.

I couldn't survive ruining another perfectly innocent baby. Not again.

"Gah!" Gavin screamed in jubilation as he knocked the last stacked tower down with his chubby hands, looking back at me for praise.

"You did it!" I cheered, smiling at him as he giggled and looked for more. "Such a smart boy."

Breathing a sigh of relief, I crept downstairs, watching the monitor for any sign that Gavin had woken. It had taken me nearly an hour to get him to sleep because he had wanted to stay up and play, fighting his tiredness. But finally, I came out victorious.

And there was a pint of mint ice cream in the freezer with my name on it as a reward.

Literally. There was a sticker on it that said '*Laila's. Eat it and die.*' in Ellie's handwriting. I'm generally suspicious of freebies; experience showed me that good deeds often had hidden downsides.

But I was trying to be trusting again, and no one here had ever hurt me before.

Which was a mantra I repeated all day every day.

I only knew the ice cream was there because Gavin's teeth had been bothering him before bed, and I remembered his frozen treats were in the kitchen. So, I risked encountering a security guard to get him some.

And now I was hooked, desperate to go back and get the ice cream I'd earned while simultaneously telling myself it wasn't worth the risk and forgetting about it.

I had made so many big-girl steps already though; I didn't want to lose the momentum to old fears. I forced my feet to move ahead, toward the kitchen and then to the freezer. Relieved, I found the kitchen empty and silent, I practically ran to the industrial-size freezer and grabbed the sweet treat, fearing I'd be caught.

The security door opened just as I reached for a spoon, and fear instantly froze me, my hand trapped in the drawer, my body screaming to react but utterly immobile.

Ryker had told his guards to stay out of the main house unless I summoned them, but I didn't call anyone. A giant body moved through the doorway, into the brightly lit kitchen, and electricity zinged through my nervous system when I saw who it was.

Zeke.

But it wasn't Zeke the way I knew Zeke. The man who walked into the kitchen and paused when he saw me was a version of Zeke I'd never seen before.

He was shirtless, wearing only a pair of black pants and matching black boots, with a scowl equally dark. Blood splattered his tattooed chest and neck, his face just as crimson stained. A nasty wound lay across the meat of his chest, directly over his heart, dripping blood down his torso and into the waistband of his pants.

"Laila?" He scowled deeper, staring at me. "What are you doing in here?" There was a slight slur to his words that instantly made me remember the way liquored-up men talked in the brothel.

Zeke was drunk.

"I'm sorry," I whispered on autopilot, dropping my eyes and staring at the floor between us as my body took over for my short-circuiting brain. "I didn't see anything. I'm sorry."

"Shit." The slow, quiet tread of his boots on the floor followed a sigh, and a muttered curse. "Hey, look at me." I forced air into my lungs, trying to forget the way the blood looked smeared across his handsome face while simultaneously reminding myself he was always kind to me.

Friend.

Ally.

Good.

I repeated those three words in my head over and over until his boots stopped right at the tips of my bare toes, crowding my view of the tile floor where I'd been staring blindly before.

"Hey." He said again, slowly reaching for my hand and taking the ice cream from it, before setting it on the counter. "I didn't mean to scare you."

"No one was supposed to come in," I whispered, taking a deep breath. "Ryker said he told the guards to stay out. Then the door opened, and I—"

"You were scared." He replied gently. "I'm sorry. I had no idea you were here, or I wouldn't have come in like this. I just needed some first aid supplies, and I'm not exactly thinking straight right at the moment. I'm sorry."

My eyes moved from the floor to his pants, slowly taking in the cuts in his pants and the wounds showing through them, then to his abs splattered in blood I didn't have to be a fool to realize wasn't all his up to his massive chest and shoulders and then to his perfect face.

"You're hurt," I stated the obvious as I relaxed out of my fight-or-flight mode. "Should I call Ryker? Or the doctor?"

The wound on his chest continuously dripped blood down his abs, and I ached to make it stop. There was only so much blood inside the human body, and even though Zeke was a giant, he was only human.

"I may need a doctor if I keep bleeding on Ellie's kitchen floor," he joked and gave me a one-sided grin. "But no, I'm okay."

"Here." I moved and grabbed a roll of paper towels off the counter, ripping a handful free and holding them out to him. "Put pressure on it."

He raised an eyebrow at me but, thankfully, staunched the bleeding with the towels anyway. "You know first aid?"

I nodded. "I patched the girls up when they—," I shrugged, leaving the rest of it open-ended. He knew what happened to the girls. "I picked up a few skills along the way."

"It's a good thing to know." He replied. "What are you doing in the mansion?" he asked again, looking around for someone else.

"The four of them went to a concert. Gavin's nanny was sick, so they asked me to watch him so they could go." I shrugged, looking from the red stain seeping through the paper towels to his bright blue eyes. "You need to get that bleeding stopped."

"I know." He nodded, reached around me to a tall cabinet on the wall, and grabbed a large bin from it. "I just needed this." He held it up and smirked. "I'll get out of your hair now."

He backed up toward the security room again and nodded to the rest of the house behind the kitchen. "Go enjoy the rest of your night, Laila."

"Where are you going?" I questioned, "Is someone going to help you with that?"

He shrugged, watching me closely. "I don't need any help. I'm just going to take the mess to my apartment."

"What if you can't get it stopped?" I rambled. "What if you need help? Can the guards help you?"

He tilted his head and kept watching me, like a puzzle he was trying to figure out. "I'm a big boy, Laila. I can take care of it."

The idea of him going to his apartment alone while I was stuck here for another few hours waiting for Ryker and Ellie to return stressed me out, so I spoke up again. "No one will know if you pass out or something. You can't go lock yourself away alone."

"Are you worried about me?" There was something so intimidating about his penetrating stare, and I, of course, dropped it, unable to even meet a weak man's gaze regularly. And Zeke was anything but weak.

"No," I replied instantly, stepping backward and shaking my head at the ridiculous notion.

"Hmm." He hummed, putting his hand on the door handle, and nodding to me. "Stupid me thought maybe you forgot to turn the clock off on our little friendship experiment the other day." He joked. "Don't worry about me, I can handle this."

"Stop." I barked, making the man freeze in his steps, once again facing me. "I'll do it. Come here." I nodded to the stool at the island and rolled my sleeves up. "Sit."

He raised his eyebrows and took a step closer. "Since when are you bossy?"

"Since you're threatening to bleed out on your apartment floor because your toxic masculinity is stopping you from asking for help. Now sit down."

He put the bin on the counter and sat down on the stool, leaning back against the bar behind him. "Can you touch me, Laila?" His voice was deep and filled with gravel that made it feel like my entire body vibrated around the words. "I'm a half-dressed man, and you have to touch me to help me."

I opened the bin and started taking out what supplies I would need to close his wound. "I'll just pretend you're someone else."

He snorted and smirked at me, and a part of me ached to see his full face without his dark beard so I could see if the dimple in his cheek was as deep as I imagined it would be.

"Who are you pretending I am?"

I poured antiseptic onto a few gauze pads and started wiping away the blood around his wound, waiting for him to flinch when the liquid penetrated the angry red muscle, but he didn't so much as blink. "A harmless old lady." I shrugged. "Too frail and slow to be a threat."

He smirked again and looked up at the ceiling with that devilish grin on his face as he let me work. "And is it helping you feel safe?"

"A little." I shrugged again, focused on my task. "Stay still," I ordered when he raised his arm, and the muscle I was working on flexed.

Do not stare at his moving pecks.

Do not stare at his moving pecks.

How did guys do that, anyway? It was unfair.

"I am still."

"You're fidgeting." I countered.

"I'm *not* a fidgeter." He scoffed. "I do not fidget."

"Now you're rambling, Granny." I deadpanned, fighting my smirk. But when he opened his mouth and laughed at the ceiling, I was in awe of him, suddenly unable to care about the volume of blood he was losing.

Thankfully, it only lasted a second before I snapped myself out of it and got back to work.

"Okay, spitfire." He relaxed, looking down at my work. "I'll be a good boy and sit still. But just because it's you."

I shook my head, grabbing the bottle of medical-grade skin glue and holding it up to him. "Are you ready?"

"This is going to hurt, isn't it?" He raised an eyebrow at me and then chuckled. "Do your worst, Doc."

"Hold still, and I'll make sure you get a sucker when you're done."

"Now you're talking my language, Doc." He closed his eyes, tipping his head backward like he was going to take a nap instead of enduring liquid fire sealing his wound together. "Praise and treats are the only way to make me behave."

"I'll have to remember that." I mused, pinching his skin together with my fingers and wincing as I quickly poured the sealant into the wound. He jerked and hissed as it essentially cauterized the muscle in his chest. The muscles in his neck were taut, but he remained still and passive otherwise, leaving me in awe of his strength.

"Don't glue your fingers to my chest." He said between clenched teeth before popping one eye open to look at me. "Unless you're looking for an excuse to continue our friendship experiment."

I laughed, pulling my fingers from his skin as the solution got tacky and dabbed at the bit of blood that escaped from the wound. It wasn't pretty, but it was sealed, protecting him from infection and more blood loss. "Friendship." I pondered, but the word didn't feel right, though I didn't offer any others in its place. "Are you actually friends with anyone?"

"Hmm." He hummed, "Ryker." He sat up again, looking down at the wound on his chest and then at me. "And occasionally your brother."

"Just occasionally?" I questioned, entranced by him again as he stood up and towered over me. "When aren't you?"

"When we're arguing over you."

CHAPTER 6 – ZEKE

Her brown eyes dilated, and her nostrils flared as she stared up at me. "Me?"

"Mmh." I nodded. "He gets possessive of you."

"Why does that cause an argument?" she asked bravely, holding my gaze.

I smirked, fighting the urge to tell her how many times a day I thought about her. Or how many times a day I envisioned her naked in my bed, head tipped back in ecstasy. "Because he's a cranky bastard to deal with when he wants to be." To avoid a bloody mess, I bypassed her, washed my hands at the sink, and thus prevented a trail of blood on the doorknobs. I was far from patched up completely, but the biggest one was taken care of for the time being. I headed for the door again, stopping next to her where she stayed frozen at the counter and leaned down until I hovered right above her ear. "And he can't stand the thought of someone like me, tainting you."

She inhaled quickly, turning her head so we were face to face. "Good thing you aren't interested in me then, isn't it?"

I chuckled humorlessly, and tomorrow I'd blame it on the amount of whiskey I drank on the way back to the mansion to numb the pain radiating through my body from a job gone sideways, but tonight I was going to indulge.

"Good thing you're the only one who doesn't see me for what I am. Because then you'd know that's a lie."

She licked her lips, "And what are you then?"

"A monster." I replied, leaning forward, and bending her back over the counter, without actually touching her. Because that was the flaw in everything. She couldn't stand my touch. "A monster with a hunger for a sweet little innocent brown-eyed girl that lives across the hall from me, screaming my name in her sex dreams, tempting me."

Her chest collapsed as I exposed her secret out into the open and exposed myself at the same moment. "Zeke." She whispered, and I closed my eyes, savoring the sound of my name on her lips again.

"Don't worry." I sighed, leaning back away from her tense body. "I'll never touch you." I shook my head and took a step back. "I know you don't want me." Although it was difficult, I walked away, leaving her because it was the right thing to do, despite the turmoil in my heart with every step.

I didn't just lust after Laila. That much was obvious.

There was something else inside of me that was drawn to her, even though I didn't understand it. I didn't understand the connection between us, especially considering we didn't know each other.

"I'm incapable of giving you anything—that includes friendship, Zeke." She called after me. "I thought I made that much clear when I bolted from your apartment after you tried to treat my burned hand." She shrugged sadly, "I'm too broken."

I stopped once again in the doorway, so close to leaving this whole situation behind me, but turned around anyway. "I don't need you to give me anything, Laila." I tightened my hand around the doorknob to keep the emotions I was feeling off my face. "And my friendship isn't conditional on you giving me anything in return. I just want to get to know you. Help you."

"I don't know how to." She shook her head. "I know nothing about you, and you don't know anything about me, and I don't know how to change that because I'm so fucked up, I can't even converse with you like a normal person." Her anxiety was turning into hysterics as she got worked up over her failures. "I can't carry on a conversation with anyone for long before the weight of it literally exhausts me."

"I need nothing in return from you." I repeated. "You already have my friendship. When you're ready to let me in, I'll listen, however you decide to communicate. And I'll return the favor when you're ready."

It had been six days since I had seen Laila during the late-night kitchen incident. Six days since I laid eyes on her with my own, and not on the other side of a security monitor.

I *had* watched her plenty from the security footage around the mansion.

Obsession.

That's the only word that I could put to what my fascination with her melted down to. Obsessed. I was completely obsessed with her, and she had no idea. She didn't even think I was interested in her. And in a way, that was exactly what I needed her to think. At the end of the day, nothing could ever happen between us. Not even counting the drama that something between us would cause for Jed, she didn't stand to gain anything from letting me near her.

All the bullshit I threw in her direction about friendship and what I was willing to give to her without the expectation of anything in return was, well, bullshit frankly.

I wanted her.

I craved her.

I needed her.

But I'd never have her.

So, I was settling for friendship. Getting just enough to ease the consuming ache inside of me to possess her.

I'd been gone from the estate as much as possible over the last six days, trying to convince myself I wasn't hiding from her after my drunken, loose lips hinted at how fucking bad I wanted her. But every night when I returned, I'd look at her door and try to sense if she was inside, resting peacefully or being haunted by the monsters of her past in her dreams.

But tonight, while I was sneaking down the hallway, something on my door distracted me from her. It was a piece of paper, folded and slid between the door and jamb, waiting for me.

I flicked my glance back over to her door and caught the slightest bit of movement in the shadows under the door, showing that she was moving around by the door.

Was she watching through the peephole?

Was the note from her?

I grabbed the paper and unfolded it, instantly aware that it was Laila's neat handwriting, and looked back at her door in confusion.

Instead of going inside my place to read the note, I stood there in the hallway and dove in. The paper was ripped out of a notebook, and there was a date at the very top.

Three weeks ago.

Skimming over the words, I realized it was a journal entry from three weeks ago.

From Laila's journal. She took a page from her private thoughts and left it for me to read.

She was communicating with me. The only way she felt comfortable.

Dear journal,

I used to love sunsets. I remember lying at the end of my bed in my parent's home as a kid, and watching the colors of the sky melt into a watercolor painting of vibrant pinks and oranges like a movie. It was one of my favorite things to do. Every night.

*Until **that** night.*

The night I was taken from my life and thrown into Hell at nineteen. I never watched another sunset again. The end of the daylight meant that the night was beginning, and every night brought pain with it. So, sunsets started representing pain and suffering to me, and I stopped watching them.

Until tonight.

Tonight, I sat on the manicured lawn of an estate I have no business calling home and watched the bright yellow ball of fire light the sky ablaze with orange and red streaks of beauty.

And I felt like a piece of my past was returned to me. With the simplicity of sitting down and watching the sunset for the evening, I regained a piece of my soul. A piece of myself.

Why can't everything be that easy?

> *Why can't it all happen so effortlessly?*
> *I just want to be happy.*
> *XO, L.*

I folded the paper back in half and looked back at her door, noting the two shadows, shoulder width apart at the base of the door, as nothing but silence met my stare.

She was watching.

She watched as she gave me something she gave to no one else.

"Thank you." I said to the door, knowing she'd hear me. When she didn't respond or open her door, I went into my apartment and put the folded piece of paper in my nightstand drawer to read again sometime.

As I showered off the day and let the hot water relax my tired muscles, I replayed her words in my head, over and over again.

I just want to be happy.

Did she not understand how much we all wanted that for her, too? How willing we all were to help her get that.

She deserved so much more than just happiness out of life.

And I was going to make sure she got it.

CHAPTER 7 – LAILA

Can you die from fear?

An internet search I never thought I'd have to make in my life, yet there I was, pacing my floor back and forth, thumbs roving over my phone screen and typing that stupid question to the internet gods.

Zeke read my journal entry.

And not only did he read it, but he stood in the hallway and let me watch him read it.

Did he know I was watching?

Holy Hell, I thought I was going to die from the overwhelming amount of fear and anxiety running through my body.

I locked my phone screen and tossed it down on my bed as I kept pacing. That had been at one am, and hours later, I was still panicking over it.

He told me both in the kitchen and on the sidewalk that he wanted to be my friend, and that he'd wait for me to be ready to communicate and share with him who I was. But I wasn't some normal girl who could just be friends with someone. Especially not a sexually arousing man like Zeke Evans.

I couldn't even talk to him without my blood pressure rising to a stupid level.

So, I thought about it repeatedly for days after the night I watched Gavin and finally came up with a decision.

I'd share the only way I knew how, and that was through my journaling.

I picked a very surface level one out of the deep and dark secret sharing entries in my leather-bound journal my therapist insisted I write in months ago.

And holy fucking shit, it had been the most nerve-wracking thing in the world.

But I did it.

It felt like I'd ripped the band-aid off and shared a part of myself with him I wouldn't have done any other way.

But now, I was going crazy trying to figure out what he thought about me after reading my poor, sappy entry about missing sunsets.

Did he think I was nuts?

Well, *I was*, so that was fine.

But did he change his mind about wanting to be my friend?

"Jesus, Laila." I snapped in aggravation. "The man woke you up out of what he clearly knew was a sex dream. About him!" I argued with myself. "If that didn't send him running for the hills, your bullshit story about sunsets isn't enough to register."

I sighed and threw myself down on my bed, frustrated with myself and the entire situation. "This is why I stay in my apartment and don't interact with anyone." I complained once again to myself.

"This is why I stay in my apartment all the time." I complained as Carly walked ahead of me into the store.

"Which is why I lied and tricked you into coming with me here tonight." She winked and held the door open for me. "Mav agreed to close the store down an hour early so we could do this," She waved her hand for me to enter, "So come on."

I groaned but rushed in ahead of her as the cool evening followed in after me. "Carly, I can't do this."

Racks upon racks of sexy clothes and lingerie stared back at me like strangers judging me.

"Yes, you can." She reassured me for the tenth time since letting me in on her plan as we left our last stop at the salon. I should have known she had more up her sleeve besides the fresh highlights and blow-out she surprised me with today. "Your sexuality is a powerful tool."

"It's a weapon used against women by predators and pearl-clutchers to trick us into thinking we somehow asked to be targeted and brutalized simply because of the clothing we dress ourselves with." I snapped back and then sighed, hating that I talked to her that way. "That wasn't fair, I'm sorry."

"It's true." She stared me down. "Sexuality can be used against us by everyone. Our family and friends, partners and first dates, strangers online, predators who attack and abuse us, the possibilities are endless."

"Then why do it?" I questioned, waving my hand out at her tight neon pink leather pants and sexy black crop top with matching pink laces tying it together over her chest. It wasn't that the outfit was particularly revealing, there was only a sliver of skin between the top of her pants and the bottom of her shirt that showed. But it was the intent of it that rubbed me wrong.

It gave off a *look-at-me* vibe.

"Because I enjoy it." She replied. "I enjoy dressing up in a way that gets attention and makes me feel good about myself. I have zero intent of doing anything about any of the attention from anyone besides your brother, but knowing that I can get it excites me, nonetheless."

"Even after everything?" I lowered my voice. "After how your reputation and appearance made you a target for those men to use you?" I brought up our time together in the brothel for one of the first times since my rescue.

"Is that what you're scared of?" She questioned, stepping closer. "Do you think if you embrace your body and sex appeal that it will draw the wrong attention and make you a target again?" She tilted her head. "Women survive every day without anything bad happening to them, dressed just like this and even more over the top." She tried reasoning.

"And women endure torture every day for doing far less than simply wearing clothes that draw unwanted attention." I countered. "I guess it's just too much risk for the reward."

Her shoulders dropped slightly, "I'm so sorry that you feel so threatened by everything. Believe me, Laila," she said, taking my hand and squeezing it, "If I had one wish from a genie, or one do-over for anyone or anything in this world, I would erase all the bad things that happened to you."

"I don't want to change it all." I whispered, surprising her. "In a way, I know things have to happen for a reason. I know things have to follow a certain path to come out the other side the way they have."

I squeezed her hand back, "Believe it or not, I still don't regret saving you from Titus that night. Because it brought you into my life, and it gave me back Jed." I fought to keep tears from my eyes. "So, I wouldn't change all of it. But I would change some of it."

"So maybe we can find a way to change some things, but not all of it." She smiled sadly, wiping away her own tears and blowing her bangs out of her face. "Small bits and pieces."

"Small bits and pieces." I eyed the racks near us and fought the smile that she always managed to bring out of me. "Just maybe."

I tugged the shirt down for the hundredth time and then groaned at how it just exposed my chest even more. Carly snickered from next to me on the sidewalk as we left Mav's boutique with bags upon bags of new clothes for me.

On Ryker's dime. Yet another debt to add to the growing list in my journal. Which reminded me I really needed to get another job.

Carly's car was parked in the VIP section of Lux Strip Club, conveniently located down the street from Mav's and also conveniently guarded by the jacked bouncers of Ryker's swanky club.

"I can't wait to see all these new clothes on you." Carly smiled brightly as she popped the trunk and helped me put the bags in.

A man from the front of Lux called out to Carly. "Hey Sunshine, here to bring some class back to Lux?" I looked over the car at the man in a flashy suit as he chatted with the bouncers before going into the club. "God knows we all miss you." He was middle age but surprisingly normal looking for a man walking into a strip club on a Wednesday evening. I always imagined that the only men who frequented places like this were seedy and gross.

Maybe that was just the men who went to brothels.

Carly smirked and gave a pretty pout. "Those days are long behind me now, Tom." She winked. "I'm a paying customer every time I walk in there these days."

"Too bad." The man named Tom shrugged good-heartedly. "See ya around, Sunshine." He called before walking through the front door and disappearing into the dimly lit foyer.

Carly shook her head, still smiling. "Do you miss it?" I questioned, nodding to the building.

"All the time." She answered honestly. "When the longing gets too big, I just go in as a customer and tip the girls big and enjoy myself as a spectator."

"Hmm." I hummed, staring at the elegant neon sign on the front of the building. We were in a decent part of town, and I was having trouble wrapping my head around what kind of stuff went on inside the black brick building surrounded by boutiques and bars.

"What is it?" Carly asked, watching me closely.

"Hmm?" I snapped out of it. "Nothing."

"Laila." She raised an eyebrow at me. "You can be honest with me."

I sighed and rested my hip against the trunk, staring back up at the building. "I've never been to a strip club before." Shrugging, I tried to seem indifferent. "Isn't it kind of a rite of passage to go to a strip club in your early twenties and, I don't know, let loose?"

Carly smiled and shrugged her shoulders. "It can be."

"Can girls dance without being touched in there?" I questioned, watching the blue and pink neon sign flicker as the pattern changed to a purple and teal combination.

"Why?"

"Answer me." I flicked my glance back to her, challenging her to be honest before I told her why.

"Sure." She nodded her head. "Girls can do stage dances for tips only. They would miss out on the big money that's usually found in the VIP room or in lap dances at least. But hypothetically speaking, girls can dance only on the stage. Now tell me why you're asking." Before I could reply, she pointed her finger at me. "Honestly. Because you have a look in your eye, I've never seen before and maybe it's because your tits look incredible in that shirt and your mile high legs are distracting me in those shorts, but I think you're about to say something shocking."

I smirked and rolled my eyes, turning my back on the building and the appeal. "I need a job."

Carly snorted and glared at me. "And you thought you'd jump right from part-time barista to stripper?"

I shrugged and crossed my arms over my chest. "I'm actually pretty good at it."

"Stripping?" She deadpanned, going all serious.

I shrugged again. "I danced throughout my entire childhood. It was the only normal part of my life for the longest time. And then when I was—" I cut off, leaving the word trafficked out, "I stripped a few times."

"And you would willingly want to do it again?" She questioned. "Because believe me, I'm all for supporting a woman's ability to sell her own sex in whatever fashion she wants to. From stripping to escorting, it's all fine with me if the woman does it safely and for her own benefit. But I'm surprised to hear you say it, considering you were against even wearing a revealing shirt two hours ago."

I stood up off the car with a nod of my head, "You're not wrong." I faced her, "Allowing my sexuality to be used in a controlled state doesn't scare me as much as the unpreparedness of just welcoming that attention from the public. Dancing in a place with armed guards," I looked over at the big hulking men at the door, "And I'm not just talking about their biceps, gives girls at least a little of security. Am I right?"

"Completely." She agreed and then sighed. "But even though I support whatever path you want to take, Jed, on the other hand would burn the entire building down if he knew you were inside of it working." She shuddered. "Scratch that, he'd burn the entire block down."

I tipped my head back and laughed. "Didn't you two meet inside there?"

"We did. But as soon as I started falling for him, I walked away, because there was just something that felt wrong about showing other men what belonged to him."

"Hmm." I hummed. "It doesn't matter either way."

She smirked and then shut the trunk, nodding towards the building. "I'm probably going to get in trouble for this but come with me."

"Where?" I followed her, scowling in confusion.

"To pop your strip club cherry." She winked. "Let's go get you a lap dance or two and I'll introduce you to my friends." She waved to the bouncers as we walked up. "Evening, boys."

"Sunshine." The men responded, nodding their heads respectfully as they opened the heavy doors. "Have a good night."

"Oh, we intend to." She purred back seductively, grabbing my hand and pulling me in with her. "Here's to a liberating experience tonight." She squeezed as the tempo of the music cascaded over my skin, igniting every nerve in my body. "Let's hope you're a changed woman when we leave."

CHAPTER 8 – ZEKE

"The order is short." I laid the paper down on Ryker's desk, letting him go over the numbers himself. "Think the A1's did it? Or do you think someone here did?"

Drugs were a big part of Ryker's business running Shadeport. And with the business, liars, and stealers were plentiful. Even among our own crew.

"How short?" He scanned the report, noticing the discrepancies.

"About a hundred thousand dollars short."

"Fucking hell." He groaned, tossing the paper down on his desk and leaning back in his chair. "The A1's wouldn't take that much off the top. They're young and stupid, but they're not suicidal." He spoke of the gang in Southern California that ran the drugs for him from the border to Shadeport.

"Then you think it's someone here?" I rubbed a hand over my head, trying to get the headache that crunching numbers always gave me to go away.

"I don't think so either." He rocked back and forth in his chair. "But who the fuck knows."

"I'll look into it." I took the burden off his shoulders; it was my job as right-hand man to figure this shit out for him.

"Thanks." He sighed, going back to his own spreadsheets on his computer screen that I'd interrupted. I walked away to the mirrored glass overlooking the main stage below, scanning the crowd absently as I played different scenarios out in my head of how a hundred thousand dollars of cocaine could come up missing in the four-day trip from Mexico to our warehouse.

But any logistics I'd been playing out mentally froze mid-thought as my eyes landed on the back of a head in the VIP section below.

I stepped closer, looking almost directly beneath the window to try to get a better view of the brunette in the velvet booth with her back to me. The heavy curtains were pulled shut, encasing the large U-shaped booth in privacy as two dancers gave a private show, just feet from the main stage. I couldn't see her face. But I didn't need to either.

I knew it was Laila.

But I also knew it wasn't.

The woman with her back to me had streaks of copper in her dark brown hair, and it was a couple of inches shorter than Laila's, but still, something inside of me recognized her.

"I'll be back," I mumbled to Ryker, leaving the room and his own mumbled response as he essentially ignored me for numbers.

I walked down the hallway to the staff entrance for main floor and exited, keeping tabs on the comings and goings in the room like always, while keeping the closed booth in my peripheral on my way to Theo, stationed at the bar watching the room.

He was the club host, tasked with matching clients and girls through the night. He knew the ins and outs of Lux better than even I.

"Theo." I called, walking up to him, "Who's in booth four?"

His eyes flicked to the curtained booth and then back to me, and his neck tightened as he swallowed. "Uh, I'll have to check."

"Theo." I squinted my eyes down at the man, who was as bad a liar as a nun. "Who's in booth four?"

"Um—," He hesitated again, flicking his eyes that way once again like he was looking for the right answer.

"Theo. I'm not going to ask again."

He groaned and pinched the bridge of his nose. "I can't say." He rushed on, "Customers deserve privacy."

I raised my eyebrows at him, and he shrunk into his flashy silver suit as he swallowed audibly.

"You're fired." I barked, stepping back from him as I headed toward the booth myself.

"What?" He cried dramatically. "I—" He stammered, "You can't—" I ignored his theatrics and crossed the room. "Mr. Evans!" He called after me, but I just kept on walking until I got to the curtain.

Taser, a bouncer who had been with the club for almost as long as Ryker owned it, watched me approach the booth with a questioning glance over my shoulder to Theo. "Boss." He nodded.

"Who's inside?" I questioned, ignoring formalities.

"Sunshine." He replied instantly, "She brought a friend and is getting a dance from a couple of girls." He looked back at Theo again, who was audibly throwing a fit. "Everything alright?"

"Who's the friend?"

Taser shrugged his shoulders, "Never seen her before. Pretty little thing. Scared as a kitten with a mile-long tail in a rocking chair store, though."

Something bloomed in my chest at the description, confirming my original suspicion.

It was Laila.

"Move," I ordered him, and he instantly stepped aside, pulling the curtain open for me to step through as he went.

The two dancers looked at me in surprise, but when they stepped aside, Carly just smirked and rolled her eyes. "I knew we wouldn't get away with it for long." She flicked her hair over her shoulder as she looked at Laila.

When I looked at her cohort, sitting next to her in the large plush booth, everyone else in the room ceased to exist. Laila's big brown eyes were wide and almost fearful as she gazed up at me. Her hair was different, she'd been to a salon today, and judging by the swell of her breasts peeking through the deep V of her fresh shirt, Carly had taken her to Mav's too.

Her long legs were crossed at the ankle as she sat still as stone, silently watching me take in the changes to her appearance. "Ladies, give us a minute," I said, never taking my eyes off Laila.

The two dancers left the room, wrapping their robes back around their bodies, covering their nudity as if I could care to look at them, but Carly chuckled and leaned back in her seat, "As if, Cue Ball." she challenged, crossing her arms. "We did nothing wrong."

"I didn't say you did." I turned my attention to her and glared. "But I need a word with Laila."

"No deal." Carly held my stare, raising an eyebrow at me. "Jed wouldn't approve."

"Carly." Laila glared at her.

"What?" Carly shrugged. "Laila's an adult and can come to a strip club if she wants. You don't get to yell at her for it."

"I'm not yelling!" I growled and then clenched my teeth at how she made me yell, even if it wasn't at Laila. "Carly, just fuck off."

"Carly, please. Just give us a minute." Laila sighed, rubbing her forehead until Carly finally threw her hands up in the air and stood up.

"Fine." She said, passing me with a finger raised, "But don't you dare try to control her."

I kept my teeth clenched to avoid retorting back at her, and when the heavy velvet curtain closed behind her, I took a deep breath, looking down at Laila.

"Am I in trouble?" she asked meekly.

"Why would you be in trouble?" I questioned, loosening the button at my throat, and taking my jacket off before sitting down on the other side of the rounded booth.

"Because you look like I'm in trouble." She leaned back and tucked one leg under her, facing me. "You kind of always look like I'm in trouble."

I smirked, shrugging one shoulder at her honesty. "I'm a serious man."

"I know." She looked up at me. "So, you're not here to yell at me?"

"No, Laila. I'm not here to yell at you for watching two women strip at Ryker's club." I raised my eyebrow at her, silently pointing out the absurdity of the whole thing.

"It was Carly's idea." She smiled the tiniest bit before biting her lip. "I told her I'd never been to a club before, and she dragged me inside. After she mutilated me at the salon and forced me into these clothes at the boutique down the street." She joked.

"I don't think you look mutilated at all." I nodded at her hair. "The gold suits you."

She held my stare with wide eyes for a second before dropping my gaze completely and blushing as she tucked a bit of hair behind her ear. "Why are you here?"

"I work here," I answered plainly.

She rolled her eyes and looked back up at me. "Here in this booth. After kicking Carly out."

"Because," I paused, trying to decide which route I wanted to take this conversation. "I wanted to see you."

Her chest rose, daring my eyes to fall to the perfect swell of her small breasts, and I gave in. I watched a flush of blush cover her perfect breasts before crawling up to her neck and her face, dragging my eyes with it.

"Zeke." She whispered before swallowing. "I don't know how to do this."

"I know," I replied, rubbing my hand over my face, feeling slightly ashamed of making her uncomfortable. The unspoken attraction between us was known, but she wouldn't act on it.

Which meant that I couldn't either. She wasn't ready, and I didn't know if she ever would be after everything she had survived.

"I'm sorry." I cleared my throat and stood up, "I just wanted to check in on you."

"Zeke, wait." She grabbed my hand and looked up at me before slowly standing in front of me. "Why are you interested in me?" She nearly whispered. "I don't understand what's happening between us."

My chest ached with the desire to take away her insecurities and poor self-esteem.

"Can I touch you?" I asked, hating how that simple question made fear bloom in her pretty brown eyes. "I won't hurt you, Laila." Shaking my head, "Ever."

She swallowed, taking a deep breath as her eyelids fluttered closed, she nodded her head. Her eyes being closed was a tactic to protect herself from whatever was about to happen, and I imagined years of her closing her eyes to block out what was done to her. While that enraged me, I would never show her I could help her heal from it without physically touching her.

So, if she needed to close her eyes for right now, I was going to let her. I slid my fingers through hers, anchoring her to me with just our hands as I looked her over. "You are hands down the most beautiful woman I've ever seen before," I said, and her lips quivered as she took a shaky breath, with her eyes still closed. "I know you don't feel like it, and you don't believe my words, but hopefully someday I'll change your mind." I ran my thumb over the pulse point on her wrist and felt the erratic beat under her skin. "There's a part of me that wants to protect you from every bit of darkness in this world. That part wants to wrap you up in the most comfortable blanket and keep you safe, tucked away from everything else, and worship you like a divine goddess that I don't even deserve to be in the presence of." She licked her lips and leaned into my touch but didn't press her body against mine like I wanted her to.

"I feel like there's a *but* coming." She whispered as the noise of the club picked up on the other side of the curtain.

"There is." I leaned forward so she could hear me and feel my breath on her face. "Because the other part of me wants to use my body to make yours scream in ecstasy." She gasped and fell forward, gripping the front of my shirt with her icy fingers as her chest pressed against my stomach. "That part of me wants to spread your sexy body out in my bed and feast on you, giving you nothing but pleasure for days straight until you don't remember any other man's touch before mine, ever again. That part of me wants to hear you beg me to claim you. That part of me wants to make you so addicted to me that you never want to leave." I turned my face to speak directly into her ear, making her shiver as goosebumps broke out over her arms. "That part of me needs you to want me as badly as I want you."

"Zeke." She moaned.

Moaned.

My Laila moaned my name, and I growled in response, unable to stop it before it escaped, and she shivered again.

"Do it again," I demanded, closing my own eyes to the darkness trying to overtake me. "Moan my name again, Laila."

She took a deep breath and gave me what I needed. "Zeke." She moaned, tightening her hand on my shirt. "I don't know how to do this."

"I know." Savoring her scent, I sighed deeply as I breathed in at her neck, appreciating her delightful fragrance. "I know you don't. But I didn't want you to doubt how badly I wanted you anymore. Because I'm nearly cross-eyed with need for you." I leaned back, sliding my hand over hers, gripping my shirt, relaxing her hold as I massaged her fingers. "I'm leaving the ball in your court. You're in charge here. If you want me, come to me."

"I don't know how—," She whined, opening her eyes finally and staring up at me. "I don't know."

"I know, baby." Slowly, I raised my hand to cup her cheek. "I'm not asking you to be in control if you don't want to be." She swallowed as I continued, "But I need it to be your decision to begin with. I need to know you want it." Her pupils dilated when I made it clear that I was talking about sex and pleasure. "I need to know you want me."

I backed up a foot away from her, leaving her swaying on her feet for a second before she got her bearings.

"Come to me when you're ready, Laila," I repeated, taking another step backward after picking up my suit jacket. "You know where to find me."

As I backed out of the VIP booth, hard and aching, I smiled to myself for the first time in days.

She would come to me.

I knew she would.

I just hoped she wouldn't make me wait forever, though I would.

For her, I would.

CHAPTER 9 – LAILA

I paced my apartment floor, wearing holes in the girly carpet Carly picked out for me when I first moved in. I rubbed my hands together back and forth, trying to create warmth between them as the cold of the night seeped in.

A noise down the hallway vibrated through the air, and I froze in place, cocking my head to hear what it was. When the heavy door of the exterior hallway closed, I raced to my door, silently pressing my body against it as I looked through the peephole.

It was Zeke.

He was wearing a black pair of joggers and nothing else but a layer of sweat as he pulled his earbuds from his ears. He stopped at his door, noticing the folded paper in the crack again, and then looked over at my door. A devilish smile pulled his perfect lips back as he pocketed his earbuds and pulled the paper from its spot.

I bit my lip to keep silent as he leaned back against his closed door, crossing one ankle over the other before opening the folded paper.

It was another journal entry.

Another olive branch of communicating with him, the only way I knew how.

I needed him to know me. The dark and messed up parts of me, so he knew what he was getting into before I gave in to my desire to give my body to him.

God, even the thought of sleeping with him made me dizzy.

I took a deep breath and watched his bright blue eyes flick up from the paper to my door like he could sense me on the other side of it before he started reading.

This journal entry was deeper than the other one.

It put a voice to my fear of moving on. It told the truth about my failure to thrive.

> *Dear Journal,*
>
> *I thought my life had been bad. When I was young, my inno-cence was stripped from me with the swing of a knife, and I was never the same again. I thought that had been the worst of it, but I was wrong.*
>
> *So wrong because it got so much worse after that.*
>
> *Yet now, as a grown woman with nothing but opportunity ahead of me, I'm left feeling like it's even worse now.*
>
> *Somehow, being free yet chained to my past by fear is sorrier than being back there, imprisoned and tortured every day.*
>
> *Freedom mocks me.*
>
> *Happiness eludes me.*
>
> *Nightmares haunt me.*
>
> *I don't know how much longer I can do this. Pretending. Avoid-ing. Acting like I wouldn't rather be back inside that brothel.*

> *At least back then, I could blame my captivity on something physical. Because right now, my captor is a figment of my imagination. Something that no longer exists.*
>
> *Yet I can't move forward. I'm stuck. Frozen in time, watching the rest of the world pass me by with curious glances and pitiful expressions when I fail to meet their expectations.*
>
> *I'm nothing. Not even a prisoner anymore.*
>
> *What if Carly and Jed tire of me? What if Ryker bores of funding my existence?*
>
> *Will I simply fade away for good?*
>
> *X- Laila*

He folded the paper and stared at the door between us, once again like he knew I was hiding behind it. "Open the door."

His deep voice echoed through the long hallway, and my breath froze in my chest.

I hadn't anticipated that.

I wasn't prepared to face him after cutting myself open like that. "Laila." He called dominantly. "Open the door."

My hand hovered over the unlocked handle but hesitated before I forced myself to turn it and step back, revealing myself to the harsh light of the hallway.

In my inability to plan for him wanting to speak face to face after reading the entry, I hadn't gotten dressed for the occasion, and as his bright blue eyes slid down my body, covered in the light pink baseball style shirt and matching white shorts, shivers erupted over my skin.

He swallowed and leaned off his door, holding the paper between his fingers. "Do you think this is going to deter me?"

I bit my bottom lip to keep the quick remark I wanted to make from flying out of my mouth. "I just want you to know."

"I know." His deep voice vibrated through his bare chest and across the hallway to me. He slid the paper into his pocket and moved closer to me. "I know, Laila. I still want you."

Swallowing, I took a deep breath. "I have nothing to offer you." I shrugged, facing the bravery I felt earlier today head-on and embracing it. "I live on Ryker's dime, I have no job, I have no future. I don't even know how to be a willing sexual partner to you, for fuck's sake, Zeke."

"Enough." He growled with that dominating tone that always made my toes curl, and my insides melt. "I don't need you to have a 401K to desire you. You're doing everything you're supposed to be doing right now, Laila. You're healing." His throat tightened as he swallowed, looking down at me. "You're finally getting to decide how you want to live your life and what makes you happy."

"Don't you want someone—" I paused, "Normal?"

He scoffed and slowly lifted his hand to the side of my face again, like he had that night in the club. He did it so cautiously; I knew he was giving me time to tell him to stop. But I didn't. Because I craved his touch. Even if it hurt and burned at the same time. "Do I strike you as a normal man?"

I sighed and rolled my eyes at him, and his body tightened in front of mine in a way that I felt to my bones.

"I kill people for a living." He warned in that deep, dominant voice. "I make people beg for death as I torture them. I steal from them. I take everything they have to give in this world and then I take more." My body shivered from the intensity of his stare as he spoke. "I'm not a normal man, and I'm not looking for normal."

I opened my mouth to retort his claim, fighting for control of the situation when everything else inside of me wanted to just roll over and give in to what he was offering. It was all too good to be true.

Before I could reply, though, he covered my lips with the tip of his thumb. "No." He stated, "No more excuses. No more trying to convince me to change my mind. I want you." He stepped forward until our bodies were flushed together, and the panic and anxiety that normally came with physical touch didn't surface. My skin flared to life against his with something else. "Decide right now if this is something you want. If it's not, I'll leave you alone. I need to know if I'm pressuring you into something you don't even want."

"I want it." The words rushed out as I licked my lips, softly brushing the tip of my tongue against his thumb still pressed against my bottom lip. "I want you, Zeke," I admitted, feeling braver than I ever had before. "I've never physically wanted another man in my life."

He growled, cracking his neck as if he were fighting for restraint. But I had none. He'd undone me, leaving me raw and exposed for this.

"Kiss me," I whispered, feeling like my heart was going to explode out of my chest at any moment, and not wanting to die before I knew what it felt like to be kissed by Zeke Evans.

"Gladly." He rasped as he lowered his face to mine. "Fucking gladly."

The second his warm lips pressed against mine, I melted and exploded into thin air, all at the same time. He was dominant and assertive with his kiss, just like I knew he would be. But he did it without making me feel like he was the one in control. He did it in a way that made me feel like he was leading me.

Guiding me.

Towards bliss.

Because, God, I saw stars with every brush of his skin against mine. I cried against him, whimpering a pathetic and needy sound of pure longing I would have been embarrassed by if not for the responding vibration through his chest. He licked my lips and tilted my head to the side, deepening the contact until I clung to his shoulders for support in fear of falling on my ass completely.

"You are perfection." He whispered, nibbling on my bottom lip as he slid his free hand around my waist and anchored me to him further. "Do you understand how fucking perfect you are?"

"It's you," I whispered, tentatively biting his lip in response, and drawing another animalistic growl from his chest. "It's this."

"You're right." He responded. "This. Us. That's perfection."

"Zeke." I moaned, sliding my hands over his shoulders to the back of his neck, desperate to be even closer to him, even though I had no idea what I was doing. I was acting on instinct and longing, trusting him to lead me.

A loud chirping noise cut off anything he was going to say as he pulled his ringing cell phone from his pocket, glancing briefly at the screen before placing it against his ear. "Yeah." He barked.

I slid my hands from the back of his neck and tried to step back to put space between us, but his grip on my waist tightened and he glared down at me with a serious look. I watched his face as he stared at me, listening to someone on the other end of the line before he replied, "Make Jed do it." He stated and then clenched his teeth as a reply barked back. "Fine." He sighed. "Give me ten minutes."

He didn't wait for a reply but ended the call and slid it into his pocket, keeping those deep blue eyes locked on me the entire time. "You have to go," I stated, trying to make the rejection in my heart disappear. It wasn't like he wanted to go; I knew that. I'd heard him.

"Yeah." He replied, "Ryker needs me." I sank to my heels, nodding my head, but he once again didn't allow me to back up. "This conversation isn't over, Laila."

A snort slipped through my lips, and I covered my mouth in embarrassment as he smirked down at me. "I didn't think this was a conversation anymore."

"I disagree." He swallowed, flicking his eyes down to my lips before bringing them back to my stare. "You communicate with me in ways that you don't even realize." He lowered his face to mine, hovering against my mouth. "Your lips speak volumes, even when words don't pass them." He kissed me, and I melted into his touch again, feeling no anxiety or fear rising inside of me like usual. "Your body begs for things you're too afraid to ask for vocally." He kissed my cheek and then down to my ear, where he whispered. "We don't need words to communicate, do we?"

"No," I whispered, biting my bottom lip as the tip of his tongue traced the shell of my ear. "We don't."

"Then, like I said," He pulled back and looked down at me again, "We'll continue this conversation at a later time." He kissed me chastely once more before sliding his hands off my body and backing up towards his door.

"Okay," I said breathlessly, sagging against my doorframe.

"Go inside, Laila." He commanded, "Or I'll be too tempted to disobey Ryker for the first time in my life."

I smirked and stepped backward into my apartment. "Go be a good boy, Zeke," I said bravely before quickly shutting my door and locking it with a giggle as a predatory growl escaped his mouth.

I ran to my bed and threw myself down in the center of it, using my pillow to muffle my gleeful giggle as excitement coursed through my body.

When was the last time I was excited about something?

When was the last time I giggled?

The brisk morning air cooled my overheated skin as I pushed through the door from the barracks to the lush yard behind it. I took a deep breath and forced my body to be still for the first time since I tore out that journal entry for Zeke at three am this morning.

He left a while ago to take care of whatever task Ryker had for him, but I was so unsettled I couldn't sit still.

"Uh oh." A voice called from across the yard, startling me as my eyes popped open in surprise. "You look—" Elora tilted her head to the side as she shifted Gavin to her other hip, "Buzzed?"

"I don't drink," I replied, swallowing down the guilt I felt at being caught being happy. Was that even a thing to feel guilty about?

"High?" She raised her brows as she watched me skeptically. "Don't think I'm judging; it's been forever since I had a good high." She sighed.

"I don't do drugs," I replied, glossing over the rest of it.

"Then why do you look so—" She paused again and then scrunched up her nose, "Euphoric?"

"Euphoric?" I rolled my eyes, playing for nonchalance. "That's too big a word for this time of day."

She smirked and pursed her lips. "I agree. So, spill."

"I'm fine." I shook my head. "No drugs, alcohol, or spiritual bliss on board here." I turned and walked toward the driveway, adjusting my purse on my shoulder. "I just slept well."

"Then it has nothing to do with the tall, strapping, tattooed man that left a while ago whistling a tune on his way to work?" She called after me, stopping me in my tracks. "Sure thing."

I looked over my shoulder at her, swallowing guiltily as she watched me, trying to come up with some cover story for my and Zeke's good moods this morning.

She held her hand up, cutting me off before I could lie or refute her claim, though. "You owe me no explanation, Laila." She smiled as Gavin babbled on in her arms. "Just thought it was worth mentioning the change was obvious in a good way." She winked. "Get it, girl."

"I didn't—" I started and then bit my lip, fighting the urge to lie about it. "We didn't—" I shook my head and sighed.

"It doesn't matter." She walked toward me, so she didn't have to yell across the grass. "You deserve to be happy, whatever the cause."

I sighed and kicked a loose pebble with the toe of my boot in uncertainty. "Jed doesn't approve," I admitted, feeling comfortable admitting that there was something between Zeke and me to anyone other than Carly, given her obligation to tell Jed.

"You're a grown-up." She stated plainly, "You don't need your brother's permission to date or be happy."

"Don't I though?" I tilted my head to the side, "I feel like I live under constant supervision." I lifted my hands, showcasing the surrounding estate. "Every time I try to go somewhere or do anything, someone always pops up."

"Yeah," She nodded her head, adjusting Gavin once again, "The men here—" She shrugged her shoulders, "Tend to be a little overbearing." She snickered, "But that doesn't mean they're right. Or in charge. Even if they don't agree."

"It's complicated." I deflected, "I don't want to do anything to upset Jed or their friendship."

"It's not, actually." She replied, "They're adults too, Laila, and only they are responsible for their feelings, not anyone else." She put her hand on my arm, and I didn't flinch for the first time in months, "Don't let anyone tell you what you can and cannot do anymore. And don't you dare worry about a grown man's feelings just because none of the men here can admit that all they want is what's best for us girls without their macho toxic masculinity getting in the way." She rolled her eyes. "Ask me how I know."

I chuckled and relaxed a bit. "Yeah, I guess you do know. Better than most, I'm sure." I hinted at her overprotective husband, who was probably the worst of all three men in charge here.

"I do." She nodded, rocking a sleepy Gavin as he rested his head on her shoulder. "So, believe me when I say, Jed will get over whatever hang-ups he has about you being romantically involved with anyone." She raised her eyebrows. "Even Zeke. Because at the end of the day girl, no one will treat you better than Mr. Serious himself." She winked again. "He was one of my dad's best friends and has been Ryker's right-hand man since he took over Shadeport, but in all the years I've known him, I've never seen him treat a woman poorly. Not once."

I cringed and backed up, "I don't think I want to imagine him treating any woman in any way. At all."

She smirked brightly and looked at me up and down as I took another step away, already knowing what was coming. "Does Laila Manning have a jealous streak?" She chuckled.

"It's anyone's guess." I shrugged, tilted my head back, laughed, and then she called out one last thing.

"I guess we'll find out." As I walked down the driveway toward my waiting ride, I waved over my shoulder.

On autopilot, I rode through the East Valley and into town, replaying my early morning kiss with Zeke in my mind.

His taste and smell wrapped around me like a blanket when he touched me, filling my thoughts. The way his hands felt on my waist and my cheek, dominant and possessive but kind and reassuring at the same time.

I didn't know if he pitied me, or if he was repulsed by the idea of what was done to me by those men, but he didn't show it. He didn't treat me like he was, but how could he not be?

I would be, wouldn't I?

The idea alone of him with women in the past was enough to raise my blood pressure in a most unflattering way.

The car I booked pulled over to the curb outside of the restaurant where I had an interview, and I waved goodbye to the woman driving as I stepped out onto the sidewalk.

Ignoring the feeling of dread and uncertainty as I walked across the cracked concrete to the front door, I kept my head held high as I walked inside.

I could do this.

I could pretend for just half an hour that I was normal.

I could be normal if I just tried hard enough.

CHAPTER 10 – ZEKE

For the first time in my entire life, I really fucking hated my job. Ryker's drug smuggling problem came to a head the other morning when our ears on the ground tipped us off that the A1s knew who shorted the last order.

Ryker called me, interrupting my first moment of true fucking bliss in decades when I had Laila in my arms for the first time, and ordered me to report for duty. I tried getting out of it, which was not in my nature. But there was no way. It was all hands on deck.

And it had been three days since that phone call dragged me away from Laila and I hadn't seen her since. I came home after long nights, and she was gone, and when she came home, I was off dealing with the fallout.

I wasn't sure where she was going every day exactly, which annoyed me. Since she quit her job at the coffee shop, she'd been looking for another one, but I didn't know if she'd gotten one.

I didn't know anything.

And that fucking bothered me.

I thrived on knowing everything. All the time.

Yet Laila was a mystery to me.

Though that was changing slowly.

Each time I came back to my apartment to shower and catch an hour or two of sleep, there would be another journal entry wedged in my door.

Her attempt to communicate with me about her past, the only way that she was comfortable. And I ate it up like catnip, consuming every single word written in her elegant, flowy script like they were a window into her soul.

Into her very being.

I wanted it all. Every morsel she gave me and everything she hid from me. I needed it.

I took the paper, opened my door, and walked into my dark and empty apartment as I unfolded her secrets.

Dear Journal,

I dreamed about that night again. It's been so long since the last time I was forced to relive that horrid evening in vivid detail, I thought perhaps I was finally past it. But apparently not.

It started just like it always does.

First, I hear the music and feel the bass thumping over my skin as I dance around the cheesy gymnasium with its paper streamers and sparkling confetti. I remember the euphoria in my heart as my friends and I sang to the stupid boy band songs blaring and laughed our way through another tacky award given to someone for best dressed, or most transformed.

Puke.

My friends and I were the farthest things from popular, so we would never be on that stage, but we didn't care. We weren't there for that.

Prom.

The night of joy and a rite of passage every high schooler should take before they're thrust out of the illusion of comfort and into the real world full of bills, responsibilities, and deadlines that were never reachable.

But that's when the dream changes, every time. Gone is the music, and the flashing lights and laughter.

Gone is the high I was riding from joy and happiness, and in its place falls something heavy. Something dark.

I didn't know when it was happening in real time, but that heaviness was a drug I'd never even heard of, let alone willingly allowed to fall into my cup of bland punch from the table by the wall. I realized too late what had happened. I realized it only when I woke up the next morning.

Broken.

Taken.

No longer Laila.

Just another girl in the room.

A boy who was three years too old even to be at a high school prom drugged me. Apparently, he did it at every dance. To some lucky girl who was so unsuspecting, she didn't even think she was in danger until it was too late.

The dream always picks up as I stumble out of the side door of the gymnasium, seeking cool air to clear my jumbled head.

Stupid.

So, so, so stupid.

That was when he swooped in. I vaguely remember him helping me, offering to get me to a bench to sit down so the world would stop spinning.

But he didn't do that.

He didn't help me.

He hurt me.

First, when he shoved me into the trunk of his car, shutting off any of the cool air I was seeking and any prying eyes or ears that may have heard me cry for help. And then again, when he dragged me into his disgusting camper by my hair because I was so far gone, I couldn't even walk. But the pain didn't stop there.

That was the night I lost my virginity.

Held down by the invisible bindings of the drug as he did horrific things to my innocent body. As if drugging and raping someone weren't bad enough, he wasn't done there. And that's the worst part of the dream, because it ends there. But when I wake up from that nightmare, I remember how he sold me to another guy like some unwanted object, ready for the taking.

And then another.

And then another until the men had no faces, and the days had no ticks of time.

And then I was sold to a new owner, and the process started all over again.

I wake up from the dream, every single time, shaking with anger and pain like I'm back in that dark and musty camper all over again. People came and went, for sex or drugs or his disgusting style of company, and no one saved me.

No one cared.

I was seventeen years old.

A child.

> *How could the world be so cruel so many times to the same person?*
>
> *xo- L*

My mind spins with the words from her latest entry.

Anger burns in my gut as I hear her voice reading the words like she spoke them to me firsthand.

"Zeke. Are you even listening?" Ryker asked, pausing the obsessive pacing that he'd been doing around his office for the last four days.

"Yes." I kept staring out the window, fighting the urge to tell him to fuck off.

"He's daydreaming like he has been for weeks now," Jed added with that pissy tone he'd been addressing me with since Laila came to live in the barracks. It grated on the very last nerve I had left in my body, and I felt myself begin to unravel.

"One warning, Jed," I growled, with my back still turned to him . "That's all you fucking get, and it's more than you deserve."

"What the fuck is that supposed to mean?" He snapped back, and I sensed him standing up from the couch.

"Enough." Ryker barked in frustration.

But there was no stopping the freight train collision that had been impending for weeks now.

It had to happen.

There was no way around it anymore.

"It means you've stepped out of line for way too long, and I'm done giving forgiveness for it."

"Forgiveness!" He roared, "You fucking prick!"

I turned as his fist swung, ducking to the side just in time to avoid it.

"Jed!" Ryker bellowed, but we ignored him.

"Learn your fucking place, kid!" I snapped, shoving him backward before delivering an undercut to his jaw. "You don't run this shit!"

"My place is putting you in the ground for being an old pervert!" He recoiled and lunged at me. His giant fist slammed into my ribs, knocking the wind from my lungs, but I didn't hesitate. Jed was mammoth, even against me, but my speed was unmatched in this fight against the giant.

"Get it off your chest now, because only one of us will have any teeth left when this is done with, and it won't be you." I swung wide, boxing his ear, and as he recoiled off of me, I hit him on the cheek.

"Stay away from Laila!" He yelled in my face, shoving me against the glass, and grabbing for my throat. "Stop thinking about her. Stop talking to her. Stop mind-fucking her every time she comes near your creepy old ass. She's got enough problems without you hovering over her with your bullshit."

"Jed!" Ryker yelled, pulling him off me as his hand squeezed my throat. But I didn't need Ryker to interfere, because I had it. I jammed my knee up into his inner thigh and dislodged him, connecting again with the side of his face as anger like no other filled my body.

"You don't know a fucking thing about her or me!" I screamed in his face, letting it out. "Don't talk about her like you know what's best for her."

"I do know what's best for her! She's my sister!" He yelled back as Ryker pushed him backward, stepping between us.

"You don't even fucking know her! Or what she's been through!" I accused, even though I didn't know that for a fact. I didn't know if she told Carly the things she told me with her journal entries, but a part of me was sure she didn't.

She kept it all bottled inside, except for me.

"Fuck you!" He screamed, lunging again, and I stood there, waiting for his body to crash into mine, willing to feel the pain for the truth.

For the claim over her.

"Enough!" Ryker yelled again, getting a hold of him at the last second and throwing him across the room with strength I hadn't seen out of him in years. Not since he took the throne. "That's enough!" He sneered at Jed before turning and pointing at me. "From both of you." He huffed. "Dammit, Zeke, I expect more from you!"

"That's your problem, Ryker. Not mine." With a shrug, I adjusted my jacket on my shoulders. "I won't have this punk stomping around and throwing his weight around like he has a fucking ounce of power over me. I've earned my place!" Scoffing, I looked at my best friend. "It's time he learned where his is! And it's not standing over his grown sister like he's her boss."

"I'm just trying to protect her!" Jed challenged, "From men like you and Diesel who can't seem to take the hint that she doesn't want you!"

"That's not true." I shook my head. "Admit it, Jed, you don't know the first thing about her."

"She's my sister! Of course I know her!" He sneered.

"You haven't seen her in decades! And your relationship with her now is superficial at best!" I took a deep breath and stared him down. "I know her." His face reddened as Ryker threw his finger at him to keep him quiet. "I know her. You don't."

"You touched her, didn't you?" He alleged it angrily. "You son of a bitch! I'll fucking rip your head off your shoulders and lay it at her feet!" He blasted through Ryker and ran for me. I braced, taking the weight of his body as he slammed into me, and we both flew through the window out onto the catwalk above the nightclub in a flurry of glass shards and fists.

We both swung at each other, over and over, rolling across the glass, beating the shit out of each other until bouncers from below finally got to us and pulled us apart.

It took six men to separate us, and when we stood a few feet apart, bleeding, chests heaving and glaring at each other, nothing else needed to be said.

Our fists said it all.

Our friendship was over.

Because neither of us would concede our claim for Laila, even if we weren't in competition with each other in the least.

But it didn't matter.

Minds didn't change after fists were thrown between men like us.

I shoved the guards off and stared him down as I walked past him toward the exit. "No one will ever take care of her like I can."

"I killed for her!" He roared. "I lost everything for her!" He thundered behind me, but I kept walking.

I scrubbed the day off in the shower, angrily washing the glass out of my wounds and letting it go down the drain. Most of them were on my back from the ride through the window, with Jed on top of me.

Cheap shot, asshole.

My fists ached and my jaw burned every time I opened it, but I didn't regret a single hit I took. Or any I threw.

They had been necessary.

But that didn't mean I didn't mourn the end of a friendship all the same.

I laid my fist against the tile wall and leaned into it, letting the weight of the day wash away with the blood.

Bang, bang, bang!

I groaned as someone tried knocking down my front door with their fists when all I wanted to do was ignore the world for a few more minutes. I contemplated ignoring it, but even as I tried, the banging continued.

"Zeke!" A feminine voice echoed over the sound of the water, and I cut the shower off instantly as both excitement and trepidation coursed through my veins.

I wrapped a towel around my waist and walked to my front door, dripping water on the floor as I went.

Before I could reach the handle, another cry sounded from the other side. "Please open the door, Zeke!"

"Laila." I sighed, ripping it open as I got the confirmation I sought after the first time the soft voice called out.

She stood in the hallway, wringing her hands together in front of her as she paced back and forth. She froze when I opened the door all the way, and her brown eyes traveled over my wet body, to the towel hanging around my hips, and then back to my face.

I expected arousal or excitement to fill the bottomless depths of her perfectly warm eyes, but ice water slid down my spine as tears filled them instead.

"What's wrong?" I cleared the doorway, alert and anxious as her shoulders fell in defeat. "What happened?"

"He did this to you?" She whispered, ignoring my panic as she stared at the wounds on my arms and face.

"What?" I felt like we were both moving at two different speeds as I tried to wrap my head around what was happening.

She shook her head, and the tears that had been building fell, cascading down her cheeks. "Oh my God, Zeke." She backed up as I took another step out into the hallway. "I'm so sorry." She rambled. "I just got home, and Jed was waiting for me in the driveway! He said you guys fought, and then he forbade me from coming to you—" She gasped and shuddered.

"Shh," I commanded, closing the space and taking control as she slid down the slippery slope of panic. I rubbed my hand across her cheek and around the back of her head, pulling her to my chest as she gripped my wrist, anchoring herself to me like a life raft in a hurricane. "Stop. Slow your breathing down before you pass out."

She shook her head against my hold and covered her shaking lips with her fingers. "I'm so sorry."

"Don't," I ordered her, pressing my lips against her hairline as she sank into my hold. "Don't you dare, Laila."

"He hit you." She cried against my chest, and I wrapped my free arm around her waist, holding her closer.

"I hit him back." I tried for levity, rubbing my hand up and down the length of her spine as she trembled. "It was a long time coming."

"Because of me." She pulled back and looked up at me with her wide, teary eyes. "He hit you because of me."

"So what?"

"He hurt you!" She cried, scanning my split lip and swollen cheek.

"I'm not the victim here, Laila. Stop treating me like one." I demanded, and she hesitated, fighting her urge to listen to me. "It had to happen."

"That doesn't make any sense!" She shuddered again and tried to pull away, but I wouldn't let her. "We're in the hallway." She argued. "And you're almost naked."

"We're the only two who live here." I countered, and she rolled her eyes, finally focusing on something other than her guilt. "Would you prefer to go inside?"

She went still as her fears and wants battled inside of her brain; her eyes flicked to the open door into my apartment behind us. "I can't."

"Your place then." I offered, "Though I have no problem standing right here, just like this." I raised an eyebrow at her, tightening my hold on her waist.

She sighed, relaxing once again in my hold before pulling back out of my grip. "My place." She twisted the doorknob and opened the door, walking into the dim space as I stood in the hallway, suddenly unsure.

"I'll go get dressed." I nodded back into my place.

"I can't tend to your wounds if you cover them up." She said, and held her hand out, inviting me in for the first time.

And she didn't have to ask more than once.

I closed my door and followed her into her apartment, locking the door behind me.

With her standing a few feet away from me, and off the edge of a panic attack, I finally took the time to look at what she was wearing. "Hang on a second." I closed the distance between us and tapped my finger against the logo above her right breast on her black V-neck t-shirt. "Explain this."

She swallowed and dropped her eyes from mine to somewhere below my chin, as she usually did when uncomfortable. "I got a job."

"At *Neat*?" I questioned naming the trendy new bar and restaurant in the city. It was a decent place, with good owners, but at the end of the day, it was still a bar.

And bars attracted seedy people, no matter how expensive the drinks on the menu were.

"Yeah, I'm in training."

"When did that happen?"

"I had an interview the other day." She licked her lips and sucked the bottom one in between her teeth. "I started that night."

"Doing what, exactly?"

"Hosting right now." She nibbled that lip distractedly. "And training to serve."

I took a deep breath and fought everything inside of me that wanted to tell her to quit. A bar was not the kind of atmosphere she needed to be in to heal the trauma of her past.

But I wasn't going to tell her to quit because, at the end of the day, she needed support more than anything.

Not another dominating asshole standing over her and dictating what she did. Jed did that often enough.

"Do you like it?" I asked.

She raised her eyebrows as her lip fell free of her teeth in surprise. "Do I like it?"

"The job. The bar. Your bosses?" I reiterated. "Do you like it?"

"Yes." She whispered, nodding her head slowly. "A lot actually."

I smiled down at her, surprising her. "Good."

"Good?" she questioned, frowning a bit.

"Is that not a good thing?"

"It is." She stammered, rubbing her fingers over her forehead in confusion. "I'm just—," She paused and tilted her head to the side as she watched me. "That's not the reaction I expected from you."

I smiled again, though I felt the darkness in it as I ran my fingers down her arm, desperate to touch her again.

"If you're happy there, then I'm happy for you," I replied, feeling the pulse in her wrist skyrocket now that I was touching her again. "Is that okay?"

"Yes." She whispered as her eyelids fluttered closed distractedly.

"Good," I whispered, lowering my lips to the side of her face above her ear. "Then nothing else matters."

She groaned and put her hand flat on my bare stomach, leaning her weight against it. "You're trying to distract me."

"How?"

"By shocking me into forgetting the whole reason you're standing here in my apartment, wearing a towel and nothing else, covered in cuts and bruises." She sighed. "Will you let me help you?"

"I don't need your help, Laila," I responded, standing up to my full height so I could see her. "I'm not that hurt."

"Will you let me do it anyway?" She whispered, and I swore I saw a bit of seduction behind the quick flutter of her eyelashes and the way she nibbled her bottom lip. Whether she knew what her body was doing or not, she was trying to use seduction to persuade me.

And the responsible man inside of me knew better than to let her do that because she deserved better from me than to let her use such tactics to get her way.

But the monster in me wanted all of her.

The shy, seductive woman, testing boundaries and comfort levels included.

"You can do whatever you want to me." I held my arms out at my sides. "You're in charge here."

She swallowed and then smirked slightly before nodding her head like she was the boss. "Then turn around so I can see all of it."

I raised my eyebrow at her seductively, "All of it?"

"Your wounds!" She gasped, widening her eyes as she realized her blunder. "On your back!"

I chuckled, letting her off the hook as I turned so she could see the cuts on my back, though I would have given anything to distract her into forgetting about the fight altogether. Because the second she saw the deep wounds along my spine, the flirty seductress that had been in the room with me a moment ago was gone and in her place was the anxious, worrisome woman who blamed herself for my wounds.

"Zeke." She sighed, gently pressing her fingers to a particularly tender spot on my lower back. "This is all my fault."

I walked away silently, creating space between us as frustration bloomed anew.

"Where are you going?" She gasped as I reached her door.

"Back to my place." I looked at her. "I won't stay here if you're going to blame yourself. Because we're both big boys." I reminded her when she opened her mouth to argue, but I cut her off. "We're responsible for ourselves. You aren't, and I'm not going to allow you to put that burden on your shoulders. So, you can either knock it off and play doctor, or you can stew in here alone while I patch up myself."

"Okay!" She rolled her eyes and then sighed. "Sit." She pointed at the couch and raised her brows at me in challenge when I didn't move right away. "I want to play doctor, Zeke." She baited me with that innocent seduction again. "But I'm the boss in my apartment, just like you said. So, sit."

"Yes, ma'am," I smirked, sauntering back to her and sitting down on the couch like she had ordered me to do. She shook her head, still smirking to herself as she grabbed supplies from her bathroom and then came back to me. "I kind of like bossy Laila." I joked as she pushed my shoulder, so I'd turn around and show her my back again as she got settled on the couch next to me.

"Be careful." She quipped, "Or I'll pour peroxide directly into this deep one."

I laughed and leaned forward with my elbows on my knees as she went to work. She worked on a few cuts, cleaning them and applying ointment before speaking again. "Why did you say this fight had to happen?" She asked quietly, continuing to work as she talked.

I mulled my answer over before giving it but was honest with her. "Because I refused to stop pursuing you," I replied as her hand stilled on my back, so I looked over my shoulder at her. Her lips were parted, and her eyes were wide as she stared back. "I want you, you know that." I reminded her. "And Jed doesn't approve."

"So now what happens?" She whispered, going back to patch me up. "Now that you've fought."

"Nothing." I shrugged my shoulder, winning a playful slap when I disturbed her work. "I won't stop unless you tell me you don't want me."

Her eyes flicked back to mine, and she blinked rapidly before looking back at my wounds as if we didn't make eye contact, she was somehow braver for it. "I want you." She whispered after a while. "You know that." She repeated my words as she worked, and my body responded to her, even as I tried to control it. "But he's my brother." She sighed, pouring ice water on my cock that was hardening under the towel I still wore. "I can't just cut him off."

"I'd never ask you to." I immediately countered because I wouldn't. Asking her to cut ties with someone so significant to her was something I'd never do. "We're men." I tried to downplay it, "We'll get over it."

"Do you really believe that?" she asked, dropping her hands from my back as she finished up and I turned to face her. "Do you think you two could be friends after this?"

"I have no ill will towards Jed, Laila." I admitted, with a hand on her knee: "But I'm not a pushover either. I'll always stand up for myself and the respect I deserve from the men inside the crew. Your bother included."

"You've earned your spot at Ryker's side." She looked at me head-on. "Everything I've heard about you since I got here has spoken of your honor and loyalty to the crew. To Ryker."

"Does that bother you?"

"Not in the least." She replied instantly. "If a man is honorable and loyal to something important in his life," she shrugged and swallowed uncertainly, "Maybe he can be honorable and loyal in other aspects of life too."

"To you, you mean." I cut to the point. "You're talking about yourself."

"Yes." She shrugged. "I've never been honored before, Zeke."

I growled, cocking my head to the side as the protective side of me fought for control. "You have no idea how good I can treat you, Laila."

"I want that." She whispered, closing her eyes as she leaned closer to me. "I want this." She put her hand on mine atop her knee. "I want you. But I don't know what to do."

"Trust me," I growled, sliding my hand up her thigh as her nails dug into the top of my hand, pulling it higher. She had jeans on, so my ascent was safe, but knowing she wanted it was what was important. "Trust me to take care of you." She nodded, clawing at my hand as she panted. "Open your eyes, Laila," I commanded, and her golden-brown eyes flicked open, hazed with arousal as she fought for focus. "I need you to see that it's me touching you." I slid my hand further up her thigh until my thumb rested near the apex of her legs, and she trembled. "No one else exists anymore. Once I have you, no one else will."

"Yes." She moaned, arching her hips until my thumb brushed over the seam in her jeans, right against her pussy. "God, yes."

CHAPTER 11 – Laila

Every inch of my body hummed in a way that only happened when Zeke was nearby. He was electric. Hot. Powerful. And my body responded to him in ways that words couldn't portray.

They didn't need to, it was natural.

Instinctive.

Right.

Everything about Zeke felt right, and I ached to just fall headfirst into what he promised me, without a second of hesitation. I was on the edge, ready to jump.

To trust.

To give in and lose myself in him.

"Open your eyes, Dove." He whispered and my eyes snapped open. I didn't even realize I'd closed them again; lost to the sensations he was giving me. "There's my good girl."

I moaned, leaning into him, desperate for his praise as much as I was for his touch. Did he know how badly I wanted to be his good girl? To be good for him?

"Please," I whispered, tilting my head back as I fell into the need he was creating inside of me.

"Please what, Dove?" He asked against my ear. "Tell me." His breath was warm, and I shivered. "Beg me."

"Please," I repeated, fighting embarrassment and hang-ups as he patiently waited for me to give him what he wanted. What I wanted.

Because the truth was, I wanted to beg. I wanted to plead with him to touch me. To kiss me. To make me feel good. To fuck me. God, I wanted to fall to my knees at his feet and show him just how much I desired this. Him.

But I didn't know how.

I had never desired a man before. Never wanted to be touched. Yet with Zeke, I couldn't think of anything else.

"I need you," I whispered. "You make me feral for it."

He smiled against my cheek and kissed a trail of erotic kisses down my neck and back to my chin. "You don't even know what that word means." He paused with his lips hovering over mine, "Yet."

The second his lips touched mine, I mewled, digging my nails into his hand again and arching into his touch, opening to his coaxing until his tongue brushed mine. His thumb brushed over my sensitive core again, matching the seductive motion of his tongue, gently flicking and rubbing me.

Cautious.

Hesitant.

Thoughtful.

But that wasn't what I wanted right now.

It wasn't what I needed.

I slid both hands over his massive shoulders and to the back of his neck, pulling him closer to deepen the kiss. I felt the power rippling underneath his skin as he responded to my need, on the edge of losing control, and for some reason, the thought of him letting go didn't scare me.

It excited me.

Elora had been right the other day when she referred to him as Mr. Serious because Zeke was always in control of himself. But right now, I needed to feel the edge of that control slip to match my own craziness.

He growled into my mouth, biting my lip as he put more pressure between my legs, and I brazenly spread my thighs wider to make more room for his hand. "I can feel how hot you are through your jeans, Dove." He growled. "Tell me that's for me."

"It's for you." I panted. "I'm so turned on."

"I'm going to make you come." He promised as he moved his fingers against my clit until I whimpered and cried out in desperation. "I want to hear every sound you make when you come. I want to watch you come apart."

"Zeke." I groaned, laying my forehead against his chin as I clung to the back of his neck. "You have no idea how close I am."

"Then be my good girl and come. Give it to me." He demanded, and my body caved, chasing euphoria like it was my last breath.

"Yes!" I hissed out between clenched teeth as I rocked my hips back and forth, coming against his hand through my jeans like a teenager.

"Fuck yes." He growled against my lips, "That's it, Dove. Come for me."

"Oh, my God." I gasped, sinking back into the couch as my chest heaved from exertion. I caught my breath and slowly opened my once again closed eyes and found Zeke smirking down at me with that predatory gaze. He looked smug and excited all at once, and I smirked back. "What?"

"I don't think I've ever seen anything so beautiful before." He winked and leaned down to kiss me, and I eagerly returned his affection, like it was natural and normal between us. I looked down between us and noticed the large bulge tenting the front of his towel, and I was secretly glad I hadn't let him go get dressed before I invited him inside.

He watched me, noting where my gaze was pinpointed. "I'm sorry." He reached down quickly and adjusted himself, not that it did any good because he was obviously large, and the towel offered no concealment. "Hey." he said, lifting my chin to look away from his lap and into his eyes. "Ignore it."

"What?" I shook my head slowly, confused.

"This isn't about me. This was about you."

"But—," I stammered, still not grasping what he meant.

"Shh." He pressed his thumb to my lips, silencing me. "Thank you. For giving me this gift. For allowing me to touch you. It was incredible to watch."

"That makes me feel like a science experiment," I stated plainly as he leaned back to get a better look at me. The hostility in my voice was palpable, but I couldn't stop it. "Are you saying that's it? We're not doing anything else?"

"Yes, that's all we're doing." He responded firmly, and I sputtered in shock. "Stop." He commanded as I unraveled, "Take a deep breath and talk to me. Why are you upset?"

"I—," I stood up, detangling myself from his hold to pace the small space. "Don't you want—?" I started, but shame burned so brightly in my stomach that I stopped before I could finish.

"Laila." He warned, catching my drift anyway.

"Never mind. Just go." I turned my back on him and busied myself with the supplies discarded on the coffee table.

"No." He argued. "Stop."

"Please just go. This is all embarrassing enough without the awkward ending." I was such an idiot to think he was actually interested in me.

He was repulsed by my body.

Just like I knew he would be.

Exactly how he should be.

"Laila." He barked as I left the living room and took the supplies to the bathroom. "Just talk to me. Don't shut down."

"I can't." I felt my walls crumbling and panic building and knew I needed to end this conversation before it got any worse. "Please just go."

"Do you think I don't want you?" He followed me and stood in the doorway, blocking my path out. "Laila, talk to me."

"I can't." I cried, closing my eyes, and hanging my head in defeat at the sink. "Please, Zeke. Just go."

"No." He stepped behind me and pressed his body against mine, pinning me to the sink with his hips. "Does this feel like I don't fucking want you, Dove?" He ground his hips again, rubbing his erection against my ass, and I groaned, hating how the night turned. "Feel how hard you made me and then look me in the eye and tell me you still think that."

"Zeke." I shook my head.

"What are you feeling right now? Tell me."

"I don't know how." I stared at him in the mirror and hated the tears that sparkled in my eyes.

"Try." He wrapped his hands around my waist and stood patiently behind me. "For me."

My desire to please him, to give him this, caused a sigh of frustration to slip from my lips. "I feel—" I closed my eyes, "Dirty."

Zeke tensed behind me, and the tears slid over my cheeks again for the second time tonight. "Because of what I did?"

"No!" I cried, opening my eyes and staring at him in the mirror. "Because you didn't want me to do it back."

"Laila." He deflated behind me and closed his eyes like the information pained him. "You're not dirty. I didn't stop this because I don't want you." He forced me to face him, and he wrapped one hand around the side of my neck, using his thumb under my jaw to keep my head tipped back so I was looking at him. "I stopped because I want to give you so much pleasure, you're cross-eyed with it before I take even a second of pleasure from your body." He kissed me, and instead of fighting him on it like I should have, I melted into it. "You've spent too much time seeing to other people's pleasure, Dove. It's time you were worshiped the way you deserve to be."

"I don't want you to make up for other people's sins." I cried, shaking my head.

"I'm not." He pressed his forehead against mine and held me firmly. "But I will heal your wounds, Laila. Because that's what someone does when they care about you. They better you and help you."

"I just want to be normal." I cried, hating that everything he was saying was the right thing. Because I didn't want there to be any right or wrong things to say anymore. I just wanted to be normal.

"You're not normal. And neither am I." He kissed my lips, slowly coaxing me to kiss him back like I had before. But instead of the carnal need behind the kiss like earlier, there was something deeper and more heartfelt in it. "I don't want your normal, Dove. I want your wounds, your insecurities, and your hesitations. It's in these that I prove to you how much I want you. It's in moments just like this one that we grow together. Tighter and stronger than a normal couple that is shallow and only surface deep."

"I don't know—," I hesitated.

"Well, I do."

I smirked and took a deep breath, trying to relax and unwind, the whole night had been a whirlwind of emotions from the moment I walked up the driveway. "If you say so."

Zeke left shortly after our moment in my apartment, going back to work for Ryker. Before he left, he kissed me and told me he wouldn't stay away for so long again this time. I didn't know if he meant it, and a part of me believed he only said that so I wouldn't feel used after what happened between us.

But I wasn't sure.

I did know, however, that I didn't feel used.

Quite the opposite, actually.

I felt like I was the user in the equation, having received pleasure without reciprocating any. Yet, that was what Zeke said he wanted. It was all uncharted territory for us both, and I think he was just being cautious, given how unpredictable my trauma and triggers were.

And I didn't want to dwell on any of it. So, the next morning, I got up, got ready for the day, and went to hunt down my infuriatingly protective and caring brother.

I had to finish the argument he started last night in the driveway when I got home from work. Unconsciously picking a side, I left him standing there last night to find Zeke and check on him.

I just wish I hadn't been put in that place to begin with.

"Ropes." Carly snickered from her front porch as I walked up, face buried in her phone as Elora looked over her shoulder. "That's so hot."

"I prefer satin or silk." Elora shrugged, "Less likely to leave bruises when Ryker gets rough."

Carly chuckled and shook her head, still oblivious to my presence as I got to the bottom step. "I like wearing Jed's mark."

"Ew." I cringed with a smirk, making my presence known, and they both looked up, snickering together.

Carly rolled her eyes and smiled at me. "Well, good morning, troublemaker."

I ignored it and walked up the steps, forcing each foot in front of the next to get closer. Would it ever get easier to walk down paths?

"Is my wrist-branding brother here?" I asked, trying to keep things light and carefree.

"He isn't." Carly set her phone down and stared at me as Elora smirked over the top of her mug. "But he'll be back in a few minutes with donuts. So, you can stay and wait."

"I'll just catch him at the garage." I hooked my thumb over my shoulder and gave a slight wave as I went to make my exit.

"Not so fast." She whipped back, halting me before my foot even lifted off the wooden porch. "Spill it."

"What?" I crossed my arms over my chest and fought for control of the panic rising.

"Jed came home yesterday, broken and bloody from a fight with a man he had been friends with for years. And then when he tries to talk to you about it, you blow him off and go searching for that same stubborn and problematic man."

"Zeke is not problematic!" I argued, scowling at her. Of course, Carly was going to choose Jed, that was obvious. But I wasn't going to let her just throw Zeke, who was a good friend of hers as well, under the bus, not knowing the whole story.

She smirked and pursed her lips. "Interesting."

"I thought she'd have a better poker face than that." Elora quipped, leaning back in her chair. "She folded like paper in a hurricane."

"Told ya she had it bad." Carly added.

I shook my head and held my hand up, ceasing their annoying banter. "What is happening here?"

"It doesn't matter." Carly took her feet off the chair across from her and nodded to it. "What does matter is you telling us exactly what's happening with Zeke."

I groaned but sat down in the chair, because to be honest, I couldn't internally dissect everything that transpired between us anymore without breaking my psyche completely. God knew it was fragile at best to begin with.

"I don't even know how to answer that."

"Start at the strip club." Carly fired away instantly, ready for this conversation long before I was. "What happened after I left?"

I shrugged my shoulders, feeling stupid for saying it out loud. "He told me he wanted me." I covered my face as Elora's lit up and Carly smirked. "And that he would wait for me to come to him when I was ready."

"Girl." Elora gushed. "He's so damn respectful." She sighed, "It's almost attractive."

I snorted and relaxed a bit in the chair.

"Then what happened?" Carly pressed on.

"I did what any traumatized and damaged woman would do when a good man was interested in her." I cocked my head to the side, as if the answer was obvious.

"You tried to scare him off." Elora guessed and laughed when I looked at her, surprised that she knew my sarcastic answer. She rolled her eyes and waved me off. "I've done my fair share of trying to run from Ryker in the past. Ask Carly," She nudged her best friend. "One time I hid at Carly's, high off my ass, and he knocked her door down, carrying me out over his shoulder like a caveman." She giggled. "It was the hottest thing in the world."

"It was annoying as hell. And you blew chunks in the front flowerbed of my building." Carly challenged with a raised eyebrow before looking back at me. "What did you do to scare him off?"

I picked at a stray thread on my jeans, feeling the familiar waves of anxiety building from the embarrassing first moments between Zeke and me. "Ripped myself open to bleed at his feet so he'd know exactly how fucked up I am."

Neither one had a quick, snappy remark to make like they were known for, and I think that was harder to swallow than what I actually said. Carly reached across the space and took my hand in hers, making my nose burn as tears tried to form in my eyes from her niceties. "It didn't work, did it?"

I smiled sadly and squeezed her hand, "He's headstrong."

"Just like you." She whispered proudly and leaned back in her seat. "If there is anyone out there strong enough to endure and carry the weight of your trauma on his shoulders for you, it's Zeke."

"I know." I admitted, no longer interested in fighting the connection that seemed to be building between us. "I tell him the worst parts of me, and he just stands taller under the weight of it." I scoffed dramatically. "It's annoying, really."

They chuckled and waited for me to continue at my own speed.

"He kissed me." I finally added. "Well, actually, that's not true." I smirked, remembering that night in the hallway after leaving him with the first journal entry. "He made me beg him to kiss me before he would."

"That sounds about right." Elora replied. "Leave it to Zeke to make sure you're one hundred percent on board."

"Was that your first genuine kiss?" Carly asked seriously, no doubt remembering my freak out when I admitted to her I'd never had consensual sex before.

"Yes." I nodded. "And it was one for the history books."

"So, are you two together?" Elora asked, cutting straight to the point.

I shrugged again, unsure. "I doubt he'd react well if I kissed someone else."

"That's probably pretty fucking accurate." Carly joked and then nodded behind me. "Here comes Jed."

The hair on the back of my neck stood up as I heard his footsteps near behind me on the sidewalk and then up the steps to the porch.

"Hey." He said when I turned to look up at him towering over me. He had two boxes of doughnuts in his hands and a face full of bruises.

"Hi." I sighed, taking in the cuts and swelling on the exposed parts of his face and arms. "Do you have a minute?"

"Of course." He handed Carly the boxes and nodded at the front door. "Are you okay with going inside?"

I glanced at the ominous door but nodded before I could talk myself out of it. "Yeah." I needed to talk to him without Carly and Elora's penetrating gazes for a few minutes at least.

He walked inside, leaving the door open behind him as he took his leather jacket off and hung it on a hook in the hallway, cautiously watching me as I hesitated briefly at the doorway. But I forced my feet forward and shut the heavy oak door behind me as he moved to the kitchen.

"Can I get you some coffee or something?" he offered, pulling the pot out to pour himself a cup.

"I'm okay." I declined. "I'm already an anxious mess without caffeine helping." I tried to joke, but he grimaced as he poured sugar into his cup. "I'm sorry—"

"I'm sorry." He said at the same time, and we both paused in uncertainty before he went first. "I shouldn't have bombarded you at the door last night. That wasn't fair to you."

"I'm sorry you're in this position." I stated plainly. "Honestly. I never intended for you to be so torn—"

He held his hand up and shook his head, "Stop." He sighed and walked around the island, pulling a chair out for me and taking the other one so we were looking at each other. "I've been wrong this entire time." He started and took a deep breath. "I guess it took Zeke physically beating some sense into me before I realized that my overbearing desire to keep you safe was ruining your chances of living your life how you see fit."

I put my hand on his and fought emotions for the second time this morning as he softened himself for me. Jed was always protective and dominant, and I was sure only Carly and I ever saw the softer, caring side of him.

"I don't want to choose between you and him. Or you and anyone else in the future, either." I stated. "Because I'll choose you. And it will only hurt our relationship to do that."

He dropped his head. "I don't want you to choose." He lifted his head. "I just want what's right for you. You deserve to have everything that you've been robbed of for so long. I want you to have the future that you've dreamed of."

"I don't even know what I want, Jed." I smiled reassuringly. "I'm figuring it out as I go, and I'm trying to heal the past as I plan for the future."

"And Zeke helps with that somehow?" Jed questioned. "He said you talk to him." His throat clearing implied the words were hard for him to utter. "That you tell him things about your past." He looked back up at me. "Things you don't tell me."

"They aren't things you should hear." I shook my head, believing every word wholeheartedly.

"I'm your family, Laila. Your blood. I can take it."

"He doesn't punish himself for my past, Jed. You do." I stood up to pace as the topic became more uncomfortable as we dived deeper. "I have no clue what the future holds for Zeke and me. I have no clue if there *is* a future for us, or if he's just someone who stars in this chapter of my life. But I also had no idea how cathartic it would be to let some of my pain out into the universe and let someone else catch it." I trembled as he watched me intently. "For years, no one has known my story. No one cared because everyone I met had it bad, so I wasn't special. But now, there is a man who wants to know me. Who wants to know the bad so he can understand why I am the way I am today, and I'm tempted—" I shrugged, closing my eyes as tears threatened to spill down my face. "I'm tempted to lean on that. For even just a moment in time."

"You're tired." He whispered, and I opened my eyes to see his pain. "My therapist says you're tired because you've been in survival mode for decades. And now you don't have to be, but you don't know how to get out of it and just live."

"You have a therapist?" I asked, deflecting from the way his words hit so true in my heart.

He smirked, onto my plan and nodded his head. "Carly made me go to one right after you came home to us." He swallowed and took a calming breath. "She said I needed to know how to help you when you were ready to let me. And if I didn't get professional help to do that, I'd fuck it up when it mattered most." He cocked his head to the side, "Kind of how I did yesterday."

"Our therapists should chat because they sound a lot alike." I joked, feeling my body relax again as we found common ground. "I just want you to live your life without worrying about me."

"And I just want you to have every single thing you've ever dreamed of before. I'd move heaven and hell for you, Laila." He got serious again. "I'd kill for you."

Flashbacks assaulted my mind to that night so many years ago when Jed found me beaten and barely alive after our father tried to kill me with his fists. "And you'll never know how much you mean to me." I smiled softly, "And how much I need you in my life, still after all this time."

"Well, good." He smiled, standing up and puffing out his chest. "Because I have no plans on going anywhere, anytime soon."

"Unless you decide to push someone else through a glass window?" I raised my eyebrow at him and smirked as he rolled his eyes.

"Would it help you to know that I ended up getting more cut up than he did?" He joked.

"No." I answered honestly, "I'd prefer if you'd refrain from going through any windows, ever again."

"Me too." He groaned, deflating his shoulders a bit with a boyish grin. "I'm getting too old to be so wild."

I tipped my head back and laughed as the front door opened and Carly and Elora walked in, eyeing us.

"Well, that's a good sign." Carly said to Elora like we weren't standing right there watching them.

"Better than we'd hoped for, huh?" Elora winked.

"Do they always do that weird commentary thing?" I asked Jed out loud, giving them a taste of their own medicine.

"All the time." he joked, crossing his arms over his wide chest, and leaning against the island as Carly walked near him. "But you kind of get used to it after a while."

"Did you guys make up?" Carly ignored me and looked up at Jed.

"If you mean, did I apologize," He stared at her pointedly, "Then yes."

"And did you accept it?" She turned to me.

"Yes." I quipped.

"Good." She perked up, like she'd been waiting for that news to go on with her life. "Because I can't handle this kind of stress in my life."

"Oh, stop it." He groaned, kissing her forehead. "You've lived for this drama since leaving the clubs."

"True." She pouted and playfully slapped his chest. "I am quite bored with this whole housewife life."

"And that's my cue to go back to work." Jed winked over the top of her head, and I looked away as they kissed and hugged goodbye. "I'll apologize to Zeke the next time I see him." Jed called out as he walked to the front door. "Try to make things easier for you two."

"Thank you." I smiled brightly at him. "But don't go too easy on him," I cringed dramatically, "Have you seen what he did to your face?"

"Brat." He groaned as he walked out the door with a wave.

It felt good to know he and I were on good terms again, considering we all lived on the same estate.

"So," Elora steepled her fingers together in front of her as she looked at Carly. "Are the results in yet?"

"Huh?" I shook my head, once again confused by their internal banter.

"We took kink tests while we waited for you two to hug and make up." Ellie prattled on as if it were a normal discussion.

"And that's my cue to leave." I shook my head, walking around the island for the exit.

"Not so fast." Carly grabbed my arm and pulled me back. "You should take one."

"No." I shook my head so fast it nearly fell off my shoulders. "Nope."

"Oh, come on," Elora sighed. "Do you know what you're into sexually?" When I glared at her, she had her answer. "Don't you think it would be better to know ahead of time before you're in the situation to be triggered by something you hate?"

"Ugh." I groaned, hating that she was right because it was such foreign ground.

"She has a point. Let's look at our results, and you can go from there." Carly said, walking to the desk against the wall and pulling up the email with their results in it.

I eyed the door longingly as they pulled out the chairs to sit and look. But I hated to admit Elora was right. I had no idea what I liked in the bedroom.

Well, besides Zeke's touch.

That got me all hot and bothered pretty quickly.

"I don't think I'm kinky." I shook my head, glancing over their shoulders as their results popped up in pie chart form. "What's the term? Vanilla?"

Carly chuckled and pulled me over until I was sitting down next to her. "A kink test doesn't mean latex-wearing BDSM shit. It just helps break down what kind of things you are interested in by using basic terms and general statements. Look." She pointed to her results and clicked the top result. "I'm a switch."

"I have no idea what that means." I deadpanned, winning a chuckle from Elora.

"It means," Carly droned on dramatically, ignoring us, "That I like to be dominant and submissive."

"I'm getting images in my head I shouldn't have." I shuddered, winning another round of laughs from the girls.

"Don't think about Jed." Carly groaned. "Think about you." She switched screens to Elora's results and snorted. "Sub." She pointed out her top percentage. "No surprise there."

"What's that term mean?" I asked, falling into the conversation purely because my curiosity got the best of me.

"Rope bunny?" Carly asked, looking at her second highest rated result. "Means I like to be tied up and tie up—uh, my partner."

"Eh." I groaned, physically shaking out the images of Carly suspended in the air like a ham at a butcher's shop.

"Do you like bondage?" She asked.

"No." I replied instantly as I imagined lying in the center of my bed, tied to all four posts, helpless and at the mercy of the other person in the room. But when I replaced that faceless monster in the corner with Zeke, the repulsion of the idea didn't hit as hard. In fact, something else tingled in my brain as I imagined it.

"Wait for it." Elora whispered as I stared unseeingly at the computer screen.

Because I was now envisioning Zeke tied down in the center of my bed. Helpless and at my mercy, with his cock hard and ready for me, desperate for my touch as much as I was desperate to feel him.

"Maybe." I tilted my head as I imagined him panting in desperation while I hovered just out of reach. "Him, not me."

"There it is." Carly mused. "See, you were all hard no at first, but now you're imagining going full dominatrix on Zeke, aren't you?"

"Skip the latex cat woman suit." I blinked, clearing the erotic images from my head as Carly somehow swam around inside of my brain like she belonged there. "But maybe."

"Noted." She winked knowingly. "What else?" She looked back at her results and scrolled over each with her cursor, giving me time to read them and form an opinion in my head.

"Degradation is a hard no." I shook violently at the idea. "No way."

"Makes sense." Carly said evenly, not dwelling on the trauma behind the emotion.

"Non-monogamous?" I questioned, "Like sister wives?" I asked as I saw her relatively high score for that topic.

"Like swinging." She replied. "Not any less committed to your partner, but willing to share under certain circumstances."

"Ha." Elora snorted. "That won't work for Laila." She shook her head confidently as my own opinions were forming in my head. "She's jealous. Possessive, if you will."

"How do you know that?" Carly scowled at her best friend, and I shrugged my shoulders because Elora was right.

"Because I mentioned how Zeke treated other women around me over the years, and Laila went full space cadet and imagined their untimely demise before I even finished my sentence."

"I did not." I rolled my eyes.

"Pretty close." She smirked. "Either way, she's not going to want to see Zeke give any other woman a second of attention around her." She stared at me pointedly, "Are you?"

"No." I answered evenly, "Not at all."

"Good to know." Carly added, scrolling again.

"What about voyeurism?" Elora asked, noting the high score on Carly's sheet again. "Exhibitionism?"

"Like screwing in front of people?" I cringed.

"Or watching others have sex."

"No." I shook my head. Too many times in my life had I seen others screwing. "People actually like that?"

Carly snorted, and Elora chuckled. "Carly has an exhibitionism kink. So yes."

My eyebrows rose to my hairline as I tried to imagine the appeal.

"Hey, don't knock it until you've been fucked up against your kitchen window while the gardener's watch." Carly shrugged non-chalantly, and my eyes drifted over to the large glass windows over-looking their lush backyard.

"I have no words." I admitted.

"That's fine." Carly nodded and clicked on a new topic. "Ooh, what about role play?"

"Like doctor and nurse?" I recoiled. "Too cliché."

"It doesn't have to be a scene like that." Elora said, "It could be as simple as using pet names for power play."

"You say that's simple, but I'm even more confused now." I replied, unimpressed.

She rolled her eyes, "Like does the idea of calling Zeke, Daddy, excite you?"

"Daddy?" I scowled. "Don't you think I have enough daddy issues?"

"Yes." Elora and Carly both said at the same time.

"But that's exactly why you'd probably be into it." Elora shrugged. "Ryker and my dad were best friends from childhood, yet I love a well-placed 'Please, Daddy' when I'm feeling particularly dirty."

"I bet Ryker eats that up like catnip, too." Carly joked.

"Spoon-fed catnip," Elora confirmed. "Just keep it in the back of your head."

"Zeke would make such a wonderful Daddy Dom." Carly mused, leaning back in her chair. "With his seriousness and attention to detail." She groaned. "I bet he's a pleasure Dom."

"Stop." I snapped, feeling my body heat increase just thinking about Zeke being kinky like that.

"There's that green-eyed monster." Elora joked. "Can't even let us talk about Zeke sexually."

Carly laughed at my expense, but I wasn't mad, because she was right. "I remember how I felt about Jed in the beginning, too." She assured me, "I was very possessive too, but that lessens the longer you're together and feel more confident in the strength of the relationship."

"No, it doesn't." Elora challenged. "I'll still cut a bitch for looking at Ryker with bedroom eyes." She shrugged. "You included." She smirked at her best friend.

"Ladies," I intervened comically.

"Okay, back to the point." Carly glared at Elora before looking back at me. "Here." She grabbed a paper off the printer as it came out and handed it to me. "Take the test, think about the answers, and then we'll plug them in and get your results."

"Take the kink test?" I droned, "No."

"Yes." She shoved the paper into my hand and closed it with hers. "You should know these answers before you enter a sexual relationship with someone who has so much more experience in the real world of sex."

"Shut up." I ripped the paper and my hand out of hers theatrically. "My green monster is growing." I glared at her as I stood up, folding the paper up and putting it in my back pocket. "I have to go to therapy."

"Have fun!" Carly called as I walked through her house. "Learn something."

"Make wise choices!" Elora called out after her. Before I shut the front door behind me, she sang, "Our little girl is getting so grown up."

I shook my head with a smirk on my face as I walked through the grass back to the barracks to drop off the offensive paper, burning a hole in my pocket before I left for therapy.

There was no way I was going to my session with that bomb in my pants.

CHAPTER 12 – LAILA

"I 've been looking for you." A gruff voice called as I stared at the cracks in the sidewalk in front of me.

"Why?" I rolled my eyes, looking up and getting blinded by the bright sunlight before Diesel Ames stepped in the way, blocking the offensive glare so I could drop my hand from my face.

"Because you keep changing your schedule." He stated plainly.

"You know you are kind of creepy when you don't filter your thoughts, right?" I mused, feeling so numb from therapy that I didn't even feel the fear I normally got from being in men's presence. Most men, though to be honest, not usually around the MC president with his menacing scars and long wild hair tied back.

His face pulled up in a smirk, accentuating the gnarly scars covering his cheeks. "Yet you never tell me to get lost." A loud horn honked from the busy street, reminding me I had been walking before he interrupted me.

"Wrong." I started walking again, and as expected, he followed. "I'm pretty sure I've told you to kick rocks almost every time I've seen you out randomly." I stopped and glared at him. "Or not so randomly."

He smirked again and moved the toothpick between his teeth with his tongue. "I had business in this part of town."

"Right." I pressed the button for the crossing light and waited, hoping he'd get on with it or get lost. "What do you want, Diesel?"

"You're snappy today." He scoffed as if he was offended, but I didn't think anything really offended the man. Other than pushing his tricked-out motorcycle down a cliff or something as extreme.

"I'm burned out." I pushed the button again. "Therapy has that effect on me."

"How's that going?" He asked, like we were old friends. And in a way, he kind of was his own version of a friend to me, I guess. I wouldn't really know how to make friends organically since the only two I had were partially related, and we all shared space on the estate. It wasn't like I met them at a restaurant and complimented them on their outfits and became fast friends or whatever girls do.

Hell, I wasn't even a good friend to Diesel, since every time he came around, I told him to get lost.

"I mean, she hasn't strapped me down and shocked me with electrodes." I shrugged, making him snort, "Yet."

"Sounds like my kind of Saturday night." He joked, though I didn't know how much of a joke it actually was. "But do you feel like it's helping? With the anxiety and stuff?"

It was my turn to snort, "And stuff?" I rolled my eyes. "Yeah, it's helping." I looked back across the street and watched people walking and passing by each other, busy and on their way with their day. Yet my only purpose was walking down the street.

Diesel said something about progress or something, but I was distracted as I watched a kid walk out of an alley across the street, with a hood pulled down deep over his head and his shoulders hunched under his baggy tattered sweater.

I glimpsed his bright blue eyes as they scanned the surrounding people on the street. Something about the mannerisms and the look in his eyes grabbed my attention and wouldn't let it go.

"Light's green." Diesel said, nudging my shoulder. "You plan on standing here all day?"

As the kid walked toward the crosswalk, I jumped forward, mumbling an apology and inexplicably following him with my eyes.

I couldn't explain it, but something had a hold of me and wouldn't let go. Diesel walked silently beside me, seemingly sensing my distraction.

I watched the kid's hunched frame scurry down the sidewalk, noticing the way his step quickened the further he got from the alley, and right before I made it across the street completely, a group of four guys ran out from the same alley. They turned around quickly, scanning the streets before one pointed at the kid I'd been watching, and they took off after him.

"Shit." I hissed, and froze right after the crosswalk, watching the young kid twist around to the mob giving chase and then took off in a sprint, right toward me.

"You know them?" Diesel asked, putting his hand on my arm and pulling me to the side as the chaos barreled toward us.

"Stop them." I said, chancing a glance up at the violent man next to me, that followed me around like a lost puppy. "Save him." I squeezed his arm, "Please."

"Fuck." He scowled at me and then shoved me toward the brick building before stepping into the path of the first kid. Diesel grabbed the kid by the shoulders and catapulted him into me against the brick building, where I caught him seconds before his face smashed off the rough wall. Those icy blue eyes I'd noticed from across the street widened in panic as I grabbed onto his sweater to steady him. Dirt streaked his face, and his cheekbones were sunken in, giving him a skeletal look.

"Stay quiet." I hissed, stepping around him and shielding him with my body as Diesel squared his big body off against the four older boys, running straight toward him.

"Where's the fire, boys?" Diesel called out as the group skidded to a stop right before plowing him over. They sputtered as they looked around the massive body standing between them and their prey. "What's the matter? Can't think and talk at the same time? Maybe you should try again after puberty."

One of the bigger boys flicked his glance from me to the kid they were chasing and back to Diesel, "He robbed us. We want it back."

Diesel chuckled and looked over his shoulder at us, where the kid slightly cowered behind me. I glanced down at him, and those icy blue eyes rapidly moved from me to the mob and back, silently trying to say something.

"All four of you?" I deadpanned, "If it was one against four and he outsmarted you somehow, you had it coming." I looked back at the tiny youngster behind me. "He clearly didn't strong-arm all of you."

Diesel played along, like we had any clue what was going on, with a confidence only a powerful man could perfect. "Take the loss and keep it moving."

"What?" The older boy sputtered angrily, "What the fuck do you have to do with it?" His boyish face turned molten red as he was told no.

"Careful." Diesel warned, leveling his finger at the bratty kid's face. "Or I'll take you over my knee right here and show your friends who your daddy is." He took a menacing step forward, shifting out of the jokester and into the notorious MC leader's role, using his scary looks to get his point across. "Get fucking lost, or I'll knock all of your crooked baby teeth out of your fucking face before I shove them down your throat." He cocked his head to the side. "You ever shit out teeth before, Peter Pan?" He flicked his finger at the boy's red hair, "Cuts like glass."

"Let's go." One of the other kids said, clearly the voice of reason over the teens when facing a lacerated asshole.

"Whatever." The leader sneered, staring right at the young kid behind me. "This ain't fucking over, asswipe."

"Ooh, original." Diesel Jazz handed the kid as he pushed him back. "Get fucking lost, now!"

The four of them turned and walked back down the sidewalk, glancing over their shoulders like they were trying to be brave with the grim reaper walking behind them until they got to the alley and turned back into the darkness and disappeared.

My shoulders sagged as I finally took a deep breath now that I was fairly confident, I wouldn't be watching the Reaper MC President beat up a couple of kids in broad daylight. Movement behind me rattled me from my thoughts, and I quickly grabbed the back of the sweater as the kid tried taking off down the street again. "Whoa, wait a second."

The kid turned around and huffed at me, rolling his eyes. "Thanks for the help, lady." He pulled against my hold on him, "But I got shit to do."

"What's your name?" I asked as Diesel leaned against the brick wall, watching over us.

"What's it to you?" The kid sneered again. I raised my brows at him and gave him a fuck around and find out look, and he rolled his eyes again and sagged into the wall, pulling his sweater from my clutches. "Kade."

"Kade." I repeated, looking him over and crossing my arms over my chest. "Did you really steal from them?"

He scowled with his bad attitude, and I saw it for what it was, a young boy's act to seem to be tough so no one would mess with him. "What the fuck's it to you?"

"Watch it." Diesel growled, flicking Kade's forehead, "Don't think because I kept the others from beating you up that I won't do it for being a disrespectful little pissant."

"Whatever." Kade sighed and pulled at his sweater, looking up and down the street. "I shorted them."

"Shorted them what?" I questioned.

"Lady, you got an off button?" He snapped, "Because you're questioning me like a cop," He flicked his eyes over Diesel again, "He don't look like no five-o, and neither do you," He glared back at me, "But you're sure riding my ass like some yuppy beat cop trying to make his quota for the day."

"What did you short them?" I repeated, ignoring his bravado.

He rolled his eyes again, and I fought the urge to tell him his face was going to freeze like that if he kept it up, simply because I was already coming off like some old Karen. But I didn't need to give him more ammo to throw insults at me. "Mary Jane." He looked up and down the street. "But they had it fucking coming." He nodded his head, "They beat up my associate two days ago and took his keep." He stood taller, "I was making it right."

"A drug dealer with a justice kink." Diesel groaned, "How original."

"Shut it." I warned him, and he held his hands up and smirked as I looked back at Kade. "What exactly was your plan to get away from them just now?" I held my hand up, silencing the smart-ass remark he was starting to make. "Cut the bullshit because if the big guy here hadn't stepped in, those four would have been stomping your face in right now." I dared him to negate that, but he just pursed his lips and looked away. "What do you get out of it?"

"Ain't it obvious, lady?" He quipped. "It's just how life goes out here. Obviously, you've never struggled in your life, or you'd get it."

I didn't correct him; he didn't need to know how wrong he was about my life. "You live on the streets?"

"Nah," he shook his head, "I got a crib up in East Valley." He sneered with the same fictitious bravado. "I just slum it down here for the fun of it." He sighed and leveled me with a look a grown-up would use with a troublesome kid. "Why'd you intervene? What do *you* get out of it?"

I shrugged and took a step back, taking the pressure off him. "Just didn't want to stand by while a kid got his ass kicked today, I guess." Suddenly I was just so fucking tired of the world and its injustices. "Guess I thought maybe you could use a break."

He didn't jump back at me with his venom or sarcasm, and I saw a bit of that bravado slip from his dirty face. "Yeah, well." He shrugged, trying to build up the act again. "Thanks."

"Don't mention it." I replied as he walked off between Diesel and me, glancing over his shoulder for a brief second before disappearing down the street with the other people walking around.

"You okay?" Diesel asked as I stared off after the kid.

"How old do you think he is?" I asked.

Diesel watched him with me and shrugged, "Hard to tell. He prob-ably hasn't eaten a full meal in months. Early teens maybe, thirteen or so."

"Thirteen years old, stealing, selling drugs, and fighting off attack-ers in the middle of broad daylight." I sighed, looking around at the dozens of other people who wouldn't have intervened if those guys had caught up with Kade. "It's just not fair."

"It's not that uncommon." Diesel shrugged. "Kids like that float in and out of crews like mine all the time. Sometimes they stay and patch in when they're older, sometimes they disappear chasing after what they're all missing in life."

"What are they missing?" I glanced at him before tracking back to the kid getting further and further away from us as the anxiety built inside of me like I should stop him.

"Love." Diesel sighed. "Compassion. Comfort. Most kids just end up finding it in unauthentic ways when they go without it for so long, unfortunately."

"Hmm." I hummed, watching that black tattered hoodie disappear around a corner down the street, gone and out of sight like we never interacted at all.

"You okay?" Diesel asked again.

"Peachy." I shook the entire bizarre interaction off and took a deep breath, "I have to get to work."

"I heard you were slinging drinks at Neat." D smirked. "At least if a customer gets rowdy with you there, you can spray them with the soda gun." He joked, referencing the time he saved me from the bitchy customer at the coffee shop.

"Don't get any ideas." I leveled a sharp look at him. "You're not allowed there. I made sure your name was on the trespass list."

He tipped his head back and laughed, "Oh baby, now I'm going to show up just to make you squirm."

CHapTer 13 – zeKe

My hands were clammy as I walked down the sidewalk towards the entrance to *Neat,* so I wiped them on my jeans.

Was this what Laila felt every time she walked down a path? My mind flipped back to that day on the sidewalk when I found her doing her therapy homework by walking down the sidewalk to help ease her trauma of being led down hallways.

I got to the front door and walked in, passing by guests waiting to be seated in the busy restaurant on my way to the hostess podium.

Which was where my prize was.

Laila.

She wore her long brown hair tied up in a neat bun with just the slightest bit of makeup on her face, showcasing her natural beauty. Her tight black uniform shirt hugged her body effortlessly, and my hands ached to slide around her waist, anchoring her to my own body.

I saw her just last night, but I was desperate to see her again. Last night I kissed her, touched her body, and made her come in my arms, and then I had to leave for work.

But not now.

I was off now, changed into jeans and a plain shirt, searching for my drug of choice.

Laila.

She was talking to a man at the podium about the wait time as I stood back and watched. She didn't notice me, but I felt her presence in every nerve ending in my body. I wanted to take her away from here and back into the serene calmness of her apartment, but she wanted to work and be normal, so I settled on showing up and killing the time she spent at her shift by watching her. At least that way, maybe the time would stop passing by at a crawl.

Any bit of euphoria I'd been feeling from having her in view again slid from my body as I watched her interact with the customer. The guy she was talking to was a millennial prick with a man bun and pants rolled up over his ankle bones like he was expecting a flood. And he was also raising his voice at my Dove.

Mine.

"What do you mean it's a two-hour wait?" He snapped, "It's five thirty. No where is that busy at five thirty."

"I'm so sorry, sir." She replied, wringing her hands together in front of her as he got closer to the podium. "We have a full reservation list for the night and only keep so many walk-in slots available, and my next one isn't until after seven. Would you like me to put you on that list now?"

"No, I don't want to wait until fucking seven to eat!" He roared, and the woman he was with sighed dramatically as she scrolled through her phone. The rest of their group grumbled their objections from the side of the lobby as well, voicing their discontent with the wait time. "There are empty tables right now!"

"They're already reserved for the reservations that have been booked." She tried again, "Like I said, I'm more than happy to put you on the list—,"

"Fuck your list." He bit, taking the last step toward the podium as he pointed his finger at her face. She whitened like a ghost as he raised his voice at her and stepped into her personal space. I scanned the lobby for any other employees working to intervene, but she was alone. And that was unacceptable. "And fuck you!"

"Sir." She gasped, backing up until her back pressed flat against the wall separating the lobby from the restaurant, but he didn't get another step closer before I clapped my hand on his shoulder and spun him around.

"Apologize." I growled. "Now."

His face went molten red as he sputtered at my interruption. "Who the fuck do you—"

I didn't let him get another word out before I punched him in the throat, closing off any chance of him finishing his sentence or any other offensive one.

"Zeke!" Laila gasped from behind her podium.

"Woah!" One of his friends came up, putting himself between me and the sissy punk that tried to act tough against a woman but turned into a simpering puss the second he faced off with a real man. "He's sorry!" His friend rushed out, glancing back at where his friend was still doubled over, trying to get air past his crushed windpipe. "He's drunk and stupid." His friend kept on. "He didn't mean it. We don't want any trouble with the Shadeport Crew."

"What's going on out here?" A voice boomed around the lobby as patrons cleared apart, allowing a path as one of the owners, Peter, came out of the kitchen, scowling at the crowd. "What happened?" He snapped at Laila, who opened her mouth and shut it, unable to form a word, before the last of the guests moved and he finally made eye contact with me. "Mr. Evans." He stopped short, glancing at the man whose face matched the shade of a blueberry, with fire in his eyes as he glared at me. "Forgive me—" Peter said.

"Where is your security?" I cut him off, looking over at Laila, whose eyes were still as wide as saucers as they bounced back and forth between me and her boss.

"They're—," Peter turned in a circle, looking for the men he paid to protect his property and business. "I don't—"

"You don't know." I snapped. "And your employees are left to handle assholes on their own because your security can't be found." He blanched as I nodded at Laila. "Rule number one in running a successful business, Peter, is to stop the riffraff from even coming through the front door to disrupt it. You can't do that if you don't have any security manning that front door."

"Right." He nodded quickly as more members of his management team filled the space. "You're absolutely right. One hundred percent. A misstep that won't be made again, thank you for intervening."

"I didn't do it for you." I stepped forward until we were chest to chest and pointed at Laila over his shoulder. "She's mine." I growled, and his eyes widened. "Do you understand what that means?"

"Yes." He stammered and nodded like he was an electronic screen glitching out. "I understand it perfectly."

"This will never happen again." I stated plainly. "She will never be left to take care of your trash for you again. Or I'll take care of you."

"Absolutely." He stiffened his spine, "This problem will be corrected immediately."

"Good."

He relaxed for a moment and then turned on his heel, snapping his fingers as two bouncers suddenly appeared from thin air. "Have this man removed." He pointed to the sniveling mess, who was finally breathing again. "He's being blacklisted from all of our restaurants."

"Yes, Sir." One bouncer said, grabbing the man off the floor and hauling him toward the door.

"Now, now." Peter announced boldly, "Let's get back to enjoying our evening, shall we?" He smiled at his guests and played the part of the host setting the mood before turning back to me. The crowd returned to their conversations, leaving us alone in ours as he lowered his voice. "My partners and I have been meaning to set up a meeting with Mr. Lawson. To formally introduce ourselves and make sure we're all on good terms—," He hesitated. "I hope this doesn't affect our chances of—"

"Rectify this situation so it never happens again, and I'll keep it between us." I paused, so he had time to understand just how fucking serious I was. "Allow anything negative to happen to her again while under your roof, and I mean anything," His eyes rounded, "And I'll wipe every single person you care about off the face of this planet. One at a time until you know it's your fucking turn. Clear?"

"Crystal." He swallowed. "She's my biggest priority now. I'll treat her like family."

"Good." I repeated, "Now point me in the direction of your office where I can have a private word with her."

"Upstairs." He hooked his thumb over his shoulder to a nondescript door along the wall by the kitchen. "Take all the time you need."

"Laila." I called, holding my hand out to her as I rounded the podium. "Come with me for a minute."

She flicked her eyes back and forth between me and Peter before sliding her hand in mine and falling in step behind me as we walked through the bustling bar to the dark stairwell leading to his office.

"Am I fired?" She whispered as she ran up the steps behind me, but I didn't answer her until we walked through the only other door in the hallway.

"Do you want to be fired?" I asked, closing it behind her and sliding my hands into my pockets as I leaned back against it. "Do you like it here?"

"I do." She answered quickly and then grimaced. "I mean, sometimes the customers suck." She shrugged. "But most of my coworkers are nice."

"You can work here for as long as you want to."

"Because Peter is scared of you?" She wrapped her arms around her waist as she cocked her head to the side. "He folded to you as if you were the most powerful man in the world. Instantly, without hesitation."

"Right now, I am the most powerful man in the bar." I said evenly. "And I work for the most powerful man in California."

Her pupils dilated slightly before she dropped her gaze to my shoes. "You were—," She started and stopped, and I forced myself to stay silent while she worked out her thoughts. Was she going to say scary? Did I frighten her with my violence? Did she flash back to the violence she saw over the years? Every second of time that ticked by dropped my heart deeper into my stomach as anxiety crawled up my spine. "Menacing." She flicked her eyes up to mine, and my heart stopped beating in my chest completely. "I don't think there's another word to describe the terrifying power I saw in your eyes when you faced that man down. You didn't even blink."

I licked my lips and forced my chest to rise, taking in a much-needed breath as her words assaulted my head over and over.

That was it. She was done.

I fucked everything up by showing her the monster inside of me like a fucking moron.

"I understand." Nodding, with my eyes fixed on the floor, I was suddenly unable to meet her gaze, just as she always struggled to meet mine. "I'm sorry you saw that side of me." I leaned off the door. "But I won't apologize for defending you. Not ever."

"Zeke." She tilted her head to the side with that curious little kitten stare she got when she was out of her depth.

"Your job here is secure, work here for as long as you want to. No one will bother you anymore. You have the crew's protection." I had to get out of the room.

It was closing in on me as I saw the one thing I'd wanted more than anything else slipping through my fingers.

"Zeke." She whispered again. "I don't understand."

"I'm sorry I scared you." Turning the handle, I opened the door, and the dim room was bathed in light from above the doorway. "I'll never do that again." Turning and walking into the hallway, I felt as if my chest might collapse and explode. I never lost control, ever. Yet there I was on the verge of losing it all because her rejection was the worst thing I'd ever imagined.

"It aroused me." She called as I stepped away, freezing me in my tracks. I looked over my shoulder at her as my brain tried to comprehend what she had just said. She held her hands out at her side and shrugged her shoulders like she didn't understand any of it, either. "Seeing you like that—," She shook her head and licked her lips as her chest rose and fell quickly, "Turned me on."

"Laila." I growled, cracking my neck to the side as I turned back to face her.

"I'm soaking wet." She bit her bottom lip, and I walked back into the room, closing the door behind me again and locking us inside. "I don't remember a time in my life I've ever gotten wet for any other man but you, Zeke." She nearly purred like she was on the verge of coming right there, from just words. "Last night when you touched me was the first time I've ever orgasmed from someone else's touch, and tonight, watching you defend me like that," her eyelids fluttered closed as her head tilted back just a little bit. "That power is the sexiest thing I've ever seen before."

"Fuck it." I cursed, closing the distance between us, and slamming my lips down on hers with my hand tight in her hair. She whimpered and clawed at my jacket as she opened her lips and licked my tongue seductively. "Tell me to stop."

"Don't stop." She panted, digging her nails into my pecks over my shirt. "I don't know how to control myself around you."

"Dove." I groaned, sliding my hands under the back of her thighs, lifting her. She wrapped her legs around my waist and clung to me as I crossed the office and sat her down on the desk.

"I should be calling you out for toxic masculinity and telling you to shove your chivalry somewhere dark, but all I can think about is how I'd rather show you my appreciation for saving me." She shook her head as she rambled. "I'm fucked up."

"You're perfect." I countered, flattening my hands against the desk on each side of her ass as she pulled me closer with her legs tangled around mine. "I thought you were afraid of me."

"No!" She gasped, biting my lip, and sucking on it like a minx. "I wanted to fall to my knees at your feet right then and there."

"Never." I growled, towering over her, and tightening my hand in her hair until she was forced to look up at me and focus. "Your knees will never touch the ground for me, Laila. You'll sit atop a throne, and I'll be the one at your feet."

She moaned and rocked her hips, creating friction between our bodies, and my cock twitched in my jeans.

"Tell me what you want." I demanded as she rocked her hips again. Her moves were frantic and uncoordinated from her inexperience.

"I don't know." She closed her eyes and tried to shake her head, but I tightened my hold around her long locks and dropped my lips to her neck, sucking on the skin above her wild pulse.

"Don't lie to me." I ordered, and she moaned, rocking her hips again, rubbing herself against my hard-on. "Tell me what you want, Dove." I sucked her earlobe into my mouth and teased it with my teeth. "Tell me what you need."

"I need to come." She panted, speaking about her needs even though it made her uncomfortable.

"You want me to make you come, Dove?"

"Yes." She cried, digging her nails into the back of my neck as she held me to her throat.

"Right here?"

"Yes." She nodded frantically.

"Say it then." I instructed. "Use your words to tell me what you need, and it's yours."

"I want you to make me come, right here, on my boss's desk." She panted and then gasped when I lifted her off the desk and laid her onto her back with her legs still wrapped around my waist as I pinned her down, hovering right above her. Her eyes were wide, and I could see the brightness of fear in them, but behind that fear was excitement.

I rocked against her, using the entire length of my hard cock pinned in my pants to rub her clit, and her eyes rolled and then fluttered closed as I did it again.

"Tell me how you feel." I whispered as I pressed my hand flat against her rib cage directly beneath her breast.

"Like I'm going to combust into flames." She panted, opening her eyes, and staring up at me as I rolled my hips again, humping her into the desk through our jeans. Twice now I'd touched her like this, but both times her clothes were between us, which was the safest way to ensure she was comfortable with it.

Until I could earn her trust with more than just her orgasms.

"I can feel how hot your pussy is, Dove." I teased, "How needy it is."

"God, yes." She moaned, widening her legs and tilting against me so she got more pressure on her clit. "You feel so good."

A flush of arousal colored her neck and cheeks as sweat beaded in her hairline. And she had never looked sexier to me.

Erotic.

She was so fucking erotic.

"I want to make you come." I admitted. "I want it more than anything else." Cupping the bottom of her breast with my hand, she arched her back, pushing it into my palm until I could feel the hard point of her nipple through her shirt and bra. "Good girl." I praised, rocking faster.

"Fuck." She whispered as her jaw went slack, and she tensed in my arms.

"Tell me."

"I'm coming." She whispered almost inaudibly, but I didn't need to hear it to know. I could *feel* it. In every nerve of my body, I could feel her orgasm cresting inside of her and tipping over the other side like a tidal wave of pleasure. Even without orgasming myself, I felt pleasure. Seeing her gain hers and being the one to give it to her was incredible.

"That's it." I commended, "That's my good girl."

"Oh God." She panted, going lax in my arms, and dropping her hands to her chest as I leisurely rolled her nipple between my fingers and slowly continued to stroke my cock against her. "Don't ever stop." She whined with her eyes closed and a satisfied smile on her lips that I eagerly tasted as I kissed her, slowing my movements and then stopping them.

Even though she told me not to stop, I wasn't going to take it any further at her job. I shouldn't have even taken it this far, but when she said she was wet—when she gave me that gift of communicating her feelings with me, I couldn't tell her no.

I couldn't resist.

"You stopped." She pouted sweetly and opened her eyes. "You did it again."

I stood up slowly, helping her upright as she fought to regain her equilibrium. "What did I do?"

"Made me come while taking nothing for yourself." She stuck her bottom lip out and as I watched her freely express herself, I realized she was the most relaxed I'd ever seen her. She was communicating and depicting what she wanted and needed from me.

"You're giving me my reward right now."

Her brow creased in the center as she slid to her feet. "What?"

"You're verbalizing your feelings to me." I said, and she froze, blinking rapidly as she realized what she was doing. "And you're alone in a room with me." I added, raising my brow at her, "With the door shut."

"Good gravy." She sighed and then smirked. "I guess I wasn't thinking about it when you led me up here."

"Does that mean you're not afraid of me?" I questioned and held my breath for her answer.

"I've never been afraid of you." She answered nonchalantly and then fought to hide a smirk as she adjusted her shirt. "You're not as intimidating as you think you are." Before she got the last word out, she fell into a fit of giggles and gave herself away.

"Funny girl."

"Hmm. The funny girl falls for the serious man." She hummed, tapping her finger on her chin. "How on earth do we expect that to work out?"

"I plan to distract you with so many orgasms; you don't see my flaws." I joked.

"And I think I plan to let you try."

CHAPTER 14 – LAILA

H e was watching me.

Staring over the rim of his glass as I moved around the bar, working and trying to focus.

Did he know how hard it was to pay attention to anything else in the world besides my need for him?

Did he know how difficult it was for me to admit to myself that I needed him?

My body tingled, aware of his stare as I tried to watch the bartender, Nicole, mix a cocktail for an order.

"You see?" she asked, topping it with a sprig of mint. "It goes directly to the top of the glass when it's poured, or you did it wrong."

"Got it." I nodded, swallowing down the lust in my body as she handed me the shaker.

"Your turn."

I took a deep breath, started gathering the same liquor bottles she used, and repeated the process.

"Good." She praised me as I poured the right amount into the shaker. "Have you bartended before?" She asked as I started shaking the drink.

"Kind of." I shrugged. "Nothing on this scale."

"Well, you've got the pour counts down, which is the hardest part for most." She watched as I strained the drink into the glass and waited to see where it would end. "Bingo." She said as the last drop left the glass completely full. "Impressive."

"Thanks." I set the glass down on the server's station with the ticket under it. "You're a good teacher."

"So, who's the hunk?" Nicole asked, nodding subtly to Zeke at the other end of the bar, watching me without recourse.

"Oh," I swallowed, rubbing my hands down my jeans before grabbing another glass and a ticket from the printer. "That's Zeke."

"Evans, right?" Nicole glanced at him and smirked. "I've heard of him before, but I'll be honest, I never understood the Boogeyman effect until now."

"The what?" I frowned, glancing at Zeke, fighting the pull his crystal blue eyes had on me as he ran the rim of his glass over his bottom lip. Did he have any idea how seductive everything he did was?

Nicole chuckled. "He's like the boogeyman. No one seems to know much about him, other than that he's scary as fuck."

"He's not scary," I argued, hating how one sentence raised my possessiveness over Zeke. "He's intimidating, sure." I shrugged, fighting to stop defending him like I had some claim over him. "That's his job."

"That's his personality." She countered, ignoring my discomfort. To be fair, she didn't know me from Adam and didn't owe me anything. "But it's cool." She winked at me as we crossed workstations. "I love a good dark and brooding man."

"Eh." I groaned to myself, fighting that knee-jerk jealousy that Elora loved to pick on me about. "Does this one get an orange?" I asked, setting down another drink on the bar, even though I already knew it got a cherry. I needed to change the subject to safer terms.

"God, that man on the other hand." She shuddered and sighed. "He looks like the kind of man that could make a girl beg for the boogeyman."

"Can we not—," I started and froze when I looked up to see her staring down at the other end of the bar.

Away from Zeke.

And directly at Diesel Ames.

Who wasn't paying her the least bit of attention, as he stared directly past her at me.

Shit. He actually fucking showed up.

I whipped my head over to Zeke, who of course already had Diesel pinned in a death glare with his hands in fists on the bar top.

Double shit.

I backed away from Diesel's end of the bar and went straight to Zeke, as if physically siding with him would ease some of the rage building behind his eyes as he stared at the Reaper's President.

"I didn't invite him." Zeke glanced at me before returning his stare to his target across the bar after my quick stammer.

"Does he come here often?"

"I don't know," I replied honestly. "I've never seen him here."

"I don't share," Zeke said effortlessly, looking back at me and leaning forward on his elbows. "Let me make that clear."

"I don't want him." His intense stare forced me to swallow my fear and keep going. "I've never invited his attention."

"You rode his bike." Zeke tilted his head to the side slightly.

"That upsets you," I stated plainly, trying to figure out the emotions in my head, battling the ones slamming into me from Zeke.

"You touched him." He tightened his hand around his whiskey glass. "Long before you ever touched me."

My mouth snapped shut in shock as his words sank into my brain.

Diesel's stare burned the side of my face as Zeke, and I locked eyes; I knew I had to be firm with Zeke to prevent the situation from worsening.

I leaned forward with my elbows on the bar until our faces were only a foot apart. "You're the only one I've ever let touch *me*, though."

His nostrils flared, and the strong column of muscles in his throat moved as he swallowed.

"Laila," Nicole called from the other side of the bar. "We've got orders."

"I have to get back to work," I said after a long pause, and I'd be lying if I said I wasn't disappointed that Zeke didn't say anything back.

"I'm not going anywhere." He finally responded, taking a sip of his drink, and leaning back on his stool a bit.

"That sort of feels like a threat."

"A promise." He clarified as I backed up.

If I thought working under Zeke's penetrating stare was hard before, it paled in comparison to the pressure of working while Zeke and Diesel sat next to each other at the bar.

And chatted.

They could have been talking about world peace or world domination, but the effect was the same.

I was shaking.

I tried staying busy, learning as much as I could from Nicole and the other bartenders after being surprisingly thrown behind the bar instead of at the podium out front. Honestly, that shouldn't have surprised me.

Nothing should surprise me anymore.

But Zeke and Diesel, chatting and drinking at my bar, was enough to nearly blow me over.

At one point I secretly snapped a picture of the two of them sitting next to each other, with their dark and dangerous tattoos and fuck-you energy, and sent it to Carly.

> **Should I be worried?**

Her response came almost instantly.

> *I'd probably lock myself in the cooler if I were you. Should I send Jed for reinforcements?*

I shuddered at the mere thought of my brother showing up at the bar as well. The whole restaurant would melt to the ground from the testosterone alone.

> *Are you trying to start a nuclear war? Best not.*

> *You're probably right. If it gets too out of hand, use the soda gun to spray them down.*

I snorted and pocketed my phone. Did people really do that?

"Hey." Nicole slid up next to me. "Head home."

"Really?" I glanced at the time, "I've still got twenty-five minutes left on my shift."

Nicole shrugged, pushing me out of her way to get to the sanitizing sink. "Peter gives the orders; I pass them down. Take it while you can get it."

"Okay." I wiped my hands on the towel and clocked out at the register. When I couldn't hesitate anymore, I slowly approached Zeke and Deisel where they sat.

They both watched me get closer and stopped talking.

"Am I interrupting?" I questioned uncomfortably.

"Just talking business." Diesel smirked with his gnarly playboy grin.

"Are you done, Dove?" Zeke asked, sliding his empty glass across the bar top.

"Yeah." I slid my hands into my back pockets uncertainly. "It's early, but I'm tired. So, I think I'm just going to head home."

He quirked an eyebrow briefly before standing up. Diesel stayed put, other than sipping from his glass as he watched me.

"Let's go." Zeke nodded for me to come out from behind the bar and then glanced Diesel's way. "Don't fuck it up, D."

Diesel's snarly smirk did little to throw Zeke off, but it sent shivers down my spine. "I wouldn't dream of messing up something so angelic." His eyes slid down my body in his dominant way, and I hurried away from him.

Zeke led the way out through the still-crowded bar with his hand possessively on my back, steering me through the masses until we hit the sidewalk.

"What were you talking about?" I questioned him as he led me toward his black car sitting at the curb in VIP parking.

"Business." He responded.

"Then why did he look at me like that when he said it?" I countered, not interested in dropping the topic with his brush-off answer.

"Because he likes to live dangerously on the edge of life and death, always one smart-mouth response away from taking a bullet between the eyes." Zeke scoffed as if Diesel were some perpetually misbehaving child he had to discipline.

I dug my heels into the concrete and forced him to stop. "Does he traffic women?"

Zeke's eyebrows creased, and he leaned against the side of his car, watching me. "Why would you ask me that?"

"That's not an answer," I complained and then took a deep breath. "I don't know what he wants with me. All of my experience outside of my interaction with you leads me to believe that he does bad things to women."

"Then why do you trust him?" He threw back instantly.

"I don't." I shook my head, confused. Then his words from earlier flew back into my mind. *You touched him. Long before you ever touched me.* "Zeke." I sighed, hating that he felt like he'd somehow come in second place when he was the first and only man to ever make my body sing for him.

"Drop it." He cleared his throat. "He doesn't traffic women. But he does have sex slaves who for the most part agree to their dynamic. Though not all of them, and I'm not going to tell you anything else about it." He held his hand up when I opened my mouth to counter that information. "What Diesel Ames does in his bedroom does not interest me, Dove. The only thing about him that I care about is business-based."

I paused, forcing my lips to stay closed until I was confident that what I wanted to say wouldn't be misconstrued. "And what about with me?" I leaned back against the door of his car so he couldn't open it and end the conversation before I was ready. "Because you're acting like I've done something wrong because he continuously pops up around me. Yet all I've done is obsess over you since the moment I met you."

He stalked over to where I leaned against his sleek car before resting his forearm on the roof of the car behind me, leaning over me. "You've obsessed over me?" He tilted his head to the side, and I could tell he was trying to let go of his frustration over the biker. So, I rewarded him. "Tell me how."

Pressing my hands to his abs, I leaned into him, like I had any claim to his body or permission to touch him. Had he not made me come hours ago on my boss's desk, I might have stressed about it. But not now. He made his interest known, and I was going to lean into it. "You've heard me when I dream." I tried my best to sound seductive, and judging by the way his nostrils flared slightly as I spoke, I was pretty sure I was doing a good job. "You've heard me scream your name. Those weren't nightmares, and you know it."

"Tell me about them." he demanded, ignoring the busy sidewalk around us, though I was pretty sure he was still aware of every person and car moving at the same time. That was just who he was, always alert. "Tell me what happened in them."

"Well," I licked my lips, and his eyes fell to them as excitement burned in my belly. "The night you woke me up specifically, you were making me come."

"Dove." He growled, stepping closer until his hips pinned mine to the car. I didn't fear him or the contact. I didn't even worry about his intent or the effect I was having on him as a man.

I craved it.

I craved the power I felt when he looked at me like that.

"Do you want to know how?" I pushed, pressing my luck and testing even my own limits.

"You know I do." He lowered his face, so his lips were right above mine. "Tell me how you came for me."

"These lips." I breathed against them, mustering up all my strength and courage, high on the attention he had given me all night from his seat at the bar, "Your tongue. And your hands." I purred without even meaning to. "God, I came for you so hard."

"Get in the car." He growled, dusting his lips over mine as he pulled the handle on my door, "Or I'm going to show everyone on this street how fucking hard I can make you come."

I ducked under his arm and slid into the front seat, high on adrenaline and hormones, running my hands over my legs as he shut the door behind me with a feral look in his eyes.

Did I just poke the bear until he turned into a beast?

Oops.

"What are you doing?" I froze as I took in the sight before me.

Zeke sat reclined on my couch with a packet of paper in his hands, reading.

The kink quiz.

We had gotten home from the restaurant a while ago, and thankfully or not, I'm not sure, the temperature between us had cooled down a touch on the way home. So I went and took a shower to wash the smell of alcohol off my skin while Zeke relaxed.

Or I thought he had been relaxing.

"Reading." He replied, not even glancing up from the paper.

"Stop it." I rushed forward and lunged for the offensive test, but he moved faster than I did and pulled it just out of reach, leaving me sprawled out across his lap, empty-handed. "Don't read it."

"Why?" He cocked his head to the side and moved the paper when I tried to reach for it again. "Where did you get this?"

"Carly." I groaned, defeated, as I tried to stand up, but he was prepared and wrapped one arm around my waist, anchoring me to his lap.

He smelled so divine up close like this, and my eyelids wanted to flutter closed and give in to the feeling of his body under mine.

"Were you going to talk to me about these things?" He raised one eyebrow at me, making me still and relax in his hold.

"No," I admitted, and his eyes widened at my answer. "I'm not kinky." I shrugged, trying to fight the feeling of inferiority trying to come over me. "There's nothing to tell."

He tilted his head back and cleared his throat as he started reading from the list. "Desire to play a role or a part other than your own during intimacy." He flicked his eyes over to me, then back to the paper, "Interested." I winced slightly, but he wasn't done with me yet as he read another line. "Desire to be dominated during intimacy." He looked right at me, "Not interested."

"Can you stop now?" I shuddered. "I'm more than mortified."

"Why are you mortified?" He laid the paper down on the couch next to him and put both hands on my hips like we were a couple that was comfortable with touches like this.

"Because you're digging into my head," I replied. "Like you always do. But I don't want you there."

"Why don't you want me to get to know you?"

"That's not—" I stammered, "It's not that I don't want you to know me."

"That's what it sounds like." He countered. "You don't want me to know what you like or don't like sexually?"

"I don't—" I sighed. "I don't even know what I do or don't like."

"Exactly." He tilted his head to the side in that unnerving, calm and controlled way he always did. "This may be beneficial for both of us."

I rolled my eyes and tried to stand up so I could think straight. The pajama shorts set that I put on after my shower left a little barrier between our bodies, and I couldn't feel all of him against my skin and think at the same time.

But he wasn't interested in letting me go and tightened his hold on my hips when I tried to move again.

"Tell me what you're thinking."

"I only took that stupid paper with me because they were shoving it down my throat." I huffed.

"Did they force you to answer these questions?" He challenged.

"No." I groaned and tilted my head back to the ceiling. "I did that after I got home from therapy. And it just further points out my shortcomings and how incompatible we are."

His brows rose, and anger flashed behind his blue irises quickly before it disappeared. "You think we're incompatible? Seriously? Even after what I made you feel in that office?"

"I didn't—" I bit my lip, struggling to find the words.

"Tell me you don't feel the connection between us, and I'll leave you alone." He said, and panic filled my heart instantly. "Tell me you really think we're incompatible and I'll never touch you again."

"No." I gasped and shook my head, "I don't know how to be interesting for you. I don't know how to give you what you need. To *keep* you interested."

He growled and wrapped one hand around the back of my neck and held me to him as he kissed me, silencing my fears. "This." He whispered against my lips, "Talking, sharing, and discussing what you like and don't like, that's how we learn what each other needs." He kissed me deeper as I softened in his hold, "I'm so fucking interested in you, Laila. Just like this. I don't need flashy kinks to get me hard." He rocked me forward in his lap so I could feel the proof of his words. "I'm always fucking hard for you, Dove."

"Zeke." I groaned, fighting the war in my head that was trying to tell me I wasn't good enough.

"Don't think." He demanded, "Just feel. Just let your body tell you what it wants."

"Okay." I panted, fully puddled in his hands.

"Read me another line from that test." He said as he dropped his lips to my neck and teased the sensitive flesh there.

"Now?" I gasped, shivering as he ran the tip of his tongue from my collarbone to my ear.

"Now." He picked the paper up and pushed it into my hand. "Be a good girl, Dove, and do what I said."

"Jesus." I moaned, hating and loving how his words sent jolts of electricity through my body. "Okay." I held the paper off to the side and tried to focus on the words as he slid his rough hands up the back of my shirt, teasing the skin right above the waistband of my shorts. "Desire to restrain your partner during intimacy." I licked my lips as my head lolled to the side, "*Interested.*"

He growled and bit the lobe of my ear, "You want to tie me down, Dove?"

"God." I moaned again and nodded my head. "Yes."

"You like the idea of being in control of me?"

"Yes." I rocked my hips and rubbed myself against him again.

"Read me another."

"Desire to be blindfolded by your partner during intimacy? Interested."

"You're a switch." He smiled against my neck and leaned back. "You want to be in control and give over some control, too."

"I don't want to be dominated." I shook my head.

"I didn't say dominated." He clarified. "I said control. There's a difference. Read me another one."

"Desire to be intimate with your partner in a public place or with someone else watching." I snorted. "Not interested."

"Good." He growled, "No one gets to see what's mine. Another." He moved to the other side of my neck and nibbled on it.

"Desire to call your partner degrading terms such as whore, pet, and sissy." I shuddered, "Not interested."

Zeke smiled against my neck and nodded, "Another."

I groaned and skimmed the page, looking for one that might be useful for the conversation. "Last one," I said, and he rolled his eyes but smirked at me, leaning his head back against the cushion. "Desire to call your partner terms associated with authority, like daddy, or master." I swallowed and licked my lips, unable to say my answer out loud.

"What is your answer, Laila?" he prodded.

"What would your answer to that question be?" I countered, pulling at a piece of fuzz on his shirt.

"Do I want to call *you* Master?" He raised a brow at me jokingly. "No, can't say as I do."

"Do you want me to call you—" I swallowed again, my throat suddenly drier than the Sahara, "Master." I shrugged. "Or—Daddy?"

His eyes darkened dramatically, and his jaw clenched tightly as he stared at me. "This is about you, Dove, and what you want."

"I need to know," I whispered.

"Then you need to be brave and tell me about your feelings about it first." He stared directly at me, as if he could grasp how fucked up I felt in the head over this. "I can tell this one bothers you, and I want to know why."

"My father tried to kill me," I whispered. "And then he killed my mom and tried killing Jed." I shivered at the memories. "That man was the catalyst that derailed my entire life."

"What does that have to do with me?" Zeke asked calmly.

"I think—" I licked my dry lips and forced myself to take a deep breath and look at him directly, "Something inside of me gets excited by the idea of calling *you*—daddy." I groaned as soon as the words were out of my mouth as a blush heated up my entire face. "And that's fucked up, considering who my real fucking father was."

Zeke stood up with me in his arms, and I shrieked, clinging to his neck in surprise as he walked us across my apartment to my bed. He didn't say anything as he kneeled on the bed and lowered me into the center of it, following me down until he lay on top of me.

Anxiety should have bloomed inside my body, nausea should have rolled through my stomach, and fear should have ignited my survival instincts from being underneath of a man in a bed again.

But none of that happened.

It was as if I were watching the entire exchange from the side of the bed. He lowered his hips, pinning mine underneath him as my hands circled the back of his neck, holding onto him instead of pushing him away.

"Say it." He growled as he slid his warm hand up my side, gathering my shirt out of his way so he could touch my skin. I leaned into his touch instead of cowering away from it.

He was addictive.

He was powerful.

He was safe.

He was everything that should terrify me, but he didn't scare me. Ever.

"Laila." He growled again and stared into my eyes, "If you want to say it, do it."

"I'm fucked—" I started to argue.

"Shut up." He barked, closing his eyes, and taking a deep breath like he was on the edge of something unseen inside of him. "Say it."

"Do you want me to?" I questioned, looking for a reason amidst the chaos that was inside my head.

"I fucking need you to." He whispered, with his eyes still closed and his jaw tight. His hand ascended until he cupped the underside of my naked breast, and my back arched, pushing my chest up into his hand like a needy slut. He smirked a devilish grin as he moved his hand higher, squeezing my entire breast and toying with my nipple.

"Fuck." I moaned, digging my nails into the back of his neck, and curling towards him, desperate for more.

"Say it, Dove." He pinched my nipple. "And I'll reward you. Do what I want you to, and I'll make you come so hard, like the good little girl that you are."

"Daddy." I all but screamed, desperate for what he was promising and determined to figure out if calling him that was as hot as my brain had conjured up when I first read it.

And my God, was it ever.

"Good girl." He growled and flicked his wrist, lifting my loose pajama shirt until my breasts were bare to him for the first time. "Such a good fucking girl, Dove." He kissed down my neck and over my collarbones until his lips hovered right above my nipple, pinched between his fingers as he rolled it back and forth. "Daddy's going to make you feel so fucking good."

"Yes!" I cried, thrashing underneath him as he flicked his tongue over my nipple and sucked it into his mouth. The man was so talented with his fingers, his mouth, and his body. And he wasn't even inside me yet. He'd never even touched the bare skin under my pants, yet he had made me come multiple times.

Never once taking anything for himself.

"Zeke!" I cried, thrashing in his hold as he expertly played with me. It was only a few hours ago that he had made me come on my boss's desk, yet here he was again, pushing me into bliss. "I want to make you feel good."

"You do." He replied, never leaving my chest as he played with my nipples.

"No." I shook my head, trying to focus as he thrust his hips to rub my clit. "I want to make you come."

"No." He shook his head, rubbing his erection against me again. "That's not what this is about."

"Yes, it is." I groaned. "Don't you want to come?"

"I will." He growled, trying to get me to drop it.

"When?" I asked as my eyes rolled to the back of my head as he bit my nipple and sucked it hard. "Fuck."

"Stop worrying about me and focus on what I'm giving to you."

"I can't." I shook my head. "I want to make you feel just as good."

"You do, Dove." He growled again as he rolled his cock against my aching pussy through our pants. "You make me feel so fucking good. Every single time you look at me. Or talk to me. Or let me touch you." He groaned. "So fucking good."

"I want to make you come." I argued, fighting for control, as I slid my hand between our bodies, fighting against his weight until I reached my prize. I wasn't tentative or shy as I gripped his hard cock through his jeans. Afterall, dicks weren't new to me. But *wanting* to touch one, was. Wanting to pleasure a man until he was reduced to sounds and feelings only, was. Wanting to make *this* man lose control was new. "Please."

"Dove," He paused, resting his forehead against my sternum like he was fighting an internal war inside his head as I ran my nails over the tight fabric barely containing his erection.

God, he was so big. He'd fill me up until I couldn't breathe from feeling so full.

And I fucking wanted it.

"Don't make me beg, because I will." I whispered, hooking my leg around his, and pulling him back up my body until his face was in line with mine and his cock was sandwiching my hand against my crotch. I bit my lip as I flexed my knuckles, tightening my hold on him and rubbing my clit at the same time. "Please."

"Laila." He whispered, pushing his cock into my hand harder and making me moan from the friction my knuckles gave me.

"Daddy." I moaned, fighting the embarrassment as my carnal need took over my good sense. "Please let me make you come, Daddy."

"God." He hissed, thrusting into my hand again as his blue eyes dilated. "I'm only a man, Dove. And you're testing my strength here."

"Give me what I want, then." I bit my lip and smirked at him. "Come for me."

"Mmh." He moaned and leaned down to bite my neck as he started humping me into the bed. "You're topping from underneath me." I wrapped my legs around his waist as he rubbed that thick cock against my pussy, clinging to his shoulders for dear life as not an inch of space existed between us anymore. "And I fucking love it."

"Yes." I moaned, feeling powerful and submissive at the same time. "God, you feel so good."

"Wait until I'm inside you for the first time." He growled, rolling his hips, and rubbing against me in a new direction. "Wait until you take me deep."

"Yes!" I repeated, "God, I'm so close."

"Tell Daddy who you belong to." He pulled back to stare down at me as he pushed against me even harder. "Tell me you're mine, Dove."

"I'm yours, Zeke." I cried out, throwing my head back as my orgasm crashed into me like a freight truck. "I'm yours."

"Yes!" He roared above me, and I forced my eyes to open and watch him come undone. His eyes were closed, and his neck was taut as he thrust against me a few more times. "Jesus Christ, Laila." He moaned and slowed as I felt warmth wet the front of his jeans.

"Oh, my God." I panted, collapsing back into the blankets, and fighting to catch my breath. "It can't be healthy to come that hard."

He smirked that playboy one-sided grin I loved and rested his forehead against mine, taking a few deep breaths before kissing me softly. "I didn't deserve that gift, Laila."

"Why?" I questioned, feeling the happy, sated feeling deflating out of my body as he negated what had just happened between us.

"Because you deserve to be worshiped. I've already told you that."

"This wasn't worship?" I countered, "I vaguely remember calling out to God."

He rolled his eyes and pursed his lips before rolling off of me and sitting up on the edge of my bed with his back to me. "I want to do this right."

It was the first time I'd seen a vulnerable side of him. His shoulders were rounded, and it made him look smaller than normal, and I found that I hated seeing him that way. So, I slowly crawled to the end of the bed and sat next to him and made myself vulnerable to match his.

"I didn't think it was possible, but somehow being the only one receiving pleasure made me feel—" I hesitated, hating the word that came to mind, but it was the right one. "Used."

He looked over at me with his brows furrowed deep over his blue eyes. "That's not—" He swallowed angrily. "I never wanted to make you feel used, Laila."

"I know." I said reassuringly and took his hand in mine. "And in a way, it was different from how I felt when I was abused. But in a way it was similar too." I shrugged and looked away from his penetrating stare. "I don't want everything between us to be about my past. And you wanting to treat me like a princess and only give without taking made me feel like my past was in control of me again. Like I was back there in some warped way." Taking a deep breath, I looked back at him. "I just want you to treat me like every other woman you've been with, that's it. I just want to be normal. I want us to be normal."

He mulled that over for a while and then closed his eyes, nodding his head. "I'll be sure to remember all of that from here on out." He stared at me, "But I will never treat you like any other woman I've been with, because I've never cared about any of those women. Not like I care about you."

"I care about you too, Zeke." I sighed, resting my temple on his shoulder and letting the easy silence fill the space. "Enough to let you lock me away in a room, all alone, without me even noticing it. Again."

He smirked and kissed my forehead. "Careful, or I'll keep you all to myself forever."

"Hmm." I smiled against the tight muscle of his arm. "I don't think I'd mind."

CHAPTER 15 – LAILA

The text lit up my phone as I stared at it, trying to make it make sense in my sleepy brain. Deciding that I was nowhere caffeinated enough yet to respond, I got out of bed, stretching and groaning with each step to the coffeepot.

A date?

Zeke had left after our hot and steamy humping session on my bed, seeking a shower and clean clothes and a night's sleep before a big day at work today. Which left me with time to ponder the turn of events between us.

Normally, that would be fine. My therapist had done a pretty good job of giving me tools not to overthink things that didn't need to be. But then he hit me with that text first thing this morning, and I was left completely unsure of how to respond.

So, I did what any twenty something year old woman did when a drop-dead gorgeous, way out of her league man gave her the tiniest bit of attention.

I panicked.

And word vomited all over him through text message.

> A date?

> Like dinner and a movie?

> Or like hanging out somewhere dark and secluded?

> Because I did that once, and it didn't work out well for me.

> Ignore that.

> I'm sorry.

> I'm awkward.

> But you know that. So anyway. What exactly do you mean by a date?

> Because I feel like I need to know that before I accept or decline.

> Have I mentioned I've never been on a date before...

> Ever.

You probably want to take back your offer now, huh?

Okay, Bye!

"Stupid." I groaned, slamming my phone down on the counter as embarrassment kept coursing through me. My phone started dancing as a reply came in, and I flinched, reaching for it, fully expecting to get a message stating I was permanently blocked by Zeke. As if that was even a real thing.

Stop texting and take a deep breath.

Little bubbles flashed on the screen before his next text came through almost instantly.

Laila, do what I said.

I rolled my eyes but took a deep breath, and another message popped up.

Good girl.

I looked around my apartment, expecting to find him watching me, but I was alone. He was just that intuitive.

Now that I have your attention. There is a charity gala tomorrow night that Ryker hosts every year. I was hoping you'd like to go as my date.

Nothing seedy or morally corrupt. Just a man in a tux, with a woman in a dress on his arm, spending the evening together.

I chewed my lips as I rolled the image of him in a black tux through my brain and fought the panic trying to keep dragging me down.

His reply came again, and I sighed, rolling my eyes again.

That was the first time I had ever put my past into harsh words like that for him. But he needed to know I wasn't an evening gown wearing woman.

I was nothing.

Trash.

So far below that kind of event, it would be disrespectful to Ryker and Elora to even show up there as their little charity case dressed up like Cinderella when I was just the maid in real life.

My phone vibrated aggressively in my hand, with Zeke's name lighting up the screen as he called me. I contemplated ignoring it, but I knew deep down he'd just call back.

"Hello." I whispered, shame pushing my shoulders down onto the floor.

"You are not beneath this." His strong, dominant voice rang through the line. "You can't embarrass me, because I stopped caring about other people's opinions years ago, Dove."

I sighed, fighting stupid tears, I had no business crying over this topic. "I can't, Zeke."

"Okay." He responded, but I could hear all the things he wanted to say instead.

"I appreciate the offer. I just can't."

"I said okay." He replied. "What would you rather do?"

"What?" I started pacing my apartment, "Just because I can't go, doesn't mean you shouldn't go."

"I'm not going without you, Laila." he said firmly. "I'm not needed."

"Then why did you invite me?"

"Because the idea of suffering through the event seemed a whole lot more appealing if I was spending the evening with you on my arm." He mocked, as if it were obvious. "But if you're not comfortable going, then we'll do something else. Some other type of date."

"Won't that get you in trouble?" I questioned.

He grunted, and I imagined that one sided bad boy grin covering his sexy face as he talked. "I'm past the point of getting my pee-pee slapped for small shit like that. Ryker will have Jed and Carly there with him and Ellie to take care of anything that comes up."

The mental image of Ellie and Carly all dressed up in evening gowns, spending the evening with their men, created some sort of jealousy in my chest. Wasn't that what I longed for all those years locked away in that brothel, being abused by men who only cared about themselves?

Normalcy?

Sure, maybe spending a lavish night in a gown at an event worth more money than I'd ever see in my lifetime wasn't exactly the definition of normalcy. But spending the night with friends and a man I cared for was.

That was the normal I always hoped for.

The normal I craved.

The normal I deserved.

"Wait." I whispered and chewed on my lip as anxiety ripped through my stomach, making me second-guess every thought rushing through my brain.

"What is it?" he asked, dropping his voice deep in that way that made my toes curl, aching to somehow feel that tone across my skin. "Talk to me, Dove."

"I think I want to go." I admitted. "But I don't know why, because I hate crowds and every other part of the evening besides spending it with you and Jed and the girls makes me want to be physically ill, but—" I paused.

"But?" He urged.

"I think I have to."

"Explain to me what that means." His rumbling, deep voice kept me grounded as I fought to keep from spiraling.

I was going to need a therapy appointment before the conversation was done.

Communication.

That was the key to taking over my life and keeping control, wasn't it?

"I don't belong at an event like that." I started and I could hear him open his mouth, ready to dispute my claim and reassure me of all the ways he disagreed, but I stopped him. "But you're worth pretending that I do for the night." I smiled at myself, almost sadly. "I think maybe it might help me see the type of things I've missed out on." To lighten the mood I'd darkened, I sighed and threw out a joke. "Who knows, I'll probably hate it, have a panic attack in the middle of the place and create a huge spectacle that Ryker's business never recovers from and in five years, tomorrow night will single-handedly be the epicenter of the beginning of the entire Shadeport Crew's untimely demise."

"Are you done?" He drawled, unimpressed with my attempt at humor.

"You can't say it isn't possible."

"I actually can." He countered, growling at the end of his words just enough to let me know he was taking control back of the conversation.

"How do you know?"

"What do you feel when I touch you?" His deep voice dropped even lower until I could feel it in my belly.

"What?" I whispered with dry lips.

"When you're in my arms, when my lips are touching your skin, when my hands are gliding across your skin. What do you feel, Dove?"

"I—," I stammered, licking my lips, trying to figure out what exactly he wanted me to say. Somehow, I didn't think he wanted my response to be *like a horny teenager*.

"Don't joke." He commanded. "What do you feel when I touch you?"

"Peace." I replied honestly. "Calm. Yet somehow erratic and crazed and energized in ways I've never experienced before."

"You've never had a panic attack with me around." He asserted. "Because your body knows that I will take care of it, even if your head doesn't yet."

"Zeke." I breathed against the phone.

"You'll always be safe with me, Laila. No matter where or what we're doing. Even at a crowded and stuffy charity event, you will not fall. I've already told you, the only one of us that will fall will be me. To my knees at your feet. Simple as that."

"I don't know what to say." I admitted, utterly overwhelmed by his dedication to me, so quickly and effortlessly.

"Say you'll be my date." He sounded almost hopeful, and I heard a glimpse of the gentle man he'd shown me when we were alone.

"Okay." I whispered, still in awe of it all.

"Good."

"But—" I started, as reality set in. "I don't have—"

"Leave it to me." He replied, stopping my statement before I could start. "I'll take care of everything."

"Okay." I replied whimsically. "Whatever you say."

"Say it." He growled, and I instantly knew what he was demanding from me.

"Whatever you say, Daddy." I whispered shyly as excitement bloomed where fear and shame had tried to take hold before.

"Good girl."

An hour later, my front door opened, and I jumped a mile from my seat on the couch, screeching in surprise and then groaning when I saw Carly's blonde hair bob her way in through the frame. "Jesus, Carly!" I gasped, "You cannot do that to me!"

"Sorry." She smiled with only the smallest bit of remorse visible as she started moving around my small apartment.

"Can I help you?" I closed the book I'd been reading and watched her walk into my bathroom and come back with my bathrobe slung over one arm.

"Yes!" She pointed flippantly at me as she started opening my dresser drawers, "Where are your thongs?"

"My what?" I squirmed. "There are things you should never borrow from someone else, Carly. Butt cheek dental floss is most definitely at the top of that list."

She glared at me over her shoulder and rolled her eyes. "Not for me, dummy." She pushed my underwear around until she found the only semi-attractive pair of black lace panties I owned. "For you." She dropped them back inside. "We'll have to buy some."

"For what?" I crossed my legs under me, even more perplexed by her sudden visit.

"For the gala!" She sighed. "Keep up."

"I'd have to be moving to keep up." I challenged, "And right now I'm so lost I can't even stand."

She sighed and stopped assaulting my granny panties and shut the drawer before turning to me. "The dresses will be here in twenty minutes. Shoes, accessories, and jewels come after that. Then there's the hair and makeup trial since I'm sure you'll want to try a couple of different styles of both before deciding for sure."

"Stop." I held my hand up, shaking my head. "English, Carly. Or take your Greek out of my place because you're giving me a headache."

"God, it's no wonder you and he get along so well. You're both so boringly dramatic when I get excited."

I deadpanned, "Get out."

"Zeke arranged for you to be spoiled like the perfect little princess you are to him, and we have to go."

"Zeke did what?"

She groaned and threw her head back as she stopped by the couch, tossing my shoes down on the floor, just stopping short of touching me and lifting me off the couch herself. Thank God even in her dramatic underwear snooping tirade, she remembered my boundaries.

I'd be sure to add my panties to that hard limit list in the future, though.

"Come on, I'll explain on the way."

"But where?" I slid my feet into my shoes but crossed my arms before following her like she so desperately wanted me to. "Triggers, Carly." I reminded. "I don't follow people anywhere, let alone blindly."

"Oh, right." She paused and took a deep breath. "Sometimes I forget, especially lately, because you don't seem so skittish all the time." She offered a small smile. "Ellie's house. To find a dress and all the fixings for the charity gala tomorrow. Zeke called and said he wanted you pampered and completely armored up for the event." She scrunched her nose at the description. "I'm not sure what armor has to do with lingerie—" She shrugged, "But whatever."

I smiled at the description, knowing exactly what he meant. He wanted me to feel like I looked the part of a gala guest to alleviate some of my anxiety and fear of falling short.

That man.

"I think I'm happy for you," She said, drawing my attention back to her standing there staring at me, catching my love drunk stargazing smile, "But I'm trying to gauge my reaction on yours, and I've never seen you so—" She tilted her head to the side like she was studying me, "Giddy."

"I'm not giddy." I rolled my eyes.

"Are too." She shrugged her shoulders as she motioned for me to walk out first. "And you have every fucking right to be, believe me. It's just uncharted territory for me." She closed the door behind us as I walked us out to the exit.

"Yeah, me too." I whispered under my breath.

"Oh my God," Elora clapped excitedly before sighing and staring at me like a blushing bride on her wedding day in a small country chapel.

"Stop it." I turned back to the mirror, ignoring her and Carly both as the stylist pulled the skirt of the dress out in a dramatic fan, letting it billow out around my legs.

The legs that were only actually covered by the fabric when I stood completely still and straight. Heaven forbid I moved my hips in one direction or the other without causing the wild and daring slit to open up completely to the revealing spot directly under my right hip bone.

Right next to my hoo-ha.

"How do you feel?" Carly asked cautiously from her spot behind me, more in check than she had been in my apartment earlier after seeing the myriads of emotions that had assaulted me all afternoon.

"Like a stripper." I groaned, "No offense."

"None taken," She shrugged nonchalantly. "I never wore that much fabric on stage."

"Me neither." I whispered, taking in my reflection as I blocked out all those nights, walking the stage for men to view me before they purchased.

"Give us a few." Elora shooed the stylist and the glam team out, closing the ornate double doors behind them, enclosing us in her lavish dressing room alone. "What's on your mind?"

I shook my head as my hands slid down the beaded bodice covering my stomach. "Unfamiliarity." I swallowed and flicked a glance at the two women, who had quickly become the only friends I had in the world. "I don't recognize that girl." I nodded to my reflection in the mirror.

"Who does she look like?" Carly asked, standing at my side, watching me close.

"Like a goddess." I shook my head. "See why I'm failing to find the similarities?"

"You know who she looks like to me?" Elora asked, taking her place on my other side.

"Hmm?" I hummed speculatively.

"Like a butterfly who just broke free from that small, confined space that held her down while she grew her wings."

"Ach," I scoffed.

"She's right." Carly gently took my hand in hers and stared at me in the mirror, waiting for me to gaze back at her. "This is who you were meant to be all along, Laila." She smiled sadly, tightening her hand in mine. "It just took you far longer than you needed to be able to stretch those wings and feel that freedom."

"I don't know her." I stared back at the dark-lined brown eyes that used to look so plain and lifeless before today. Now, they looked fierce.

Strong.

"That's okay." Carly reassured me. "We all have to find ourselves once we finally have the strength to walk away from what we used to know."

"It was like that when I reconnected with Ryker." Ellie smiled wistfully. "I was just a kid the last time I knew him, and life was *not* kind to me between then and when we ran back into each other."

Carly scoffed, bugging her eyes out. "That's putting it lightly." She said and then paused. "You know, you both kind of had similar shitty introductions to the real world, if you think about it."

"How so?" I asked, not believing that the Queen of Shadeport ever really struggled like I did, but at the same time, she had darkness in her eyes now and then that seemed familiar.

Elora chuckled humorlessly. "Well, it started when my dad, who was my very best friend, was assassinated and died in my arms in the middle of his own turf." My stomach cramped at the information and the dead look in her eyes as she said it. "And then my drug-addicted mother stole me away from Ryker and any bit of stability I had left in the wake of my father's death. Only so she could steal the money he sent her for my care to spend on drugs and men." She raised her eyebrows as I turned to face her. "Oh, and then there was the time she locked me in a motel room and had a line of men outside, paying her for a go with me when I was sixteen. One even paid an extra few bucks to take my virginity."

"Jesus." I hissed. "I had no idea."

She shrugged her shoulders and then stiffened her spine. "I was luckier than you were, Laila, because I escaped before any of them touched me." She said firmly, "But then I was homeless and starving, working a dozen dead-end jobs, just trying to survive."

"And that's when I found her." Carly smiled sadly at her, pulling her into her arms. "And I nursed this little birdy back to health and kept her fed when she'd let me until she found Ryker again."

"Now look at me." Elora winked at her best friend. "The Queen. Married to the dark and dangerous King, with a perfect little prince."

"It's like a fairytale." I smiled dreamily at her as she took my hand and squeezed.

"The specifics may be different, but there are a lot of similarities to our lives. Which means you can get your happily ever after too. Even if you don't think so."

I felt the familiar prickles of doubt trying to shut down the tingles of excitement and hope building from her testimony.

"You mean I can have my turn with the dark and dangerous King now?" I winked at her and then turned back to the mirror as she glared at me good-heartedly.

"Careful." She warned. "You may be Carly's sister-in-law, but I'll still kill you for that man."

"Don't doubt her," Carly added with a laugh. "She watched Zeke kill her mother while she fucked Ry in the next room."

My eyes bugged out as an icy chill bloomed over my spine, and I could tell from the nonchalant shrug Elora gave she was telling the truth.

"I'm not exactly proud of it." Elora chirped, "But I'm not ashamed either." She pointed her finger at me with a pointed glare. "So don't get any ideas."

Raising my hands, I shook my head. "I'm apparently more interested in the man who did the killing than the fucking." I shrugged. "Who knew?"

Carly snorted, "This conversation got weird, quick."

"But hey," Elora pointed out, "You forgot all your worries pretty quickly, didn't you?"

I chuckled and glanced back at the reflection of the done-up woman staring back at me. "Yeah, I did. For now, at least."

CHAPTER 16 – ZEKE

"**G**round rules." Jed barked authoritatively from the back seat.

"Here we go." Ryker sighed, rubbing his fingers over his forehead as I glanced at him out of the corner of my eye.

"Before you say another word," I adjusted the rearview mirror to stare at Jed where he took up the entire backseat of Ryker's large SUV, "Just know that whatever you tell me not to do, I'm going to do ten times worse just because you thought you could be the boss." I raised my eyebrow at him as his jaw clenched while I drove through busy downtown traffic, nearing the event. "So please continue."

"I fucking hate you." Jed complained but turned to look out the window, ending any further rule-giving he was about to do.

"Yeah, I know." I sighed, pulling the SUV past the police barricades to the private entrance behind the swanky hotel the event was being hosted at.

I parked the car and got out, scanning the buildings around us and the barricades on the street, keeping the riffraff out and allowing only the most elite of the VIP guests in for the evening.

"Perfect timing." Ryker nodded to the black limo pulling up, sandwiched between two of our cars filled with men, convoying the most elite guests of the event in. "You look nervous, old boy." He hit my stomach with the back of his hand as I buttoned my tux up, staring at the blackout windows, hoping for a glance inside.

"She deserves a perfect night." I tore my eyes away as Elora's personal guards flanked both sides of the car and opened the back door.

"She does." Ryker admitted, pointing a glance at Jed, who squinted his annoyance at him.

"I'm not going to fuck it up." He said defensively.

Before either of us could counter that obvious lie, Elora stepped out of the limo, smiling brightly at Ryker and stealing away the attention of everyone around.

She looked stunning in a dark blue velvet dress that reminded me of the obscenely big sapphire that old lady dropped into the ocean in that movie. But fuck it, she deserved her perfect night too, so I gave her a nod as she winked at me, stepping aside so the next woman could get out as Ryker guided her to the pristine carpet laid out just for them.

I could tell by the shoe alone; the next woman was Carly. Flashy and blindingly encrusted with jewels, it matched her white sparkly gown. It did some weird tuxedo thing where the skirt was short and tight around her thighs with a sheer tail of sparkling fabric flowing down to her ankles.

It was so Carly that it was painful yet entertaining to watch.

"Damn." Jed grunted, stepping forward out of his trance to take his woman's hand and walk her over to where Ryker and Elora waited at the entrance.

Which meant Laila was the last one inside.

Was she inside?

Did she back out and leave me standing here like a fool?

Did she let her fear get the better of her?

The earlier anxiety I felt shifted to a more acute form of nervousness the moment that incredibly alluring foot touched the ground.

My feet were moving before my brain processed anything until I was pushing the guard aside and holding my hand out for my date.

"Dove." I sighed as her warm brown eyes stared up at me from the seat with relief and nervousness burning bright in them.

"Hi." She gave me a small smile and slid her hand into mine, squeezing it for dear life as she stood up.

"My God." I growled, scanning her from the top of her soft, curled chocolate hair to her shoulders bare above the modest yet romantic heart-shaped neckline of her strapless red dress. Her makeup was dark, and it made her look like a Viking warrior, and I loved every single inch of it. "This dress." I slowly slid my eyes down her lush body, stepping back to take in the whole package as she blushed and made a small spin for me.

"Do you like it?" She slid her hands down the tight corseted top to where the fabric loosened under her hips and pooled around her legs. "It's daring." She shifted her hips a little, and a slit opened up, baring her entire leg to my hungry eyes. The black strappy sky-high heels she wore tied the outfit together.

"It's nothing compared to you." I brought my eyes back to hers. "Do you have any idea how brave you look right now?"

"In my armor?" She asked, raising her brow at me with a smirk. "Thank you for this, Zeke." She slid her hands down the gown again. "I feel like a goddess."

"Because you are." I leaned forward and kissed her cheek as Carly cat-called from behind us.

"You two want us to give you some alone time?" she asked, and Laila chuckled shyly, pulling back to look up at me.

"Are you ready?" I asked, sliding to the side, "It's not too late to change your mind, and we can go get takeout in our evening wear." I winked, and she leaned into me.

"Promise me you won't leave my side?"

"Not for a second." I replied instantly, meaning every word.

"Then I'm good." She smiled brightly, took a deep breath, and looked at where our friends were waiting for us. "Let's do this shit." She giggled.

I tipped my head back and laughed at her tough-guy voice and slid her arm through mine, anchoring her to my side as we joined our group. "Let's do this shit."

I watched Laila from the corner of my eye as we made our way into the event, already in full swing. Socialites, politicians, billionaires, celebrities, and professional athletes mingled across the gold floor with their overpriced clothes and obnoxious attitudes. I didn't care one way or another, I never had. They weren't my people after all, just the people I worked for. But I was interested in Laila's opinion of it all.

Her wide brown eyes flicked over everything so quickly, I wasn't sure she was even processing half of it, but I knew what she was looking for.

Danger.

Threats.

Escapes.

She just needed to trust she'd never need any of those things at my side. I'd protect her.

I'd give her the escape she needed.

"Wow." She whispered, watching Ryker and Jed lead the girls to the table at the front of the room before he pulled Ellie off to shake hands and mingle. "Do you always attend events like this?"

"Not if I can help it." I grumbled, smirking down at her perfect face.

"You fit in well." She patted the front of my tux with a smile on her red lips. "Even with the tattoos peeking out."

"I don't belong with these people." I slid the backs of my fingers up her bare arm, admiring the goose bumps as they grew on her skin. "Most of these people—" I looked out over the crowd with disdain, "they view me as a tool." I looked back down at her instead of at the people I hated. "The boogeyman they hire to do the bad things they're too weak to do themselves."

"You've built your reputation on being the man willing to do those things." She tilted her head, "But it doesn't mean you have to be."

"Hmm." I hummed, "It's hard to suddenly become something different after so many years."

"But not impossible." She smiled sadly, "Look at me," She fanned her hands over her evening gown, "The poor captive girl, turned charity gala goer." She shrugged, "Nothing's impossible at the end of the day I suppose."

"Perhaps." I leaned down and gave in to the urge to kiss her that had been plaguing me since she got out of the limo. She leaned into me, sliding her hands over my chest when I lingered against her lips. "But you have belonged here all along." I pulled back and quirked my eyebrow down at her body. "You're a perfect fit in a gown."

She snorted and rolled her eyes dismissively, "It's just lipstick on a pig." She said nonchalantly and then stopped me as I called her out for degrading herself, "But thank you anyway."

"Zeke." A voice called from behind us, silencing anything else I wanted to say to her about her negativity, and we turned to the approaching guest.

"Howard." I nodded, sliding my hand around Laila's waist and pulling her against my side. "I didn't think you were coming tonight." I said pointedly to the seedy, sniveling, pathetic excuse for a man that was trying his best to act like he fit in with the surrounding crowd.

"Pfft." He waved his hand dismissively with a shrug, "Clerical error between Ryker's people and mine, that's it." His eyes left mine and slid down to where Laila leaned against me fully, like she was trying to hide within me, but her face gave away no sign of distress. I could tell she just wasn't comfortable with strangers, but she wasn't upset. And she was an impeccable judge of character, meaning she probably could pick up on what a snake Howard Sheffield was.

"Interesting." I drawled, refusing to go further into the fact that the man was not only not invited tonight, but he was also blacklisted from the event completely. Yet there he stood, chatting me up like he belonged.

"Anyway, not the point." He moved on, "I really just wanted to talk to you about the Hoffman organization—"

I moved fluidly, sliding Laila behind my back, and stepping into Howard's space, towering over the top of him until his fat, grotesque stomach pressed against my front. "If you want to keep that disgusting piece of fat you call a tongue inside of your mouth where it belongs, then I suggest you stop using it to do anything other than swallow the free food you no doubt already gorged yourself on. Because if you dare to use it to speak to anyone in this room about anything other than the fucking charity we're here to support tonight, I'll cut it out in the middle of the dancefloor." I sneered down at him as his eyes flicked from side to side, as if he'd find a hero amongst my men. "Get the fuck out of here." I snapped my fingers over the back of his balding head, and two security members from the crew stepped up immediately. "Remove him," I growled, "and ensure he doesn't fucking dare to come back."

"I was invited!" Howard cried as the guards pulled him backward. "I want to talk about the merger!" He yelled desperately, dragging the curious gazes of other partygoers as they watched the drama unfold. "I need in on that merger!"

One of the guards delivered a well-placed punch to his side, knocking the air out of his lungs and effectively silencing him as they pulled him from the ballroom and to a holding room where they would no doubt deliver a few more hits to get the point across.

"Pathetic." I sneered, trying to shake the mere thought of him from my memory. I turned and froze when I saw the look on Laila's face as she watched the man being dragged from the room before her doe eyes flicked up to mine. "Dove." I exhaled as panic set into my spine.

I fucked up.

Again.

She dropped her eyes and licked her lips, feigning an attempt to adjust her skirt as she composed herself, but I couldn't find the words to fix this.

"It's fine." She rushed out but still wouldn't look at me. "I was just surprised by the—," she paused and took a deep breath, "Intensity of it."

"I'm sorry." I sighed, reaching up to brush her arm again, but stopped short.

"Don't." She scowled, and anger filled those brown eyes. "It's exactly the same thing that happened the other night at the restaurant." She stopped, widening her eyes. "It excited me. Which always catches me off guard."

"Zeke." Another voice called out, and I clenched my teeth, fighting the urge to punch the owner of this voice for interrupting us again, but stopped, because punching my girl's brother was off limits. Tonight anyway.

"What?" I snapped, twisting around to face Jed as he stopped short with Carly right on his heels.

"You good?" He glanced at Laila, who still stood at my back, as she slid her arm through mine and pressed her body against my side.

"We're great." She answered for me. "Doesn't that type of thing always happen around you, men?"

Carly smirked and shrugged. "Kind of, yeah."

"Exactly." Laila nodded curtly before looking up at me. "Nothing to see here."

"Then let's sit." Jed said pointedly, "Before anyone else wants to interrupt our night with business bullshit."

CHAPTER 17 – LAILA

"**I** need a drink." Carly said, rolling her eyes as Jed smiled at a middle-aged woman who had been chatting his ear off for no less than fifteen minutes.

He was charming her, sure. But only for her money for the cause. I knew that. Carly knew that. But I could see the jealousy burning in her eyes at losing his attention for so long.

Zeke had been dutiful all night long, staying not only by my side like he promised, but keeping his skin pressed to mine, physically aligning ourselves. And it was working.

As people came and went to our table, pulling the guys into boring business talks, or hushed whispers of shady dealings, I never got worked up or uncomfortable. Maybe it was because Carly and Elora were just as bored as I was, but it felt—normal?

Tedious, sure.

But normal.

"Come with me." Carly slid her hand in mine and pulled, but Zeke tightened his hold on my waist, never breaking the conversation with the man I recognized from the big city news station. He merely glared at her for a moment, mid-sentence, and continued without missing a beat.

Which, of course, made me giggle because the ridiculousness of the whole thing was just too much.

Zeke, Mr. Big, Bad and Serious, was being attentive and caring, while continuing on with his dark business dealings.

It was all a bit mind swirling to keep up with.

"Oh, come on, Cueball, let her come with me to the bar." Carly whined, pulling my arm again. "If not, I'm going to cause a scene, and that's bad business." She droned on dramatically.

"It's fine." I whispered to Zeke, glancing over at the bar across the room. "Just come find me when you're done." I leaned up and kissed his cheek, drinking in the open affection between us. "I'll be okay with her."

"Dove." He warned, flicking his glance at the bar. "I made you a promise, and I intend on keeping it."

"I know." Smiling up at him, "I'm trying to be a good friend, too." I shrugged, "Help me figure out how to do both."

"I don't like it." He said, and I could feel the growl in his chest as the man he was talking to stared at us openly like he was witnessing history in the making. I could almost hear his newscaster's voice shouting out the headline of our affair.

"Come find me in a few minutes, then I'll let you steal me away, even if Jed is still being a bad boyfriend."

He looked over at Jed's big back as he laughed at something the woman said, and Carly's nails dug into my wrist as her bright blue eyes darkened like a storm was brewing. "I'll make sure he wraps things up quickly." Zeke said perceptively, loosening his hold on my waist and letting Carly pull me away into the crowd.

"Slow down." I hissed as she weaved through one elegant evening dress at a time until we were pressed up against the elaborate mahogany-topped bar. "Jesus, Carly."

"I was going to tear her fake ass chlorine green extensions from her ugly fucking head if I stayed put one more second." she muttered, waving down the bartender intensely. "Four shots of tequila, top shelf." She demanded without so much as a *Hi, how are you.*

"Uh, I'm not drinking." I corrected, sending an apologetic smile to the young girl readying the glasses.

"None of them are for you." Carly snapped her fingers as the bartender froze, "Four shots. Now. Please." She added, and if she hadn't added the please at the end, I probably would have slapped her.

I bit my tongue as the girl set the glasses and the limes down on the bar top, eager to leave us to help more polite guests, I was sure. When she was out of earshot, I slapped Carly's arm. "That was so rude."

"I'm sorry." She sighed after tipping back the first glass and hissing in her exhalation. "I'm wound up and angry and horny and none of those make for a clear head."

"Ew." I shivered and shook my head. "I didn't think you got jealous." I mused, "What with the whole exhibition kink and all."

She scoffed, downing her second shot. "I'm rabid when it comes to other women trying to get what's mine, on a good day." She shivered and grimaced at the second shot. "But it's ten times worse lately."

I put my hand on top of hers to stop her from throwing back number three in rapid-fire succession, "Wait." I pushed it away. "Just slow down."

"I can't!" She whined in a way that was so very not like her, I was shocked. "I can't fucking stop because I can't get control over my emotions!" She looked at me with wide blue eyes, and I recognized the panic in them. "I'm positively manic."

"Take a deep breath." I ordered and picked up the two shots and handed them to a passing woman, "Here, on the house." I winked, trying for confidence I didn't possess, and the woman paused only for a moment and then smiled.

"Thanks."

"No problem." I waved it off and turned back to Carly, who looked like she was either going to burst into tears or vomit. "Okay, back to the problem at hand. Jed chatting with a woman nearly—" I looked out over the crowd back to the table where the woman brushed her hand over Jed's upper arm like she was feeling for muscles and I cringed as Carly groaned, "Twice your age," I fibbed a little to make her feel better, "It doesn't actually bother you; I know that, and I think you know that." She rolled her eyes and huffed, but didn't contradict me because she knew I was right. "So, there's something else pushing these emotions up to the surface, or perhaps something you're subconsciously trying to cover up with the very unlike you jealously. So, which is it?"

She hesitated and looked around the space as if she were looking everywhere but at me.

"What is it?" I urged and then held my hand up, thinking better of it. "If you don't want to tell me, I understand, but maybe you should at least talk to Jed about it. Something tells me he has no idea you're upset about something."

She sighed and leaned against the bar, "I'm late."

My mind swam as I tried to figure out how she could be late to an event she was already at, and then it clicked.

And millions of different emotions buzzed through my head at lightning speed creating panic before I forced myself to imagine that the panic was a physical thing inside of my head and I grabbed it mentally, forcing it to stay still and stop causing mayhem like my therapist had taught me. I glanced back at the table for Zeke, knowing I was going to need him ASAP if this conversation went the way I thought it was going to go, but he was mysteriously missing. And he was nowhere between there and the bar, on his way to me.

He was gone.

"Say something." Carly whispered, and I forced myself back to the present, pushing Zeke's absence to the back of my mind as I tried to give my future sister-in-law what she deserved most.

Support.

It was exactly what she had given me, unwaveringly, since she whispered my name to Jed that night in the brothel and set the wheels in motion to rescue me.

"Have you taken a test?"

She shook her head as her blue eyes misted over. "I'm too scared to."

I nodded and picked her hand up from the bar top, squeezing it tight and forcing her to look at me. "Does Jed know?"

She silently shook her head and stared at her feet. "I don't know how to tell him that there's a chance I could be giving him something he's always wanted," She looked up at me with those tear-filled eyes, "When I'm not sure I want it at all."

My chest ached with her words, but I fought it down.

It was not about me.

It was about her. I had to focus on her because she deserved it. I owed her.

I just wasn't sure how much it would cost me to give it to her.

"You don't know if you want kids?" I asked quietly, glancing around us to make sure there were no prying ears. "But Jed does."

She swallowed and nodded her head, "Since Gavin was born, it's all he talks about." She shuddered, "But I'm not sure I'm meant to be a mom. Even if he was born to be a dad." She covered her face. "I drank. Fuck!" She yelled behind her hands. "Just another fucking sign I'm not cut out for this!"

"Shh." I hushed her, rubbing my hands over her arms as she started panicking. "Go to the bathroom." I said firmly, "Get it out. I don't think it can actually hurt a baby this soon if it's not a lot, but I don't know, and I'm not willing to let you put something else on your conscience."

"Jesus." She cried. "I'm fucking everything up."

"It's okay." I reassured her, "You're allowed to be scared, either way. This is huge," I leveled my stare at her, "You're not a bad person for being scared or in doubt."

"Maybe." she said weakly.

"Can I get you Jed?" I asked, "Or Elora?"

She bit her lip. "I just want Jed." Her perfectly lined lips trembled slightly, "I shouldn't have kept this from him tonight like I could just pretend everything was fine." She groaned, "I should have just tested at home first!"

"Shh," I hushed her again, "Don't build yourself up. Okay, just go to the bathroom and I'll get Jed for you."

She nodded with a ghostly white face. "You're right." She nodded again, "Okay, thank you, Laila." She hesitated and then decided to just grab me and pull me into a hug, "I needed your surprising calmness right now."

I chuckled, "Glad I could keep it together for you." I joked and pushed her off toward the bathroom.

Having watched her disappear into the restroom, I turned back toward the table, intent on finding Jed for her as promised. It shouldn't be hard, considering he was a seven-foot-tall Viking. But alas, he was missing from the damn spot he'd been held up chatting with that woman for half an hour.

"Fucking perfect." I cursed under my breath as I started weaving through the crowd, trying to find anyone from the crew I knew to ask if they could find Jed for me. My phone was in Zeke's pocket because sexists fucks that made dresses never sewed pockets into them. I ducked around a group and tried to cut back toward the edge of the room to where it wasn't so crowded, but a figure stood up from a table and I slid on the skirt of my dress and smacked straight into it, hard enough to rattle my teeth. "Oof." I grimaced.

"Careful now." A smooth voice called out as two hands grabbed my upper arms to steady me. "Don't want to fall on your ass in the middle of a crowd."

I was anything but steady as I jumped backward, fighting the tight hold on my arms until he let go. My ears rang violently as my heart seized completely in my chest, creating a catastrophic pain to ricochet through the empty cavity where my heart used to beat.

That voice.

"Are you okay?" he asked again, stepping back into my personal space as the darkness of the outer edge of the room cut us off from most of the other guests.

That fucking voice.

Darkness crowded my vision, blocking anything in my peripherals until all that existed was him.

It felt like I was back in that room.

Tied down.

And gagged.

As a monster mutilated my body because of this man standing in front of me.

Ruined me because of this man. Stole my future because of this man.

His inky black hair, styled to perfection, seemed poised to take flight like a toupee in a gale. His fake-tanned skin and his ul-tra-bleached teeth contradicted each other as he smiled down at me. "You alright darling, you look like you've seen a ghost." He said with that sadistic humor he loved to use when he was torturing young girls. But as I fought the urge to throw up on his shoes, and forced myself to focus on escaping his clutches, I realized he didn't know who I was. "What's your name, sweetheart?" He asked, reaching out to touch me again, and even though I tried, I couldn't control the flinch as I evaded his touch.

"Don't touch me." I snarled, feeling a rage inside of me like I'd never felt before. All my adult life, I had experienced such tumultuous emotions that most days felt like they controlled me more than I controlled them.

Fear.

Pain.

Disgust.

Anguish.

Pain.

Grief.

Sorrow.

Pain.

But right now, facing off with the man who single-handedly de-stroyed my very body and soul—all I felt was rage. Blinding rage that left me imagining what it would feel like to stab something sharp into the fleshy part of his neck, severing the arteries and veins necessary for blood flow to and from his brain, and then watch him bleed out at my feet.

Would I feel justice?

More grief?

Perhaps pain?

"Whoa now." He smiled and held his hands up theatrically as a man passing by heard my snarl and looked on curiously. "I just wanted to make sure you didn't fall, that's all."

"Move out of my way." I demanded, realizing he was blocking my path back to the bar where I at least would be in the glowing lights of the party again, and not tucked into a dark corner like I was.

I watched him closely as the entertainer's smile slid off his face and a more serious look clouded his eyes. "You look familiar." he said, squinting and tilting his head like he was trying to see me clearer. "Have we met before?"

"Ah, there you are." A female voice cut through the buzz of the crowd as Elora pushed past the man who was blocking my path. "I've been looking for you." She said pointedly to me as she slid her arm through mine and stood at my side. "Senator Lupold." She addressed the monster in front of me. "Harassing one of my guests. *Again*. Why am I not surprised?" Elora didn't mince words, nor did she cover the disdain in her voice as she addressed him.

I reveled in her strength and power, witnessing the Queen in her element for the first time since meeting her.

"Elora." The monster replied, adjusting his jacket as he stood up to his full height, like he hadn't just been cornering me in the dark.

"*You* may call me Mrs. Lawson." She whipped her retort back at him, reminding him who and where he was. "I don't care for your bought title, but here," She glared openly at him, "Amongst *my* people, you will respect mine."

I flicked a glance at the man who had haunted my dreams for years as Elora knocked him down a dozen pegs of manhood and power with words alone, in awe of her.

"My apologies," He replied, but I could feel the barely restrained anger in his words, "Mrs. Lawson. I was simply chatting with your friend here—" He paused, tipping his head and waiting for one of us to give him my name, which was obviously sought after.

"No, you were harassing her." Elora snapped, "And make no mistake, Charles," She spit out his name like it was disgusting, "There are no less than a dozen men in this room watching you right this second, ready and very, *very fucking eager* to make a worthless, greedy, pathetic man like you disappear." She stood up even taller, "For good."

His face reddened, and his jaw clenched as he looked from her to me and then out over the crowd, like he was looking for proof of her threat. "I've always been in good standing with Ryker," He challenged, as though that would give him any credit in the conversation, "You simply don't know what your—"

"Enough." Elora snapped and pulled me away from the corner and the sniveling man, who she handled in ways I always dreamed of. "Get out of my sight or I'll make sure you never talk through that disgusting mouth of fake teeth ever again."

He sputtered, but Elora didn't wait for any rebuttal he had to give at her dismissal and walked us across the busy floor.

"Easy." She said soothingly, "Deep breath."

I realized then that I was clinging to her like a life raft in a hurricane and nearly hyperventilating from the entire scenario.

"Jed." I whispered, closing my eyes, and fighting for control of my body and emotions, but I was losing. Spiraling directly into a panic attack that would rival any other I'd ever had before. "Carly needs Jed." I needed to finish my task of helping my friend, and then I needed to get the fuck out of this event and out of this dress. "She's in the bathroom."

"I'll get him, but what about you?" she asked firmly, leading me through the tables like she had a destination in mind when all I could do was manage to put one foot in front of the other on autopilot. "What do you need? What happened?"

"I need to find Zeke." I cried, losing my grip.

"He's right here." She turned, and we cut to another dark area of the room where Ryker was conversing with men in the shadows, reminding me that so much of the men's lives were shady and dangerous.

But at that moment, all I could see was Zeke's serious face watching us as we approached. He didn't say anything, simply moved through the crowd of men and was on me in an instant.

He slid both hands over my cheeks and around the back of my neck as I buried my face in his jacket. Embarrassment and grief didn't even have a chance to take hold of me as I fought the terror of memories and flashbacks, trying to stay on my feet.

"Get her out of here. Take her home." Elora commanded, but Zeke was already pulling me, still wrapped in his arms and shielded from any prying eyes as he opened a door I didn't even notice and pulled us through into an empty service hallway.

"Dove." He groaned as he scooped my legs out from under me and held me to his chest as he flew through the hallway away from the party. "I'm sorry. Hold on to me. Hold on to me, Laila."

"I'm so broken." I whispered as every bit of sorrow crashed over me, consuming me, and drowning me in it until I didn't think I'd ever reach the surface again.

CHAPTER 18 – ZEKE

"Tell me what you need." I implored as she paced back and forth in the small meeting room. It was the first place I could get her to after carrying her from the ballroom. She was spiraling and needed privacy, and it would have to do until I could get her outside and home.

Fuck, I never should have made her come to the gala in the first place.

She clawed at her neck and mumbled to herself as she walked the length of the room before turning back and going in the opposite direction, only to do it again at the next wall. "Dove, please." I begged, trying to break through her haze.

I let her down. Something triggered her after I left her alone, but I didn't know what it was.

Ten minutes. That was it, I was only gone for ten minutes.

"Laila." I raised my voice, "Stop." She froze like she was finally even aware of her surroundings and blinked at me.

"Sorry." She whispered, swallowing and dropping her hands to her sides. "I'm sorry." She looked at the locked door behind me. "I fucked up."

"No." I stepped forward, and she stiffened, so I stopped. "You didn't do anything wrong, Laila." She flicked her glance at the door again, and I tried not to get offended by her obvious discomfort at being alone with me. We'd been making such progress with closed spaces, I thought we were past it, but maybe the triggering caused her to regress. "Talk to me though, tell me what happened while I was gone."

She shook her head before the words were even out of my mouth and started pacing again. "No." She kept shaking her head. "I can't."

"Okay." I recanted, "Okay, then tell me what you need. Tell me how I can help you."

"You can't." She tipped her head back and closed her eyes as desperation took hold of her. "I just need to escape."

"Escape." I took a step closer to her now that her eyes were closed, and she wasn't watching me. "Escape how?"

"My head." She slapped the palms of her hands against her temples repeatedly. "I just want to get out of my head!" Her anxiety climbed with each word. "I don't want to be inside my head anymore!" Her face crumbled. "I hate it inside here. All there is—is pain!"

"You aren't trapped." I closed the distance, fighting the anxiety growing inside of me as she broke. "You are free." I slid my hands over her arms, and she leaned into me instead of bolting out of my hold like I thought she would. God, I needed her comfort right now as much as I needed to give her some, too.

"I'm not." She cried, "One second. That's all it took, and I was right back there. Chained up and captive."

"You aren't." Again, I said, "You're free, and I'm right here." I pressed my lips against her forehead as she melted into my touch. "I'm right here."

"You weren't though." She shook her head, gripping the front of my tux. "You weren't right there."

"I'm sorry." I kicked myself, hating that she got as far away from me as she did. "Fucking hell, Laila. I'm so fucking sorry."

"Make me forget." She clung to me tighter. "Make it all disappear. You're the only one that makes my head just—stop."

"What do you need?" I pulled her face back so I could see her, "Whatever you want, it's yours."

"Touch me." She whispered with her eyes still closed. "Make me feel good the way only you can."

"Dove," I groaned, fighting the demon inside of me that ached to take what she was offering.

"Please." She begged, "I need to escape, and you give me that out." She opened her eyes, and tears swam in the chocolate depths of her irises. "Please."

I growled in my chest, unable to stop the predatory noise. "Promise me this is what you actually want." I fought to stay in control of my body as my need to consume her and help her rose inside.

"I promise." She agreed eagerly without hesitation, "I need you, I'm tired of you treating me with kid gloves. I need you."

After cracking my neck, I ran my hands down her waist to her hips, drawing her close against me. "I'm not fucking you in a conference room amidst a panic attack, Dove."

"Zeke, please—" She cried desperately.

"Enough." I commanded, and she stopped and bit her lip to stay quiet as I stared down at her. "The first time I slide into your body, you're going to be mindless from all the orgasms I've already given to you. You'll be drunk on the need and the pleasure, desperate for me exactly how I've been for you every single second of every single day since I first heard you moan my name in your dreams."

"God." She panted, rocking her body forward as my erection grew against her stomach.

"I'm not fucking you here, but I'll make you feel so fucking good you won't even notice that I'm not buried deep inside of you."

"Please." She mewed, licking her lips, and sliding her hands up and down my chest. "Please, Daddy. Take care of me."

"Stay still." I commanded, leaning down to kiss her lips and then down to her neck. "Don't move."

"Okay." she whispered, loosening her grip as I backed away from her delicious body.

I pulled an armless chair off the wall and sat it in the middle of the room, watching her as she trembled where I had left her, watching me. I undid the tie around my neck and pulled it free, laying it over the back of the chair before unbuttoning my jacket and taking it off, adding it to the tie. She watched me silently, with her hands gripped tight in front of her like she was fighting her desire to disobey me and move.

I undid the cufflinks on my wrists and rolled my sleeves up, watching her stare at every move I made as I sank down onto the chair. I leaned back and spread my feet wide.

"Sit." I commanded, running my hand up and down my thigh.

"What?" She stammered as her eyes flicked from my thigh to my face.

"Straddle my knee. Now, Dove."

Her chest rose and fell quickly above the neckline of her dress. "Zeke, I—" She shook her head, letting fear and uncertainty fill her head instead of the lust she was consumed with moments ago.

"You can." I corrected, spreading my legs further apart. "Straddle my knee and ride me until you come."

"I don't know if I can."

"I already told you; you can." I patted my knee, and her throat bobbed as she swallowed, "And you will. Because Daddy told you to."

She took a deep breath and blew it out slowly before taking one step, and then another, toward me until she stood at my feet.

"Good girl." I praised her, and she smiled cautiously at me. "Pull your skirt open and sit." I patted my leg again, "I want to feel your hot pussy right here, Dove."

She reached for the slit of her dress with shaking fingers, pulling the skirt open, revealing a sexy pair of red lace panties underneath it as she elegantly stepped forward, straddling my thigh and slowly lowered herself down onto it. We were eye to eye as she trembled in my lap.

"You begged me to touch you." I feathered the back of my fingers over her cheek to her neck, over the erratic pulse point and then to her delicate collarbones right above her breasts. Breasts I ached to see and taste again, but I fought my own needs to fulfill hers. "To make you forget." I skimmed my fingertips over the swells of those tempting breasts, and her head tipped back as she pushed her chest forward into my chest. "Make yourself forget, Dove." I slid my hands over her waist and then into the opening of her skirt to hold her hips. "Ride my thigh and come all over me. Be my good girl and take what you need from me."

"Zeke." She moaned and tentatively rocked forward on my thick thigh. "Mmh." She licked her lips and did it again, closing her eyes and rocking further forward and back, finding the right pressure and rhythm. "God, I'm so horny." She dropped her head forward and slid her hands over my tense stomach, using it for leverage as she rolled her hips in a circular motion at the front and back of every rock. "You make me so needy."

"Even at your most needy, you don't come close to feeling how deprived I am of you." I growled, moving her hips with my hands as she lost her rhythm to her need. "How fucking desperate I am to consume you."

"Yes." She panted, "I want to touch you."

"I'm right here." I replied, drifting my fingers around to her back and making quick work of her dress, unzipping it and revealing her bare breasts to my hungry eyes. "You're so fucking perfect."

She palmed my erection through the fabric of my pants and squeezed, before dragging her nails up the length of it and making my eyes cross as I leaned forward to flick my tongue over one perfect nipple.

"Daddy." She moaned, gripping me as she rocked faster and slid her hand around the back of my head, pulling me against her chest. "Fuck, you feel so good."

"Use me." I growled, nibbling on her nipple, and sliding my thumb between her pussy and my thigh as extra stimulation against her clit. "Come all over me."

"God, I'm going to. I can't stop it. I'm coming." She panted before her entire body convulsed as if she was electrocuted and wracked by waves of pleasure as she came.

"Good girl, Dove." I praised, pinching her nipple between my fingers and watching her as she kept rocking back and forth on my thumb and thigh, squeezing my aching cock. Her lips were parted, and her face was flushed as she gasped for breath. "My perfect Dove."

"Fuck." She gasped, collapsing forward and resting her head on my shoulder as she trembled from the aftershocks. "Thank you." Her warm breath tickled the hair on my neck as I lazily ran my fingers up and down her spine as she came down from her high.

"You took what you wanted." I reminded her. "You provided for yourself."

She chuckled and leaned back to look at me through hazy eyes. "What a marvelous tool you allowed yourself to be for the cause, too."

"I didn't say I was perfect." Her shriek of surprise pierced the air as I lifted her into my arms and stood. "I didn't say I was entirely selfless, either." Ominously, I sat her down on the conference table while standing between her parted thighs. "I didn't say I would not take what I wanted in return."

Her eyes widened in uncertainty, and I smirked at her confusion as I slid my hands up her smooth thighs to the band of her red lace panties still peeking out at me through the fabric of her dress. I gripped the band and slowly tugged them down, sliding them down those perfect thighs as I stared deep into her eyes.

"It's my turn to get what I need." I growled, slowly sinking to my knees in front of her as I pulled her panties off and laid them on the table next to her. "It's my turn to taste you." Her plump lip found its way back between her white teeth as she bit it. "It's my turn to feel you come directly on my tongue. Just like in your dreams."

"Zeke." She moaned.

"Daddy." I corrected, pushing her thighs wide and exposing her perfectly pink pussy as I blew a teasing breath on it. "When your legs are wrapped around my ears and my beard is tickling your thighs, you will call me Daddy."

"Fuck." She moaned as I ran the tip of my finger up through her wetness before spreading her lips open to reveal her clit. "Yes, Daddy."

"Good girl." I praised and flicked my tongue over her clit before sucking it into my mouth as she gasped and rocked forward onto my face. "That's my good girl."

She looked breathtaking with her dress draped around her waist loosely, with her marvelous tits exposed and her legs spread for me, with the flush of an orgasm already on her skin before I even touched her pussy directly. She was a goddess. I was unworthy.

But fuck if I was going to stop from taking what I needed desperately from her.

Her hands went to the back of my head, and she let out a guttural moan as she arched her back, riding my face like the sexual goddess she was. "Oh my God, oh my God, oh my God."

"You taste like heaven." I hummed against her body, watching her as I slid two fingers into her tight body. It was the first time I felt her from the inside, and my cock leaked, just imagining how good she was going to feel wrapped around me for real. "You feel like heaven." I curled my fingers forward, and she gasped, widening her legs. "I need to taste your orgasm, Dove."

"Yes." She panted, opening her eyes again and staring down at me with her lips parted. "I'm so close again."

"Come for me." I demanded, sucking her clit into my mouth and rocking her forward and back with my hand. "Give it to me."

"Zeke," She screamed, tipping her head back and orgasming just like I told her to. "Holy fuck." She gasped, collapsing back onto the table as she panted and came down again.

I chuckled, licking up the evidence of her orgasm and twirling my tongue around her clit, making her twitch for good measure, before standing back up. She pried one eye open and smirked lazily at me before she sat back up, readjusting her dress to cover her chest. "In terms of not being fucked when I demanded to be," She shrugged, "I'm still going to mark that one down as a win."

I tipped my head back and chuckled at her dry humor and then kissed her lips, leisurely tasting her and relaxing her. "Are you ready to get out of here?"

"Mmh," She hummed, sagging into me. "I don't think I can even walk."

I zipped her dress back up for her and then slid my jacket over her shoulders to protect her flushed skin from the cool evening air. "Walk to the car, and I'll keep your legs in the air the rest of the night."

"Deal!" She cheered eagerly, sliding off the table and winking at me.

And gone were the anxiety and fear that had been consuming her when we walked into the room. And in their place, there was peace and humor. Which was exactly how it should be.

But as she leaned into my body and wrapped her arm around my waist for support as we walked out the rear exit of the building to my waiting car, I vowed to make sure whoever put her into that panic to begin with would never feel peace again.

No, they'd only feel terror and pain when I figured out who hurt her.

Because someone in that room tonight hurt my girl. And I wasn't dumb enough to think they did it tonight.

They were from her past.

And I was going to end their future.

CHAPTER 19 – ZEKE

Her breathing was even, the soft flow of it branding my skin with each exhale. It assured me she was alive and well, *whole*. Because without feeling her breath, or the steady beat of her heart, my brain wouldn't believe she was fine.

There was a disconnect between rational thought and fear. And I was stuck living somewhere between them since meeting her.

When Carly wanted to take her away from my side at the gala, I protested, tightening my hold on her in a physical rebuttal to the idea. Then Laila had assured me she would be fine, a mere fifty feet away while I stayed and finished my conversation.

She didn't realize I was clinging to her for my own sanity, not just protecting hers.

So, I let her go. Gave her space to spread her wings and find her footing with her bravery fully in place and the strong and fiery Carly at her side. One interaction followed another, and a call to duty arose that I couldn't refuse; Ryker was pulled from our central location in the room and into the shadows to conduct business. I was his second, so I couldn't stand outside of that circle during that conversation. I had no choice.

Ten minutes.

That was all it had been from the moment she left my side until her panicked and agonized face came through the crowd where she clung to Elora, searching for me.

Ten minutes, and she was broken.

She wouldn't tell me what happened, instead, demanded that I make her forget all about it with my touch.

With my body.

She had no fucking clue how hard it was to resist the urge to slide deep inside of her for the first time, after holding back for months with nothing but small glimpses into the pleasure I'd find in bed with her.

The only reason I denied her when she begged me so prettily was that she deserved so much better for our first time. She deserved romance, and worship, and things I didn't have time to give her with the busy party carrying on right outside the door.

Instead, I gave her what I could.

I gave her power.

Watching her ride my thigh and make herself come was one of the most erotic things I'd ever seen before. And I hardly touched her at that moment.

But tasting her.

Jesus fuck, tasting her sweet pussy for the first time, spreading her thighs and pushing her body into ecstasy again so soon after her first orgasm, was pure selfishness on my part.

Sure, she enjoyed herself. But I did it for myself.

I needed to taste her, to keep myself from bucking into her right then and there like a wild animal, intent only on leaving a part of myself inside of her body. Claiming her as mine.

By the time we got back to the barracks, she was dead on her feet from worry and orgasms. Leaving me to carry her into her apartment, strip her down and dress her in her cute, innocent little pajamas and tuck her into bed. I had planned to kiss her goodnight and leave her to rest, so I didn't encroach on her safe space too much with my presence. But as I turned to leave, she rolled over and held her hand out to me with her sleepy smile on her perfect face. "Stay with me." She whispered, "Please."

As if I could have denied her request.

Never mind the fact that the idea of leaving her side at all, after how I found her at the gala, felt like I was physically putting myself into a grinder and losing parts of my soul in tiny chunks.

So, I stayed.

I stripped down to my boxers, and slid in behind her, molding my body to hers and feeling her unusual calmness settle into my bones like it was my own.

I was always calm.

Calculated and in control.

Yet from the first moment I touched Laila, I was a wreck. I was unhinged. I was desperate. For whatever she would give me, while trying to protect her fragile soul and heart from the darkness inside of me.

It was exhausting and rewarding in ways I'd never experienced before.

It was the *more* I'd gone my whole life without feeling that others did when they found love.

It was everything.

She was everything.

And she was hurt. She had been hurt, because of a number of men that I couldn't even comprehend. And believe me, I had tried. I had forced myself to do as much digging into Laila's past as I could. Beating heads together and peeling skin from muscle in search of a list of names to turn my attention to so I could offload some of the fury in my heart from her pain.

But there was no list.

The men who had abused and assaulted her were so plentiful, there was simply no way to track them down. She had been abused so regularly that the faces of men who went into her room blurred until the people I interrogated simply couldn't name them.

It was single-handedly the most helpless feeling I'd ever endured before.

I had to do something. I had to even the score; *it was what I fucking did*. It was what was ingrained in my DNA at this point in life.

So as the early morning sunlight started peeking in through her blinds, I slid from her bed, having not slept a wink as my mind ran all night long, and began my search for answers.

And stop number one was in Ryker's kitchen.

I walked in, surprised to find Jed and Carly at the counter, both nursing cups of coffee like they'd been up all night long as well. The bags under Jed's eyes said there was far more at play between the two of them than I was privy to, so I didn't bother asking.

"How is she?" Carly asked, skipping pleasantries.

Before I could answer, Ryker walked in, tying the string on a pair of pajama pants as he flicked his glance at all of us. "You all look like shit." He went to the fancy coffee machine and pushed the button, filling a cup and handing it to me before starting another for himself. "How's Laila?" He asked.

"She's fine." I responded, angry, that they all seemed to know how close to losing it she came last night. "But I need to talk to Ellie."

"She's on her way down." He replied, turning his attention to Jed and Carly, "You two figure your shit out?"

Carly wouldn't meet Ryker's stare, and Jed just clenched his jaw. "We're fine." He turned his attention back to me, deflecting as usual. "What the fuck happened last night?"

I bristled at the accusation in his tone and fought the urge to throw my cup of steaming coffee at his face for the fun of it. If Carly wasn't in the splash zone, I wouldn't have thought twice about it.

"Enough." Ellie called, walking into the room wearing a cream-colored lounge set and looking rested, but angry. "I won't have any of your bullshit in my kitchen at this hour." She pointed her finger at Jed and then turned to me. "How's Laila?"

"Will everyone stop fucking asking me that?" I snapped, clenching my jaw to keep from screaming through the anxiety building inside of me with each passing minute spent away from her. I took a deep breath, noting Ryker's glare over his wife's shoulder as she leaned back against his chest and tried again. "She's sleeping. She has been out all night."

"Good." Ellie nodded.

"I want to know what happened." I cut to the chase. "Before you brought her to me."

Ellie sighed and flicked a glance over at Carly, "Let's start at the beginning then, because I only have part of the story."

I turned to Carly, "What happened when you two got to the bar?"

She ducked her head again, and Jed tensed, and if I wasn't mistaken, it looked like Carly brushed away a tear as she pushed her hair back and sat up straighter. "She talked me off a ledge about Jed and his obnoxious flirting—"

"Flirting!" Her boyfriend roared, rolling his eyes. "I was fucking talking to the wife of a—"

She cut him off, dominating the conversation, "I don't care." She snapped, and he huffed, closing his mouth as if he were physically fighting back the words trying to escape. "And then I felt—" She paused and swallowed, losing some of the bravado, "sick. So, she went to find Jed while I went to the bathroom. That was the last I saw of her."

I turned to Jed, "What happened when she got you?"

"She didn't." He sighed, "Ellie came and found me, but said you'd already taken Laila home. I never saw her after she went to the bar."

I turned back to Ellie and put my hands on my hips, fighting the urge to scream at them all for the fucking answers. "So, what happened between the bar and you finding her?" Ellie's body was tense where she leaned against Ryker, and I instantly felt dread come over me. "Someone fucking hurt her." I stated thickly, fighting emotions from cutting off my voice completely.

"Not last night, they didn't." Elora whispered angrily as her eyes misted, "I don't know when it happened. But I know who it was."

"Who?"

She swallowed, and Ryker ran his hands up and down her arms, giving her silent support, showing she had already told him what she knew.

"I found her cornered in the darkness, and she looked like a wild animal." She shuddered, "I haven't seen that look in her eyes since you rescued her from that brothel that night."

My body tightened as I got closer to a name. A face. A body to enact some vengeance on. "Who, Elora?" I demanded again.

"Senator Lupold." She spat out, grimacing at the mere mention of his name, and my blood ran cold. "I don't know what happened before I got there, but he recognized her. He didn't know where from, though. And she was ready to tear herself limb from limb to get away from him."

My heartbeat echoed in my ears as the slimy face of that man blurred my vision, in time with the memory of that day on the sidewalk.

She was stopped outside his house. Frozen in time. Staring up at the brick exterior in a daze and when I asked her what she was doing outside the Senator's home, she grimaced at the title.

"That man did something to Laila." Elora croaked as she fought her emotions. "I don't know what it was exactly, but it was something catastrophic."

"I'll kill him." Jed sneered, glancing up at me. "*We* will kill him."

"Not yet." I shook my head, looking back at Ryker. Senator Lupold was a disgrace to humankind, but he was powerful. Whatever we did, it had to be smart. "We can't make a move on him." I hated saying those words, even if they were true. "Not right away, at least."

"Why the fuck not?" Jed snapped, standing up from his spot at the island and tipping his stool over. "We all fucking know what that scum bag did to her." He yelled, losing his composure as his imagination ran wild. Where his mind was racing, mine slowed down. Moves I could make played out in perfect succession like a chess match, showing me the right and wrong ones in cinematic fashion.

"Because he deserves worse than that." I replied, and Ryker smirked, already knowing what I was thinking from years of working side by side.

"He'd be too prepared for it." Ryker added, holding his hand up to Jed as his temper boiled over. "Zeke's right. Killing him swiftly for whatever crime he committed against Laila is too kind of a fate. And his security is too tight for a blitz attack."

"Then what the fuck are you suggesting?" Jed threw his hands up. "We finally have a fucking name, and you want to sit here and strategize? Fuck that!"

"No." I shook my head, staring at the countertop. "There's only one way to do this." I glanced up at Laila's brother and finally saw him for what he had been all along. Her biggest protector. It was ingrained in his DNA to keep her safe, and knowing he had failed had led him to act out and fight for control of the situation. "We have to do this her way."

"Her?" He froze, "You seriously think she should be involved in this? He abused her! She nearly lost her mind last night just from seeing him!" He turned to Ryker, pleading for reason. "You have to agree that involving Laila in any of this would just hurt her further."

"I don't agree." Ryker said easily. "I think it should be up to her completely." He nodded in my direction.

"Like my mother." Ellie stared at me head on, before glancing at Jed. "I killed my mother for what she did to me." She shrugged, "Okay, maybe not firsthand," She smirked almost ironically, "But I gave Zeke the command on when and how. And it gave me an incredible sense of power when I did it."

"No." Jed started pacing. "No!" He roared, and Carly stayed peculiarly quiet in her chair as her man lost it further. "I don't want her near death!" He turned on me. "I fucking lost everything to protect her from it the first time! I'm not going to just make that all for nothing by forcing her to expose herself to it now!"

"She's not a kid anymore." I tried reasoning with him, even though I could empathize with his panic. "And neither are you, Jed." I leveled with him, "She's stronger than you give her credit for. And she thrives on being in control of things, even if she doubts her ability to do so at first. She deserves at least to have a say in it."

"It will just re-victimize her." Carly said quietly from her spot, which she hadn't moved from. "You didn't see it." She shook her head and closed her eyes as haunting tears spilled over her cheeks. "You didn't see what it was like for them." Her voice cut out as she opened her eyes and stared right at me. "You didn't see what they did to her." She shook her head, causing more tears to spill, and my chest ached from her pain. "Don't make her relive it."

"She relived it last night." Elora added calmly, trying to reason with her best friend. "She was right back inside that building last night when I got to her."

"And what do you think killing the man who tortured her will do?" Carly snapped at Ellie as she stood up. "Because I did that." Her whole-body shook. "I killed Frankie for what he did to me, and I regret it every single fucking day. Every single fucking day I remember that moment, I know you all are so fucking desensitized to the brutality of murder—" Carly cried before turning to me, "But I'm not. Laila's not." She grabbed her coffee off the counter and poured it down the drain. "I don't know if it's up for a fucking vote or not, but my vote is to leave her out of it." She looked to Ryker and Ellie, "I've spent the most time out of all of us working with her through her trauma and I'm begging you," She turned to me and pled with her teary eyes, "Don't put more darkness on her soul."

She turned and walked out of the kitchen towards her house, and Jed hung his head in frustration, moved by her plea. "My vote is no." He tossed his hands up in the air, looking from me to Ryker, "But we all know you two don't care what my opinion is where my sister is concerned. Or you would have respected it from day one. I brought her here because I thought she'd be safe." He turned and walked out after Carly, leaving a thick silence in his wake.

"He sacrificed everything for her." I stated to no one in particular, "Maybe he has a point."

Ellie shook her head, standing up out of her husband's arms and taking a deep breath. "My vote is we ask her opinion, at least." She stared at me with eyes that reminded me so much of her father's unwavering stare. "But we can all agree that the man will die."

"I'll agree to that much." I nodded, already knowing that Lupold didn't deserve to breathe the same air as Laila any longer, but not sure of anything else past that, thanks to Carly and Jed's opinions.

"My vote is with Ellie." Ryker gave his input, "But that puts it at a tie." He put his hand on my shoulder as he passed by me, "Which means at the end of the day, it's up to you." He sighed, lending me his years' long friendship with just a touch. "No one here knows her better than you do, Zeke. Think about it and let me know. Either way, you'll have my support." He smirked, "Not that it would stop you if you didn't."

I smirked humorlessly and nodded my head, "No, not when it comes to her, it wouldn't."

"The old boy has officially been bitten by the love bug." He joked, "Who would have thought we'd see the day." He left the kitchen, pulling his wife with him as I stood there, now more unsure than when I walked in, hell-bent on vengeance and burning the world at Laila's feet for her.

"Sure as hell not me." I muttered, taking another sip of my coffee, and walked out back to the barracks.

Back to her.

When I got back into her apartment, she was standing in her bathroom with her toothbrush hanging out of her mouth. "Did you use your key?" She mumbled and then rinsed her mouth before propping her hip up against the doorframe.

"Does that bother you?" I questioned, taking my shoes off and walking toward her, unable to stop the attraction pulling us together.

"Not in the least, actually." She smiled, letting her eyes rove over my body as I slowly started unbuttoning last night's shirt I put back on this morning. "Where did you go?"

"To the mansion." I undid the last button as I came toe to toe with her and pulled it off, tossing it onto the chair next to her bed. "But I'm back now."

"Hmm." She smiled against my lips when I leaned down to kiss her. "I thought you were gone for the day, off being Mr. Important Boogeyman."

"Boogeyman?" I sucked her bottom lip into my mouth and bit it lightly. "I thought you weren't scared of me."

"I didn't say I was." She placed her hands against my bare stomach, and her eyelids fluttered closed as she explored, and whispered, "Do you have to leave?"

"Not today." I replied, though I knew I had plans nearly every hour of the day. But fuck every single last one of them. The mood in the room told me I wasn't going to leave this apartment any time soon. "Today, I'm yours." I left out the part where I needed to erase all of the thoughts of her past by perfecting her present. I needed to give her whatever she wanted.

"Mmh." She moaned, leaning into me. "Make me yours." She licked my lip shyly as I gripped her hips and pulled her closer. "Make it real."

"Say it." I growled, sliding my fingertips under her shirt and across the smooth skin of her flat stomach to the cute little bow at the front of her pajama shorts. "Tell me what you want."

"I want you." She whispered, raising up on her tippy toes so my fingers slid inside the waistband, right above the bare skin of her pussy that I had explored last night. "I need to feel you inside me, Zeke."

"Say it." I repeated, hanging on by a thread to my sanity. "Say the words, Laila. The dirty and depraved things that you're requesting."

She faltered, but took a deep breath and pushed forward. "I want to start with exploring your body." She slid one dainty hand down my stomach to the tented front of my slacks, palming my cock where it grew down my leg. "I want to touch and taste every inch of you. I wanted it last night, but you told me no."

My cock jumped in her hand, and I felt it leak from her dirty words. "I don't want to take anything from you, Dove." She tightened her hold on my cock, and I groaned, fighting the urge to thrust it through her tight hold like an animal. "I just want to give to you."

"Then give me this." She flicked the button on my pants open, and teased the zipper down, one metal tooth at a time until it was all the way down before she slid her hand inside. "I need to feel you lose yourself to me. And then I want you to make me yours."

"Fucking hell, Dove." I growled, cracking my neck as I fought to remain in control. "I don't know how to do that without triggering you. How to *take* without reminding you of everything else."

"I don't remember anything else when you touch me." She urged, pushing my pants and boxers down and freeing my cock into her bare hand for the first time. "Feel how wet I am." She whispered against my lips, reminding me how close my fingers were to her sweet center, and they moved on their own. Down to the delicious cream that her body was making specifically for this purpose. "You're not taking anything I'm not willingly begging you to have."

She locked her eyes on mine as she slowly sank down to her knees. "Dove." I growled in warning when she ended up with my cock aimed directly at her pink lips.

"Do you want me to beg you, Daddy?" She purred, "You talk of worship like I'm not capable of being the one on my knees for you." She leaned forward and used just the very tip of her tongue on the head of my cock, tasting my pre-cum. "Like you don't deserve my devotion."

"I'm not." I tightened my hands into fists but didn't move away from her like I should have. Weeks ago, when I first touched her, she was timid and unsure of every single move she made. But last night she had ridden my thigh and then my face, and now she was on her knees at my feet, licking my cock like a goddess, and everything I thought I knew evaporated.

"Wrong." She swirled her tongue around the head of my cock and sucked on it. Laila looked like a vixen, but I felt her uncertainty in every move she made. She didn't know what to do, but knew she wanted to try it. "You've unleashed something inside of me, Zeke." She wrapped her fingers around the base of my cock, and it twitched and wept for her again as she kept those honeyed brown eyes locked on mine. "Something I want to explore and experiment with." She sucked the head of my cock into her mouth, staring at me. "With you. I've never wanted any man like I want you."

"Fuck." I lost my resolve as she sucked on me again and started moving with her lips wrapped around me. She pushed her mouth down until she gagged and then used her hands around what she couldn't reach with her lips. I tried focusing on the pleasure she was giving me and not where she learned her skills from, but it was like an internal war raging inside my brain and body. After learning the first name on the list of men to abuse her, I should have been doing literally anything else in the world besides taking the best goddamn head job of my life. Yet there I was, head thrown back, stomach tight, cock buried in the sexiest mouth on earth and so fucking close to blowing my load I should have felt embarrassment. "That's it, Dove." I gritted out between clenched teeth and gave in to the pleasure she was tempting me with.

"Good boy." She smirked and then dove back down before I could reprimand her for her sass. There was something so powerful passing between us as her eyes stayed locked on mine. Something formidable grew deeper inside of us as we crossed another wall meant to keep us apart. "I love watching you come undone." She licked up the entire length of me as she dug her nails into my lower stomach with her other hand and hummed as she licked my balls.

"Fuck it, Dove." I gasped, "I'm going to come if you keep it up."

"Do it." She challenged, tightening her hand around my cock as she stroked me and sucked on my balls. "Give it to me, Daddy. I want it so fucking bad."

"No." I fought through the haze and pulled back, stepping out of her hold on me and scooping her up in my arms and then tossing her down on the bed. "I've taken enough from you." She panted and smirked up at me with wild eyes as I grabbed the band of her shorts and pulled them down her legs, revealing that bare and glistening pussy I felt earlier. I grabbed the hem of her shirt and ripped it up over her head and tossed it with the growing pile on the chair as I kicked out of my pants and stood over her.

She relaxed back onto the bed and bent her knees, slowly spreading them for me as she watched me with desire in her eyes. I lowered my hand to my cock and stroked it, from root to tip, rotating my hand around the crown just how I liked as she stared, mesmerized. "That's so sexy." She purred, seductive without even trying. It was incredible to see her come into her sexuality without a reason behind it other than desire.

"No, Dove. You are sexy." I slid my hands down her knees to her inner thighs and pushed them wider apart. "Every inch of you was made for me." I crawled up the bed and kissed the inside of her leg, creating goosebumps in my wake. "Tell me you want this."

"I need this." She soothed, running her hand over the side of my face and pulling me up her body until we were face to face. "I need you."

"You have me, Dove."

"Prove it." She wrapped one leg around the back of mine and urged me forward until the tip of my cock lay heavily against the wetness of her pussy. "Don't make me wait anymore, please."

"Keep your eyes open and on me. The entire time you're taking me; I want your eyes open. I want you to know who's fucking you."

"Mmh." She groaned as she tilted her hips so that the head of my cock pressed into her, just a bit. "Yes, Daddy. Please give me your cock, I want to take it so deep I don't know where you end and I begin again."

"Dove." I growled, pushing in an inch and reveling in the shocking heat of her body as it wrapped around me for the first time. "You're so wet and hot for me."

"All for you." She laid her head back on the pillow and ran her hands up the sides of my neck as she rolled her hips, taking me deeper. "God yes, do you have any idea how good you're making me feel right now?"

"I can't—" I growled, pulling out and pushing back in. "I've never felt like this."

"Me neither." She purred, kissing my lips and rolling her hips to rub herself against my body with each down thrust. "I'm already so close to coming for you. Because of you."

"Then do it, Dove." I fought the urge to finish with her as her body tensed, head tipped back, mouth parted in ecstasy, pussy spasming around my cock in a vice grip. "Good girl," I hissed, slamming into her over and over again. "That's it, so fucking good for me."

"Please," She cried, burying her nails in my neck and pulling me even closer, "Come for me, Zeke."

"Condom." I growled, angry with myself, "Are you on the pill?"

"I'm safe." She gasped, hitching her foot against the back of my thigh, pulling me closer. "Come inside of me."

My body needed nothing more to be said on it, it let go, giving in to her pleasurable promise as fire lit up my spine.

"God, Zeke," She screamed, staring up at me as I pumped her full. Eyes so wide, and body limp underneath mine as our hearts raced against each other. "Oh, my God."

I rolled off her, but her tight grip around me didn't waver, and she rolled with me until we lay on our sides staring at each other, letting our breaths slow and bodies relax.

"Talk to me," I whispered, brushing my fingers through her hair, pushing it off her forehead. "Tell me how you are."

Her eyes watered over, but the tears didn't fall as she smiled at me. "I think I was meant to find you." She whispered as I held my breath, "I think maybe you're the one good thing I'll ever find in life, and if that's how it's supposed to go for me, then I'm okay with that."

"Laila—" I whispered.

"I'm falling for you, Zeke." She smiled cautiously, "And I'll be honest, I don't have a clue what a healthy relationship is supposed to look like, but I know it's how I feel."

"We don't have to know it to feel it. Together." I kissed her lips gently before pressing my forehead to hers and breathing her in.

CHAPTER 20 – LAILA

How was it possible to be living like nothing changed, when in reality, every single thing inside of my brain was different?

Somehow, Zeke had rewired certain parts of my brain to process thoughts and feelings in a new way. A healthier way.

It was stupid in hindsight to credit mind-blowing sex with trauma healing. I knew that. But I couldn't explain it in any other way than how feeling the ecstasy and the connection forged between us when we were in bed changed the hormones inside of my brain to just kind of—relax.

It wasn't just the orgasms either, as earth-shattering as they were. It was something deeper than that. I felt refreshed when I woke up and felt the sunshine streaming through the blinds. Normally, I'd contemplate my need to get up and out of bed, trying to come up with any reason to stay buried under the blankets in my safety cocoon. Yet today, I was up with the sun and ready to face just about anything the world tried to throw at me. Believe me, I'd been served my fair share of shit sandwiches by the world, so that was saying something.

And stop number one for my fresh and easy-going morning—Carly.

I had seen no one since the gala, thanks to Zeke's intent to keep me naked and screaming his name all day yesterday, not that I was complaining. But she had been going through some deep shit when I last saw her, and I wanted to check in.

Even if I knew the conversation had the potential to derail this sunshiny feeling that bloomed deep inside of me.

When I walked up her front path, I had hoped she would be on the porch, as usual, with a cup of coffee and a welcoming smile. But her chair was empty, and I felt uncertainty trying to claw its way up my neck at what that meant.

Did she not want me to visit?

Was she mad that I couldn't deliver Jed to her like she needed at the gala?

Was she mad at me?

Before I could dwell on my insecurities and let it darken my mood, I climbed her stairs and gently knocked on her front door.

"Come in, Laila." Carly's voice called from inside, and I entered her serene space, something that used to cause such panic inside of me, yet lately, it only gave me mild prickles of unease.

And today, nothing.

"Hey." I said, sliding my shoes off and nodding to her where she sat curled up on the couch with a book and a fluffy blanket. "Is it okay that I'm here?"

Her nose scrunched up, and she closed her book. "Why wouldn't it be okay for you to be here?"

"Well—," I paused and sat down at the other end of the couch. "You weren't out on the porch." I stated plainly.

She rolled her eyes and patted my knee before tossing part of her blanket over my lap, welcoming me into her comfort. "I'm avoiding your brother." She pursed her lips, "If I'm on the porch, he can keep eyes on me through the security cameras."

I smirked at her wisdom, "But if you're inside, he's dark. Sneaky, I like it." I relaxed on the couch. "What happened after—" I paused, not sure what to call it exactly since I wasn't sure what she knew, "After I left the gala?"

She took a deep breath and played with a string on the blanket, "I'm not pregnant." She shrugged her shoulders and tears welled in her blue eyes as she huffed and stared at the ceiling. "I can't seem to stop fucking crying about it, though."

I fought the urge to remove myself from the situation completely, and instead slid closer to her, taking her hand in mine with a gentle smile. "You don't have to talk about it if you don't want to. But I do want you to know I'll listen if you do."

She chuckled and rested her head on my shoulder, wrapping both arms around mine and taking a couple more deep breaths. "I didn't expect you to be the calm, cool, and collected one while I was having a freak out." She joked, "But I kind of like leaning on you." She tapped her head against my shoulder for emphasis before sitting back upright. "I don't quite know why I'm sad. I didn't want to be pregnant at the gala, the idea alone terrified me." She sighed, and I squeezed her hand, giving her my silent support while she worked through it. "Yet, I think a part of me is disappointed that it was negative. Does any of that make sense?"

"You can be terrified of something and still want it." I replied, looking down at our arms linked together. "I used to be terrified of physical touch," I patted her arm, "And now look at us." She chuckled again, even as her tears slid over her lashes. "But it doesn't mean it doesn't still scare the shit out of me. It just means I'm choosing to welcome the benefits of it without dwelling on the negatives that could maybe come from it as well."

"Well, when you put it that way."

"Do you know what it is about the idea of parenthood that freaks you out?" I questioned.

She shook her head, "That's what's weird. I love babies, and I love little Gavin with everything inside of me. There isn't a day that goes by without me wanting to be involved in his everyday life, and I spend so much time with him that I can honestly say it's not the responsibility or burden of parenthood that scares me."

"Then what is it?"

She looked at me with wide eyes and whispered, "I think it's the chance of bringing a perfectly innocent little baby into this world just for it to chew them up and spit them out." My heart seized in my chest as I realized what her fears were, deep down. She wasn't naïve about the cruelty of the world, especially the one she lived in, and after being kidnapped, trafficked, and assaulted, she was well within her rights to be terrified. "I wouldn't survive something bad happening to my baby, especially if it was because of the life I chose to live."

"I get it." Nodding my head, I offered my complete understanding. "No one in the world will grasp your fears like I do, Carly."

"So, you don't think I'm crazy?" She cringed, "Or selfish?"

"Did Jed call you selfish?" I scowled at her, feeling anger building in my chest for the injustice he delivered to her trauma.

"Not in as many words." She sighed, "He just aches to be a dad, and I've been able to hold him off so far with small excuses, but I think this—scare, lit a fire inside of him that made him realize he really wants a baby."

"And if you asked him to leave the crew to dispel some of your fears in exchange?" I asked and then thought better of it, "*Can* he leave the crew? Is it like a blood in, blood out thing?"

She snorted and shrugged her shoulders, "I don't think Ryker would kill him for leaving if he wanted to. But I also don't think he'd ever willingly leave the very thing that saved him when he was a teenager, lost, scared and all alone."

"What a pickle." I mused, leaning back onto the couch as she chuckled her agreement from next to me.

We sat there in silence for a while before I ended the serenity of it all with word vomit. "I saw someone at the gala."

She looked over at me but didn't say anything right away, giving me that supportive silence my therapist always used when she wanted me to expand on a thought without shaping it with her own words.

So, I went on. "Out of all of them," I swallowed, and she tightened her hold on my arm. "He was the worst." I don't know why I felt the need to tell her, but there was a part of our relationship, a bond made in the hellhole of that place, that made me feel like she would understand.

"Is that why you fell into a panic attack?" She asked, so she must have heard something about that night.

"He didn't know who I was." I laid my head back against the couch and chuckled humorlessly. "I guess I'm hard to recognize in an evening gown and not tied down to a table so he could torture me—." The words dried up in my throat like sand, and I closed my eyes to quell the anger and panic burning in my gut. "I've never felt rage like that before." Her sad blue eyes met mine when I opened them back up, I said, "I didn't even recognize myself. I don't know what kind of scene I would have caused if Elora hadn't rescued me from the entire situation."

She questioned something I wasn't even willing to think about yet. "What were you thinking of doing?"

I hesitated, then admitted the truth. "Exposing him. Telling everyone the depths of his depravity and decaying soul. Destroying him, like he destroyed me." As soon as that fantasy popped into my head like a bubble, my excitement deflated. "I could never go through with it though, because in order to expose him, I'd have to expose myself." I clenched my teeth at the pure impossibility of the entire situation. "And I wouldn't survive that."

"What if—" She paused and sat forward on the couch and looked at me over her shoulder. "What if he silently paid for what he did? What if the world never knew, but you knew that justice was served?"

I regarded her, trying to understand what she was saying as darkness took root behind her usually bright blue eyes. "I don't understand."

She swallowed and looked at the floor, so I leaned forward to sit even with her as she carefully plotted her response. "Frankie was my friend at one point." She spoke of the guy responsible for her kidnapping, and while I didn't know all the details of the ordeal, I knew he betrayed her. "We hooked up on occasion, but it was casual. So, when I got with Jed and told Frankie I wasn't interested in that kind of relationship with him anymore, I thought he'd be okay with it. But he wasn't." She played with the tiny gold bracelet on her wrist as she talked. "I'd never felt betrayal like that before in my life. I thought it was going to cost me everything, and I'd have no way to even the score."

"But you did." I whispered, remembering the way she left me behind that car during the gunfight to enact her own revenge on her kidnapper.

"I didn't plan it." She shook her head and looked at me with haunted eyes, "I don't even remember making the decision to pick up the gun or to pull the trigger."

"Do you regret it?" I asked the impossible question, "Would you go back and change it if you could?"

"Yes." She nodded softly, "I can't get the image of him as I shot him out of my head. Some nights it wakes me up, and I'm right back in that dark parking lot all over again."

"Do you feel like revenge could have felt differently if he'd have died in the shootout or something, not at your hand?" I questioned, imagining my own demon facing the end of a gun, but I couldn't tell who was holding it and pulling the trigger.

She tilted her head to the side sadly, "Are you asking for me, or yourself?"

"I don't know anymore." I admitted in defeat.

"All I can tell you is it gives me peace knowing he can't hurt me again." She acknowledged. "But I don't know what that means for me or my soul."

"I think my soul died sometime around my twentieth birthday."

I stayed at Carly's for a while more, relaxing in the silence of her understanding and healing something in the ease of it. But I couldn't hide anymore, even though she was intent on locking herself inside all day to avoid Jed.

I wasn't going to get involved in their relationship differences, be-cause if I had to put my guess in, I'd say Carly just needed some time to get her head wrapped around the idea of bringing a baby into the world. She didn't seem completely opposed to the idea, especially with her reaction to her negative test. They just had to move toward the common ground together on their own.

Plus, it's not like I had any fucking experience worth throwing in to help them figure it out.

And never would.

So, I'd busy myself in other ways.

More pleasurable ways, if I was lucky.

I hadn't seen Zeke since he slid out of my bed sometime in the morning before the sun came up to go do something dark and spooky for the crew.

I contemplated calling him. Or texting him something witty. Sexy? Seductive?

Rounding the shop between the barracks and Carly's cottage, I pulled out my phone with the intention to try anyway despite know-ing nothing about seduction.

I wasn't totally sure what went on inside the ominous building between our homes, but the aura coming off of it led me to believe I never wanted to end up inside.

I pulled up my message app and watched the cursor blink at me, waiting for the seduction to roll off my thumbs and into hyperspace on its way to Zeke, but I was blank.

"Cut it out." A voice snapped from the side door of the shop, where a black box truck was backed up to the entrance. "I said fucking stop it."

I kept on the path to the barracks, but couldn't tear my eyes away from the truck as I moved around it.

That voice.

There were men unloading boxes from the truck, and some of them nodded to me, with slightly guilty looks on their faces, as they caught me staring. They were crew members whom I'd never been introduced to but knew from their coming and going from the estate.

"Pick it up." One of the men snapped, using his boot to kick a box across the ground toward the door. "You're taking forever."

"They're fucking heavy." That same familiar voice cut back with venom. "And it doesn't help when your boys fucking throw them at me from ten feet up." The voice walked out from behind the truck with a box three times the size of him in his arms, covering his face.

But I recognized the ratty black hoodie with holes along the sleeves.

"Kade?" I called, turning back, and going to the truck. The men unloading the boxes stopped as the young kid from the street the other day dropped the box and scowled at me.

"You?" He snapped. "Are you fucking following me?"

"Hey!" A large voice boomed from the back of the truck, and Jed jumped down, landing powerfully on both feet. "I know I didn't just hear you talk to her like that." Jed grabbed Kade's hoodie and pulled him back to face him. "The fuck is wrong with you?"

"Hey!" Kade cried, scrambling to get free as he stared up at one of the most intimidating men he'd probably ever seen.

"Jed!" I clawed at his arm, trying to loosen his hold on Kade's sweater as panic filled the young kid's eyes. I recognized the fight-or-flight burning behind his bright blue irises. I remembered that feeling as I begged Jed, "Let him go."

"What's going on out here?" Another voice demanded, with less volume than Jed's, but with so much more authority. It sent shivers down my spine as it washed over me, calming and simultaneously exciting me.

Zeke.

I swung around to find him walking out of the shop with that perfect scowl on his face as he found Jed and me in a game of tug-of-war with a child.

"Dove." He said, flicking his glance at Jed and then down to Kade.

"Dove?" Kade mouthed off, and I cringed before the next words came out of his mouth. "I thought you were that big, gnarly biker's old lady."

"Shut up." I snapped, glaring at the kid I had contemplated harming and saving on two different occasions. "If you want to live to see the sunrise tomorrow, keep your smart-ass mouth shut."

Jed snorted and loosened his hold on Kade's sweater as I risked a glance up at Zeke.

As expected, that dark scowl was even darker after Kade's comment about Diesel.

"Wait." I shook my head, turning back to Kade and effectively removing Jed's hold completely. Kade shook free, adjusting his sweater, and I watched as that big tough guy act morphed back into his body language now that my brother wasn't threatening to clobber him. "What are you doing here, Kade?" I ignored the imposing men all around us.

"What's it look like, lady?" The mouthy kid scoffed, "I'm working here."

"With the crew?" I cried, turning to look at Jed and Zeke, who stood shoulder to shoulder, both staring at me like I had three heads. "He's a child!"

"Excuse you." Kade reacted as if he was offended. "I'm not a fucking child. Just because you're middle-aged—"

"Enough." Zeke snapped domineeringly, and both Kade and I shrunk a little under his stare. "How do you know each other?"

"We don't." Kade snapped. "She's a stalker trying to kidnap me and turn me into a skin suit."

I pushed the kid on the shoulder, frustrated with his smart mouth, and enjoyed the look of outrage as it covered his face. "I stepped in and saved him from getting his ass beat by some kids the other day."

"Wrong." Kade snapped, and I suddenly had the image of my hands around his neck, shaking him. "Her big, bad biker man saved me. She just mouthed off to them as the bike man scared them off."

"You don't value your life, do you?" Jed questioned with a raised brow as Zeke glared at me.

"You can't have him here." I ignored the overwhelming judgment from Zeke, Jed and the other crew members watching the entire shitshow unfold. "He's too young." I felt outrage building inside my body. "He was dealing drugs the other day and nearly got his ass beat doing it. He's just a kid!"

"You want me to fire him?" Zeke asked emotionlessly. "Fine. You're fired." He nodded to Kade. "Get the fuck out."

"Are you serious?" Kade cried, throwing his hands up in the air. "That's not fucking fair! I work my ass off for this crew!"

Zeke didn't even bother looking at the kid again as he stared at me, and suddenly I got the feeling that I was the one in trouble. "Are you happy now?" Zeke asked me. "Does it soothe the injustice of it all for you?"

"Maybe." I deflated a bit as Kade paced back and forth angrily. "Not really."

"Good." Zeke deadpanned. "Because without this job, without this *crew*," He pointed his finger towards Kade as he angrily towered over me, "He doesn't eat! So, if your morality can't handle the fact that the street kid does street kid shit to survive, then maybe you can stomach the fact that you just took away his chance of existence."

"Zeke." Jed warned, watching Zeke wind up even more in anger.

"I didn't—" I swallowed, feeling small and guilty.

"No, you didn't." Zeke snapped, "You didn't stop to think that this crew is the only chance he has."

"He's a kid." I whispered as stupid tears burned behind my eyes.

"Most of us were kids when we got in. I was younger than he is." He leveled and I let my gaze roam over the crew members staring at me, finding confirmation in their eyes. "Without this, none of us would have survived."

I took a step back from him, not recognizing his anger now that it was coming toward me. Not once had his rage been aimed my way before. I hated the way it made me feel.

I hated the hurt that bloomed from it.

"Just because this world chewed us all up and spit us out, doesn't mean we should help it do it to others." I said, and some of the darkness in Zeke's eyes lessened. I looked at Jed and pleaded with him to understand me. "What's the point of bringing new life into this world if you're going to let kids fall victim to it?"

Maybe it was a low blow.

Maybe it was the practicality he needed so he could understand mine and Carly's view on it, but my brother's shoulders deflated, picking up what I meant through my cryptic message.

Now I was angry. I was angry about the injustice of it all. I was angry at the cruelty of it all. Mimicking their wisdom-imparting stances, I squared my shoulders, and deepened my scowl, feeling their authority settle upon me. "If the kid is hungry, *feed* him." I gritted my teeth as more fury burned. "When did you two climb so high that you forgot to look back down at the ones beneath you once in a while?" And then I walked the fuck away before I did something stupid.

CHAPTER 21 – ZEKE

I couldn't find her.

I couldn't breathe without knowing where she was.

She was gone, and it was my fault.

I scanned the sidewalks, searching for the angry brunette who shoved my ego down my throat and twisted it so deep before pulling it back out that it brought my conscious back up with it. Something I hadn't seen in decades.

God, she was pure and innocent, and I threw that into her face because I was jealous that she had spent more time with Diesel.

And now I couldn't find her.

She ran from me when I became the monster I'd always been, but this time to her.

"Where are you?" I whispered to myself as I turned another corner and drove further into Shadeport's dark streets. She had no business here, but something in my gut told me it was exactly where she would go.

My phone rang through the car speakers, and I mashed the call button on my steering wheel when Carly's name popped up. "Did she call you?" I asked in place of a greeting.

"No." She sighed, and I could hear Jed muttering in the background. "But I know where she is."

"Where?" I snapped.

"Lux." She replied. "Theo called me."

"Lux?" I bellowed, even as I whipped a U-turn in the middle of the crowded street, heading toward Ryker's strip club. "Why would she be there?"

My imagination was running rampant as I flew through the city. Why would my broken little Dove go to a place where women were objectified?

"If I had to guess, because it's the last place you'd expect her to be." She sighed, "Maybe you should let me come get her. I don't think she exactly wants to see you right now."

"No."

"Zeke." She huffed, "Think about it. She's running away. What happens if she sees you and bolts further?"

"I can't." I shook my head, tightening my hand on the steering wheel as my chest constricted. "I can't breathe without her, Carly." I admitted, hating how fucking weak I felt with the rift between Laila and myself.

"God, Zeke." Carly sighed, and I envisioned her rubbing her forehead at my plight. "Be gentle with her. I don't care if you have to get on your knees in the middle of the damn club, but be gentle with her."

"I know." One of the bouncers ran around the line toward me as I pulled my car in front of the door. "I'll let you know when she's safe."

"Good." Carly said and then hung up as I got out.

"Park it, or keep it here, boss?" Teenie, the obnoxiously big bouncer, asked as I shut the door behind me.

"Keep it here." I rounded the front of the hood, "I'm not staying."

"Got it." He nodded, moving back to the line as another bouncer opened the front door for me.

I used to love coming to this club. The loud music and dark mystique behind the events happening just on the other side of the velvet curtains or in the VIP rooms upstairs used to entertain me. But now, walking through as I searched for *my* girl, in a room full of other willing women, I was dangerously close to losing it all.

"Boss." Theo met me right inside the front lobby, and I could tell by the edge of his gaze, he knew why I was here.

"Where is she?"

"In your office." He fixated on one of his cufflinks as he explained. "Willow recognized her." Willow had been trafficked at the same time Carly had been and ended up in the brothel that held Laila captive for years. "As soon as I talked to Carly, I approached her, and before I could even say anything, she asked to go to your office." He shrugged almost sadly, "Like she knew you would be coming for her."

"Did anyone bother her before that?" I glanced over the crowd, looking over the men in attendance and half expecting to see a scar-faced biker sitting amongst the crowd, lurking for another chance to steal my girl.

"No, boss." Theo shook his head theatrically. "She was giving off—" He grimaced, "Well frankly, she was hostile toward anyone that came near her. She just sat at the end of the bar and drank."

"Is she drunk?" I questioned, moving toward the staff entrance to the back offices.

He shrugged leaving me to go on my way, "Kind of hard to tell when there's that much anger radiating off of such a small woman."

"Thank you, Theo." I called, but didn't wait for his reply as I moved through the dark hallway to my office. To be honest, I never wanted her to be in this place. The space I used for such carnal things over the years felt like it was tainting her perfection.

I could see the desk lamp on through the frosted glass of the door and hesitated outside. Theo said she was angry. And Carly said to be gentle with her.

But what did my Dove need? Would she bolt and run away from me again?

Would she yell and fight?

Would she cry and crumble?

Before I could dwell on it, I turned the brass doorknob and took in the sight before me. "Dove."

Laila sat in my office chair, with her feet up on the polished desktop and a glass of red wine between her fingers. She wore the same clothes from earlier, and as she looked at me from over the rim of her glass, I could almost physically feel the fatigue through her stare.

She didn't say anything to me but watched me with those dark eyes I'd fallen in love with from the very beginning. Usually, they rounded with fear and excitement when I called her Dove, but tonight, they stared flatly.

Something wasn't right.

"Are you okay?" I asked, loosening the button of my shirt at my throat as it started choking me with the anxiety in the room.

"I'm fine." She replied, taking a sip of her wine. "How did you find me?"

"Why were you hiding from me?" I countered, leaning back against the door and sliding my hands into my pants pockets. It was a power move to pretend I was unaffected by the entire thing, and probably the wrong decision altogether. But I was grasping at straws, desperate for some control.

I was always desperate to hang on to the control around Laila.

"You embarrassed me." She lowered her bottom lip to the rim of the glass and held it there. "Why did you do that?"

I regarded her, hearing the steadiness of her words. At first, I thought she would be drunk. Yet when I walked in, my assumptions were proven wrong.

No, something else was wrong.

"You spent time with Diesel." I admitted exposing my weakness to her. She wasn't my enemy; she was someone I was trying to make into my partner, so I gave her my vulnerability without her even asking for it.

"Wrong." She sipped from her glass. "He followed me around on the street like a little lost puppy dog." She leaned back and rested her head on the chair, "The same way he has since I first met him. I've never given him anything, especially not my time. Yet you punished me for it."

Her backbone was iron-straight as she stared down her nose at me.

And my God, what a magnificent sight she was to behold.

I'd never seen her act so sure and strong before.

Yet now, and even earlier today at the shop, she told me off.

"Correct." There was no point in lying, we both knew why I did what I did.

"Did you feel big?" she asked and cocked her head to the side with a bit of a sneer on her perfect wine-stained lips. "Did it make your cock hard to push me down into my place?"

I raised an eyebrow at her and leaned off the wall. No woman had spoken to me like that for years.

Not one that lived long afterwards, at least.

"No." I slowly stalked across the office toward her. "But I'm getting harder now by the second." Her eyes ignited, and I couldn't tell if it was anger or arousal behind them. "I was wrong." Her thoughts eluded me, and I hated it. "I was jealous. And a fool."

Her teeth clenched, and she looked away from me for a moment before she snapped those beautiful eyes back at me. "I don't think you grasp how it made me feel." She pursed her lips before taking her feet off the desk and leaning forward in the chair to stare up at me directly. "The things it made me feel—," She hesitated, "They took me back."

She didn't need to say where or when they took her back to. I knew. And my stomach rolled at the mere thought of causing her any sort of flashback to that time. That was why she looked so detached when I walked in. She was disappearing back into survival mode, where she disassociated from her surroundings to protect herself.

I took the glass of wine from her fingers and set it on the desk. Her breath caught, and for a moment I thought she was going to yell at me, but she didn't, sinking into the space in her head meant for escape. Slowly, so she wouldn't be alarmed, I sank to my knees at her feet, sliding my hands over her thighs as I tried to connect us. Her inky black eyelashes widened as she watched me present myself in a way I'd never done for another woman before.

"I'm sorry." Kneeling before her, I met her gaze as my thumbs gently circled the tops of her thighs, connecting us through my touch. "I was wrong to talk to you like I did. I've never had to share this part of my life with a woman before. I'm not used to explaining what I do or why."

"He's a kid." She repeated the same mantra she had fought with earlier over the scrawny street kid that had started with the crew a few weeks ago. "He deserves a chance."

"We can't save every kid." I reasoned with her. "But we can give them an opportunity to earn the things they need. No one else gives them that."

"In exchange for what, though?" She pleaded, and the indifference in her eyes shifted to the glowing life normally burning so brightly when she was passionate about something. "Their life? Don't try to tell me they aren't doing dangerous things on the street for you and Ryker, because I already saved him from a beat down once." She jabbed her finger into my chest. "Over your drugs."

"Not my drugs." I grabbed her hand and held it tight so she couldn't jab me again. "And what he did to deserve the beat down was his choice, not the crew's."

"Whatever." She scoffed, fighting my hold, "We're obviously not going to agree on this."

"Why is it so important to you?" I asked, reading her body language, watching as she went from fiery and passionate to cold and defensive. "Why does he matter to you?"

She licked her lips and stared off at the lamp on the desk as her mind took her far away from me and that room. "He should matter to someone."

"Like you didn't, you mean." I added, but she still didn't look at me. "This is about you, not that kid."

She shook her head, "No. It's about him. Because something can be done to help him. No one helped me."

I was hesitant to interpret her veiled language, apprehensive about saying something that might cause her emotional distress or revive bad memories. It felt like walking through a minefield blindfolded. But I'd do it, again and again, to help figure her out.

"Okay." I sighed and squeezed her thighs as she looked over at me finally. I gave her a small smile and lifted my hand to her cheek, when she leaned into my touch, I breathed deeply for the first time. "I'll help him. Because he matters to you."

"I don't want you to do this for me. I don't want you to resent me for it later."

Shaking my head, I stopped her before her worries grew. "You matter to me. That's the only reason I'm doing it. That's not something to resent you for later."

"But you don't agree with me on it." She countered, and I hated that she was hesitating to take what she wanted from me, like she was expecting a trick at the end.

"Do I think it will make the grand change to his life that he needs, to suddenly be successful and thriving? No." I admitted. "But I can see how he's struggling as much as you can, and maybe I ignored it because I'm desensitized to it at this point in life. So instead of ignoring it, I'll help him." I squeezed her thighs again, "Because he won't get a fair chance at life from anyone else but you."

"I don't know why I'm drawn to him." She admitted relaxing her shoulders for the first time since I had walked into the room. "But I can't seem to shake the need to intervene."

"Then let's agree that there was a reason you met him on the street that day. And go from there."

"And you won't hate me?" She chewed her bottom lip.

"Never." I promised immediately. "Especially not over your generous heart."

She sighed and offered me a small smile. "I'm sorry I ran."

"I'm sorry I yelled."

"Yeah, I really didn't like that." She widened her eyes and pursed her lips.

I chuckled and rose from my knees. "Make me a promise?"

"Uh oh." She droned, standing from the chair with her hand in mine. "What is it?"

"That if you need space from me like this again, you are free to leave. But please tell someone where you're going. Even if it's Carly or Jed. Just don't go dark on us again."

She swallowed and nodded her head, "I won't do it again." And then fluttered her eyelashes, "Sorry Daddy."

I growled and cocked my head to the side in warning as a smile pulled on her full lips. "Careful, Dove." I leaned down until my lips were hovering above hers, "Because I've thought of nothing else all day except how sexy your moans were when I slid deep inside of you each time yesterday. And I'm on edge, barely containing that need, until we get back to your place."

"Hmm, and if you didn't contain yourself?" She questioned, "Would you fuck me before we got back."

"Minx." I groaned, tightening my hands around her waist and pressing my ever-growing erection into her stomach as she giggled and licked those lips. "Car. Now."

"Yes, Daddy." She whispered, leaning up to peck my lips briefly before all but running for the door.

Trouble; Laila Manning finding her footing and backbone was nothing but trouble.

And I was ready to fucking thrive in the chaos of her strength.

CHapTer 22 – Laila

"Tell me what you meant about no one helping you." Zeke said, tightening his fingers on my thigh as we drove through the dark city streets of Shadeport.

He found me at Lux, and I had half expected his anger when he showed up. Hell, I'd been ready to match his anger with my own.

But he was only gentle and understanding. Firm and protective, but understanding.

"Just in life." I shrugged, trying to avoid the memories that burned behind my eyes like a horrific movie.

"When I got to you, you weren't all there." He said, glancing over at me as I looked at him questioningly. "You were disassociated from your surroundings."

"How do you know that?" I wondered out loud.

"Because there was no life left in your eyes." He held my stare as he drove without caring for the surrounding traffic, like a pro. "There was no warmth or even fear. You were hollow."

"That's a cruel thing to say." I deflected, looking back out the window.

"Not if it's the truth."

That was the thing about Zeke, he was unapologetically curious about me. Even when it was rude or difficult. He pushed.

He prodded.

He investigated.

At first, I used to get bothered by it. I felt like he was trying to pry into the dark and disgusting parts of me, like I was some experiment he was trying to solve. But the more he did it, the more he questioned the why behind the what, I realized he was trying to know *me*.

I couldn't remember another time in my life when someone actually tried to know me. Not just the things that happened *to* me or what I could offer to them.

So, I took a deep breath and faced my anxiety head-on in light of his devotion. "I escaped once." He didn't say anything, but a tense pause settled in his muscles where his hand still lay on my thigh. "It was before I ended up at the brothel. I don't really remember when exactly. But I lived in this run-down motel room with three other girls." Just talking about the room made the rotten smell of the carpet invade my senses, like I was right back there. "One night I escaped from a passed-out John, who left his car keys and wallet in his pants pockets on the floor." I remembered the fear pumping through my body that night as I eyed them for an hour before I got brave enough to make a move. "I made a break for it and managed to get into his car and take off in the middle of the night."

"What happened?" He asked with that calm seriousness he always had when he was in business mode.

The memories of that night assaulted me even as I tried for indifference. Looking out the window, I shrugged my shoulder. "I crashed the car a couple of miles away. I didn't have much driving experience, and with all the adrenaline—" I sighed, "It was a crowded city street, kind of like this one. I got out of the car wearing a dirty oversized t-shirt and nothing else, not even shoes." A shudder ran through me as I recalled my fear that night. "People lined the streets, going in and out of clubs and bars, and I begged someone to help me. I told them I'd been kidnapped and assaulted—but no one would even make eye contact with me."

"Jesus." He grunted, tightening his hand on the steering wheel.

"The cops showed up, and I thought that I'd finally found my saviors to end the hellish ordeal for good." I swallowed down the pain, "But they called the guy who owned the car, and he convinced them that I was his daughter who was mentally unstable and had stolen his car." I sank into the seat under the weight of it all. "My pimp showed up with him and dragged me back, kicking and screaming, in the middle of a crowded street, and no one did a damn thing to help me. Right before he slammed me back into his car, one of the cops, a woman, sneered at me and said, prostitutes weren't allowed to cry rape."

"I'm so sorry, Laila."

"I think that's why I can't just let this go with Kade." I turned to look at him in the dark car, and he was staring back. "I think that's why I can't seem to just turn away when he's desperately in need of help."

"I get it now." Zeke nodded, glancing back at the road as we turned back into East Valley. "I understand the depth of it now."

"I didn't." I admitted, "Until right now."

"Most of the time, we don't grasp why we do what we do in the moment until we take time to sit back and think it through. Talk it out."

"Maybe." I mused, "Or maybe there's just something about you always digging around in my head, knowing all of my darkest secrets that brings it out." I tried joking, bringing up what I said to him that day on the sidewalk, but instantly regretted it when I remembered what I was doing when he found me that day. When I remembered whose house I was standing outside of.

"You're doing it again." He gently squeezed my leg, and I noticed he passed the turn to Ryker's estate, taking the next street instead. The street that skipped the Senator's home. "Drifting away into yourself."

"You know, don't you?" I watched the warm streetlights blur as we passed the houses.

Zeke sighed and turned down the next street, taking us back toward Ryker's estate. "I think I know a small part of it."

"I wish you didn't know any of it." I admitted sadly.

"I wish none of it had been done to you in the first place." He asserted, parking his car next to the garage and turning it off, leaving us bathed in darkness and silence. "You don't have to cut yourself open any more than you already have tonight, Dove." He took my hand in his and raised it to his lips. "But I won't lie and tell you that I don't wish I knew the facts so that I could protect you from any more hurt." He sighed, "So you aren't left vulnerable like you were at the gala ever again."

"I don't want to feel like a child, always being watched." My past meant I knew I'd always be treated cautiously, so my argument lacked conviction.

"You don't get it, do you?" He gently shook his head and then kissed each of my fingertips. "I'm not watching you like a child, Laila." He dropped our hands to his lap and stared directly at me until I could feel his gaze in my heart. "I'm trying to worship you like a goddess, worthy of every single second of my attention simply because you exist, and I'm so fucking obsessed with you I have no choice but to focus on you." He leaned over the center console and slid his hand around the back of my neck, pulling me to him until our foreheads pressed together, breathing the same air. "What I'm offering you is my *devotion*. My loyalty in protecting you, in honoring you, in caring for you isn't one out of pity or guilt. It's out of admiration." He pressed his lips to mine, "One out of love."

"Zeke." I gasped against his lips, physically moved by his declaration.

"Don't say anything." He spoke gently, rubbing his thumb over my jaw. "I didn't realize how deeply in love with you I was until you left me today, so I don't expect you to say it back. But I didn't want you to misunderstand what I feel for you as anything other than love, ever again."

"Thank you." I whispered, unable to form any other words as his moved through my brain and heart. "Thank you."

I worked my shift at Neat, learning as much as I could as I tried to focus on anything but what was happening out on the streets outside the building. There was no identifiable source of what caused the repetitive loop of intrusive thoughts I was stuck in, but I couldn't get out of it. Honestly, if I looked at my entire life for the last ten years, I could get a pretty good idea, but still, there had been no recent trigger.

Nonetheless, I was stuck on a hamster wheel imagining the worst of the worst happening to everyone I loved, right outside the doors of Neat. And it was making it hard to function.

Was it some dark and twisted version of a sixth sense, or was it trauma?

I'd put twenty on trauma.

Nicole, the head bartender, nudged me on her way past with a bottle of high-end whiskey. "Hey girl, you're all set. Beat feet."

"Oh, thank God." I joked, wiping my hands on a towel as I stared down at the dozens of glasses I'd just washed. "I was afraid my fingerprints were never going to return if I washed anymore."

She chuckled and shrugged, "Newbie dues. You'll be off them once the next person starts training, and then you can pass the dish towel off and never look back."

"Good to know there's light at the end of the tunnel." Using the register, I clocked out and pulled out my phone to order a ride. "I'm going out the back, do you need me to take anything to the dumpster?"

"Yeah, take that garbage, if you don't mind."

"Got it." I tied the bag closed and walked away with a wave, eager to get out of the bar and into the fresh air. Even though the fresh air smelled like trash as I neared the full dumpster. It was almost dark out, but there was still a serene peacefulness to the sky as it started turning purple above the city lights. At least, there was if you could ignore the smells and sounds of the city too. I wasn't a big fan of living near the city, but there was a stark difference in the vibes of East Valley, even if it was only ten minutes from downtown.

I guess money bought serenity.

As I swung open the gate to the dumpster fence, three shadowy figures jumped in surprise around the side, making me freeze mid-step.

Drugs.

Doing or selling, I couldn't tell. But I was between them and the exit, and that wasn't good.

"Fuck you looking at, bitch?" One of the figures snapped with aggression as he walked out of the shadows.

"Just taking the trash out." I murmured, trying to calm my erratic heart rate as I shoved the gate open all the way. "Go about your business."

"My business." The man sneered, rounding the dumpster and standing in my way of it, "You're fucking with my business." He was twice my size and looked dirty and diseased, making me shiver as he got closer.

"You should get a better office." I snapped back, running off pure adrenaline and anxiety. Or maybe I was running off of trauma and mental illness, who the fuck knew. But either way, that was not the best thing to say, when all I really wanted was to leave, unnoticed.

"Maybe you should learn your fucking place." He pointed his fingers at me, shaped like a gun as he grabbed his belt. "Maybe I'll help teach you a lesson."

My mouth was as dry as sandpaper as I took a step backward across the wet pavement. I watched as the two other figures came out of the shadows, wiping their noses and looking a little less clear-eyed. I was terribly outnumbered and—angry.

I was so damn angry at being caught in the stupid situations, over and over again, just like this one.

"Wait." One of the nose wipers said, pushing his way out to look at me through red, glossy eyes. "Fuck. It's you." He was young, maybe barely eighteen, but unlikely, and looked as dirty as the first one.

"You know her?" The first druggie snapped, looking me up and down with disdain.

"Yeah," The kid said, elbowing the third guy. "Zeke's girl."

"Yup." The third one slurred with a slow nod, "The one with a hard-on for Kade."

"Zeke?" The first one questioned as my blood ran cold. Were they friends or enemies of Zeke and Kade, or of all of Shadeport, for that matter. "Zeke Evans?" He sneered, "With you?"

The second kid shrugged with a laugh, "I don't get it either, but yeah, I think she's related to Jed somehow too."

The first guy walked closer to me, but I stayed frozen in place, it wasn't like I'd get away if I tried, in a way it felt like all those times I forced myself to stay still and let it happen in the brothel.

Sometimes fighting back made it hurt worse.

"It's your lucky day, cunt." The first guy said, checking his shoulder into mine as he walked by. "Tomorrow won't be, though, so stay out of my business."

I clenched my teeth to keep from retorting something smart-mouthed back to him, as it seemed I'd earned my free pass. The other kid went with him, but when the third went to go by, he paused, flicking a glance out after his buddies and then at me.

His slurred speech was painful to listen to, and I wasn't sure how he was standing on both feet still, but he asked, "Have you seen Kade lately?"

My icy cold hands started sweating instantly when I deciphered the concern behind his blood-shot eyes. "No." I replied, forcing my tongue off the roof of my mouth, mentally counting the days since I saw him at the estate the day I yelled at Zeke. "A week or so I think. Why? Is something wrong?"

The kid shrugged, looking back after his buddies as one called his name before disappearing down an alley. "He's not been around much the last few days. That's weird for him."

"Are you in the crew?" I asked, and then quickly tossed the trash into the dumpster as he stumbled away after his friends. "Wait, he hasn't been around where? Where is he usually?"

He shrugged again, walking in a stumbled pace toward the dark alley I wouldn't be caught dead in willingly. I had to get my answers from him before he walked into the darkness or I'd never get them.

"Dunno. Around. But not for a few days now." He slurred.

I stopped following him as the shadows swallowed him up as a million thoughts ran through my head from his cryptic questions and answers.

If Kade's druggie friends were worried about him, then something was wrong.

Maybe that was why the doomsday feeling had been clinging to my neck like a noose all day long. I had to find him.

CHAPTER 23 – ZEKE

I wiped the steam off the mirror above my sink when my front door banged open. Leaning back, I caught a flurry of brown copper hair coming through my door before the doorknob had even stopped vibrating from the dent it had left in the wall.

"How can I find Kade?" Laila demanded in her haste, with her hands on her hips as I turned and walked out of the bathroom completely.

"Hello to you too, Dove." I replied, crossing my arms over my chest as I leaned my shoulder against the wall. "How was your day? Mine was fine, thanks for asking."

Laila rolled her eyes and dropped her fists from her hips as a deep breath filled her lungs. She still wore her work uniform, and her cheeks were pink and flushed, breathing life into her light skin. "Hi." She gave me a soft smile, and then it was like she finally paid attention to the fact that I stood before her in just a towel, fresh out of the shower. Her warm brown eyes traveled down my body, and her pink lips parted momentarily before her dark lashes snapped back up to my face and her cheeks got even more color to them. "My day is getting better by the moment."

I chuckled, standing up off the wall and crossing the space to her. We'd only been together for a short while, but my hands knew her body like they'd never been without the feel of her skin against them, and when she was in reach, she leaned into me as I hugged her. "I missed you." I whispered against her ear, and she pulled back to kiss me.

A few weeks ago, she wouldn't have been able to be in the room with me alone without panicking, yet now she openly came to me and physically relaxed in my hold instead of tensing. The weight of her trust settled upon me, a powerful and incredible feeling.

"I'm pretty sure I missed you more." She pouted comically, resting her cheek against my chest and holding onto me.

"Did something happen?" She was on edge when she walked into my apartment, and even though she relaxed with my touch, I could still tell something had her rattled.

"No, I mean, not really."

"Hmm." I grunted, pulling her over to the couch and into my lap, adjusting her until she lay against me with her head tucked under my chin. "Tell me."

She snuggled in deeper, and her breath warmed the flesh of my neck as she spoke. "I ran into a couple of junkies out back behind Neat. One of them asked me if I'd seen Kade lately. Apparently, he hasn't been around, and I guess he thought I knew where he was."

"Street kids tend to come and go, Dove." I replied, mentally tracking the last time I saw the scraggly bag of bones kid. But I couldn't think of any times past the infamous day here at the estate when I fired him. He wasn't actually fired, and I let him keep unloading the truck with Jed. Since then, though, he had been gone.

"The kid said it wasn't normal for Kade, though. If he's not here with you or the crew, where else would he be?"

I shrugged because, to be honest, I didn't know where the kid hung out or slept at night. I had never cared to check in.

Laila cared, though, and that meant I should have cared. "I'll ask around. See what he's up to."

"Yeah?" She leaned back and looked up at me with hope in her warm chocolate eyes. "Really?"

"Really. He's probably just off doing riffraff shit, but I'll check on him."

"Thank you." Laila murmured, sounding slightly surprised still.

"I'd do anything you asked of me, Dove."

She snorted, "The last time we talked about Kade, you yelled at me. Pardon me if my confidence is a little shaky on that topic."

At first, I wanted to rebuke her claim, arguing that she was wrong. But she wasn't, not really. I didn't remember yelling at her exactly during that exchange outside of the shop, but it didn't matter. I failed her needs at that moment by reacting to the news that she had once again been with Diesel and taking it out on her.

"Just promise me one thing." I said, running my fingers through her hair as she leaned back again to look up at me.

"I'll try."

"Promise me that if he's a lost cause, you'll let him go."

"Zeke," She started, but I shook my head and silenced her.

"Some people can't be saved. Some things are out of our control, and not everyone even wants help. So, I'll get involved and help you, but I don't want you to hold yourself to blame if it doesn't go your way in the end. Not everything can be fixed."

"I know." She sighed. "But I want to try. I can't explain the draw to him, but it's there. Something bigger than you and me is telling me that I need to try. Past that, I don't know what will happen, but I think he needs us."

"Us." I repeated, rolling the word around in my mind as she smiled against my neck.

"Unless you want me going off on my own again—" She joked. "I seem to be a magnet for trouble, though."

I scoffed, adjusting her on my lap until she was face down over my lap across the couch. She giggled, wordlessly telling me she was okay, so I went further, rubbing my hand over her ass in her tight jeans before squeezing one of her plump ass cheeks. "I think I like when your trouble is only found here with me."

"Mmh," She wiggled her hips and looked over her shoulder at me. "Can we try something?"

My dick throbbed under her as I nodded.

She was nervous, I could tell by the way she nibbled on her bottom lip and avoided eye contact. "Will you spank me?"

My hand tightened on her ass cheek, and my breath hitched in my throat as my heart raced like it had just been electrocuted. For the last few days, she had been working through her list—the kink list. Asking me questions like they were hypothetical and not specific to her, but I knew better. "Why do you want to try that?"

"Because I think I'd like it." She licked her lips, "When you touch me, I—" She sighed, "I burn, Zeke."

"What does spanking have to do with that?" I questioned, rubbing my palm over her ass, dipping my fingers between her thighs ever so slightly and rubbing.

"Because I throb when I think about you doing it to me." Laila's sweet innocent voice speaking such filth nearly broke me.

"If you want it, you have to prove it." I slid my fingers between her legs and pushed them against her hot and apparently throbbing core. "Stand up and take your jeans off."

She blinked once, and then scrambled from my lap, flicking the button of her pants open and then pushing them down over her flared hips. The entire time I sat on the couch, leaned back, watching her, letting her see the hunger in my gaze as she gave me the only thing I ever craved from her—her words.

There she was before me, in a pair of black panties and her black uniform shirt. "Take your shirt off, Dove."

Laila didn't even hesitate as she pulled it up over her head and tossed it on the floor with her jeans. "Now what?" she asked softly.

We were toeing the line of right and wrong, safe and dangerous, yet I ached to see how far she would go with me. Because with me—she was safe.

"Lie down like you were." I ran my palm over my thigh, still wearing only my towel from my shower, but my good girl crawled across my lap, just like I said. "That's a good girl." I praised, running my knuckles down the long length of her spine, teasing the clasp of her matching black bra before flicking it open so I could trace a line from the base of her skull to the base of her spine. "Tell me what you like most about the idea of me spanking you."

She swallowed, the noise audible as she laid her cheek on the couch so she could look at me. "I don't know exactly." She took a deep breath, "It started spinning in my head the other night at Neat. When you were all aggression and testosterone and so—" She groaned, "So damn sexy."

"And you think if you feel that strength and testosterone, that you'll what? Enjoy it?"

"God, I hope so," She groaned, "Or this will all be incredibly embarrassing."

"No, it won't." I admonished, tracing the edge of her panties over her ass cheeks, dipping between her thighs and back over the seam of the fabric, tempting and teasing her. "Anything we learn about each other is invaluable information to have. You need to remember that. And anytime you want something from me, just tell me, and it's yours. Anytime you don't like something, just tell me and I'll never do it again."

"What about you?" She whispered. "This—do you like this?"

"You on my lap in your panties?" I questioned, though I knew she was talking about the idea of spanking. "I love it." Dipping my thumb under the seam of her panties, I pushed it between her thighs to find her dripping center, she was soaked already. "And spanking you—" I moaned as I pushed my thumb into her and then circled her clit with it. Her thighs widened, and she arched her back, presenting her ass just the slightest bit for me. "I think we're both going to enjoy it, Dove."

"Spank me, Zeke." She begged, curling her fingers into fists and bracing as she shimmied in my lap. "Please, I'm begging you."

"No." I mused, torturing us both. "Not until you're so delirious with need that you don't know any better."

"Zeke." She whined and then moaned when I changed the angle of my thumb, replacing it with my finger and pushed it into her pussy, going deeper. "Mmh, okay." She gasped, "Whatever you say, just don't stop that."

Sliding her panties down over her ass until they tangled around her knees, I used my fingers to spread her cheeks apart so I could watch my fingers disappearing into her body. What a fucking privilege it was to be inside of her, any part of my body, it didn't matter. I just wanted to exist inside her pretty pink pussy.

I curled my finger inside of her while playing with her clit, making her wiggle and shift on my lap. "Tell me how that feels."

"Like I'm going to burst into flames." She moaned, "Like my skin is on fire."

"What do you want?"

"You to spank me. And then fuck me." She gasped. "Or hell, fuck me and spank me at the same time, I don't care. I just want to come."

"Are you ready?" I asked, using my free hand lazily to palm her plump ass cheek.

"Yes!" She all but screamed at me, and I grinned as I laid my palm down in a sharp slap across the supple flesh. I didn't go easy on her, that wasn't what she wanted. She wanted to be spanked by a real man, to find pleasure from it. So, I started rough, and I could always lighten up if needed.

"Fuck yes!" She groaned, fisting the couch and pushing back into my hand. "Again."

"Beg for it."

"Please, Daddy, again!"

I spanked her again. And again, she let out a guttural groan that sounded like part of her soul was being freed, piece by piece with each spank.

I kept my fingers working on her, pleasing her with the pain so she didn't slip into her traumatic past, but with every moan and plea for more, I trusted her words more. "I'm so close." She moaned, looking over at me with wild eyes. "From you. Because of you. For you."

"That's it, Dove." I pulled my fingers free from her body and slid out from under her before laying over her back, letting my big body dwarf hers on the couch. "Beg me for more."

"Please, I need to feel you, everywhere."

I ripped my towel off and pressed the tip of my dick between her wet thighs, letting them stroke my cock from root to tip as I teased her before switching my angle and giving her just the head. "You're such a good girl for me. So fucking perfect."

"Fuck me, Zeke." Laila begged, pushing back onto me until I was buried halfway inside of her tight little body. "Just like that," She purred as she laced her fingers through mine, holding me to her.

I gave it to her, pushing deep into her body and clenching my jaw to keep from biting her shoulder as she gasped and took it. "You take me so perfectly, Laila. This pussy was always meant for me. Your body will only know mine for the rest of forever."

"Promise me." She cried, and I pulled back, lifting her hips until she was on her knees, and slammed into her as I spanked her ass for emphasis.

"Mine." I vowed, and she shot off before the word even died on my lips. Screaming my name in ecstasy as I fucked her harder than I had yet. It was primal and raw, and everything she was craving from me.

And it meant everything *to* me.

She meant everything to me, and I would never let her go. Whatever she wanted out of life, was hers. Me included.

CHAPTER 24 – Laila

It took me a solid four days of psychotic stalking before I found Kade. Four freaking days, even with Zeke and Jed backing my endeavor to find him. Eventually, I'd give him credit for being so elusive and street smart, but all I felt the first time I laid eyes on him again was worry. He looked different.

In a good way. He was clean and had fresh clothes on.

His hair was even cut and styled.

He looked like a normal kid walking down the streets in Shadeport, and not like a street kid, lurking in dark alleys, running shady dealings in the shadows.

I should have been happy that he looked so good, but there was something in my gut, burning and raging loud enough to force me to acknowledge it. And it felt a lot like intuition. The clean-cut look made him look youthful and fresh, too. It made him look vulnerable.

Which made me angry.

"I've been looking for you." I announced, catching him off guard as he walked past the bistro cafe I was sitting at, having a cup of tea. Finding him at that moment hadn't been planned, I'd simply been taking a break from walking the streets, looking behind dumpsters and abandoned buildings, searching for him. And then there he was, walking down the street in a new name-brand hoodie and fresh sneakers like he hadn't been missing at all.

His bright blue eyes always reminded me of Zeke's, and when they snapped at me, filling with irritation almost instantly, I brushed it off. "You don't quit, do you?"

"Sit." I snapped my fingers, kicking the metal chair across from me out and lifting my cup to my lips. He scoffed and waved me off, walking away from me without a second glance as I called out, "Or I'll tell Zeke."

I sensed him coming to a stop behind me, right before I could feel his glare in the back of my head, followed by his groan in frustration. He stomped back to my table and threw himself down in the chair, leaning his elbows on the table to glare at me. "What the fuck is wrong with you, lady?"

"Laila." I replied, sipping my tea again as he squinted at me in contemplation. "My name is Laila."

"Why should I care what my stalker's name is?"

I shrugged and smiled at an older couple who walked by, both with canes holding hands. "If I wanted to stalk you, I'd order a hit out and have you sent to the shop so I could *watch* you there."

I had zero clue if anything I said made sense; I didn't even know what went on in the ominous building behind the barracks. Hell, I didn't even know how to order a hit on anyone or if that was even how things were done in the crew, but it sounded good. And it must have sounded good enough, because his youthful features whitened a bit before he leaned back in the chair, defeated.

"What do you want?" He asked with far less malice in his voice, and I waved the server down, drawing her to the table.

"Spare me a few minutes, get yourself a drink, and let's chat. Without all the false bravado and jabs flying." I stared at him pointedly, "From either of us."

He sighed but turned his attention to the waitress, "I'll have a watermelon boba."

"Please." I replied pointedly, and he rolled his eyes but added it.

"Please. Thank you."

"Good job." I smiled as the server walked away, and an awkward silence fell between us. I hadn't planned exactly what I'd say to him when I found him, but I knew if I didn't start soon, he'd bolt. "Your friend asked me if I had seen you a few days ago. And it took me this long to lay eyes on you. Which is impressive, considering Jed and Zeke were helping me."

"I've been busy." He shrugged, watching the cars drive down the street. "I got a new job."

"How old are you?" I questioned, "Before with the whole gloom and doom look, I would have guessed thirteen, maybe. But now, you look even younger."

Ty scoffed with a snort, "Dirt ages you."

"Tell me about it." I droned on, sipping my tea.

His blue eyes finally found me again and squinted. "Like you know anything about being dirty. I'm sure you've never lifted a single manicured finger living in the East Valley."

"Except I only just moved to Ryker's Estate a few months ago. Before that, I lived in conditions far worse than anything you could dream up in that smart-mouthed little head of yours."

He opened his mouth to say something but stopped himself, as if he was physically trying to be—nice. I'm sure the tough-guy act was a hard one to drop after perfecting it for years.

"I'm twelve." He replied after a while. "But it's just a number. When you've been on your own as long as I have been, it doesn't mean anything."

"How long have you been alone?" I sipped my tea, watching silently as he gave the young server who delivered his tea a flirty smile before he responded.

He stared back toward the traffic with a slight shrug. "Four years on my own. Three in foster care before that."

He had been on the streets since he was eight years old.

I wasn't even allowed to cross the street alone at eight, but now look at the both of us. We were both products of the world, chewing us up and spitting us out. "I'm guessing that somehow, the street is better than your foster care was?" I asked, and he just rolled his eyes with a shrug, telling me all I needed to know. "What new job did you get?"

He shrugged again, looking out over the street. "Taking care of some stuff."

"Stuff?" I deadpanned, "For whom?"

"Why do you care?"

"Because you're a kid. At the end of the day Kade, you're a kid. And I'm trying to make sure you're not being taken advantage of. So, who are you working for?"

He rolled his eyes with annoyance, "A rich lady in East Valley." He huffed, "She has me do odds and ends around the property."

"A rich lady?" I speculated, "Doesn't she have staff for that?"

There wasn't a single house in the Valley that didn't have land-scapers and handymen on staff. There were people milling around constantly.

"She doesn't trust people in her home, she said." He took another long drink of the tea, "It's a cushy gig, I organize shit and get paid big time. She even got me new clothes, she said she couldn't have riffraff going in and out of her home because she had an image to protect."

"Kade, that sounds—"

"Don't." He snapped, leaning forward and holding my stare in a way that kids never did. "It's not too good to be true. It's just a good opportunity to get out of what I've been doing. That's it."

"I thought you liked the crew?" I questioned, "Wasn't that why you freaked out on me."

"No one likes selling drugs to low-lives on the street, Lady." He scoffed, "And this new gig pays far better."

I sighed, and he took his opportunity, standing up from his chair and tossing his half drank tea into the trash bin. "Look, I got to go. I've got places to be."

"Okay, wait," I rose and called after him, waiting for him to dramatically turn back. "Just know that if you need help with anything," I said, "Come find me. No questions asked. I'll always help. I promise."

"Yeah right," He waved me off, "Questions are your middle name, lady. K bye!"

He walked away, and I let him go. My stomach was gnawing at me to do something more, to stop him from leaving now that I had finally found him. But I didn't. I watched him walk away, hoping to God that he was telling the truth and trying to find a way to make my body trust in someone else's words. If he said it was a good gig, why did I automatically think he was wrong?

Oh, yeah—experience.

I walked the path to Carly's without so much as a trembling nerve or worried stomach in sight, even as I climbed the steps and knocked on her front door.

Was I healed? What did that term even mean? But I was finally happy.

Wait, was I? What the hell did *that* term mean?

"Come in, Laila." Carly called, and I shook the thought from my mind as I walked in. Carly was in the kitchen, wiping down the countertop with a sweet little tune humming in her distraction. "Good morning, Sunshine."

I paused, looking behind me and then smirking when she rolled her eyes at me. "You're in a good mood this morning."

"Make-up sex does that to a girl." She shrugged, and then paused, cloth in hand, "I mean, hate sex does that to me too, and role-play sex—"

"Okay, we get it, you like sex." I chuckled, taking a seat at the island instead of burrowing myself into the chair in the living room like usual. "What else is going on?"

"I'm actually leaving in a few for a nail appointment, want to come with me?" She asked. "You could get a manicure with me."

"Thanks," I eyed my bland natural nails compared to her fancy designed acrylics. "But I have to work in a little bit. Besides, all the dishes would chip the paint off in two seconds flat."

She grimaced, "Still stuck on dish duty, huh?"

"For now," I shrugged, "But I don't hate it."

Carly paused and held my stare. "I'm proud of you, you know that?"

I waved her off and slid from the stool, "Yeah, okay, the cleaning spray is going to your head." I smirked as I walked back toward the front door. "Have fun with your nails!"

"'Kay bye!" She called with a chuckle.

As I left Carly's cottage, I went toward the mansion; the day was just too beautiful to go back to the concrete building. Especially since Zeke was gone for the day working.

Had he been in the barracks, I would have eagerly joined him for some more of his naughty activities.

When I got to the side of the garage, I heard voices inside and paused before walking around the front. The big overhead door was open, and the security room was off the garage, so no way was I walking in if it was crawling with crew members.

But as I listened to the voices, I recognized them. And I wish I hadn't, because what they were saying broke my heart.

"It's not your place, Jed." Ryker sighed, and I could almost imagine him rubbing his hand over his face.

"It is!" Jed barked back, "She's my sister, Ry. Mine. My flesh and my blood. No one else. We had a vote, and it ended in a tie, but she deserves to be shielded from this. He was her abuser, for fuck's sake! It will traumatize her all over again! He's a monster, why should she have to face that? Everything I've ever done has been to shield her from the monsters out there, and it was all for nothing! But not this. *This* I can protect her from!"

My heart sank into my gut as I covered my lips with my fingers to keep from crying out.

"She needs to know." Zeke snapped. "That's the end of it."

"Then why haven't you told her?" Jed bellowed. "Tell me why we had this discussion over a week ago, and she still doesn't know that we're killing the Senator for her?" Jed's voice turned lethal, and my skin pebbled. "Let me guess, you've been too busy using her body for your own selfish pleasures instead of talking to her about what actually fucking matters!"

A sickening thud echoed, and then the scuff of feet as Ryker yelled for them to separate.

"Tell me." I stepped around the corner and found Zeke on top of Jed, arm pulled back, ready to strike. But the three men went still when I appeared. Ellie stood along the wall, and her face fell when she saw me. "Tell me!"

"Dove." Zeke uncurled his fist from the front of Jed's shirt, and my brother shoved him off as they both got to their feet.

"Tell me." I repeated with a lethal calmness I couldn't remember ever feeling before. It was similar to how I felt when I turned my brain off during a job in the brothel. My brain and my body were two separate entities, and that was the only thing keeping me standing on my own two feet as Zeke stared at me, looking gutted.

"Laila," Zeke started, but Jed cut him off, staring at me like an equal instead of a victim.

"Senator Lupold." Jed said evenly. "We know he was one of the men who assaulted you." He took a step forward as I stared at him, emotionless. "We don't know the details, but we've agreed he'll die for what he did to you. So will anyone else we can identify."

I turned my gaze to Zeke, feeling the anger radiating off me. "Why didn't you tell me? The other night in the car, when I realized you knew, why didn't you tell me you knew *this* much!" My voice ended in a scream as I lost my grip on my emotions.

My skin crawled as the three men, the strongest men I'd ever known, stared at me like I was a filthy, broken little piece of trash. And then I heard the voices of my attackers in my head, sneering their vile words into my ears as they raped me.

You don't matter to anyone.

No one ever loved you.

You're a dirty, disgusting whore, nothing else.

You're ugly and vile.

You're good for nothing but this.

Zeke finally spoke, "I didn't know if you should be involved or not."

"Involved?" I gasped. "Yet you think you should be?" I accused, tasting bile in my throat. "Or were you just too worried that if I knew what you were planning to do, that I wouldn't be such an easy fucking lay for you! That maybe my trauma would get in the way of you getting your dick inside of me!"

"Laila, take a deep breath." Ellie walked forward and touched my arm, but I ripped away from her, dragging my nails down my arm to erase the feeling of her touch. Blood pooled in the gouges left, but I hardly felt them as it ran down my fingers and onto the floor. How many times did I bleed the touch of others from my skin before this? Too many.

"I'm sorry that this keeps happening." I kept my face to the ground as I took another step backward. "I'm sorry that you all had to have secret meetings about my fucked-up life." My breath caught as my throat felt like it was going to close up from the anxiety. "I'm sorry that my past keeps interrupting your perfectly poised and polished lives."

"Stop it." Zeke snapped as he came closer to me, but I flinched when he went to touch me, a haunted look crossing his face before he schooled it. "None of that is true. We were trying to come up with the best way to handle it."

"To handle me!" I screamed, shaking like a leaf as I stared into his blue eyes. Eyes so clear and captivating that I had lost myself in them as he made love to me, just that morning before he left to talk about my trauma like I didn't exist apart from it. "You should have left it alone! Instead, you all made up your minds, my feelings be damned!"

"We're trying to protect you." He clarified, as if it made a bit of difference.

"You can't." I shook my head, hollowed out by it all. "If you knew what he did," My voice broke, "What he stole from me." My chest heaved, and I pressed my hand to my heart, praying the organ wouldn't go into cardiac arrest from the erratic beating. "I can't—" I shook my head, backing away from him as I turned to Jed, holding my brother's broken stare. "If you want to kill the man, go ahead. If you do, make it fucking hurt. But I don't want to know anything more about it. Promise me that much."

My big, strong, and immovable brother nodded his head, brows furrowed over his dark eyes, "I promise you."

And no words ever felt more real to me.

In a tornado of secrets and hushed whispers, I couldn't find my footing when it felt like everyone felt the need to make decisions for me, without even asking my opinion first. But in Jed's eyes, in his firm conviction, I found the assurance I was in desperate need of.

He would kill the monster who stole my whole life from me. I could count on that.

"Please don't walk away again," Zeke tried, taking a step toward me as I turned away, "Not like this."

"I can't." I shook my head, unable to meet his eyes. "I can't be a part of this. Because Jed was right, I shouldn't have to face this all over again."

"I'm sorry." Zeke called out, defeated, but I simply shook my head in response. "God, Laila."

"I can't. I need to be alone." And I walked away, leaving my heart in the dirt with the men who thought they knew how to care for it better than I did.

Little did they know, my heart stopped carrying weight in my chest years ago. It was just something that happened when you lost everything worth hoping for.

CHAPTER 25 – ZEKE

I sat on my couch, staring through my open front door to Laila's closed one. I knocked, but she wouldn't answer. Calling her ended up with a full voicemail box.

She wanted to be alone, so I was trying to honor her wishes, but dammit, it was hard.

It felt impossible.

It killed me.

So I sat, waiting, simply praying for her to come to me, or let me in. Anything.

The longer I waited, hearing nothing from the other side of her door, the less sure I became that she'd ever open it for me again.

Lost in thought, I never heard the exterior door open until a shadow crossed my threshold as Carly paused between our doorways. She looked from Laila's closed one to me and leaned on my frame. "Anything?"

I shook my head, rocking my jaw back and forth as I stared at a spot on the floor. "I really thought what I was doing was right." Knowing Carly was safe overshadowed my self-consciousness about sounding shattered. "I just didn't know how to tell her without—breaking her. Telling her would break her, and somehow keeping it from her did the same."

"Let me try to talk to her." Carly said, "I'll see what I can do."

I didn't agree, or give her permission, but she didn't wait around to see if I did. She knocked softly on Laila's door and leaned toward it, "Laila, it's Carly."

"Come in." Laila's gentle voice called out from within, and I sat up straight on the couch, ready to follow her inside, but Carly waved me off, with a stern glare before disappearing inside the dark apartment.

I hung my head and scrubbed my hands over my face with a loud growl. Sitting idly went against everything I'd spent my entire life becoming. I was the type of person who took care of shit, fully, and without question. But Laila didn't know that, because we hardly ever talked about me. It was my fault, my efforts were always to dig into her head, while keeping her out of mine.

But no more.

If she forgave me for fighting with Jed again and for hiding that I knew more than I let on, then I'd bare myself to her from now on. I'd share.

I'd protect.

I'd love.

Fully.

It felt like hours passed, more time spent sitting on my couch staring at the bolted door before it opened again. This time Carly came out first, but Laila was behind her, frozen in her doorway.

My breath caught in my throat when her red-rimmed eyes found me and watered up.

"Be gentle." Carly said, looking at Laila and me. "Listen, without having to refute or explain yourself." She took Laila's hand and squeezed it before giving me one last look. "Be open and honest in ways you've never had to be before, either of you. That's the only way."

"Got it." I nodded to her as she walked down the hall toward the exit, but my eyes never left Laila.

She was curled in on herself, and she hid behind her hair. It had been weeks since I'd seen the broken and scared version of her, part of me almost forgot she existed inside of Laila's newfound confidence and comfort around me.

God, I was stupid. I thought telling her about Senator Lupold was a good idea because she had been so strong, conquering her fears with me and finding a new kind of normalcy, but I forgot how fragile she really was inside still.

I didn't push her; I didn't speak or try to crowd her—instead I slowly lowered myself down onto the floor in the opening of my front door, crossed my legs and looked up at her. She had to decide what she did next; I couldn't do it for her.

Finally, she bent her legs and lowered herself to the floor opposite me, in her doorway and brought her knees up to her chest before resting her chin on them. She wore cozy thick sweatpants and a cardigan, almost disappearing inside the long sleeves and baggy pants, but I could see the bandage peeking out from the sleeve and my stomach cramped knowing she hurt herself because of what I did. The moment Ellie touched her, she was back inside of that building, because of me.

Still, I stayed silent, giving her my support without expecting anything.

We sat there, letting the surrounding quiet fill the space until finally she swallowed and started talking.

"I was pregnant once." She licked her lips and took a deep breath, finally looking up again to hold my stare. "I had just turned twenty, I think, and at the time, the man that held me captive had some big-name clients." Her shoulders shuttered as my hands tightened in my lap, but I didn't move an inch. "The Senator was one of them, though he wasn't a senator then."

I stayed silent, so afraid that she'd shut down if I said something wrong, even though my brain was screaming in agony.

She went on, picking at a thread on her sleeve. "He bought me exclusively around that time, so he was the only one who got to—" She cracked her neck as her eyes closed, tears falling down her cheeks, "To rape me." Licking her lips again, she went on, and I had no idea how she shared her story with me without breaking. "So, when I got pregnant, I knew I was in trouble. I just didn't realize how brutal he'd be about it."

"What did he do?" I asked, my voice hoarse with emotion.

She looked up at the ceiling as tears rolled over her cheeks while her lips trembled, "He took everything." Her voice was no more than a whisper as she cut herself open for me. "They tied me down and brutalized me, taking everything from inside of me that made me a woman so it wouldn't happen again."

My blood ran cold as her shoulders broke under the weight of her horrors. The scars on her abdomen, the ones that were faded but still visible—those were from him. I asked her once about them, but she brushed it off, saying it was from a surgery she had years ago. God, I had no idea.

"I screamed bloody murder and fought them until I passed out from the pain," Her body shook with sobs. "But when I woke up, it was too late, they had mutilated me and stolen my future. When I was a kid, the only thing I ever dreamed of being was a mother. I wanted a house full of babies to love the way I wasn't, and he stole that from me simply because he couldn't risk his favorite toy carrying on his DNA and creating a scandal." Her face contorted in anger as she screamed to the ceiling, "He stole everything from me! It didn't matter if I escaped that hell, I would always be trapped because of him!"

I slid forward, and she dropped her head, staring at me with wild eyes, filled with so much fear and anger as I sat just out of reach. "Can I touch you?" I asked, and she nodded, falling deeper into her own despair as I wrapped my arms around her, cradling her into my body as if I could absorb her pain if I held her tight enough.

She sobbed, rocking in my arms on the hallway floor for hours as she broke apart from the pain she held in her heart.

And I did the only thing I could do; I held her tighter and told her over and over again how safe and loved she was at that very moment. I told her she wasn't trapped and I'd give her anything she ever wanted out of life, however I could.

"I'd like to tell you why I am the way I am, if that's okay." I said quietly, as I continued stroking my hand up and down Laila's back. We were on my couch, I was lying on my back, and she was lying on top of me with her head in the very center of my chest. Something about hearing my heartbeat soothed her, even before tonight, and if she wanted this contact to ease some of her grief, I would gladly give it to her.

"What do you mean by that?" she asked, turning her head to look up at me, resting her chin on her hand. Her eyes were less red, but they were still sad, and that killed me. "You make it sound like there's something wrong with you."

I brushed her chocolate hair back off her forehead and gave her a smile, "In a way, there is." I said, "A lot of things. But in this case, I mean when it comes to the insane drive I have to make you happy."

She pressed her lips to her hand and shrugged, giving me permission to start.

"I was four the first time I slept on the streets." Her perfect eyebrows creased over her nose, and I smiled humorlessly, rubbing my thumb over it to smooth it out. "I had a mother who loved me, so I wasn't alone. She just had no idea how to be an adult and provide a stable home for me. She was only thirteen when she had me."

"Jesus." Laila sighed.

"We lived at her childhood home, with my grandparents until she was seventeen and they had a falling out." I resumed rubbing my hand through her hair to ground myself. "Part of me wants to think that they loved me and didn't want us to end up on the street, but I'll never know."

"How did she navigate the streets at that age?"

"She didn't. Not really, which was the problem. We couch-surfed from what I remember, and then that stopped, and then we were spending our days on the streets, in parks and public buildings, and our nights in shelters if we were lucky, or on those same park benches."

"I can't imagine how scary it was for you at that age."

"She tried." I reasoned, "I think she did, at least. Maybe it was just the innocent rose-colored glasses view I had of the woman I loved more than anything else in the world. In a way, she could do no wrong in my eyes."

"Until she could," Laila whispered, "I feel like that's what you're not saying."

I took a deep breath and let her warmth ease me. Not once, in my entire life, had I told anyone about my mother. In a way, it was my shitty secret to keep, and I didn't want anyone else knowing I was human.

Imperfect.

Weak.

"I was thirteen when she started dating a man who was a particularly mean son of a bitch. We had bounced in and out of places, depending on who she was dating. She was always looking for a man to fix all of her problems, as if she needed one to feel worthy. But this one, was a breed of bastard I couldn't compete with, I couldn't protect myself from either. So I made myself scarce, avoiding him at all costs."

"Getting into trouble on the streets, I'm sure." Her cheeks flicked the tiniest bit of movement, as if she thought about smiling before moving on from the idea.

"Of course." I smiled for her, "That's what young boys do with no supervision, trying not to become a victim and trying to learn how to be a big dog."

"Is that when you found the Shadeport Crew?" She asked, and I turned us so she was tucked between the back of the sofa and my body so I could kiss her. I didn't, of course, she was still too raw. But I wanted to.

"Sort of. Back then it was another crew, led by a man who was ruthless and he used brutality to earn your obedience." I sighed, "Ryker was coming up about that same time. Him, Gavin and I kind of fell into a pack, using our different skills to make a name for ourselves as a crew. And then it just grew from there until Gavin was king, and Ryker and I were at his side."

"What skills did you each bring? What were your differences?"

I smiled slightly, remembering those years as a teenager running shit we had no business being involved in, with Gavin and Ryker at my side.

"Gavin was the thinker, God that man could craft a plan and execute it to perfection, every single time. It was like watching a movie unfold as his plans went into motion. And Ryker, he was always known for his dominance. People wouldn't risk going against him, simply because he never gave them the notion that they'd win if they tried."

"And you?" She asked.

"Me?" I nudged my nose against hers as she snuggled in against my body more. "I was the boogeyman. I earned my place in blood. If someone tried to fuck with Gavin's plans, and Ryker's reputation didn't convince them otherwise, they sent me in."

"To hurt them." She whispered.

"To obliterate them." I corrected her, "To make an example out of them. For every one example, four more could be avoided before the shock factor would wear off and I'd have to remind everyone."

"Jesus." She swallowed, "That's a lot of bloodshed on your hands."

"It is." I agreed, "But it's shaped me into the man I am today, and I can't take that back or change it now."

"Would you? If you could? Would you change the way people thought about you when they saw you walk into a room?"

Firmly, I answered, "No."

"Why?"

"Because the mere mention of my name will keep you safe." I reasoned and her eyes widened. "The mere mention of my name will make even the most ruthless pieces of shits turn and walk the other way someday, and if it keeps you safe, than it's worth everything else."

She scooted up on the couch, "It already has. The title of being your girl has turned men around when I thought they'd hassle me or try something. But I never looked at it that way."

"I couldn't protect my mother from men like that. She openly chose them over me, time and time again, desperately searching for love and acceptance, and they beat the shit out of her and me for it. They used her, and abused her, got her hooked on drugs and broke her because she was a nobody, with no one to watch over her. But that will never happen to you, not for as long as I live."

"Where is your mom now?" she asked sincerely.

"I don't know anymore. I ran into her a few times over the years, but not in the last ten or so."

"Would you help her if you did now? Would you give her the love she so desperately searches for, but in a different way? The result would still be the same Zeke, she'd finally feel like she was worth it. Could you put it all behind you?"

I paused, unable to answer her truthfully. "I don't know."

"That's fair." Her warm brown eyes found mine as she leaned into my face, gently rubbing her nose against mine like I had hers, but it was her decision. "I don't think I'll ever put my pain behind me. But I want to try."

"Tell me how, and I'll help you anyway I can." I stated confidently, firm and with a strength she didn't have.

"I want to find a way not to be reminded of it. I just want to walk forward, down a different path that doesn't take me back there in any way, and never look back."

"Is that why my decision to come to you about the Senator triggered you so much?"

"Yes." She admitted, "But that's not your fault, because you had good intentions. At the time I just couldn't see them."

"Do you see them now?" I asked, breathing her in, "Because the road to hell is paved with good intentions, Dove. And I'm not going to get it right, every time, even though I'm going to try my hardest."

"I know you will." Her lips brushed against mine as she closed her eyes and sank into me fully. "And I have to find a way to trust you with my pain, instead of trying to keep them separate things. Because they're not, are they?"

"No, they aren't." I replied, "But that doesn't have to be a bad thing."

"Hmm," she hummed, licking her lips and tasting mine. "Trust."

"Trust." I replied as she shifted in my arms, hitching her leg over my hip and curling further into my body.

"I think I want to try trusting you with all of me." She purred, "The good and the bad. The past and the future."

"I'll be here, Dove." I replied, running my hand over her hip and thigh as she rocked against me slightly. "For all of it. If you can't trust in anything else, trust in that."

"Okay." She whispered before softly pressing her lips against mine, "I can try."

"That's all I need from you. Let me take care of everything else."

CHAPTER 26 – LAILA

It was there again.

That doomsday feeling, crawling across my skin like a slithering eel of bad news, was just waiting to strike and ruin my day. Or worse—my life.

I scrubbed glasses behind the bar, making small talk when I could, and mentally counted to ten a million and a half times, but still, I was on edge.

"Hey, are you alright?" Nicole asked as I stood frozen, lost in thought, with my hands hovering over the water pan.

"Yeah, I'm fine. Sorry!" I blinked away the distraction and started washing dishes again, but then stopped. "Actually, you know what? I'm not okay." I grabbed a rag and dried my hands off. "I'm sorry, but I have to leave."

"Uh, okay." She stuttered in surprise, "I'll let management know. Can I do something to help you somehow? You seem really rattled."

"I'll be okay, I just have to—" I paused, trying to find the words. "Find someone."

"Okay." She stepped aside as I quickly clocked out. "Good luck."

"Thanks."

As soon as my feet hit the pavement outside, my skin burned to life with anxiety, and it felt that if I didn't keep moving, it would split into a million pieces, shedding off of me.

Something was wrong. And I was done ignoring it.

I pulled my phone out of my pocket and dialed Zeke. He was on a job with Jed, no where near Shadeport. I didn't think it was him, but I had to make sure.

"Dove." His warm, thick voice answered on the second ring. "Are you okay?"

"Are you?" I replied, walking toward the dumpster corral. "Is Jed?"

"We're fine. Why?"

I lifted the lock with the toe of my Converse and swung the door open. "I'm fine. But something or someone isn't. I have a feeling, and I know it sounds stupid, but something is wrong, Zeke. Somewhere. I just don't know with whom yet."

"We're fine." He repeated, "Where are you?"

"I'm leaving work. I couldn't focus, and I couldn't shake the feeling, so I called you, figured I'd start there and work down the line." Even before I said it, I knew it was stupid. "I think it's Kade."

"Okay." He replied, and it was refreshing to have someone believe me. No questions or doubt, just support. "I'll reach out and check on him."

"That didn't work last time, remember." I walked around the dumpster, finding it empty of the junkies that frequented the dark space to get high. "But okay. I appreciate it."

"Promise me something." He said, and I rolled my eyes, already knowing what he was about to say. "Be safe. Let me get some crew to come with you."

"If that's what you need to do, fine. But I'm not waiting for them to show up. I'm going to claw my skin from my bones if I stay still, Zeke. I can't describe it or make it make sense—"

"I get it." He cut me off with the strong, unwavering power I craved and relied on. "I'll get them to you. Is your location on?"

"For you, always." I smirked, remembering the way he insisted on being able to find me after the last time I bolted. The last time we argued about Kade.

"Good. I'll have them meet you. Keep your head on straight."

"Yes, Daddy." I purred, feeling brave with his support.

He groaned, and I reveled in the sound. "I love you."

Now I was melting. Those words.

Something I never imagined hearing from someone with such genuine truth behind them.

"I love you too, Zeke."

And then I hung up, heading toward the dark alley.

Before I could get there, a truck pulled into the parking lot, blocking the space. Instead of that unusual sense of dread that always overcame me when people were near, I ignored everything else and went to walk around it. Part of me dared someone to stop me. Or even try.

I was too fired up with the need to find Kade and settle the fear building in my chest to let someone get in my way.

"You seen the kid?" A gruff voice called out, and I stopped, looking at the driver's side window that was rolled down.

"Diesel?" I peered inside, confused to see him in a truck and not on his bike. And then his words struck. "The kid? Kade?" I walked to his window, "No, why, have you? What's wrong?"

His gnarled face tightened as he looked back out the windshield. "He's MIA. And I don't have a good feeling."

"What do you mean?"

"I've been watching him." Diesel said, looking back at me. "For Zeke. For you. But he's gone dark and I—" his jaw tightened and so did his hand on the wheel. "I think he was trafficked."

My heart sank into my stomach as my knees threatened to buckle. "No." I whispered, shaking my head as my eyes widened. "Don't say that. Don't you dare—"

"He was working for Clarissa Lupold."

"How do you—" My stomach rolled as the name shattered the hope in my gut, swirling the possibilities around like bile and fire until there could be no other explanation. Clarissa was the senator's wife. Oh, my god. "No!"

"I found out too late." Diesel grimaced. "And now I can't find him."

I replayed everything Kade said to me the other day at the cafe. He said he worked for a rich lady in East Valley, doing odds and ends around the property.

"Oh, my God." I gripped the frame of the truck door as my legs gave out. "No, D. No! We have to find him. He's just a kid." Tears burned my eyes as I stared at the scary man that had befriended me for some reason. Begging him silently to help me.

"I know." He gripped my hand and nodded to the passenger side. "Get in. We're going to find him."

I didn't think twice; I didn't hesitate to worry about being in a vehicle with practically a stranger who was clearly a psychopath. Should I have? Probably. But I couldn't think of anything but what Kade was possibly experiencing at that very moment because of Lupold and his wife.

I ran my hands up and down my legs as he started driving. "Where do we start?"

"I don't know." He replied. "My contacts are digging for info on Lupold's holding spots, but I don't know where he'd keep a boy."

"A boy." I cried, rubbing my head as panic threatened to take hold. "That doesn't make sense, he doesn't like boys." I didn't know how much Diesel knew about me and my past, but I didn't care. "He has a thing for girls. Teenagers."

"Then why—" Diesel shook his head.

"Her." I whispered, remembering the vile vibes I got from her that day I walked with Zeke on the sidewalk of East Valley. She was slimy and predatory with every word that fell from her crimson lips. That day I had been too distracted with jealousy over thoughts of Zeke entertaining her, I missed them. "His wife. Oh god I'm going to be sick."

"Hey." Diesel reached across the seat and gripped my hand as he drove. "Take a deep breath."

"She lured him into her home!" I cried in a panic, "He said she bought him new clothes and paid him—she was *grooming* him! And I fucking missed it!"

"You didn't." Diesel said, turning the truck toward the Valley, and my blood ran cold. "You didn't have any reason to suspect that someone would do that to him. Not there, not in the Valley."

"She's married to the worst monster in the world!" I screamed, "Of course I should have automatically suspected that someone who took a street kid in with some flashy made-up job was doing it for their own sick desires! I should have fucking known that! But I missed it!"

"We're going to get him." Diesel sped down the road, but we were still so far away. With every mile between us and that house of horrors, I felt that same feeling, like my skin was going to rip from my bones.

"But what will it cost him first?" I asked, gutted by the reality. Diesel didn't answer me, because the answer was too cruel to say aloud. I pulled my phone out and dialed Zeke, hoping he was back at the Estate. Again, he answered instantly. "She has him! That fucking vile snake of a woman has him! I missed it, Zeke!"

"Who?" His voice was calm and lethal as I broke.

"Lupold's wife! Diesel picked me up and told me Kade was working for her. He's missing!"

There was a commotion in the background, and then Jed's voice filled in the gap as he spoke to someone while Zeke talked to me. "Where is she keeping him, Dove?"

"I don't know." I cried, "The house maybe? Diesel said they were digging into Lupold's holdings but he wouldn't keep a boy there. He has a very specific type," my stomach rolled again as a cold sweat broke out over my skin. "I think she had him right down the fucking street the whole time."

"We're coming." Zeke replied menacingly. "Jed's assembling the crew that's at the Estate. Where are you?"

"Pulling into the Valley." I cried, holding onto the door handle as Diesel took the corner on two wheels. He didn't stop at the gatehouse, smashing through the barrier with the hood of his truck as the loud roaring of bike engines followed us through the wreckage from the other side of the street.

The Reaper MC crew was following us in, and the Shadeport Crew would meet us there.

My heart felt like it was going to beat out of my chest as we turned down the street, racing to the house.

"Laila, don't go inside." Zeke roared through the phone as the house came into view. "Laila!" He yelled to get my attention, "Do not go inside that house, do you hear me? Please!"

"I have to." I whispered, looking over at Diesel, who glanced out of the corner of his eye at me. "Kade needs me. I have to."

"Fuck!" Zeke roared, knowing there was nothing he could do because he wasn't close enough to stop me. "D, keep her safe!"

"On it." Diesel replied, slamming the truck into park out front of the house as black Escalades skidded to a stop from the direction of Ryker's estate. "Let's go."

"I love you." I said into the phone, and then hung up as I jumped out of the truck. My muscles felt like they were being electrocuted as I ran with the armed men that came from both crews at the drop of a hat.

Armed guards ran from the home as we got close, but they were so outnumbered, they hesitated for just a moment before opening fire.

But it was long enough.

The Reapers and Shadeport Crew took them out, some using guns, some using their fists, and within moments I was running through a door behind Diesel into the home.

Please be here. Please. Please. Please.

I was sick to my stomach, hoping that Kade was inside of the home of a known predator, but not knowing where he was, left him more vulnerable because we all knew he was in trouble. There was no other way around it.

"Who the hell do you think you are?" A screeching, shrill voice screamed as the evil wife of the senator came around the corner, staring down the men in her home like she was any sort of threat. "Get out of my house!"

"Where's Kade?" I snapped, stepping around Diesel's massive body to stand in front of her, that electrocution feeling coursing through my body in a way I'd never felt before. In every other situation, I froze, I shrunk, I disassociated from what was happening around me until I couldn't even see or hear. But not now. Now, it felt like fire nipped at my feet, and if I didn't act, I'd die. "Where is he?" I screamed.

But she just pressed her lips together with a smug look of superiority as she looked me up and down. "You." She sneered, "I knew I recognized you that day I saw you walking with Zeke." She scoffed as she put her hands on her hips. "You pathetic, disgusting whore! Look at you, out of the dirt and filth and living the life of luxury like you're something worthy of this life!"

My blood ran cold as I realized what she meant.

She recognized me.

Recognized me.

As her husband's torture toy.

She took a step toward me and pointed her manicured nail at me, "He should have killed you when he cut that bastard baby out of you! But he was too obsessed with you! With fucking you! Whore!"

I didn't think or decide—I didn't even know what I was doing until my fist slammed into her face. Pain vibrated up my wrist and arm all the way to my shoulder as her head snapped backward, blood spraying across my face as she fell on her ass.

There was no noise surrounding me, though I could see her mouth opening and closing as she screamed more vile things at me, but I couldn't hear them.

I couldn't feel them.

I just attacked her.

My hands grabbed handfuls of her perfectly styled hair, ripping it out in clumps as I slammed my hand into her face, over and over again, gouging and scratching, pulling pieces of her flesh apart with each swing of my arms.

I should have stopped, I should have left her to someone else to deal with, but I couldn't.

For the first time in my life, I had the upper hand.

People moved around me, men searching the house and securing other staff on the property, holding them at gunpoint.

But I didn't stop until she stopped fighting back.

Was she dead?

Did I care?

"Laila."

The voice sounded so far away I ignored it at first. But then something touched me, a hand on my shoulder, and I turned, slashing my hands at the new outlet.

"Whoa," Diesel said, gripping my wrists tight in his hands and immobilizing me as his eyes roamed my face. "You did well. She's done. You did well."

His words weren't quite penetrating my brain, as if there was an invisible force field scattering them into a garbled mess.

But then he said something that made it through.

"We found Kade."

My muscles stopped tensing against his hold. My bones locked up tight, immovable as my brain fought for control again. "What?" I asked, not even sure it was clear.

"He needs you." Diesel said, loosening his hold on my wrists but not letting go completely. "It's bad, Laila."

"Where?" I yanked my arms free, blinking off whatever rage-induced tantrum I had fallen victim to and focused, "Where is he?"

"Come on," Diesel nodded, and I followed him, glancing down at the woman lying in a pool of blood, chunks of flesh missing from her plastic face. "This way." Diesel stopped at the top of a set of stairs leading to a basement.

I could tell even from where I froze behind him that it was nicer than any basement I'd ever been in before, but still.

Basements rarely had other exits.

"Don't touch me!" A hoarse scream ripped through the air from below, and my heart cracked when I recognized the pain in it. "Don't come near me!"

"Oh God." I whispered, pushing past Diesel and running down the stairs and down a long hallway. Men cleared the way as I shoved past them, some patch members, some Zeke's men as I got to the opening.

A cell.

A cell of horrors, I found so many familiar similarities to the one I lived in for a while.

And inside of it, curled into a ball of skin and bones, bruises and cuts, was a little boy who would never be the same because of it.

"Kade." I whispered, as the rest of the guys cleared out, leaving me alone with Diesel and the boy. The door to the cell was open, but Kade was curled behind the metal bed, with his face buried behind the fabric of his bare mattress. "Kade," I said a little louder, "It's me, Laila."

Something dripped down my face, and I swiped at it, pulling my hand away to find tears mixing with Clarissa's blood on my fingers. I was crying, and didn't even realize.

Piercing blue eyes peeked out from behind the mattress, a mop of dirty brown hair stuck to his forehead.

God, he was so small and hurt.

"Kade, you're safe now." I tried again, lowering myself to my knees in the middle of the cell. "No one is going to hurt you. I promise you." More tears fell from my eyes, but I tried to keep my voice calm and strong for him. I tried to be everything I dreamed of in finding a rescuer when I was in his place. "I promise you."

"You're covered in blood." He replied softly, sitting up a little higher to see more of my body over the bed. "Who's?"

I swallowed, "Hers." Saying her name felt too personal. He knew who I meant. She was the villain in his nightmare. We all had one.

"Is she dead?" Kade asked, gripping the metal bar of the bed frame to pull his body out just a fraction of an inch from where he was sandwiched against the wall. "Is that enough blood to kill someone?"

"I don't know." I said honestly. "But if it's not, I'll get more." I raised my eyebrows at him and nodded once. "If she's not dead, she will be. I promise."

"Promises." He shuddered, "I fucking hate promises."

"I'm sorry." I deflated slightly, trying to figure out how to help him when I didn't even know what had happened to him.

"Don't be." He swallowed and moved an inch more toward me. "You've never broken any to me before. You're probably the only one."

My heart broke for the little boy, who sounded like a worn and tired man instead of a twelve-year-old. "And I never will."

"Neither will I." Diesel said from behind me, and I looked over my shoulder as he took his leather cut off, and then took his giant flannel off, handing it to me. "What do you say we get out of this fucking place, kid?"

I held the flannel, still warm with Diesel's body heat, out to Kade, who eyed it before he said, "I never came to you for help, like you told me to. I was too fucking late." His shoulders shook slightly as he fought to keep from breaking with that statement. When I last saw him, I told him he could always come to me, no questions asked.

And he made a joke about questions being my middle name.

What I wouldn't give to go back to that moment and do it all differently to save him from what happened between then and now.

"You're not too late now. And my offer still stands." I leaned forward, holding the shirt out closer to him. "Let me help you, Kade. As someone who knows exactly what you're feeling right now. Just take my hand and let me help you."

"Okay." He whispered, bloodshot eyes watering up even as he refused to let them fall. He was so strong and so broken, all at the same time.

"Okay." I crawled forward, wrapping the shirt around him, engulfing him in it as he got out of his hiding spot. "I got you."

The shirt was so big it fell to his knees, and I wrapped my arms around him, praying it wouldn't trigger him, but he leaned into me, burying his face in my chest as I squeezed him with everything inside of me.

Human touch could destroy every belief a person had in humanity. Or it could heal it.

CHAPTER 27 – ZEKE

As soon as I laid eyes on her, I'd settle the monster in my chest, trying to claw its way out through my flesh and bones.

That was what I kept telling myself as I raced back to Laila after her panicked call earlier. Of course, I was hours away on a deal, leaving me feeling like part of my body was being cut off with every minute back to her.

I had gotten status reports from the crew about what happened at The Senator's house; I knew about Kade and the horrors they found there. But I had to see them both with my own eyes before I'd settle.

"Drop me at the Lupold's." Jed said as we finally pulled into the East Valley. "Go to Laila and Kade and I'll finish the cleanup there."

"You sure?" I asked, understanding just how much that cost him to stay away when he wanted to check on her as much as I did. But she wasn't alone. And Kade didn't need more spectators right now.

"Yeah." He nodded firmly, "Just don't touch that slimy bastard before I get there."

The Senator.

Ryker ordered the hit on him the moment I called him with Laila's suspicion, before we even had confirmation that Kade was there.

And now the sitting Senator was hanging from chains in The Shop.

Alongside his wife.

Though she was still unconscious from the injuries that Laila had given her. Pride didn't even fucking cover the emotions that hit me when I heard what Laila had done, facing the wife of her biggest monster.

She did it for Kade. She did it for herself.

And I would finish it for her.

"You have my word."

When we got to the Lupold Mansion, police had the property marked off with caution tape, keeping reporters and media at bay. As the police officer waved us through the barricade, Jed jumped out, gave me a pointed look, and approached the Police Chief, who nodded to me as I drove away.

The story broke an hour after Laila left with Kade safely in her arms.

And the headlines all said the same thing, thanks to Ryker's influence.

Tragedy Strikes at California Senator Charles Lupold's Home: Murder-Suicide or A Bitter Betrayal Between a Jaded Wife and Wandering Husband?

The world thought they were already dead. Which meant they wouldn't care what we did to them at The Shop. The world would never even know.

Which was a kinder fate than they deserved, to be sure. Their victims deserved to know how much they suffered, but there were limits even to Ryker's powers. But Laila and Kade would know.

Ryker's estate was crawling with Crew—armed guards covering every inch of the place while we held the Lupold couple in The Shop. Last I heard, there had already been 3 offers sent to Ryker looking to exchange cash for the privilege of killing them. But they'd never leave the property.

They'd live there for as long as we could keep them alive while torturing them, and then they'd be cremated and disposed of from there. Until there was nothing left of them.

When I parked at the building Laila and I shared, Ryker and Elora stood outside talking with Carly, who had just walked out.

Carly handed me a to-go cup of tea that I recognized as Laila's favorite. "She wouldn't drink it, but she needs it."

"Is she with Kade?" I asked, taking the cup.

"He's asleep in her bed, the doctor sedated him." Ryker replied. "He didn't want to go to the hospital, so I brought one here."

"And Laila?" I asked, but he looked away at Carly.

"She showered at your place, and I sat with Kade. That was the only way she'd leave him. She was terrified he'd wake up alone in an unfamiliar place. She was covered in blood, Zeke." Carly warned, "But she didn't seem shaken by it."

"She did it for him." I gave her a small shrug, "Maybe that's why. Either way, thank you." I said, and they all cleared to let me pass. I silently walked down the hall, finding both of our doors open, though I knew where Laila would be.

Her apartment was dark, only the light from the hall lit up the floor inside the doorway, and that's where I found her. Sitting on the floor next to her couch, staring at the tiny unmoving ball curled up asleep in the center of her bed.

I didn't say anything, but she must have sensed me because she looked over her shoulder as I walked in. Instead of trying to convince her to do something that would be impossible for her, I lowered myself onto the cold floor behind her, bracketing her with my legs and pulling her back against my chest. "Lean on me, Dove."

She pulled my arms around her body, engulfing her in them as she snuggled into me. I hated that I wasn't there for her today, but I was with her finally, and I'd be whatever she needed me to be.

"They hurt him, Zeke." she whispered, staring at the curled-up boy. "She abused him."

"I know." I groaned softly, kissing her temple. "And you'll never know how sorry I am for not seeing him for what he is—a kid. I should have protected him like you asked me to, but I let my own jaded experience keep me from seeing it your way."

"It's not your fault." She sighed, "It's not even my fault. We can't burden the faults of abusers on our shoulders; that's their weight to carry. But now we need to figure out how to help him heal from this." Laila turned and looked up at me with her big wide eyes, "I can't let him go, so please don't ask me to."

"What are you saying, Laila? You want to keep him? He's not a puppy."

"He's a kid," She shrugged, "He needs someone to take care of him, the way he deserves to be taken care of." Looking back over at Kade, "The way you and I both deserved."

My shoulders deflated, and I rested my chin on her head. "Whatever you want to do, I support you."

"Really?" Laila asked, almost surprised.

"Yes." I tightened my hold on her, "But that doesn't mean I'm going to let him abuse you the way he has. If he's here, if he's going to stay, then he's going to learn respect and gentleness. For you."

"For me." She replied wistfully. "I've never had respect or gentleness. Not until I met you."

"That's the only thing you'll ever know again." I looked over at Kade as he rolled over in his sleep, facing us. When he was clean and peaceful in slumber, he looked like a fragile little kid, not the snarky, sarcastic pain in the ass he had been when he was around the crew. "I'll teach him how to be a man. A good man."

Laila sniffled, looking up at me with those warm brown eyes swimming with unshed tears, "You're a good man, Zeke Evans."

"Only for you." I kissed her gently, "And now for him, too."

Hours later, I stood in the doorway to Laila's place, coffee in hand, watching the boy as he started rousing from his sedation. Laila was asleep across the hall in my bed, both of our doors were open when she finally agreed to crash a few hours ago, just in case he woke up.

Kade tossed again and then his eyelids cracked open, squinting into the bright morning sunrise shining in through Laila's blinds. And then he sat up like a bolt of lightning, touched his toes and his eyes found mine across the room.

Fear burned in them.

That was understandable.

I hadn't always treated him fairly.

"Good morning." I said gently, walking in to lean against the kitchen counter as I took another sip of coffee. "You're safe."

Kade looked around the empty apartment, probably looking for Laila, before he pushed his floppy hair off his forehead. "Is she here?"

"Laila." I corrected him. "And yes, she's asleep at my place across the hall. She didn't want to leave you, but she was exhausted."

"You want me out." He said, not asking, instead assuming. "I get it." He swung his legs off the edge of the bed, and the basketball shorts he was wearing slid above his knees, revealing cuts and scrapes covering every inch of his bare legs below.

"Stop." I said, and he paused, feet hanging above the floor. "That's not what I want. Not at all."

"I don't understand." He looked up at me, confused. The thing about Kade was he always said what was on his mind, sometimes to a fault. He was crass and sarcastic, but he was mostly honest. And young. Fuck, he was so damn young.

"Laila wants you to stay with us from now on." I took another sip of my coffee and stared at him straight on. "And I do too."

"Why though?" He squinted, laying his hands in his lap and leaning on his elbows. "A few weeks ago, you yelled at her because of me. Fired me, even."

"That's something I regret on both of your behalves. I'd like to say it'll never happen again, but that's not something I can promise. So, I won't lie. But what I will do is tell you the truth. Does that work?"

He straightened his spine and nodded his head once. "I can respect that."

"I don't know what it is about you personally that caught Laila's attention, but you got it. And she's not willing to let it go. She has the biggest heart and a suitcase full of baggage to work through, and she thinks that helping you is what she's meant to do. Which leaves you with two options."

"Okay." He murmured hesitantly.

"You can choose to walk away from her and have the backing of the crew in whatever you want to do. You can go on being a street kid, or go back into foster care, or whatever. You'll be protected and taken care of by Ryker and myself, all of our members will be your big brothers. But you won't find any love there, just camaraderie."

"And the second option?"

"You can stay." I replied firmly. "You can let go of everything that's happened to you since you were forced into this life not meant for you, with mine and Laila's help, and you can be a kid. A real fucking *kid*. Not a smart ass with a chip on his shoulder and a foul mouth who aims it at anyone who sticks around long enough to catch it. You can get therapy, and go to school, and do normal kid stuff like play video games and ride a bike and be innocent of everything else you've already witnessed, for a few more years, until you're ready to face it all on." He swallowed, and his chest rose and fell under his shirt. "You can let Laila love you because she will. God, she'll fucking love you, and you'll never think you deserve it, and you'll mess it up, and you'll fight it, and you'll make her cry. But she'll love you, nonetheless. And eventually, you'll be better at it. And eventually you'll start to believe that you're worthy of it. That will be when you realize how fucking lucky you were to run into her on the street one day, and from that moment on, you'll work hard every day to prove to her that you aren't a mistake, that you deserve what she's giving you. And that's a damn good life, Kade, compared to the other."

He took a shuttering breath and looked at the window, watching the trees behind the barracks blow in the breeze as he mulled it over. Finally, he looked back over at me, with those eyes that seemed so much wiser than his years, and spoke. "That's what happened to you, isn't it?" He asked and went on, "She loved you, and you messed it up, and you fought it, and you made her cry. But she loved you anyway."

"Yes." I nodded, "And I work hard every fucking day to prove to her I'm worthy of her gift, because that's what it is. A priceless gift that I'll never find anywhere else, not like this. And neither will you."

He dropped his gaze and looked at his lap. Tears silently hit the covers lying over his legs. "I don't want to leave. But I don't know how to stay. I don't remember how to be a kid."

"I'm not asking you to know how just yet." I said, setting my coffee down and walking over to the bed to sit on the edge next to him. I didn't want to crowd him out, or scare him, he had already been through so much, but I wanted him to know I was near at the same time. "I'm just asking you to let yourself learn. To accept help from the most selfless and loving human being either of us street kids are ever going to meet."

"And you?" He looked over at me, showing me his fear and his vulnerability. I couldn't remember another time he had ever acted his actual age around me, so openly before. "Are you a package deal, because I don't want to mess up what you two have going."

"You won't." I shook my head, "Because I'd move heaven and hell for that woman. I'm not going anywhere."

He mulled that over, and I let him, sitting silently beside him as he thought. Eventually he nodded his head again, staring down at the blankets in his lap. "I think I'd like to have a home again." Kade's voice was so small and exposed as he spoke to his lap. "I think I'm ready to just be a kid."

"Then welcome home." I put my hand on his back, gently lending my strength to him, and he threw himself at me, wrapping his arms around my waist as he started crying, letting it all go. "You're home, Kade. You're safe here."

I heard something and looked up to find Laila standing at the door, hand covering her mouth, with tears on her cheeks as she watched us.

Last year I was a bachelor, who only ever cared about my work and my crew. I was alone and content with it, as everyone around me found their own versions of happiness in partners and families.

And then I found Laila, my brunette angel with scars as deep as mine and enough love to cover them all. And now Kade, a little boy with demons I'd chase away as long as I was on this earth, to keep him and Laila safe and happy.

Nothing else mattered outside of that.

CHAPTER 28 – Laila

The sun was scorching, but in the shade, with the cool breeze that so rarely found its way into the middle of the day, felt nice. Carly's porch had quickly become a favorite place for Kade, just as it had for me when I first moved onto the estate.

It was a Thursday, or maybe Wednesday, I lost count.

All I knew was that Kade had been living with us for almost two weeks, and it had been the most fulfilling two weeks of my entire life.

He was quiet and withdrawn a lot, but he was—calm. He wasn't rushing off to the next job, or worried about who was coming after him out of a dark alley. He wasn't thinking about money, food, or sleep.

Kade was just being a kid. And I found healing in helping him heal.

Zeke found healing in making Charles and Clarissa Lupold pay for what they did with pain. He spent every day at The Shop, with Jed and Ryker, as if other business didn't matter. The three men were focused on doing something to make up for all the harm those two individuals caused countless others.

I didn't want to know what was happening behind the soundproof walls. And neither did Kade, though Zeke gave him that choice.

Kade was intent on just being a kid again, like the mission of experiencing all the things he never got to do as a carefree child could occupy his mind enough to silence all the darkness there.

Kade lay on the floor of the porch, on Carly's fancy rug, rattling a toy for Gavin, trying to convince him to take a step toward him.

God, that kid loved Gavin. We all loved Gavin. A world full of people with darkness and scars on their skin, melted for the innocent, and silly little baby.

"Come on, I know you want to do it." Kade said, sitting up on his butt and holding the toy closer to Gavin. "You know you want your first steps to be to me."

Ellie snorted but kept her opinion on that matter to herself from her spot on the porch swing, sipping her tea and watching the boys. Carly was in her favorite rocking chair, smiling at them and peeking over at me.

"What?" I asked.

"Happy looks good on you." She replied wistfully.

"Happy?" I scoffed gently, "I feel like I'm just trying not to shit my pants twenty-four seven."

Carly chuckled, and Kade popped his head up, looking at me over his shoulder. "Two bucks in the swear jar."

I rolled my eyes, and Elora snorted, "I'm sorry, what?"

"Their rules." Kade held his hands up innocently, but we all knew he was anything but. "I'm just sticking to them."

"Zeke and he have a bet going—two, actually." I huffed, glaring at the boy, who winked at me with a charismatic charm so similar to

Zeke's. "First bet is to see who can stop swearing first. They both have atrocious sailor's mouths. And then the second one is to see who can make me fill the swear jar up first, because they both seem to draw curse words from me like magic." I glared at Elora. "Men!"

Elora chuckled, shaking her head, "Oh, I like this plan. Do I get a cut if I make her curse, too?"

Kade shook his head, "Nope. I have a dirt bike on the line for that jar. No chance."

I rolled my eyes, already dreading the day that Zeke showed up with a death trap on wheels. I knew it was going to happen, the second Zeke and Kade started talking about those things, I knew Zeke would fold and get him one. The big, scary man was obsessed with making Kade happy. But in a careful way. It was so fun to sit back and watch the two interact; they bonded as if they had known each other their whole lives, instead of for just a few months, living together for only a few weeks.

Almost as if there was something deeper connecting them in this weird, wild world than just their similarly icy blue eyes.

My alarm dinged on my phone, and I turned it off, feeling the energy around Kade shift even though he didn't even look at me. "Time to go, bud."

"Yeah," He leaned over and gave the toy to Gavin before standing up and wiping his hands off on his shorts. "Thanks for letting us hang out again." He said to Carly and Elora, like a polite gentleman.

"Anytime." Elora smiled.

Carly nodded, "See ya later, kiddo."

Kade and I fell into step together, heading back to the barracks to leave for our therapy sessions, and I put my arm on his shoulders and pulled him into me. "Nervous?"

"No." He said firmly with a shrug as he kicked a stone with the toe of his sneaker. "You?"

"Always." I said and smirked before I added, "I feel like I'm going to shit my pants at therapy every time."

He scoffed and shivered dramatically, "You got poop problems?"

I tipped my head back and laughed as I shoved him lightly. "Not compared to the smells you make with your butt."

"Rude." He scoffed, pushing me back and cracking a smirk as we rounded The Shop. We both gave it a wide berth, but when the doors opened as we got to the front, we both hesitated when Zeke came out.

He looked like the powerhouse boogeyman he always did, but his suit jacket was gone, and his black shirtsleeves were rolled up, exposing parts of the tattoos that covered his entire body. The ones that made my mouth water. And between his perfect lips was a cigarette.

Which meant that whatever was going on inside that building was affecting even his hardened exterior.

"Hi." He called when he saw us, taking one last drag off the cigarette before crushing it beneath his shoe as he walked to us. "Going to therapy?"

"Yeah." I said breathlessly, staring up at his handsome features. "Everything okay?"

"Yes." He said, pulling me into him and kissing my forehead as he turned to Kade. "Do you have your notebook ready for your therapist?"

Kade nodded, sliding his hands into his pants pockets. "Yes, it's inside."

"Go grab it so you're not late." Zeke said, nodding to the barracks behind us.

"Yes, Sir." Kade turned and jogged into the barracks, where we did some new configuring. He was still at my place, and I was across the hall with Zeke. There were other studio apartments in the building, but none of us were interested in switching it up right now.

No one else was allowed to come in or out of the barracks since Kade moved in, so we just kept our doors open and moved in between as needed. Besides, it gave Kade the space to have a little privacy to settle into his new routine, without us being too far away from him when he needed us.

"Are you okay?" I asked Zeke, wrapping my arms around his waist as he squeezed me tightly. He would never tell me if he weren't, but I didn't need his words to confirm my suspicions. The way he clung to me gave me everything I needed to know. "I'm sorry."

"Don't be." He sighed, threading his fingers through my hair and breathing me in. "Sometimes it is just more intense than others. Forgive me for coming out to find you and interrupting you with it on your way out."

"Did you?" I asked, leaning back to look up at him. "Come out to find me?"

"Yes." He cradled my cheek in his palm. "I needed you. Just a moment with you."

"I'm here." I whispered, falling into his embrace as he exposed his needs to me. Too often I doubted my ability to be something the beautifully tragic man in front of me needed, but it proved how wrong I was. "I can cancel—."

"Don't." He took a deep breath and pressed his lips to mine, gently, as if he was savoring the taste on his tongue before he rested his forehead against mine with his eyes closed. "I just needed a moment with you."

"You can have more when we get back." I kissed him again. "Just like this."

"I'll meet you in town after therapy." He kissed my nose with a soft smile. "We'll grab dinner, okay?"

"Really?" I asked excitedly, trying not to sound like a teenager getting asked on a date. He was usually just so busy, and I was busy with Kade most days now, too. "Are you sure?"

"I'm sure." He pulled back and let his hands fall from my body. "Just the three of us." He gave me one of his earth-shattering smiles that only I saw, "If you're a good girl, I'll even buy you ice cream for dessert."

"Pfft," I rolled my eyes as I took a step back, feeling playful. "Being good is overrated."

"Careful, Dove." He warned and then waved. "I'll see you in a few hours."

"See ya." I waved and walked to the front of the barracks to find Kade leaning against my new car.

Zeke surprised me with it last week, and at first, I refused it, but when he pointed out how many appointments and things Kade would need from me, there was no denying that I needed to be able to get him from point A to point B without ordering a car every time.

It was a Subaru, pearly white and, honestly, the cutest car I'd ever seen before. It wasn't flashy or over the top, but it was the top-rated in safety, and I loved that even more. Especially now that I was responsible for Kade's safety.

Elora had called it my new mom mobile, and she had no idea what those words meant to me. She didn't know about my forced hysterectomy years ago.

She didn't know about the dreams I'd never experience firsthand.

But in a way, Kade was giving me some of that. Even if I had no idea how to raise an almost teenager, I would figure it out for him.

And he had no idea how to be a son, letting someone mother him and parent him to keep him safe and healthy, but he was trying to figure it out too.

"Shoot, I forgot my helmet." Kade joked when I got to the car, and I glared at him as he got in.

I had my driver's license, but I hadn't had many years behind the wheel before I was taken, and to be honest, I was rusty.

I was trying nonetheless—for Kade.

Because he needed me, and I would rather walk into that brothel than let him down. Ever.

Hours later, I waited for Kade to get out of his session, flipping through a magazine when he came out of the room. His eyes were red-rimmed, but he was smiling at his therapist, Andy, when he walked him over to me.

We both saw therapists at the same clinic, which made it nice for lining appointments up as well as updates and progress checks, though Kade just started.

It seemed like he liked the two different therapists he worked with in tandem, and I was happy if he was comfortable and happy.

"You ready?" I asked, standing up to throw my purse strap over my head.

"Yep." Kade said with a confident nod. "I'm starving."

We walked out the front door to my car, "Well, lucky for you, Zeke's buying, so you can get whatever you want."

"Fuck yes!" He fist-pumped and then his shoulders rose to his ears as he sank into his seat. "I mean, heck yes."

I rolled my eyes, chuckling to myself. "How was your session?" I asked, turning out into traffic and heading towards the restaurant I picked and texted Zeke to meet us at earlier.

"I don't know." Kade said, looking out the window. "I don't know what to say all the time." He sighed, and I peeked over at him. "Turns out I'm fucked up from more than just the—" He didn't say the words, but I knew he meant the kidnapping. "Life fucked me over far before all that."

"Hey," I reached over and took his hand, "Same."

He looked at me and gave me a gentle smile. The day I found him in Zeke's arms, crying his little eyes out, I gave him a condensed and mostly child-safe explanation of what I'd been through. I told him of my parent's death, and my own kidnapping and exploitation.

I told him how Zeke, Jed, and Ryker rescued me. I even told him that Diesel and the Reapers were there too, just how they were for his own rescue.

I needed him to know that he was understood, even if he didn't understand what he felt and thought, and that Zeke and I were a safe place for him to talk when he wanted to, and a safe place to simply exist when he didn't.

To say we bonded through that would be an unjust description of the feelings that happened. It was like we linked up, an invisible force binding us together like the links of a chain, welded together into an unbreakable promise.

Nothing would scare me away. Nothing would turn Zeke away.

We were there for him, in ways he didn't know he'd need until that time came.

"The journaling helps." He said after a while, letting me into his brain a little more. What a gift it was to be let in, too. I stayed silent as he expanded, "I don't always know how to put my thoughts into words in the moment, but when I do, I write them down, so when I go back, I have them to read to Andy. I think it makes it easier to talk too, like reading them doesn't feel as awkward."

"Good." I smiled at him, pulling into the parking lot and looking for Zeke. It seemed we had beaten him. "I'm glad you're finding a way to communicate with your team. And me." I winked at him as we got out of the car. When we started walking up to the restaurant, I went on, "I like having you around, kid."

He snorted with the same sarcastic class clown attitude he had when I first met him. "Duh, I'm cool."

"Yeah," I ruffled his hair as he groaned and tried to fix it. "And I'm the weirdo still following you around."

"Meh," He shrugged, "You're not half bad."

He walked up to the host and told them we wanted to sit outside, and I paused, taken aback by the smallest little compliment he threw my way without a second thought.

There was no way that a preteen kid knew what those words meant to someone like me, but I'd hold on to them either way.

In a way, we were healing each other just by existing.

"She said there's a ten-minute wait." Kade said, coming back to meet me. "Cool with you?"

"Yeah," I looked around the downtown scene, "Zeke will be here soon, anyway." I pulled my phone out to make sure he hadn't texted me or anything when I heard someone come around the building like they were in a rush.

"Kade!" A voice hissed, and Kade whipped around as an older woman grabbed his arm. "Where have you been?"

"Whoa." I grabbed her hand and pulled it off Kade's arm without even thinking. "Don't touch him."

"Excuse you!" The woman snapped, scowling at me as she glared my way. "Stay out of it."

Kade slid in front of me, hardly blocking me at all from the woman's vile glare, but I recognized it for what it was—his attempt to protect me from it.

Jesus Christ, my heart almost ripped in two. I needed to get my silly feelings in check; I couldn't melt every time he did something that made me feel like he didn't hate my guts anymore. I was too damn old to be silly.

"Stop it." Kade bit back with menace. "What do you want?"

"What do I want?" The woman's eyes were rounded with shock before they darkened with anger. "You haven't shown up with my money. I have bills to pay!"

"Okay," I shook my head, pulling Kade backward. "I don't know who you are, but you need to go away. Now. We're not doing this."

She turned her glare my way again as I pulled Kade back another step, but she followed us. We were on the edge of the brick restaurant, thankfully away from the guests, so we weren't causing a scene. It didn't take me long to realize the woman was a junkie; she had scabs on her arms and hollowed-out cheeks and wild eyes.

That was a look all too familiar to me from my years dealing with addicted girls falling victim to more than just drugs.

"Damnit, bitch, try to pull my son away from me again, and I'll cut you!" The woman hissed, pulling a short pocketknife from her pants and flashing it at me. My stomach dropped as I eyed the dirty blade in the middle of the bustling city.

"Mom, stop!" Kade groaned, once again pushing himself between me and the woman. There was no way she was his mom. She looked way too old, but I couldn't tell if it was an illusion from the drugs or the dirt caking her skin. The moment my brain caught up though, I recognized the icy hue of her blue eyes behind layers of caked on black eye makeup and God knew what else. "I'm not working right now." Kade hissed, "I don't have any money."

"You got money to be at a restaurant, boy!" She yelled, getting irate. "Don't lie to me!"

"He's not." I argued. "I'm paying for his food. And his shelter. And his life, since you're clearly incapable of caring for him as his biological mother!" I snapped, anger radiating through my body at the injustice of it all. "And you dare to demand money from him? He's twelve!"

"It ain't your business, bitch!" She exploded, taking a menacing step forward with the knife still clutched in her bony fingers.

"Enough." A menacing voice snapped, seconds before her wrist twisted and the knife fell to the ground, clinking off the cement. Zeke pressed his body in front of Kade and me as he stared the woman down. "You need to leave."

I pulled Kade back further as Zeke went into boogeyman mode, and he let me. I thought he would have fought me, but he didn't, he simply stayed behind me and watched it all unfold.

"That's my kid!" the woman spat out, shooting her arm out around Zeke. "You don't get to tell me what to do with my damn kid! He owes me money!"

"You're wrong." Zeke slapped her hand away, "He's my kid now. You didn't deserve him. You didn't love him. You didn't care for him. Therefore, you've lost your claim to him and anything else you manipulated him into giving you over the years. It's done. It stops here. If you ever come near him again, I'll slit your fucking throat and let you bleed out in the streets, I don't care. You fucked up your chance time and time again. And now he's going to be loved and cared for by us, so leave. Before I lose my patience and make an example out of you, proving to everyone just how fucking tired the Shadeport Crew is of deadbeat parents fucking their kids up like they're not the most precious thing on this Earth."

My heart beat wildly in my chest as the woman sputtered in indignation, no doubt ignoring everything that Zeke said to her. But I didn't.

And neither did Kade. He stared up at Zeke with eyes so full of wonder and awe as the man claimed him as his own. As ours. I knew Kade was before that moment, but we hadn't openly told him about our intentions for the long term.

I was glad it was out there though, so he knew how serious we were about keeping him and making a family out of our own messed up little dynamic. I threaded my fingers into Kade's ice-cold ones, and he squeezed me back instantly, looking at me with questioning eyes.

"He's right—every word. You're home."

The woman stumbled backward as Zeke advanced on her, proving how serious he was, and then she glared at Kade before I pulled him behind me completely, squaring up to her.

She hissed at the boy, "You always were useless to me, anyway! Good for nothing ungrateful little shit who ran his mouth more than his feet!"

"Get out of here!" I snapped, cutting off any other things she could have said to the innocent kid. I turned and held him in a hug. "She's wrong."

"I know." He wrapped his arms around my stomach and held on to me with a sigh. "I just really hate her."

"I'm sorry." I hugged him tight as Zeke stood at my back and ran his big hand over Kade's hair.

"She's gone." He said powerfully, with that dominance I leaned into so often.

"Thanks." Kade muttered, pulling back to look up at Zeke. "I'm sorry—"

"Don't." Zeke cut him off and gave him a one-sided smile, but there was something so dark raging behind his gaze. "She doesn't matter."

"Okay." Kade nodded and then he peeked at me. "Will you be mad if I don't want to stay for dinner anymore?"

"Never." I shook my head, saddened for him. I hated that five minutes ago he was young and carefree, excited to eat and have a nice meal together, almost as a family, and now that woman ruined it all.

His mom.

What a fucking privilege she didn't deserve.

"Let's go home." Zeke led us back toward the parking lot, with Kade between us. "Leave your car here, and I'll have someone pick it up and drop it off later."

I didn't argue, even though I hated the idea of someone else driving my shiny new Pearl. I didn't want to leave either of their sides.

We got into Zeke's massive SUV, Kade silently climbing into the backseat as Zeke drove us back to East Valley. There was no talking, or even music on the radio as we drove, all of us in our own minds.

Zeke's silence felt heavier than normal, though, and when I looked over at him, the lethal look in his eyes should have scared me.

It should have warned me away from the power lying under his tailored suit and taut, inked skin. But I didn't shy away from it. No, that would have been something the old Laila did.

The new me wanted to burn in its power and authority. Sliding my hand over his where it rested on the center console, I scraped my nails down his knuckles before weaving my fingers between his.

His piercing eyes flew over to me, and I could feel the heat in them, without using a single word to describe it. If we had been alone in the car, I probably would have climbed over onto his lap to use his body to calm the unrest raging in mine.

Instead, I stayed seated, crossing my legs to stop myself from doing something embarrassing. Like begging him.

When we pulled into Ryker's Estate, the lawn was crawling with people, crew members and even their girlfriends and wives. Kids played soccer on the manicured grass, and Ryker and his men set up grills in the driveway, filling the air with smoke as they cooked.

We all got out, and a few of the guys called to Kade, inviting him over to their game of catch with a football. A few weeks ago, they had teased him mercilessly for being so small and mouthy, but now, with Zeke's protection at his back, they welcomed him into their groups with no more hazing.

"Is it okay?" He asked, nodding to the guys.

"Only if you want to." I agreed with a smile, "If you don't, I can pretend to be a bitch and you can tell them I said no."

He grinned with a roll of his eyes and took a step backward towards the guys. "I don't think anyone would believe that you have a mean bone in your body. But thanks."

"Have fun." I waved to him as Zeke slid his hand over the back of my neck under my hair, tightening it enough to catch my attention.

His voice was low as he lowered his lips to my ear. "I'm taking you into the Shop. You won't see anything you don't want to. But you'll come with me, no questions asked. Understand?"

I stared up at him, on the edge of telling him there was not a fucking chance in hell I was going into that building, no matter the reason. Before I could, though, there was something nagging at the bottom of my stomach that begged me to find out what he wanted from me in the horrid place, so I nodded once.

"Promise me you won't hurt me in there?" I asked. Part of me was asking it jokingly, part of me needed his assurance before I followed him blindly into the place known for pain and torture.

He growled and pulled my body flush to his, with the same wild look in his eyes as he lowered his lips to mine. "I promise you that you'll feel nothing but pleasure."

I moaned and sagged into him, ignorant of anyone else around us. "Deal."

"Let's go." He turned us and started toward The Shop with his hand on my ass, leading me. When we got to the grills, Jed gave him a suspicious look as we went past, but Zeke just pointed off to where Kade was. "Don't let him out of your sight, would ya?"

Jed saw Kade and then looked at us and rolled his eyes. "Sure thing."

I kept my feet moving to keep up with Zeke's long gait, as he paused only briefly to use the keypad at the door into the place, unlocking it, and ushered me inside.

The first thing that hit me was the air, frigid and blowing like it did inside of a hospital. The white, nondescript walls of the entrance gave nothing away as he turned, leading us down the long hallway. I had imagined the inside of the building a million times since moving in, and I had always envisioned blood-coated concrete walls, with plastic curtains hanging like inside of a slaughterhouse, screams echoing throughout the space.

It wasn't that at all.

Or at least it wasn't where we were. Maybe that part was deeper inside.

Before I could give it much thought, Zeke pushed me into a dark room that lit up when he slammed the door shut behind him.

My chest rose and fell in a rush of excitement and fear as I realized where we stood.

The walls of the room were padded, including the floor. White and blank of anything but the padding and lights glowing through the metal grates at the ceiling.

"Zeke." I whispered, but even I heard the moan fall from my lips at the end.

"Are you afraid of me?" he demanded as he crowded me in against the wall.

"Should I be?" I licked my lips, and he tracked it with his eyes.

Jesus fuck, he was nearly feral.

And I was hungry for it. Eat your heart out, Zeke, I'm ready for you.

"I'm not scared of you." I redacted, sliding my hands over his abs through his shirt, letting my sexuality free in the safety of his love. "You need this, don't you?"

He let an animalistic groan fall from his lips as he put his fists against the wall above my head and leaned into them. "I was going to use your touch to settle me." His hips bucked when I slid my fingers behind the tightness of his belt. "But it seems that you want to use your touch to do something else to me."

"What am I doing to you, Zeke?" I purred, pushing his belt through the buckle, undoing it. "All *I'm* doing is letting my body respond to the power I see in your eyes and feel in your touch. It makes me want to purr like a kitten for more."

"Dove." He growled as I pulled the button of his pants free. His dick was hard, growing in his pants and tenting the fabric as I dragged my nails over the length through his slacks.

"Why did you bring me here?" I lifted my lips to speak against his. "Why in here, and not in your bed, if you needed me to settle you?"

"Because I'm going to make you scream, and a soundproof room sounded better than a concrete box across the hall from our son." He promised, licking my lips and grinding his dick into my hand. "I can feel your energy through just your fingertips, Dove. And you're just as wild as I am right now. You don't want my tenderness, do you?"

I slowly shook my head no and then bit his lip. "Right now, I want your rawness." I sucked it into my mouth, making him moan. "You make me want to use my sexuality to my advantage."

"Do it." He urged, challenging me. "Do your very worst to get what you need from me. Whatever you want, you can have it. Onetime offer."

I smiled, already knowing what I wanted from him, if he was going to let me have free rein. Slowly, I slid down the wall until I was on my knees at his feet—a place he told me I'd never be allowed.

Zeke's nostrils flared when I pulled his zipper down, "Laila." He warned.

Pulling his cock out of his pants, I kissed the tip of it as I looked up under my lashes at him. "I think I might come from sucking your cock alone."

"Fuck." He moaned, rocking his jaw as I teased the tip of him with my tongue. "Laila."

"Dove." I argued, sucking him deep into my mouth and making him hiss when I dragged my teeth over his shaft. "When your cock is in my mouth, I'm your Dove. Don't disrespect me by using my given name when I'm on my knees for you."

His body shook as I sucked him, using every single skill and technique I knew to drive him wild. I pushed his button-down shirt out of the way so I could see the deliciously deep V up his stomach and then demanded, "Take it off for me. I want to see all of you."

He leaned off the wall and pulled his shirt buttons undone, ripping it off his chest as he threw his shirt and jacket to the side while I kept pleasuring him. I pulled his pants and underwear down as he kicked his shoes off and stripped until he was completely naked for me.

Almost every inch of his skin was tattooed, and I loved deciphering the ink like a story playing out in front of me, but right now, I wanted to leave my own mark on his skin. Digging my nails into his abs, I dragged them down, pulling a hiss from his lips as he pushed into my touch more until his skin pebbled with red marks under the black ink of an Icarus portrait above his groin.

"That's it." He growled, lifting my hands to his sides and pushing my nails into him again as I took his cock deep into my throat. "Again."

Dragging my nails down his sides, I left more marks as his pre-cum coated my tongue. "You want to come for me, don't you?" I flicked my tongue across the hole in his cock, and he bucked.

"Wrong." He lifted me under my arms and pushed me into the wall as he held me with a gentle hand around my neck. His fingers ripped my clothes off one-handed until I was as naked as he was, writhing and grinding against his skin in desperation. "I want to come inside of you."

"Mmh," I moaned and squealed when he lifted me and pinned me to the wall, my legs wrapped around his hips instinctively. He lined up and pushed deep into my wet body without warning, and I eagerly took him. I needed him as badly as he needed me. "Fuck me, Zeke." I dared, biting his fingers when he pushed them into my mouth as he caught my hands in his other hand, pinning them above my body. "Own me."

"As if there was anything else to call this." He snapped, slamming into me with strong thrusts until I was clawing at his body, dragging more marks across his back and neck as I rubbed my clit against his groin. "I own you. And you own me, Dove. I've never belonged to a woman the way I do to you. Never."

"I love you," I cried, coming on his cock with my declaration in the air, vibrating off my screams as he punishingly thrust into me. "Don't stop." Begging him for more when he had already given me so much was rude, but I didn't want it to stop. I didn't want him to go back to being that cool and collected man who kept control of everything around him.

Right now, I wanted him to crumble for me.

Because of me.

With me.

He pulled me off the wall and we landed on the floor, with him on top of me as he rutted deeper into me, widening his hips and spreading my legs around his waist to leave me unable to do anything but take him.

And God, did I take him.

"Yes, baby." I moaned as he bit my neck before flipping me onto my hands and knees. "Fuck me hard."

His hand peppered my ass, and I arched my back as he gave me every inch from behind. He was possessed and feral as he fucked me, biting, squeezing, spanking and marking me. Filthy things spoken into my ear and his cock relentlessly pushing my body into orgasmic bliss, time and time again.

But not once did I associate his roughness with any from my past. Not once did I slip into a nightmare, lost in thought and memory. His touch, even rough, his brand never scared me. It consumed me and built my need for him even more.

I was in love with Zeke, and I no longer feared my past. I no longer felt trapped there.

Finally, his hips lost their rhythm, he was kneeling over me, with me on my side, leg hugged to his chest as he fucked me into his own orgasm. The whole time I watched him.

Eyes screwed shut, sweat beaded on his shaved head, black ink on display, muscles taut and twitching with each flex of his hips until he stilled, roaring my name, filling me up and giving me every last thing I begged for.

Mine.

He was mine.

And I was never going to let him go.

When he rolled to the side, he didn't pull out but dragged me with him until we lay out in the middle of the floor of the padded torture room. "This room should repulse me." I finally said with a half-smile when he snorted.

"You're saying it doesn't?"

"Not anymore." I shrugged, admitting the truth. "I'll never think of this place for anything other than whatever we just did."

His smile slipped as his eyes closed.

"Will you tell me what pushed you over the edge?" I asked after a while. "I think I know you pretty well by now, and I don't think just the run-in with Kade's mom did all of that."

He swallowed and tightened his hold on my body. "I—" His lips parted and then closed as he struggled with whatever he wanted to say but couldn't.

I leaned up on my elbow to look down at him, using my finger on his chin to turn his face toward mine. "Please Zeke. Whatever it is, I'm still here with you. I promise. I'm not going anywhere."

His stare held mine for what felt like an eternity before his lips finally parted again. But what he said shocked me enough that I fell backward and out of his embrace as if he had physically hit me.

"I think I'm related to Kade."

CHAPTER 29 – ZEKE

We needed to talk; I knew that. But I didn't even know how to start. Laila brushed her hair in my bathroom, glancing at me in the mirror as I sat on the edge of my bed, head hung, elbows braced—just watching her. We came in from The Shop an hour ago, but I was still raw.

I fucked her for hours. Using her body to alleviate the burn in my gut, and she let me. As if my cock could silence the questions in her mind, like her body silenced the fears in mine. Now that we were back in the barracks, my hands were idle, and I was losing control again. Kade was in his apartment across the hall, he said he didn't want to talk about what happened earlier and just wanted to go to bed.

I didn't know how to speak to him, with the noose of knowledge around my throat tightening with every minute that passed. How could I have been so blind? How did I not see it until his mother made her appearance today?

Finally, I spoke, my voice hoarse, and it felt like thousands of needles with each word. "She's—my mother." I swallowed, dropping my head further as her brush paused mid-stroke before she slowly turned to face me.

"The woman from the restaurant?" Laila asked with a scowl. I nodded once, forcing my gaze to stay on hers. "Are you sure?"

I nodded again, hating how sick to my stomach I was from just speaking it out loud. "I should have killed her years ago."

"Zeke." She whispered, but I shook my head, feeling that uncontrollable rage building again.

"She did it to him." I hissed. "She got knocked up again and exposed him to this life! She had a baby and then threw him to the wolves to be chewed the fuck up like I was!" Clenching my jaw so hard my teeth nearly cracked, I fisted my hands into balls. "I should have fucking killed her before she had the chance to ruin someone else like she ruined me."

"Baby." She fell to her knees at my feet, but I shot up to stand and get away from her. I couldn't take her gentleness. "Tell me what you need." Laila begged, pleading to me with her eyes as I paced my studio apartment. "Just tell me, Zeke."

"I need—" I cracked my neck and scrubbed my hand over my face before making my decision. "I need to end a life."

"You can't kill her." She whispered. "Not like this."

"I know." I paused, feeling that calm power trying to take over the manic rage inside of me. "But I can kill someone else. Someone who has it coming. Someone who's already mine to kill."

Her pretty pink lips parted as her eyes rounded. She rose to her feet, the hem of my oversized tee shirt skimming over her thighs as she stared at me. Fuck, maybe I could lose myself in her again instead. My cock hardened just looking at her, and her nipples pebbled under the worn fabric of my shirt.

Slowly, as if she were afraid of spooking me, she crossed the room until she gently laid her hand on my bare chest. "You're going to kill the man who ruined me?"

"No," I shook my head, covering her hand with mine. "But I'm going to kill the man who *tried* to ruin you. He failed. You won."

Her neck tightened as she swallowed, and I ached to feel it on the inside of my palm like earlier. "And you think it will settle you?" Her warm eyes looked up at me through her inky black lashes. "You think killing the man who hurt me will make your pain lessen, so it doesn't swallow you whole like it is right now?"

"Laila." I groaned, hating how on point she was with my emotions. How clearly she saw me.

"Do it." She leaned up on her toes and offered her lips to me, and I eagerly took them, kissing her deeply until we both panted and moaned for more. "Kill him. Destroy him, Zeke. Because you're right, he didn't win. I did." Laila fell back down onto her heels, staring up at me. "Your mother didn't win either. I did. Because I have you *and* Kade. Not her. Me. I fucking won, Zeke. You and I are the victors."

"Fuck." I groaned, lowering my forehead to hers before standing back up, feeling like my chest was going to break apart and darkness would spill everywhere if I didn't get it out of me in another way.

"Go feed your demons, baby." Laila said firmly, patting my chest again. "And then come back to us. We'll be here when you're ready."

I kissed her hard enough to bruise her lips, and she gave it right back to me. Not once had I felt her strength so profoundly as I did at that moment. She believed in me. She trusted me. She was mine.

And she was right.

We fucking won.

Walking out of my apartment, I exited the building out into the dark night. Torches burned across the lawn, the crew and their families still partied, and the firelight danced in my vision as I walked across the blacktop, still hot from the sun that set hours ago.

I probably looked like a deranged monster, barefoot, wearing a pair of black shorts and ink as I marched toward the shop in the midst of a party. I caught Ryker's eye across the lawn, and he paused mid-sentence with someone as he stared at me. He looked behind me, and I followed his gaze to Laila standing in the doorway of the barracks, arms crossed over her chest as she watched me walk away. The flames of the torches swayed in her bottomless eyes, and she had never looked more regal than she did in that very moment.

Ryker stood up from his seat and silently joined me on my way down the path. Jed was next, his silent presence joining in on my other side as we walked toward the shop.

Tonight wasn't about justice or righting a wrong.

Tonight was about revenge.

The debts of men, earned from pain of others, would be paid in full.

And my family would be freer by the morning sunrise.

The screams echoed around the room, vibrating off the walls around us and singing a tune in my mind like a siren song. A melody of pain feeding the demon inside my chest, desperate and starving for the bloodshed of those who hurt Kade and Laila.

Body parts littered the floor, blood flowed like a river down the drains, and it coated my skin like war paint.

Fingers, toes and noses were first.

One by one, Charles and Clarissa Lupold were unburdened of those parts, and as expected, Charles tried to die twice from those twenty-one cuts alone. Pussy.

Normally, I would go for the tongue next, and on Clarissa I did. Her nasally voice grated on my last nerve, and taking away her ability to beg, borrow and then threaten for her life, pleased me.

The drugs pumping into their bodies through their IV lines kept their hearts beating even after their other organs shut down from malnutrition, shock, sepsis and blood loss.

And now, they both hung, missing pieces, unable to die yet begging for it to a room of monsters. They thought they were the biggest and baddest out there, and then they messed with the wrong crew.

"So, we're going to try this one more time." Jed spun his knife around between his fingers like a menace as I chugged from a bottle of water. "Do you know the muffin man?"

Clarissa gurgled instead of screaming as her cut-off tongue bled into her mouth.

"That's a shame." Ryker mused, crossing his arms over his chest as he leaned on the table next to me. "It's a simple answer."

"Okay, throw a dart." Jed flipped his hands with a shrug. "She loses a point for not playing my game."

"Got it." I picked up the needlepoint darts off the table and chucked one at her, hitting my mark perfectly. Her scream made my blood pump faster as the dart stuck out of her eyeball. "Bullseye."

Jed chuckled and plucked it out, digging her eyeball out with it. "Pun intended."

He held the dart up with the eyeball attached and then threw it at the wall, pinning it to the wall to hang there.

"Well," Jed stopped in front of Charles, who hung limply in his chains with piss and shit covering his legs. At least his wife had some balls and fight in her, he, on the other hand was a worthless piece of shit who earned every single thing he had gotten so far. "What do you say, Chuck?" Jed asked. "Dick or balls first?"

Ryker scoffed and walked up to stand at Jed's side, "Do you think you could even cut his dick off? It's almost a vagina at this point, it's so shriveled up."

"I could make it happen." Jed shrugged. "You could always hold it out for me with pliers."

"Mmh," Ryker nodded, "That would work. So, Chucky, pick. Which goes first?"

"Please." Charles whined uselessly, "I'm sorry!"

I rolled my eyes, tired of his bullshit for the hundredth time. From the moment we unblindfolded him in the shop, he had begged non-stop. Pathetic. "I vote for flame."

"Ooh," Jed rubbed his hands together. "Melty."

I picked the blow torch up off the table and stopped right in front of the man who raped, and tortured Laila, before forcing a hysterectomy on her, aborting the baby he left behind in the wake of his torture, and stealing her dreams of ever being a mother.

"How many girls have you raped over the years, Chuck?"

He shook his head back and forth weakly until I clicked the trigger on the blowtorch, shooting a three-inch flame out of the tip and held it in front of his face. Then he finally found the energy to talk.

"I don't know!" He screamed. "They all ran together after a while."

"Well, he's honest, at least." Ryker deadpanned. "Finally."

"Dozens?" I adjusted the flame on the torch, lengthening it. "A hundred? More?"

"I don't know!" He yelled, panicking again.

"Try." Jed warned. "Make an effort here, Chucky. You're ruining my fun."

"Hundreds!" Charles snapped finally, "Thousands!" His bleary eyes found mine, and he held my stare like a man would, but we knew he was anything but. "Is that what you want? I fucked thousands of women over the years! Thousands of young bitches who cried and begged for me to stop! But you know what?" He sneered, and I already knew what he was doing. He was baiting me, and before he even finished his thought, I knew he was going to make me want to kill him for whatever he said. "Yours was my favorite." Rage. "She cried so fucking prettily for me to start with. And then she learned that made me fuck her harder, so then she started playing along how I liked. She learned to beg for it. She would get on her hands and knees the second I walked in the room and spread her legs for me, begging me to fuck her!"

I lowered the flame to his shriveled-up little dick, making him scream in agony as I stared at his contorted face while I melted his skin and flesh from his body. His body rocked as he hung from his chains, the smell of burning flesh assaulting my senses, still I stared directly into his soulless eyes.

"Well, now we don't have to worry about that ever happening again. Do we?" I lowered the flame to his balls, melting each of them and then continued dragging my flame across his body. Sure, dousing him in lighter fluid and igniting him would have sped up the process, but that wasn't the point.

The point was for him to have a long, long time to regret what he did to Laila before death finally took him. I could feel the grim reaper standing in the room, ready to take him, so I kept burning him. Melting his flesh from his bones until it dripped onto the floor at my feet.

The others were silent as I killed him by boiling him inch by inch. I imagined every moment of pain he inflicted on my perfect brown-eyed girl the entire time I hurt him. I held space for her pain, while I gave him his.

A hand laid on my shoulder after a while, and I let the trigger go, killing the flame as I stood up to my full height, the mark of my torch sizzling across Charles's eyes.

"He's dead." Ryker said easily from my side, and I flicked my gaze to the monitor on the wall displaying his vital signs.

"Finally." I replied, setting the torch down.

"And her?" Jed asked, nodding to the one-eyed woman who abused Kade over four days before we found him.

"You can decide." I stared my friend in the eye. "My gift."

"To get revenge for my nephew?" Jed said, turning to face the woman who once thought she was invincible. "Hmm, I'm thinking meat grinder."

"Nice choice." Ryker added as Jed pulled the industrial-size meat grinder from the wall. "Feet first, of course."

"Of course." Jed said, flicking the button and turning the machine on. I sat down in the chair along the wall and watched silently as they used the hydraulic lift to lower the vile woman into the machine, her screams stopped about the time the blades made it to the tops of her thighs.

The machine stopped when she was completely gone, and finally there was only silence in my mind.

My demons had been fed. Revenge had been served. And the scores had been tipped back in our favor.

And all I wanted to do was lay eyes on the two people I belonged to, in their peaceful slumber. I'd destroy the world while they slept just like this, every single night, if that was what it took to keep them safe and happy.

CHAPTER 30 – LaiLa

I felt his presence, even in my dream sleep, and I reached for him with my eyes closed. Months ago, fear would have engulfed me as I imagined a shadowy figure lurking above me in bed. Now though, the only shadow that got near me was Zeke's darkness, and it turned out I craved him.

I didn't open my eyes as his naked body pressed against mine from behind, arms and legs entangling around me to pull me impossibly close to him. His skin smelled like soap, but not his. Which meant he had showered at the shop before he came to me.

Turning in his embrace, I laid a kiss against his jaw as I finally cracked my eyes open. It was still dark, and I was glad he was with me before sunrise. "I love you." I whispered.

His reply came in the form of his lips on mine, hungry and powerful, possessing me as his hands roamed my body. "I love you." He replied finally as he rolled me onto my back, with him instantly finding that place between my thighs that he fit perfectly.

I was wet from his release earlier, and he slid right in without another word. We didn't need them though, our bodies knew how to communicate.

He took me slowly, torturously slow, rocking his thick, veined cock into me from root to tip while he sucked and bit my skin, leaving marks and soothing ones from before. I tipped my head back and silently cried out his name as I came for him, giving in to his pleasures as he followed me over the edge.

The only noise was our breathing and the erratic beating of my heart in my chest as he pulled out and lay on his side facing me.

I could just make out the features of his face in the darkness, and I ran my fingertips over the chiseled muscles of his jaw. "Is it done?" I asked after a while, unable to imagine the outcome any longer.

"Yes." He whispered. "It's done."

"How do you feel?" I asked.

"Calm." He licked his lips, "Finally."

"Good." I nuzzled my nose against his and took a deep breath. "Sleep now, baby. Everything else is okay for now. Just rest."

"Mmh." He hummed, closing his eyes and settling with me in his embrace.

"Where's Kade?" Zeke's voice rumbled, breaking through my thoughts as he pulled a short-sleeve shirt over his head, fresh from the shower. My pulse skipped, my body reacting without permission as I tried to ignore the way his tattoos caught the light, the way his muscles flexed with every movement.

I licked my lips, struggling to untangle my thoughts. "The gym," I stammered, the words heavy in my mouth, fighting to control the way my body betrayed me. "He went with Jed."

Zeke's eyes shifted to me, an almost predatory gleam in them as he started to move toward me, his confident stride purposeful. The weight of his presence, the raw energy he exuded, made my knees weaken. He didn't need to touch me for me to feel his power, the kind that commanded attention and respect, and somehow... safety.

"Good," he murmured, his voice low and steady, but the smile that tugged at his lips promised something else entirely. "We have somewhere to be."

My body tensed. "No," I whined, sagging against him. "I thought you were asking because you wanted to—"

"Oh, I do," he interrupted, stopping in front of me, his fingers lightly grazing my skin as he held my gaze. "But there's something I need to show you first."

I groaned in frustration, but there was no denying the excitement stirring inside me. Zeke was always full of surprises, and as much as I hated unpredictability, I craved it with him. He was the chaos to my calm, and I couldn't help but love him more for it.

"Ugh." I sighed, defeated by the way he always had a way of pulling me along with him, even when I wasn't sure I was ready. But I followed him without another word, helpless to resist.

Last night he killed two people because of me—yet this morning he chuckled and flirted with me like he didn't darken his soul for me. And I loved him so deeply because of it.

When we left the barracks, he opened the door to his sleek car, and I hesitated before slipping into the passenger seat. The hum of the engine was a strange comfort, the vibration beneath me like a steady pulse I could depend on. We pulled out of the driveway, and I half expected him to turn right toward the exit of the gated community, but he veered left, then left again, entering a private driveway down the street. My confusion deepened as I glanced at him, his jaw tight as he focused on the road ahead.

"Explain." I demanded, unable to hide my curiosity.

"Just wait," he said, a grin tugging at his lips.

We passed through a manicured front yard, the house coming into view, its elegant colonial structure standing tall behind grand pillars. A basketball hoop hung over a garage door, a peaceful scene that seemed so out of place, yet oddly perfect in its own way.

It was smaller than the mansions that lined the streets in the community, but it had so much charm and warmth, it felt like a *home*.

I couldn't help the way my thoughts wandered—thoughts of Kade, the kid who deserved to grow up in a place like this, a place where he could be safe, loved, and free. It was the kind of life I would have wanted for him, and yet, none of us had grown up the way we deserved.

"Come on," Zeke urged, pulling me from my spiraling thoughts, taking my hand in his and leading me toward the front door.

"What are we doing?" I asked, my voice unsteady as I followed him through the grand entrance. "Zeke, what is going on?"

"I want to show you something." His words were firm, but his touch was gentle, guiding me forward as he opened the door and walked right in, as though he owned the place. I stopped in my tracks, my heart pounding as I glanced around. "Zeke!" I hissed, dragging my feet. "We can't just walk into someone's house."

"An hour ago," he said, his voice casual, "it became my house."

I stared at him, wide-eyed. "What? You—what?"

"I bought it," he said, his grin widening as he pulled me inside. "Ryker didn't want the house next door to his estate being sold to someone else, so instead of letting some stranger take it, I bought it."

The weight of his words slammed into me. My mind struggled to process it. "You—bought this? For us?"

Zeke nodded, the intensity in his eyes softening. "I don't want the two of you in the barracks anymore. You deserve more than that. More than I ever had growing up. I want us to have a place of our own, a real home, together. I don't care where it is—this house, another one—I just want you and Kade to have something we can make ours. A place where we can heal."

Zeke ran the pad of his thumb over my cheek tenderly, "I've worked my entire life for other people's glory, and I've saved every penny of my money the entire time. Waiting for a rainy day to spend it. Waiting for someone worthy to spend it on." His face softened, "And I have that now, with you. And with Kade." I opened my mouth to say something, but I couldn't come up with anything. So, Zeke kept going. "You deserve a home, Laila. And I know this place isn't the biggest house out there, and it's not as modern or updated as it could be, but we can make it whatever we want. We can make a home here. We'd still be close to Elora and Carly, we can put a gate in along the property line, or we can sell this and buy a house wherever you want. I don't care. I just want to get you both out of the barracks and into a home where you can both start building something. With me."

"Jesus Christ." I flung myself at him, throwing my arms around his neck as he lifted me into his arms. "I don't know what to say, I don't know how to feel worthy."

"You are. And you don't have to say anything other than yes or no." He pulled back. "This house or a different one, but I want you, me and Kade to have something like this. Something that we can fill with love and laughter and happiness." Pushing his nose into mine, nuzzling me, "God knows the three of us could use some fucking happiness to settle into."

"Yes." I whispered, nodding emphatically, "Yes we do."

"Good." He grinned, beaming at me as I slid down his body, looking around the home he wanted to give to me. I pushed down every doubt-filled, unworthy feeling that tried to surface, and embraced the gift of love I never imagined finding. I forced myself to let the excitement and happiness fill me instead of worrying about the catch or the fallout on the other side like I normally would.

I deserved this.

Zeke deserved this.

Kade deserved this.

And my god, I was going to make the house a home worthy of both of them, as if it was my only purpose in life. The three of us were going to find our own happiness within the walls of this home, and we were going to heal.

No, fuck that.

We were going to *thrive.*

CHAPTER 31 – ZEKE

"I don't understand." Kade blinked with a blank stare, and I could feel the anxiety radiating from Laila at my side. "What do you mean, *welcome home*?"

"We bought this house." I looked around the expansive kitchen that Laila spent all day organizing with the brand-new appliances and dishes she picked out. Last week I told her the news, and she had secretly spent all week turning the empty house into a home, worthy of a little boy who never had one. "And we're staying here, from now on. We'll grab everything from the barracks as we go."

He looked at Laila and then back to me before glancing around the open living room behind him. "I'm happy for you two." He said, "But can I still stay at the barracks? Or should I plan to leave there now that you guys are moving out?"

"No, Kade." Laila rushed on. "We want you to live here, with us."

"But—" He shook his head, "Don't you want to be alone?" His eyebrows pinched in the center as he shrugged, "You've both been incredibly generous to me and stuff, and I'm grateful. But don't couples want to be alone to be freaky and stuff?"

I groaned, and Laila blushed.

Walking around the massive island, I pulled a stool out and motioned for Kade to sit as I took the one next to him. "See, the thing about a house this size is there's plenty of space for all three of us to exist without being on top of each other."

Kade's eyes squinted slightly, and I could tell he was weary of openly accepting what we were trying to give him. Which meant I had to come clean with him completely about the circumstances. "There's something we haven't told you yet, something I wanted concrete proof of before I opened my mouth."

"Okay." He replied hesitantly.

I pulled a photo from my pocket, unfolding the worn paper that I'd stuffed in a safe years ago. It had felt like a piece of my past at the time, something I didn't want to think back on. Yet it had come to be part of my future when I met Kade, even without knowing it. "This is a picture of me when I was three years old." I said, forcing myself to be brave. "It's the only picture I have of my mother."

I laid the picture down and slid it across the marble countertop to him, watching his face as he picked it up and stared at it.

"Does she look familiar to you, Kade?" Laila asked gently, leaning over the counter with her hands laced together.

"I don't understand." He shook his head gently. "She looks like my mom."

"She does." I nodded, "Because it is. She was just a lot younger in this picture." His icy blue eyes snapped to mine, and I put my hand on his shoulder, trying to offer him something akin to comfort as I told him the news. "I hadn't seen her for almost fifteen years before that day at the restaurant. But it didn't matter, it's hard to forget the face of the woman who chose everyone in the world over you, even decades later. Even as a grown man that no longer needs her."

"You're my—" He stumbled, so I caught him.

"Half-brother." I finished, fighting the emotions of claiming the only blood relative I knew of besides our mother. "She was only thirteen when she had me. And I was already a grown man when she had you." Taking a deep breath, I went on, "I had no idea that you existed, Kade. I walked away from her when I was your age. I ran for my life from the abuse and drugs she exposed me to, and I never looked back. But had I known about you—" My voice broke as his eyes teared up. "I would have saved you far earlier than I did. I would have taken you from her had I known, Kade. I'm sorry that I didn't. I'm sorry I wasn't there to protect you."

"You're my brother." Kade whispered as he took a shuttering breath. Turning to look at Laila he shook his head dumbfounded. "Did you know when we met?"

"No." Laila whispered with teary eyes. "But I don't doubt for one second that it was why I was so drawn to you, even without knowing why. I think God put me in your path that day for a reason."

Kade crumbled in bewilderment, trying to process it all before he scowled and looked at me. "You said you weren't going to say anything until you knew for sure. You know for sure?"

"I do." I pulled the other folded paper from my pocket and opened it up, pointing to the DNA results I ordered, using samples taken from Kade's check-up with the doctor Ryker hired to treat him after his kidnapping. "There's the proof, though it would be impossible to ignore our similarities now that I know."

"You have the same eyes." Laila smiled.

"And the same stubborn pigheadedness." I added.

Kade smiled gently, warming up to the idea. "And good looks."

Laila let out a relieved chuckle, "And we can't forget the dry humor."

Kade and I both let out a scoff and then laughed before I pushed on. "You may be my brother, Kade, but if you don't object, I'd like to be more than that to you."

"What do you mean?" he asked cautiously.

"We'd like to adopt you." Laila added, walking around the island to stand between us, holding my hand in hers and taking his. "We'd like to give you a forever home with us. Legally."

"Forever." He whispered and then let out an enormous sigh. "Are you sure? I'm kind of a pain in the ass."

Laila pulled him into a massive hug, and I stood up, wrapping them both up in my arms with a chuckle. "Really? We hadn't noticed."

EPILOGUE – LAILA

"Oh my God, no he didn't!" Ellie roared, tipping her head back and cackling as Carly shared more of her night away with Jed last week. They went to their property in the hills for a spicy night of fun and, apparently, things got interesting.

"His entire dick!" Carly gasped, holding her sides, "He thought it was going to be some sexy s'mores dessert for me to lick up, but the fluff was so fucking sticky, everything in the wilderness ended up stuck to his dick. Pine needles, grass, bugs—you name it! It was hilarious!"

"I'm guessing he didn't think so." I snorted, sipping my lemonade as I rocked on Carly's front porch. Two years ago, I moved onto the property, scared of everything, even life. And now I was thriving, surrounded by people I didn't deserve and love I'd never be worthy of. Tuesday night porch dates were our norm, and I was finally able to enjoy life without worrying about the fallout.

Besides, there was no time to think about the endless things that could go wrong in life when the estate was crawling with new life. Our hands and our hearts were full.

"No, he most definitely didn't!" Carly chuckled. "Let's just say his dick wasn't coming anywhere near me until we broke out the Dawn dish soap to break down the marshmallow."

"Child present," A voice called out from the edge of the porch, and I looked over as Kade held his hands over his ears as he walked around the railing from the backyard. He was shirtless and covered in so much dirt and grime, I could hardly see his skin. But what I could see was his beaming full smile as he joked with Carly.

"You can't claim child status anymore." Ellie deadpanned when Kade leaned up against the porch railing on the bottom step, "You're like eight feet tall."

Kade's smile got even brighter, and I rolled my eyes as he puffed his chest out with pride. "Don't even get me started." I sighed, sipping down the last of my drink. "Between his latest growth spurt and the work he's been doing with Jed, I can't keep good jeans on that boy."

"I'm not complaining," Carly shrugged, "He's a workhorse and has been here every day, sun up until sun down helping Jed with the addition. God knows we're going to need the space." She chuckled, rubbing a hand over her still nonexistent baby bump.

Considering she was already two months along with a four-month-old inside sleeping, who knew how many kids they'd end up with before Jed was done building their family and healing his own childhood trauma.

As if on cue, my brother walked around the house, guzzling a bottle of water, shirtless and covered in grime, wearing a tool belt and jeans. "Here you go."

He held a hand out to Kade, and they did some weird boy hand-shake where I never quite saw what was passed between them, but I figured it wasn't drugs or hookers, so I was fine with it.

"Thanks." Kade nodded to him and put his loot in his pocket. "Tomorrow again?"

"Nah," Jed shook his head, "It's Sunday and I'm sleeping in."

Carly snorted, "Like hell. You're on baby duty, and I'm sleeping in." As if on cue, the monitor next to her echoed out the call of her daughter Annie, from her crib where she was taking her afternoon nap inside. "And you can start right now." She smiled sweetly up at Jed, and he scoffed with a roll of his eyes.

"Give me your tits and I'll go feed her, no problem." He said, and she groaned, pairing it with a fake pout.

"I have to go, anyway." Ellie looked at her watch. "Dawson will be back with Gav and Gabriella any time now." She rose and stretched above her head. I'm sure she was enjoying her own break from her sweet son and newborn daughter, born a week after Annie. "Thanks for therapy." Ellie winked, and Carly waved at her best friend. "See you next week."

I chuckled, rising to my feet, "As if you won't be back over here for some reason by morning."

"More like Carly will be in my kitchen at sunrise eating Margaret's Sunday morning spread." Ellie said, and I chuckled.

"What time is that again?" I joked. "I think I'm free."

"Mom." Kade groaned, "We have plans."

Be still, my heart. Even months later, hearing his sweet voice call me mom, still made my heart flutter.

"Ah," I nodded like I'd forgotten, playing it cool. "Right. The plans. Um—" I pointed at him with my finger, "To do what exactly?"

"Ugh," He groaned dramatically. "You're impossible!"

I laughed, and Jed winked at me, rubbing his hand over Kade's head as he came up the steps. "Oh yeah, the dirt bike."

"Exactly." Kade smirked, like he was glad I finally remembered. To be honest, I hadn't thought of anything but it for days now, since Zeke told me that Kade had earned it, probably ten times over by now, and that he was going to buy it for him. I'd managed to drag my feet for over a year. It seemed as though I was out of time, though. "Let's go, I've got to finish putting together the accessories that came in today."

"Yeah, yeah, yeah," I droned on, walking down the steps as he slung his arm over my shoulders, since he was taller than me now, and I only cringed slightly when his teenage body odor hit my nose. The boy had been working like a dog all day in the California heat, so I couldn't hold it against him. "After a shower."

"Pfft," He scoffed, and I pinched his side. "Okay, fine!"

"Good." I said as we fell into a comfortable silence, walking across Ryker's backyard to the gate in the hedge to our yard next door. When Zeke had surprised me with the house last year, I had envisioned nights just like this in the dreamy fantasy that came to mind as soon as I saw the beautiful home.

We walked together as dusk fell, showing off the lightning bugs munching on the flower gardens I planted around the yard, and the peacefulness was palpable.

Kade must have felt it too, because as we got to the back patio of our house, he took a deep breath like he was soaking it all in before he jogged up the steps. "Tell Dad I'll be ready by seven. The store opens at eight." He looked over his shoulder at me, and I grinned, waving him off.

"Shower. Dinner. Sleep." I reminded him, "And if you do all of that, then I will let Dad take you to buy your death trap."

"Mom." He groaned again, like I was the most tiresome person in the world. Once upon a time, he would have made some smart-ass comments about my rules or questions, calling me names or something to deflect my attention, but now he just pouted.

Like a normal kid.

"Kade." Zeke's deep timber voice warned from inside the kitchen as we walked through.

"Sorry." Kade took a deep breath and gave me a small smile. "I'm just excited."

"I know." I gave him a smile back before winking at my husband across the room. "And I'm just giving you a hard time. Go get cleaned up. I'll put your dinner in the oven to re-heat since you were too busy to come home in time earlier."

Kade looked sheepish as he backed down the hallway to the stairs, "Sorry. Thank you!"

"Night."

When he was out of earshot, Zeke looked at me, wiping his hands on a dishtowel at the sink. Watching my bogeyman doing something as normal and mundane as dishes, sent me down a rabbit hole of awe that I couldn't quite label. "Dove." He stated evenly, but the deep vibration of his voice sent shivers through my body. "Careful."

Of course he picked up on my thoughts, without me even saying anything.

"What if I don't want to be careful?" I licked my lips and leaned back on the counter, tipping my knee just right so my long summer skirt's slit opened, showing off some skin. "What if I want to live dangerously?"

He stalked toward me, and I ate up the image of him, shirtless in a pair of jeans and barefoot as he slid so effortlessly into his dominant role that I loved. "You want to feel danger on your skin tonight, Dove?"

"Yes." I purred when he stopped right in front of me. "This boring housewife life you've provided for me doesn't quite quench my thirst like I thought it would."

He growled, and slid his fingers around my throat and bent me backward over the counter, hovering over me. "Be careful, or I'll take your hungry little cunt right here on the kitchen counter and fill you up."

Melting into his hold, I rubbed my hands up his washboard abs. "Please, Daddy."

"Bed." He said through clenched teeth. "Now."

I grinned, having won what I wanted by poking at the monster in his chest enough to get him riled up and ready for me. "Good thing you soundproofed the walls, because tonight I'm going to ruin you in the best way possible." Licking my lips, I tilted my chin down, and he let go, thinking I was going to do his bidding and run to our bedroom on the opposite side of the house from Kade's room upstairs. Instead, I bit the webbing between his thumb and forefinger, and he hissed but didn't pull away as I left a mark on his flesh. "Tonight, I want to be in charge."

"You know I love it when you take the lead, Dove." He said, eyeing the mark on his hand as I licked it. "What do you plan to do with me?"

"Hmm." I pulled the button on his jeans free and fluttered my eyelashes up at him. "I think I'm going to start with you on your back in our bed." I hummed, watching his bright blue eyes dilate, "Tied down, and at my mercy."

"Damn." He groaned.

That wouldn't stop me though, "And then I think I'm going to try out that new grinding toy you bought me." A few days ago, he came home with a mysteriously blank box in his hand. Inside, was a silicone toy that was full of ridges and points meant to stimulate every single inch of my pussy. But the thing that made me nearly fall to my knees when he gave it to me, was the straps that attached to the top and bottom of it.

Straps to hold it onto the thigh.

Zeke's thigh.

So, I could ride him, just like that night at the gala so long ago. The night that unlocked a new kink for the both of us.

"You want to torture me, Dove?" He asked, with a lifted brow. "Because we both know I can come from simply watching you lose yourself for me."

Truth. He had. Many times.

"I want to drive you wild before I use you." I licked my lips again. "So, I'm only going to say this once, Zeke Evans." I pulled the zipper on his pants lower as I leaned up on my tippy toes to speak against his lips. "Bed, now."

"Whatever you say, Laila Evans."

The End.

OTHER BOOKS

Did you know Ally writes across so many other types of tropes and themes?

Check out some of her other books here.

Looking for Series and Duets?

The Line Walkers Series:
https://a.co/d/bx376wq
Beauty In the Ink Series:
https://a.co/d/6tc8M7M
Bailey Dunn & Co Duet:

https://a.co/d/i9gwqL2

<u>Shadeport Crew Series:</u>

https://a.co/d/dVzGcyo

<u>Kings of Hawthorn Series:</u>

https://a.co/d/h1AITKM

How about some spicy standalones?

<u>Sinister Vows:</u>

https://a.co/d/gbe35fF

<u>Guilty For You:</u>

https://a.co/d/1ef3UPU

<u>Secrets Within Us:</u>

https://a.co/d/cTZ04XQ

AUDIOBOOKS

Did you know that the entire Line Walker Series is getting Audiobooks? EEK!!! I know, I'm so excited too!

Make sure to check out website- www.ammccoybooks.com, social media – Twisted After Dark: A.M. McCoy's Reader Group – on Facebook, and Audible for more details!

Also, did you know that my Beauty In The Ink Series got their very own audiobooks as well? Find those on Audible too!

STaLK Me!

Want to stay up to date with all of my shenanigans and upcoming news? Pretty Please?

Check out my website: www.ammccoybooks.com

How about TikTok, are you there? https://www.tiktok.com/@amm ccoy_author?is_from_webapp=1&sender_device=pc

Facebook? I've got a readers group there! Twisted After Dark: A.M. McCoy's Reader Group is mostly unhinged and full of exclusive news! https://www.facebook.com/share/g/b41rkBMkSurWz43i/

IG? https://www.instagram.com/ammccoy_author/

Amazon?
https://www.amazon.com/stores/A.-M.-McCoy/author/B07QNRJ

MLB?ref=ap_rdr&isDramIntegrated=true&shoppingPortalEnabled
=true

I think that's all for now!

www.ingramcontent.com/pod-product-compliance
Lightning Source LLC
Chambersburg PA
CBHW030736310726
48969CB00005B/1244